Bo's Ace

STEVEN WOODS

Bo's Ace
Copyright © 2022 by Steven Woods

All rights reserved. No part of this publication may be reproduced,
distributed, or transmitted in any form or by any means, including
photocopying, recording, or other electronic or mechanical
methods, without the prior written permission of the author, except
in the case of brief quotations embodied in critical reviews and
certain other non-commercial uses permitted by copyright law.

ISBN
978-1-957378-60-2 (Paperback)
978-1-957378-59-6 (eBook)
978-1-957378-61-9 (Hardcover)

Table of Contents

The old man seemed to be sleeping peacefully in his bed while his four legged friend of two years lay nearby on a tattered throw rug. Even though it was obvious to the caring canine that the old man had grown to love him in the days that followed his unexpected arrival, he had been named simply "Dog." That was fine with him, though, especially after the old man had explained that it was, in fact, a name of honor. Having always been a deeply religious African American man of the Baptist faith, it was the only name that he even considered appropriate. Little did old Lester know that the bullmastiff he had named Dog already knew and fully understood why such a simple and seemingly stupid name was chosen.

He looked at his temporary master, knowing that his first mission on his return to the earth was within hours of finally being over. Dog's big droopy brown eyes looked even more penetrating and fuller of wisdom tonight than on any other night he had spent with the old man. That pesky itch was still bothering him behind his right ear. He sat back up and curled his spine before whacking the irritating area with his right rear paw a half dozen times. Having alleviated that annoying feeling, he slumped back down, resting his chin on his front paws once again.

Dog finally arose so he could see his aged first master, who had rolled onto his back a few minutes earlier, initiating his usual evening serenade of singsong snoring; and unfortunately, it was in the key of "Lester." The big bullmastiff slowly padded over to the edge of the bed, gently nudging the old man on the shoulder with his massive drooling snout. The act produced the same results as when Lester's dearly departed wife, Annie, had resorted to the same tactic almost every night of their forty-six years of marriage. The old man rolled back over on his side, the unwelcome serenade ending after two shivering final snorts.

It was at that moment that Dog's keen ears picked up a sound coming from the kitchen in the back side of the house. He heard the back doorjamb click open. His sensitive nostrils picked up another human scent. Dog's heightened hearing started tracking this human trying to walk slowly and cautiously on the creaky linoleum floor. Most definitely, another human was now in the house. Dog knew that any other human whom the old man knew would have announced his or her arrival before entering. The old man had probably forgotten to lock the dead bolt again, a careless act that could someday be his undoing, considering that the neighborhood he lived in certainly wasn't the safest in North Omaha by any means.

The bullmastiff decided not to bark. He was afraid he would startle Lester. Instead, he chose to go quietly by himself to investigate the source of the sound and smell, letting the old man sleep peacefully into the night.

Several miles away to the south, a high school wrestling dual meet was nearing its conclusion. It was late winter in the year 1969. It was one of those strange February Midwestern days that could feel like a harbinger of the warmer weather that was just around the comer in the early afternoon and quickly give way to an Arctic-like evening.

The school gymnasium bleachers were filled with parents and students who were cheering on their respective teams. The group of Papillion (Nebraska) cheerleaders were waving pompoms and trying to excite the hometown crowd. The visiting Plattsmouth High School wrestling team had become Papillion's archrival in recent years, even though they weren't even in the same district. A match was currently underway on the mat in the center of the gym.

While two wrestlers were struggling with each other in the heat of battle, a muscular young man with curly blond hair was stretching on the floor next to his coach while they both were intent on the action in front of them. His one- piece wrestling uniform with the thin-strapped top and short clinging bottoms was sticking to him like a second skin. His headgear was lying on the mat close by. The young wrestler Bo Bozell turned around for a second and took a quick glance up at his parents, who were sitting in the bleachers behind him.

Martha Bozell smiled and waved back at her youngest son before her husband, Henry, resumed their conversation. "Well, Martha, it looks like it's going to be up to our boy again to get the win for Plattsmouth." "I hope Bo's not too nervous, Henry," said Martha. "There's a lot of pressure on him. That boy that Bo has to wrestle tonight is so much bigger than he is." "Ah, heck, Martha," answered Henry as he gestured with his long bony hand, the blond and gray hairs on the back of his hand glistening in the steamy gym, "Bo doesn't let anything like that bother him. He'll be just fine. He's been in this situation before."

Henry's reassurances didn't seem to help Martha too much as she continued to fret and stew. Despite Henry's early predictions of being the perfect parent, he had often been missing in action because of the demands of owning his own body shop business through the years, seldom an eyewitness to his youngest son's escapades. An incident involving a minikitty-parade when Bo was only three, riding buck naked down the middle of the highway on his tricycle while pulling his little red wagon filled with terrorized kittens, had just been the tip of the iceberg. Martha knew that her husband always thought he understood. "I know, Henry, but to still be undefeated and only be a sophomore . . ."

"That boy has his heart set on going to state undefeated, and nothing's gonna stop him! He's a Bozell!" Henry emphatically exclaimed to Martha, as well as several other unintended recipients of his proclamation. "1 know he's just a sophomore, Martha, but I can't help thinkin' this could be his ticket to college, a full-ride wrestling scholarship. 1 know we could help him some if he really wanted to go to college, but to foot the whole bill would be hard on our retirement plans. A wrestling scholarship would make it so much easier. 1 just hope college coaches don't think his hearing loss will hold him back any."

Martha thought about her husband's concerns as she reached up behind her and flicked her brown hair away from her slightly sweaty neck. It was still a painful subject to discuss for her. Try as she might, she had never stopped blaming herself for her son's hearing loss. She knew that

Henry had never openly blamed her, but it still didn't stop those painful memories from coming back again. Many pregnant women in the Midwest had developed complications in the early fifties from rubella. Martha never understood why she had to be one of the unlucky ones.

She looked down to the gym floor at Bo, who was still stretching near the edge of the wrestling mat, before looking back into the eyes of her husband. "They might, Henry. I'm sure Bo doesn't always hear things correctly, and you know it's sometimes hard to understand what he's saying unless you're used to listening tohis awkward pronunciations. His hearing aids help a lot in the classroom, but without them on the mat... I don't know. He's been getting by with good lipreading and an understanding coach, but college wrestling is another story. Besides, he needs to start doing a better job of applying himself more in the classroom than he has so far this school year. He's so obsessed with wrestling. If he expects to be offered a wrestling scholarship, he needs to understand that he'll also have to have good grades. If he spent as much time in his room studying as he does on that chin-up bar out in the garage and running the stadium steps at school, I wouldn't be so worried about him."

Henry nodded in agreement. "I know, Mother. I've been meanin' to have another talk with the boy about that. We know he's got the smarts. He just needs to start thinkin' about how important a good education is nowadays. I don't want him to have to sweat his tail off every day like I do just to earn a halfway decent living. The boy can do more with his life if he wants to. John's a good son and a hard worker for me, but like Ben, I never figured him for a college boy. Besides, somebody has to take over the family business once 1 call it quits someday." Bozell Body Shop was located near Downtown Plattsmouth, Nebraska, a small town on the Missouri River about a half-hour drive south of Omaha.

The current wrestling match was mercifully over as the referee held up the Papillion wrestler's arm in victory over his Plattsmouth opponent. The match ended with the Papillion wrestler winning by the lopsided score of 12-2. The partisan home crowd applauded and cheered. The defeated Plattsmouth wrestler walked toward his teammates and coach with his head down.

Bo got up from his stretching exercises, grabbing his headgear as he rose. He pulled it over his ears and adjusted it for comfort before walking over to his teammate and patting his friend Tommy on the shoulder. Tommy turned away, grabbing a towel and plopping down on the bench, burying his sweaty face behind the white terry cloth.

Bo stepped over to his coach for last-minute instructions. The crowd's noise drowned out what the coach was telling him. Teenagers in the crowd were stomping their feet like a drumbeat as they stood on the foldout wooden bleachers. The resulting vibration was probably a little unnerving and annoying to the grandpas and grandmas who had come to see their grandsons wrestle. No one in the crowd had left yet as Bo Bozell was about to wrestle the most important match of his young life.

Dog padded slowly and silently out of the bedroom, heading cautiously in the direction of the intruding sound and smell that was still coming from the kitchen. He thought about how ironic it was that this was happening on the last night that he would be there for Lester. Dog knew that he hadn't been sent to protect the old man, just to comfort him. He also knew that he wasn't always privy to the Master's plan, something that he had always accepted but was not always prepared for.

As he padded along the darkened hallway, nearing the open doorway, he could see the intruder standing in the kitchen, with a flashlight illuminating the kitchen cupboards. A neighbor's back porch light provided some limited light as it shone through the shear white curtains covering the old man's two kitchen windows. Dog could see that it was a thin young black man in dark clothes with big frizzy hair. It was not surprising that he was of the same race as the old man as the neighborhood was, in fact, predominantly black. However, Dog was thinking that this young man must not be someone who lived close by; or else, he wouldn't have been so bold as to enter a house knowing that a big dog was living there.

The thief was holding a white pillowcase that was still empty as his flashlight scanned along the top of the cupboards. Apparently, he hadn't seen anything yet worth taking as he turned toward the open doorway that would allow his entry into the rest of the house. As soon as the intruder's flashlight beamed down the hallway, revealing Dog standing there near the open door, Dog showed all his teeth and began a threatening low, guttural growl.

The young punk's eyes jerked wide open. The wild whites of his eyes gave away his seemingly sudden metamorphosis from daring to delirious as Dog could tell that the thug's desperately planned deed had apparently given way to panic and preservation. The big bullmastiff didn't even bother to run the boy down in the kitchen as he watched him drop his pillowcase and wheel around on one heel before heading for the door. Dog heard him saying "oh shit" over and over as he raced out of the kitchen and threw open the back door, disappearing into the night.

Dog was so pleased with himself that, apparently, he had been so scary that he didn't even have to start barking. If he had, he surely would have frightened and awakened the old man. He padded over to the back door and pushed it closed until he heard a click before turning the dead bolt with his teeth to securely lock the door.

When Dog turned to leave the kitchen, he realized that the scent of Lester had become too strong for him to still be back in his bedroom. Sure enough, the old man was standing just inside the doorway from the hallway in his nightshirt, holding a shotgun still trained at the back door. "You didn't really think you scared that boy away so easily just by growling, did you, Dog?" he calmly asked between a toothy grin. "You were just lucky he didn't have a gun, boy. What would you 'a' done then?" Dog somehow knew that he would find out the answer to that question someday soon.

The announcer keyed his mike. "Ladies and gentlemen, the final match of the meet is the heavyweight class! Wrestling for visiting Plattsmouth is Bo Bozell!"

The small contingent of Plattsmouth fans and parents cheered for Bo after the introduction.

"And wrestling for Papillion is Matt Duncan! Matt Duncan, ladies and gentlemen!"

The Papillion faithful cheered and applauded loudly as their cheerleaders chanted, "Go, Matt, go!"

The announcer continued, "I would like to take this opportunity to thank everyone in attendance for your support. And a special thanks to the referees and other officials who helped make this spirited competition a successful event. This has been a closely fought dual meet between two very good high school wrestling teams. Papillion is leading, going into this final match of the evening by the score of 21-16." The Papillion boosters had drowned out the smaller Plattsmouth contingent after the announcer finished speaking over the public address system.

Matt Duncan's father yelled out to his son on the mat, "Come on, Matt! You can beat this guy! You're way bigger than him!" Mr. Duncan had only stated the obvious. His son was probably a good three inches taller than Bo and outweighed him by at least 40 pounds. Duncan had a big barrel chest and tree stumps for legs. His close-cropped dark hair went well with his steely deep-set hazel eyes. Matt Duncan weighed in at 250 pounds versus Bo's 210 pounds. It was an imposing difference, even to the casual observer.

Bo's wrestling coach huddled up with him before he stepped away. Bo intently watched his coach's lips as he went over what they had discussed earlier in the visitor's locker room when he still had his hearing aids in. The intensity of a rigorous sweaty wrestling match prevented him from wearing them out on the mat.

Bo's hearing loss, discovered shortly before his fourth birthday, was irrelevant now. He was on an even playing field, not dependent on his sense of hearing as being a factor in the outcome of the battle that awaited him on the mat. It was just one-on-one once the whistle blew. Only being able to hear the dull thunder of the crowd allowed a focused, hearing-impaired person some possible advantages over his opposition. The clues of the opponent's body language, one's own basic instincts, surprising quickness, and a bold, unrelenting determination were the qualities that separated the great wrestler from the good, and the sense of sound had nothing to do with any of that.

The coach spoke slowly and deliberately as Bo's eyes stayed squarely on his face and his exaggerated mouthing of the words he spoke. "Okay, Bo, this guy's a senior with more experience and plenty of size. He hasn't lost this year, but he did lose one match last year, so you know he can be beat. Don't let him try to outmuscle you and drag this match out for the full three periods, or he's going to wear you down. You need to catch him off guard in the first period. You're quicker than he is, so use that to your advantage. We can still beat Papillion if you can get the pin for the six team points."

Bo nodded in response to his coach's instructions. "Gotcha, Coach."

The referee blew his whistle to alert the wrestlers that it was almost time for the first period to begin. The two wrestlers walked to the center of the mat, joined by their referee. The ref briefly tried to tell the two combatants what his expectations were concerning a clean match as he was practically shouting over the crowd noise. Bo watched the ref's face intently as he spoke, ignoring the fact that Duncan was trying to stare him down. The referee finally concluded his remarks and told the two wrestlers to shake hands before the match would begin. As Bo reached out and took Duncan's hand to shake, he abruptly turned his head away toward his parents in the bleachers.

As he was looking away, Duncan said, "You're going down, Bozell. You're not only going down. I'm also gonna make it hurt."

Bo turned back toward Duncan as the two of them let go of each other's hands. "Did you say something?"

Duncan had a sinister scowl on his face. "You heard me, Bozell!"

As Bo turned back around, waiting for the first-period whistle to blow, he was grinning and silently thanking his friend from another school who had tipped him off about Matt Duncan's prematch history of trying to intimidate his opponent before they even began wrestling. He was also amused that, apparently, no one had tipped off Duncan about his hearing loss. The Papillion wrestler had acted like he was sure that Bo had heard what he'd said.

Bo and his opponent both adjusted their headgear for the last time before facing each other in the middle of the mat. The referee blew his whistle again, and the two wrestlers started moving around in a circle in slightly crouched positions, sizing each other up and looking for an opportunity to make a move. They locked hands with each other a couple of times and then released them.

Matt Duncan suddenly reached down and tried to grab Bo behind his left calf, but Bo backed off quickly enough to avoid his intended grasp. The crowd was cheering wildly. They continued to circle around in the center of the mat. Both wrestlers appeared to be sizing each other up, staring intensely into each other's eyes. Apparently, neither wanted to be the first to make a tactical mistake. "Let's go, gentlemen. Wrestle," said the referee.

The two wrestlers moved in closer to each other and simultaneously grabbed the other's shoulders as they were both bent over into their opponent. Without tipping off his intentions ahead of time, Bo moved his left arm with lightning speed and leveraged his opponent's arm, lifting him enough to throw him off balance backward. Then he ducked his head under Duncan's right arm and performed a fireman's carry, using the Papillion wrestler's momentum to flip him onto his back.

For those who could see Matt Duncan's face as he landed on his back on the mat, there was an obvious look of surprise and shock that he was suddenly in such a vulnerable position. Bo immediately took advantage of this by rolling the bigger wrestler up into a cradle pin. The Papillion wrestler was lying helplessly, with his shoulders stuck to the mat. Bo had Duncan's right leg and lower torso up in the air using his right arm while he wrapped his left arm around the big boy's neck, forcing the chin down into the sternum.

The defined muscular body of Bo was glistening now with sweat. He was what body sculptors referred to as ripped. His arm and leg muscles rippled with intensity and definition. All those chin-ups out in his garage and the running on the stadium steps had paid off for him. His sculpted body had come to define who he was and what he wanted.

The referee flopped down close to the Papillion wrestler's pinned shoulders and slapped his hand on the mat three times. And just like that, the match was over. Bo had pinned his bigger opponent before the first two-minute period was over.

The Papillion faithful looked stunned. The partisan crowd stood in silence for several seconds as Bo's coach and teammates were jumping up and down, throwing towels into the air in celebration. Bo's parents were standing and hugging each other as they bounced up and down in the bleachers. The small contingent of Plattsmouth parents and boosters were also celebrating the quick victory. The final score showed "Plattsmouth, 22 ; Papillion, 21."

Bo was hopping around on the mat with a big smile on his face. The referee then grabbed his hand and that of Matt Duncan, who was now standing, and lifted Bo's hand and arm into the air as the victor. The public address announcer keyed his mike for his final remarks of the event. "With the pin by the Plattsmouth heavyweight, Bo Bozell, Plattsmouth wins this dual meet by a single point! It doesn't get any closer than that, folks!"

The announcer continued, "Once again, I want to thank everyone for coming out and supporting his or her team, and please drive home safely. I've been asked to tell everyone that there's been some sleeting and freezing rain going on outside since this meet began, so please take it a little slower as you head home. Good night."

The crowd began to file out of the bleachers as the teams gathered around their coaches before heading into their respective locker rooms. Henry and Martha slowly stepped down the center aisle with part of the departing crowd and waited near the edge of the wrestling mat. The two teams then headed for the showers as Bo walked over to Henry and Martha before joining his teammates. Bo had a big grin on his face as he talked to his father. "How did you like that, Pop?"

"Mighty impressive, son, mighty impressive."

Martha looked at her son with a sense of relief. "I don't know why I fret so much before each match. I was worried about how much bigger that other boy was."

"You know what they say, Ma. 'The bigger they are, the harder they fall."

"Yes, dear, 1 know," Martha answered. She had mixed emotions about Bo's new love for wrestling. It had made him self-assured and almost cocky compared with his apparent lack of esteem during his early grade school days, when he had been teased incessantly. In her son's first days in school, simple mispronunciations in class would elicit a chorus of snickers from his fellow first graders. Little Bo could never actually hear the snickers, but he could see them, and worst of all, he could feel them. For that reason alone, Martha knew that she must accept and embrace Bo's passion. However, only she would ever know and understand how scary it was for a protective mother to worry immensely as she watched her youngest son go into battle like a modern-day gladiator.

Martha fried to put her concern out of her mind. "Do you want us to wait for you in the parking lot after your bus gets back?" she asked.

"Nah, I can catch a ride with Tommy."

Henry seemed to look a little concerned himself. "Okay, son, but the public address announcer said it's starting to sleet outside now. Make sure Tommy drives slower once you leave the high school. We'll see you at home." Henry and Martha turned and headed for the exit as Bo walked to the visitor's locker room while dabbing sweat from his brow with a white towel. The strong smell of popcorn was overwhelming to him as he passed by the closed-down concession stand, reminding him of how long it had been since he had eaten.

Bo had walked about halfway to the door to the locker room after parting from his parents near the edge of the wrestling mat when a voice called out from behind. "Hey, Bozell!" yelled Matt Duncan. Henry and Martha were already outside. Since Bo didn't have his hearing aids in, he was oblivious to the fact that he was being yelled at.

Duncan, apparently still unaware that Bo had a partial hearing loss, had no way of knowing that the sophomore from Plattsmouth who had just embarrassed him in front of his hometown crowd couldn't hear him. He looked incensed that Bo was ignoring him as he quickened his pace, just catching up before his victorious smaller opponent had reached the visitor's locker room entrance. He tapped down hard on Bo's left shoulder. Bo wheeled around to face him, looking a little annoyed.

Duncan's eyes were all red rimmed like he might have been crying. They looked blackened as if charred from a burning fire. He was almost nose to nose with Bo before saying through clenched teeth, "1 was talking to you. What the hell's the matter with you, Bozell?"

Bo still had a surprised look on his face. His awkward speech in response served as supporting evidence of his claim to Matt Duncan. "I'm partially deaf. My hearing aids are in the locker room."

With that bit of news, Duncan seemed to get even angrier than before. Bo knew not only that his bigger opponent lost his first match of the year to him, a smaller wrestler who was only a sophomore, but that it was to an opponent who had a disability as well. Duncan was still close enough to rub noses with Bo, something neither one of them was probably contemplating at the time considering the circumstances. Besides, Duncan had bad breath. "There's something you need to know, Bozell, something I don't want you to forget. You haven't seen the last of me. You hear me? You haven't seen the last of me. We will meet again!" Duncan turned around and started to stomp back to the home team locker room.

"Is that a threat, Duncan?" Bo asked.

Duncan turned his head in Bo's direction as he continued to hastily walk away. "No, Bozell. It's a promise."

Bo just shook his head in disbelief as he walked through the locker room door, thinking how tired and lame that old cliche was. It's a promise. It was a simple answer to a simple question that would be the foretelling of a sequence of unsettling events.

Daniel Duncan was finally relaxing in his favorite leather chair in front of the fireplace, having kindled what had now become a blazing fire by the time he had plopped back down to unwind before going to bed. He was holding the business section of the local newspaper in front him while smoking his favorite pipe filled with cherry tobacco. Because of the Wednesday night wrestling meet that his son had just participated in, it was the first chance in his busy day to get caught up on the news.

He looked quite fatigued, having endured several high-level meetings at his railroad company's headquarters in Downtown Omaha that day. Normally, his half-hour commute in his comfortable cream Cadillac to his spacious home on the outskirts of Papillion was a time to unwind. But the early evening wrestling meet had caused him to speed home that night, ensuring that he was in the bleachers with his wife when his only son emerged from the locker room with his teammates.

His wife, Katherine, was sitting near him in another leather chair in their spacious family room, thumbing through her favorite fashion magazine that had arrived with the late-morning mail. Occasionally, she would reach up with her left hand and adjust her black bangs to the side of her forehead, having been told by her husband a few weeks ago that he would like to see her hair long again. Since she had spent most of the afternoon at the West Omaha Country Club, which they belonged to, it was her first chance of the day to get caught up on the latest fashion news. It was a subject she had followed without fail through the years, especially after landing a big catch like Daniel.

The only thing she had probably regretted about marrying her executive husband, a big man capable of producing a big son, was the twenty hours of labor and delivery she had endured when giving birth to Matt. He was the spitting image of his father—big boned, tall, and stocky with thick jet-black hair and piercing dark hazel eyes. At least Daniel had seemed happy that his heir apparent had been born, not protesting too much when Katherine had made it quite clear that she wouldn't ever go through the possibility of another twenty hours of labor again.

Thus, Matt had turned out to be their only child—a very spoiled child according to the many teachers, administrators, and other people outside the home that had tolerated his bullying behavior through the years. He was always the biggest child in the class, a physical advantage that their son had always taken full advantage of. Mrs. Duncan had become firstname friendly with all the vice principals and principals at Matt's schools through the years because she had found herself standing in front of them quite often, having been called to come and pick up her son for the day. The worst suspension he had ever received was a whole week when he headbutted and then pounded into bloody submission a supposed new bully in town who had challenged him on the first day of school in the sixth grade.

The front door suddenly opened and slammed shut. Daniel and Katherine Duncan then heard their son rattling around in the kitchen a few seconds later. Mr. Duncan dropped his paper into his lap and temporarily removed the pipe from his mouth before turning his head in the direction of the kitchen door. "Matt! Come in here for a minute!"

"I'll be there in a second!" his son yelled back, sounding like he must have had his head stuck inside the refrigerator with the door open.

Matt Duncan finally came stomping into the family room. His parents had to have known that he was very agitated, judging by the scowl on his face and his puffy red eyes. Daniel Duncan was peering over the top of his newspaper, staring at his son. "Where have you been? The match was over a good hour ago. Besides, it's snowing outside."

Matt Duncan stayed standing between his two parents' high-back leather chairs. "I was just driving around for a while, that's all."

"Son, you need to settle down. It's just one loss. You can still win the heavyweight championship at state this year."

"He was a deaf-mute."

"Who's he? What are you talking about?"

"I said that young punk from Plattsmouth who got lucky against me is a damn deaf-mute, a retard. I lost to a retard tonight!"

Mrs. Duncan had been involved in a lot of charity work, with many of the recipients being physically or mentally impaired in one way or another. She had a big frown on her face as she looked up from her magazine at her son. "Matt, 1 know how disappointed you must feel right now, but it's very wrong to refer to a hearingimpaired person as a retard—or even as a deaf-mute for that matter. He might be a very smart young man that simply has a disability, that's all."

Mr. Duncan removed the pipe from his mouth and placed it upright in the fancy ashtray that was sitting on the mahogany table next to his chair. "Yes, son, you need to learn to be more respectful of other people who are different from you."

Matt Duncan wheeled around and stomped out of the room, mumbling under his breath, "That's a bunch of bullshit." He walked away toward his bedroom, where he must have decided to stay secluded for the rest of the evening.

Duncan's suspension at the start of his sixth-grade year was said to have been an embarrassment to his parents, although privately his father had confided in a coworker about how proud he was in the way his son had "taken care of business" that day. Daniel Duncan surely had heard what his son had just mumbled as he left the room, but it was obvious that he "let it go," just like he had apparently chosen to do on many other occasions when his son had gotten into trouble through the years.

Katherine looked at her husband. "Don't you think you should go have a little talk with him?"

Daniel Duncan raised his evening paper back up in front of him. "Maybe later." He glanced back in the direction of his son's bedroom before resuming his reading. He had never seemed to act embarrassed over the years when opposing coaches had often accused his son of being a dirty wrestler. He had told his wife early on that his son needed to have a little bit of a mean streak in him if he was going to be as successful as he had been in climbing the corporate ladder of the largest railroad company in the country.

Both parents had resumed their reading. They were seemingly oblivious to the loud noises that were now coming from their son's bedroom. They were probably just hoping that he hadn't punched a hole in his wall again.

Duncan's sudden shocking loss to Bo Bozell must have been devastating to his ego. He had never been beaten so quickly and so convincingly ever before. He had told anyone who would listen that he was going to go undefeated in his senior year. The match with Bo was the last one before qualifying in the district. Bo Bozell had been responsible for destroying a perfectly planned season by Duncan. Everyone at Papillion High School knew that Matt Duncan had never been a stranger to rage. Now it seemed that he had a new motivation and emotion—revenge.

The Plattsmouth wrestling team and coach were riding on the school bus, traveling in the late evening from Papillion to Plattsmouth. The coach took a seat in the middle of his wrestlers about halfway back. His team knew that he did that so he could have conversations with some of them on the way home. He would discuss what they had done well and the not so well during their matches.

Bo was sitting with his friend Tommy. After Tommy's lopsided loss, he had asked Bo as they were walking to the bus if he wouldn't mind sitting with him in the back. Bo knew why his friend had made such a request. It was so he could take refuge in the back with the star performer of the dual meet, thus avoiding getting his ear chewed off on the way home by Coach Brody. However, Bo was wishing they had chosen a seat closer to the front where it was warmer. All that either one of them was wearing was nothing more than thick, hooded sweatshirts and sweatpants over their underwear after showering in the visitor's locker room. Leaving their winter coats in Tommy's car had been a dumb idea, although neither of them had heard the weather forecast earlier in the day when it had been unseasonably warmer. Some of the upperclassmen on the team had winter coats on over their sweats, demonstrating that their additional experience was not just limited to their knowledge and abilities on a wrestling mat.

Tommy had been sitting slouched in his seat with his head down before he finally looked at Bo. "Man, I still can't get over how fast you put a lickin' on that big dumb ass from Papillion."

Bo could hear his friend's teeth chattering as they both rocked back and forth on their mutual bench seat. "Give the guy a break, Tommy. Just because I beat him doesn't mean he's that dumb. I just caught him off guard, that's all."

Tommy looked a little surprised after Bo's restrained response. He looked out of the window for the next few seconds at the falling snow before looking back at his friend and teammate. "Whatever, it was still cool to watch. At least for a few minutes, it helped me forget about what happened to me tonight."

Bo thought again about Duncan's threat after the match. What am I doing defending the big boob after what the jerk has said to me afterward, especially after I have won the match fair and square? Bo replayed Duncan's threat in his head. He had sounded like a bit of a psycho when he had gotten in Bo's face. "You know, the more I think about it, you might be right about Duncan."

"What do you mean by that, Bo?"

Bo didn't answer Tommy at first. He kept staring forward like he was deep in thought before he finally turned his attention back to his friend. "He stopped me outside the door to the locker room after the match. He got in my face and was telling me some crap about me seeing him again someday. I'm not sure what he meant by that. I guess he figures we might face each other at the state tournament. He was obviously pissed off that I beat him." "If he was that pissed off now, he's really going to be pissed when you beat him again at state," answered Tommy.

Bo decided it was time to change the subject. He didn't want to dwell on Duncan's threats anymore. "You know, it's not too late for you to turn things around before we get to the district finals. I hope you're still not too bummed out about your match. You've got to remember, your guy was state champion last year."

"I know, but I still sucked. I wasn't aggressive enough. I let him intimidate me too much."

Bo couldn't help but agree with Tommy's self-critique. "Yeah, it kinda looked like you did. You gotta go at it with the attitude that you're capable of beating any guy you face, no matter what his record is."

"I know," said Tommy. "You're right. I'll keep workin' on it. I'm gonna come out more aggressive in my first match at the district meet. You'll see."

The school bus continued to travel down the highway as Bo and Tommy stared forward in the darkness. The temperature had been steadily dropping since the bus had departed the Papillion High School parking lot. The ice and sleet had turned to a wet snow.

Both boys were so absorbed with wrestling thoughts that they had no idea what Bo's uncle Leonard was dealing with at the same time in the front of the bus. Especially as a rookie bus driver with limited experience, he was stressing out, trying to get his nephew and the others safely back to Plattsmouth. He was having one of those white-knuckle experiences. His vision was sometimes limited as the wiper blades that were swishing back and forth on the flat windshield were icing up more now.

The snow began to come down harder, covering the highway to the point where it was getting more difficult to determine if he was still driving in his lane or not. Poor Uncle Leonard had beads of sweat breaking out on his forehead, and his eyes looked wild with fear. He was wondering why the hell he had picked driving a school bus as a part-time job.

Finally, Tommy broke the silence. "Say, isn't that your uncle that's driving our bus tonight?"

"Yeah, that's him. He just started driving a couple of weeks ago. I guess my dad doesn't pay him enough at the shop. Either that or my aunt's medical bills have put them in a bind. She was in the hospital for over a week after her gallbladder surgery. I guess he's been trying to figure out ways to supplement his income." Tommy's question reminded Bo of something that his mother had asked him to do earlier in the day. "Hey, I'm glad you just mentioned Uncle Leonard. My mom told me to invite him and Alice over for dinner tomorrow night, and I forgot to tell him. My brother Ben's leave time is up on Friday, and he's headin' over to 'Nam now."

"Your brother has to go to Vietnam? Aren't ya all worried?"

Bo had been immersed with his wrestling passion most of the evening until his friend's concern and comment jolted him back to reality. The reality that his brother was heading over to a war zone had been temporarily pushed aside in his mind as he had prepared for and won his own little war that night. "Oh yeah, especially Mom. She cried when Ben first told her the news."

"How's Ben feel about it?"

"Doesn't seem to bother him none. He's one of those gung-ho marines, I guess. Anyway, I better go up and tell Uncle Leonard about tomorrow night before I forget again." Bo got up and walked to the front of the moving bus, grabbing onto the seat backs as he walked forward to steady himself.

The coach yelled at Bo after he walked past him. "Bo, you need to sit back down! Bo!" Bo either didn't hear his coach or simply ignored him as he walked up the aisle toward his uncle, who seemed to be concentrating very hard on his driving.

Bo's uncle Leonard glanced over briefly to see that it was his nephew and then turned his full attention back to the road, at least what he could see of the road through the frosty, partially iced-up windshield. "You shouldn't be up here, Bo."

Bo responded to his uncle's concern as he held on to a pole next to the inside entrance stairway to the bus. "I know, Unc. I just wanted to talk to you quick about tomorrow night."

Before Bo could continue talking, a deer darted across the road in front of the bus. Leonard made a rookie mistake by applying the brakes too hard as he took a firmer grip on the steering wheel. With the weight of the bus, any veteran bus driver would have known to simply allow the impact of the deer rather than suddenly brake hard on a snow-packed highway that was hiding bottom layers of intermittent ice.

Bo was caught off balance and slammed into the front windshield. As he tried to right himself, the bus hit a patch of ice and began to slide sideways while he desperately tried to grab onto something, anything.

Leonard yelled out to everyone on the bus. "Hold on, everybody!"

The wrestling team and coach were yelling and trying to grab onto anything they possibly could. The deer had run across the road by now, and Leonard had somehow managed to miss her. But the bus was still fishtailing back and forth, hitting more patches of ice. Luckily, there weren't any oncoming cars or trucks in either direction on the two-lane highway at the time.

As Bo grabbed for something, he unfortunately grabbed the door mechanism. The doors popped open just before the bus fishtailed again. The rear of the bus had swung out into the oncoming lane. The sudden movement of the bus caused Bo to lose his grip on the chromed door handle. He would never remember how helpless he felt at the time. Although it was a grim reality that people generally chose not to dwell on, everyone's life can be changed or ended in a split second. He fell backward out of the open doorway and landed on his head on the snow-packed asphalt highway before rolling onto his stomach, unconscious from the blow to his skull.

Leonard finally realized that he needed to keep his foot off the brake as he regained control, letting the big yellow school bus roll to a stop as he carefully steered it off onto the shoulder of the road. The bus had rolled at least three hundred feet farther down the road since Bo had fallen out of the open doorway. "Coach! Bo's lying in the road!" yelled Leonard. "We've got to get to him before another car comes along!"

The players started scrambling to get off the bus. The coach leaped to his feet and quickly moved to the front entrance, grabbing and shoving boys back down into their seats on the way. He turned around and yelled at his team, "Everybody should stay on the bus!"

Leonard had already gone out of the open doorway, running down the highway, with Coach Brody several feet behind him. The packed snow and ice crunched under his shoes. His heart was practically pounding out of his chest. He couldn't feel the cold, even though the pelting snow was striking him in the face, limiting his ability to see ahead of him. An adrenaline rush had quickly taken hold, propelling him forward with one clear objective—to save the youngest son of his elder brother.

Both men were having a hard time running on such a slippery surface. They both took a tumble on the icy surface as they tried to run as fast as they could, scrambling up and trying to run more cautiously. A few of the wrestlers had already exited the bus, disregarding their coach's orders. Leonard wasn't thinking about the mistake his nephew had made by standing in a moving bus that was traveling along an icy, snow-packed highway. He was blaming himself for what had just happened.

Just then, some headlights appeared from around a curve, traveling in the same direction as the bus had. It was still several hundred feet from where Bo was lying, but it wouldn't be long before the car would be on him. Leonard had seen the oncoming car. "Oh my god!" He tried to run faster, but it didn't appear that either he or Bo's coach, who was gaining ground on Leonard, was going to get to Bo before the quickly approaching car. The oncoming headlights of the car were getting closer and closer. Bo's limp body was about to become an unannounced speed bump in the road. The unconscious boy wasn't dead yet, but he surely would be within the next ten seconds.

Dog materialized between two tall trees. Immediately, the falling snow— driven by a gusty winter wind—began to pelt him in the face. His nostrils began to blow out a visible, misty steam that would be expected on such a cold winter night. As he regained his bearings after his split-second journey through time and space, he suddenly felt even more saddened than before that he might never see the old man again. Oh well, he thought, *at least 1 already am able to stay a lot longer with Lester than on some of my previous missions I have spent on Earth. Plus, he knew he had been given a bonus on this trip— multiple missions this time around.*

His thoughts were abruptly interrupted. He was being instructed that he had precious seconds left to act, or else, his second mission on the same trip would already be over before it had barely begun. He bolted through the remaining trees toward the widest gap up ahead, where he could see some light beaming between the last set of trees that seemed to give way to some type of clearing.

Just when Leonard and Bo's coach had seemed to give up hope, a dog came running out of the ditch, appearing out of nowhere. In an instant, the dog was at Bo's side. The big dog looked up to see the oncoming headlights of the fastapproaching car. He dug his nose under the boy's left shoulder and rolled him onto his back. Then the mastiff bit down into his sweatshirt hood, which had flipped up next to his head. The massive mystery dog pulled him off the road and onto the safety of the road's shoulder, taking advantage of the fact that Bo's limp body was lying on a patch of ice.

The fast-approaching car had hit its brakes, the driver finally spotting the more visible dog that was just off to the side of the road. It started to fishtail a little bit as it attempted to stop. The white sedan's driver regained control of the wheel just in time to miss Bo and the bullmastiff by inches, finally pulling off onto the shoulder of the road once he was a safe distance beyond them.

Leonard and Bo's coach ran off onto the shoulder as well, where the footing was a little more predictable, slowing their pace upon seeing the mysterious dog's surprise rescue of the boy. He was lying unconscious on his back as the dog sat by his side, occasionally lapping his face. A middleaged couple got out of the fourdoor white sedan as Leonard and Bo's coach raced past them, together reaching the motionless body that was lying in the snow on the road's shoulder.

Bo's coach crouched down next to him as did Leonard on the other side while the dog got up, giving the two men more room. The bullmastiff sat down again just a few feet away. The coach felt for a pulse. "He's still alive, Leonard."

Leonard wiped his brow as he looked down at his nephew. "Thank god! You're lucky to be alive, son!" It was a well-intentioned blessing that fell on deaf ears.

The coach motioned toward the school bus as he looked back at Leonard. "Run back to the bus and call an ambulance on the CB!"

Leonard jumped up and took off on a dead run for the bus, falling and getting up once again as he hurriedly but gingerly made his return trip to the school bus, whose engine was still idling with the emergency brake on. The whole wrestling team passed him on their way to Bo. As they and the couple from the car circled around, Bo's coach finally glanced up again. "I thought I told you boys to stay on the bus!"

Tommy, Bo's close friend who was sitting next to him moments before the freak accident, spoke for the team. "We just thought we might be able to help, Coach. We're like family. How could you expect us to stay on the bus at a time like this?"

Coach Brody didn't answer Tommy. He was staring back into Bo's expressionless face.

Tommy asked the coach one last question. "Is Bo going to be all right?"

The coach continued to look down at an unconscious, helpless-looking boy who was his star performer of the evening only a little over an hour ago. "I don't know. He's unconscious but breathing. I know we don't want to move him. Give me a couple of your coats so we can keep him warm."

The husband of the middle-aged couple offered to help. "We have a blanket in the trunk."

"Great, that would be even better," replied the coach as he glanced up at the husband. The man wheeled around and ran back to his car to get the blanket.

His wife looked at the dog while her husband was away. "Did you see what this dog just did?"

The coach temporarily looked away from Bo and up at the woman. "Yeah. 1 saw it, but 1 still don't believe it. When I think of a guardian angel, a dog just doesn't come to mind."

It was late evening, shortly before midnight, and Bo was lying in a hospital bed. He was still unconscious, and there were restraints to keep him immobilized. There was a neck brace around his neck. Bo's mother, Martha, was sitting by his side in a chair, holding his limp left hand. There was another chair next to her that was empty.

Just then, a young doctor walked into the room. Martha glanced up at the doctor, temporarily taking her gaze off her son. "Where is your husband, Mrs. Bozell?"

"He went down the hall to get some coffee out of the vending machine. He should be back any minute."

The door opened, and Henry walked into the room, holding a small paper cup filled with coffee. Martha slowly lifted herself out of the chair, grimacing slightly as she rose, feeling some stiffness in her lower back from the prolonged sitting. The doctor looked at Henry. "I'm glad you're back, Mr. Bozell. We have some preliminary X-rays and test results, so I wanted to tell you and your wife what we know at this point."

Martha was dreading the news of the test results. Her brother-in-law, Leonard, who had been struggling to keep the bus on the highway, hadn't seen the fall out of the bus door, but some of the others on the bus had described what they had seen. With what she had been told, Martha knew that it would be miraculous if Bo had somehow escaped serious injury.

It was so out of character for Martha's husband, Henry, to appear gloomy, scared, and sad. But she could see it in his eyes after he had come back into Bo's hospital room, seeing the doctor there. She knew that it took a family tragedy— like with his brother, Leonard, several years ago—to temporarily take away his usual self-assuredness and spontaneous, smirky smile. He stared down at his sleeping son before looking into the eyes of the young doctor, who still stood on the other side of the bed. "How bad is it, Doc?"

Even though Bo was seemingly unaware of any conversations going on around him, the doctor walked over to the far side of the room near the window and motioned for Henry and Martha to join him. He spoke very softly, slightly above a whisper, after Bo's parents had huddled next to him. "I'm sure it doesn't come as any surprise to you to know that Bo has a pretty bad concussion. But what concerns me even more is the fact that he has fractured the second and third cervical vertebrae in his neck."

Martha looked startled by the doctor's news. After everything her youngest son had been through, now there was yet another major setback for him to deal with. Her eyes quickly welled up with tears, which began to run down her cheeks as she tried to regain her composure enough so she could speak. "You mean Bo could be paralyzed?"

The doctor must have recognized that Martha was now thinking the worst. "We won't know the full implications of his neck injury until he regains consciousness, Mrs. Bozell. The possible extent of nerve damage, if any, won't become clear until Bo himself can tell us and show us how he feels. The second and third cervical vertebrae are part of the seven vertebrae that are found in the neck. We don't see any other broken vertebrae in Bo's spinal column or any other serious injuries or broken bones. Hopefully, he should regain consciousness soon, and then we'll be able to make a better prognosis of Bo's chances for full recovery. Right now, there's considerable swelling around his spinal cord where the breaks occurred in the upper region of his neck."

Henry and Martha turned their attention away from the doctor, and they both looked at Bo. Then they looked back at each other. Martha, who bravely had been trying to hold back her tears, began to cry uncontrollably. Henry put his arms around her and consoled her. "Don't cry, Mother. Bo's a tough young man. He's going to be all right."

The doctor headed for the door. Before leaving, he turned back toward Martha and Henry. "All we can do now is wait and pray. I'll still be here for the next few hours, and the nurses will be in regularly to check on your son's condition."

After the doctor left the room, Henry and Martha sat back down in their chairs next to Bo's bed. Henry took the lid off the coffee he'd brought back and began to sip from the cup while he and Martha continued to stare at their youngest son.

Martha was dabbing her eyes with a white hanky that she had pulled out of her purse. She noticed that the smell of the fresh coffee was contrasting sharply with the overall sanitized smell of the hospital room. Martha started to feel like her head was floating, and her mind began to drift. Memories began to fill her head. Knowing that she needed to stay focused on her son, she attempted to will them away, but it was useless. She remembered the times when she had to be strong for her family. Her thoughts from the past came rushing back to her like a movie reel of her youngest son's life in chronological order.

Martha's worried mind was racing, and there was nothing she could do to slow it down as she held her youngest son's hand and stared at his closed eyelids. Memories of his birth, his infant years, his first steps as a toddler, and so on went racing through her mind as she looked on his face. She cursed God for allowing this tragedy to happen. It just wasn't fair. Bo had already overcome so many obstacles in his life. Why now did this have to happen to him? He had endured the frustration of his early grade school years—the teasing and the taunting of his young peers, the inability to understand everything the teacher was saying in the classroom.

She remembered the expression on his face when she and Henry had told him that they were sending him away for a while to a special school in Omaha. It was early summer after his fourth-grade year. "Do I have to go, Mommy?" he had asked with that pained look on his little face. She remembered how she had fought back the tears, trying to put on a good front, while her stomach was churning over into knots, and her heart was aching more than anyone would ever know.

It was his fourth-grade teacher who had recommended that he be sent to the Nebraska School for the Deaf. She had frankly told Henry and Martha that she probably shouldn't have passed him out of the fourth grade. The teacher said that she was a bit amazed that he had even made it to the fourth grade without having been required to take the first, the second, or the third grade over again.

Such talk had especially seemed to hurt Henry. Her husband had always been such a proud man. Martha knew that it had been a hard pill for him to swallow that his youngest son was struggling so. Even though Martha had borne the brunt of the child-rearing years, Henry had spent a lot of time with his sons whenever he could. He taught all three of his sons how to ride a bike and throw a baseball when they were young and how to drive a car after they had reached their fifteenth birthdays. One of the reasons that Martha loved her husband so much was that he had always been there for his sons when they really needed him and when they had looked to him for guidance.

Martha was glad that she didn't have to be in the car when the driving lessons were going on; however, judging by the expressions on the faces of father and sons when they returned after the first lesson or two, somehow they had all successfully learned how to drive. And someday all three sons would look back with appreciation at their father's efforts. In fact, John and Ben— their two eldest sons— probably already did. In Bo's case, the memories of the driving lessons were still too fresh in his mind. It would probably take a few years before a true appreciation would take hold. Martha knew how memories usually tended to soften with time.

She was just glad that it had been her sickness during pregnancy that the doctors had surmised was the cause of Bo's partial hearing loss. Martha knew had Henry thought that he had somehow been to blame, it probably would have almost killed him. She could handle the guilt to herself, never telling Henry how much it hurt inside to know that she was the one responsible for her baby boy being less than perfect. Sure, the doctors had explained that it really wasn't her fault. They had said that she was not alone—that many pregnant women during that period had abnormalities in their newborns upon birth. But such assurances hadn't made the pain inside her hurt any less.

Henry, bless his heart, had been so supportive. Yes, he sometimes got under her skin. Sometimes she just wanted to hit her stubborn husband over the head with her frying pan, probably a feeling that had been shared by her three sons after their first driving lessons. But then she would always get hold of her emotions and remind herself how lucky she was to have such a softy beneath that rough exterior of a man. Then she thought about how Bo was so much like his father in many ways. Her tears and her thoughts flowed on and on as her son continued to lie in a coma before her troubled eyes.

A few minutes passed before a nurse entered the room. Martha's reminiscing helped her realize that she had the same resolve now as she had long ago. She would be strong for her son. She sat quietly as the nurse checked the monitors that were hooked up to Bo. The nurse felt his forehead before holding his wrist while she looked at her watch for a minute.

She turned around and faced Henry and Martha. "His vital signs are all good, Mr. and Mrs. Bozell. I'm sure it won't be long before he regains consciousness."

She passed by where Henry and Martha were sitting and had almost reached the door before she stopped suddenly and wheeled back around. "Oh, by the way, do you folks own a big dog? It's a male. It's one of those large breeds that looks really muscular with short reddish-brown silky hair and a really big head."

Henry and Martha both looked at each other. "You don't suppose it's the dog that Leonard and Coach Brody kept talking about after we got here, do you?" asked Henry. He directed his attention to the nurse before Martha had a chance to respond. "My brother, Leonard, and Coach Brody claim a dog saved our son's life."

Martha turned away from Henry and looked back at the nurse with a quizzical expression. "Why are you asking about the dog?"

The nurse looked at the only window in the room. "Some of the staff have noticed that this big dog has been sitting outside near the emergency entrance ever since they brought your son in by ambulance. If you look out the window, you can see the dog sitting there from here."

Henry and Martha got up, walked over to the window, and peered through the curtains. Sure enough, a big bullmastiff was sitting near the entrance, staring at the emergency entrance door. Luckily, the snowstorm had subsided about an hour ago. The dog was very visible as he sat directly beneath an exterior lamppost. He was sitting there so motionless that only his visible breath from the crisp evening air revealed that he was alive and not some giant stuffed animal.

The nurse continued her explanation as Henry and Martha watched the dog through the window. "One of our orderlies tried to shoo him away, but he keeps coming back. He seems gentle enough, so we decided that maybe we should check with you folks before we call someone to take him away."

Martha turned around from the window and looked at the nurse. "Please don't have the dog removed. If it's true what we've heard, that he saved our son's life, we'll look after him."

Henry looked visibly upset with what Martha had just proposed. She knew how much he had loved the family's last dog, a male German shepherd named Rex. Rex had turned out to be dad's dog. He was Henry's constant shadow whenever he was home. He used to take Rex for long walks almost every night after supper. It had been several years now, but it was obvious that Henry still hadn't gotten over the loss of such a good and loyal friend. "Martha, you know how I feel about another dog ever since we had to put Rex to sleep."

Martha vehemently dismissed her husband's complaint. "That dog saved our son's life for god's sake. At least for now, Henry, until we've had a chance to see if we can find the dog's owner. The poor thing's probably cold and hungry."

Henry tilted his head to the left side and lifted his right eyebrow while holding his hands up, which was the signal to Martha that she'd won the argument, even if it was temporary at best. Martha knew that she was going to have her way, at least for now. She also knew how hard Henry had taken Rex's death, so she was appreciating his reluctant willingness to allow this mysterious new dog into their lives. "I wonder how he found his way to the hospital."

"The accident only happened two or three miles out of town. That's not far for a dog to travel," Henry replied. He then looked at the nurse, who was waiting for a final answer on the dog. "Okay, tell your staff not to worry about the dog. We'll handle it for now."

"Very well, Mr. Bozell, as you wish." The nurse then left the room. Martha sat back down in her chair while Henry remained standing. She turned her attention away from Bo and looked at her husband. "Will you go outside and check on the dog? See if he has a collar on him with some identification. And maybe you can find a dish for some water and buy a sandwich or something for him to eat. I'll have someone come and get you if Bo suddenly wakes up."

Henry let out a deep sigh. "All right, Mother, if it'll make you happy." He slouched out of the room.

Martha took Bo's limp left hand and caressed it between her own soft, warm hands. Tears streamed down her cheeks again as she softly sobbed, rocking back and forth on the edge of the chair.

It was shortly after sunrise. Henry was sitting, slouched over, asleep in one of the two chairs next to Bo's bed. Martha was standing closer to Bo. She leaned over his bed while she held Bo's left hand, and she caressed his cheek with the back of her other hand.

Bo suddenly opened his eyes and then closed them again. His eyelids fluttered partially open and closed and then opened and closed again. Martha reacted with a big smile and a look of relief on her face. "Bo, can you hear me, honey?"

Bo's eyes finally stayed open. "Of course, I can hear you, Ma. Where am I?"

"You're in the hospital, dear. Henry! Wake up! Bo's come to!" she exclaimed.

Henry shook his head back and forth a little bit as he sat up straight in his chair. He opened his eyes and looked over to see that his son was looking at him.

Bo had a look of irritation on his face. "Ma, did ya have to talk so loud right next to my ear?"

Martha's face got a little flush as she realized how loud she must have been as her son had suddenly awakened. "I'm sorry. It's just that I was so excited to see those beautiful baby blues of yours again. You really had us all worried."

Bo looked around on either side of his bed using his peripheral vision since his head was so immobilized. He could feel the weight of his hearing aids in his ears. In fact, both ears ached from having to anchor Bo's "bridges to auditory comprehension," where the simplicity of sound was taken for granted by the hearing world but never by those like Bo. "Why are my hearing aids in? You know I never sleep with them on."

Martha gave Bo a little pat on the shoulder. "We thought it might help you wake up easier. Your uncle Leonard noticed they weren't in your ears after the accident, so he searched the road with a flashlight until he found them."

Bo scanned his hospital room again, with his eyes darting from left to right. "Why is there a dog in my room?"

Henry and Martha turned around to look behind them where Bo had just focused his attention. There was no dog. "You must be hallucinating, son. There's no dog in this room," Henry replied.

"What did he look like, Bo?" Martha asked.

"He was really big, with a big head."

Henry and Martha both looked at each other with astonished looks on their faces before Henry walked quickly over to the window, oblivious to some small puddles of melted snow that he had just walked through, before peering out between the curtains. The bullmastiff was sitting exactly where they had last seen him. He walked back over to the bed before turning his attention to his wife. "Nah, couldn't be. Must be the drugs he's on." "But how did he know what he looked like?" Martha asked. Bo was already afraid and confused. "What are you two talking about?"

"Sorry, honey. I'll tell you later, once you're feeling better," Martha answered as she smiled back at her son.

"How did I get here? What happened to me?" His anxiety-filled, rapid- fire questions mirrored the same ones asked by many a victim of similar circumstances when their lives had been turned topsy-turvy in an instant. It was all about waking up from a nightmare, only to find out that it had been a reality. Bo was now a fullfledged member of the Lost Consciousness Club, a membership whose dues were paid with the precious loss of time, a state of mind unrelated to the nightly need for sleep.

Martha bent down so she could look directly into her son's eyes. "You don't remember?"

"I remember talking with Uncle Leonard in the front of the bus. I remember the bus swerving, and I hit my head. Then I tried to grab onto something. I lost my grip, and I remember falling backward and a sudden rush of cold air. That's all I remember."

Bo looked down at the two sets of straps that were holding him in place in his bed. One was across his chest, and the lower strap was across his legs, slightly above the knees. He could feel the brace that was securely fastened around his neck. His head was throbbing, and he knew that the pain and tightness he was feeling in his neck wasn't just because of the neck brace. It was slowly starting to sink in that he must be badly injured. He was afraid. *Just how bad am I hurt?* He almost was too afraid to ask. "How come I can't move?"

Martha shot a horrified glare at her husband. "Oh my god! Did you hear what he just said? He can't move, Henry!"

Being a Bozell, Bo wasn't about to let it show that he was scared. He not only was a Bozell but he also was the youngest one. He had always felt like he had to act tough, trying to rise above the fact that he was, and always would be, *the baby of the family.* He started grinning after listening to his mother's ranting. "What are ya gettin' all excited about?" asked Bo.

"You just said you can't move!" Martha snapped back.

Bo clenched his teeth, doing his best Kirk Douglas impersonation. "Well, of course, I can't move. Why do they have me all strapped down like this?"

Martha, apparently finally realizing what her son had just said to her, relaxed from her previous nervous state of confusion. "It was for your own protection, in case you came to when no one was watching you. They were concerned that you could fall out of bed or something." "Do you think you can move, son?" asked Henry.

Martha interrupted Bo before he could answer his father. "Don't move a muscle yet, until we get the doctor in here." She looked at Henry without saying anything.

Henry turned and headed for the door. "I'll go try and find the doc."

Only a few minutes had passed since Henry had left the room and found the doctor with the good news that Bo had awakened from his coma. Martha and Henry were standing off to the side as the young doctor and an older nurse was tending to their son. The nurse was unbuckling the straps that had been restraining Bo while the doctor was shining a tiny, little flashlight into his eyes at close range. "Will you follow the light back and forth with just your eyes, please?" Bo did as the doctor said.

"How many fingers am I holding up?"

"Two."

"Very good, Bo. What's your mother's name?"

"Ma—I mean, Martha."

"Okay then." The doctor dropped his little flashlight back into the top front pocket of his white smock and placed the first two fingers of his left hand into the boy's right hand that was resting palm up. "Okay, Bo, I want you to squeeze my two fingers as best as you can." Bo gripped down on his fingers. The doctor's face grimaced. "Okay, Bo, you can let go now."

Bo released his grip. The doctor took his young patient's other hand, but this time, he placed his whole hand inside of Bo's as if to shake hands with him. "Just squeeze my whole hand this time, Bo, but briefly." Bo gripped the doctor's hand and then relaxed his grip. "Very good."

The doctor walked to the foot of the bed and pulled the covers off Bo's feet. "Can you wiggle your toes?" Bo wiggled his toes for the doctor.

Henry and Martha were watching intently, smiling broadly as their son was able to do everything that the doctor asked of him. The nurse was standing on the other side of the bed observing. The tall young doctor walked around next to the nurse and faced Bo from the side, looking directly at Martha and Henry. "Well, so far, I'd have to say that your son is very lucky. The swelling around the spinal cord does not appear to have caused any paralysis. Mr. and Mrs. Bozell, would you please step out into the hallway with me for a minute while the nurse finishes up with your son for now?"

Henry and Martha followed the doctor, with Martha—being the last one to leave the room—closing the door tightly behind her. She was looking at her husband standing next the doctor when she heard heavy footsteps quickly approaching up the hallway to her right. "Leonard, you're back awfully early this morning."

Leonard bent over and touched his knees, exhaling deeply as if to catch his breath. "Couldn't sleep, Martha. I had to know how Bo was doing." The doctor glanced at Leonard without speaking.

"It's okay, Doc. This is my brother. Go ahead and say what you were going to say," said Henry.

"We'll be monitoring your son's progress closely. As soon as the swelling in his neck has gone down sufficiently, we'll be doing some more testing to determine the need to insert some pins into his broken vertebrae."

Henry got a funny look on his face. Martha knew that he must have just fully digested everything that the doctor had told them. "My son's wrestling days are over, aren't they, Doc?"

The doctor let out a sigh. "Yes, Mr. Bozell. I'm sorry to say . . . you are correct."

Leonard looked at the closed door to Bo's room. His eyes suddenly looked moist. "It was my fault... all my fault. I've managed to mess things up again for this family."

Henry reached over and threw his arm around his younger brother. Henry was practically on his tiptoes as his younger brother was a big, tall man. "Now, Leonard, don't be so hard on yourself. It really wasn't your fault. Bo shouldn't have left his seat in the back of the bus. He's awake now. You can go on in." Henry removed his arm from around his brother. Leonard nodded to Henry and Martha before opening the hospital room door and walking in, closing the door gently behind him.

Just like her husband and Leonard, Martha looked visibly upset by the news, understanding how tragic this development would be for her son. She knew how important wrestling had become for Bo. It had finally allowed him to make his mark in life. His confidence had been soaring as he had remained undefeated ever since his very first match. "My son is going to be heartbroken to hear that bit of news."

Heartbroken was an understatement. Bo had always exhumed an aura of uniqueness about himself, even from a very early age—a mischievous toddler who broke the mold when it came to the exploration of his surroundings and learning all that God's green earth had to offer. He had known no fear. When Henry and Martha had finally figured out why he seemed to ignore them, why he didn't always come when they called for him, why his speech seemed slurred, they were devastated.

Martha and Henry's youngest son had a disability—a fact that they both had had to come to terms with in their own way. It was amazing, and a credit to Bo's early tenacity, that he was almost four years old before his partial hearing loss was diagnosed. Once Bo became old enough to realize that he was a little different from the other children his age, he lost a lot of that swagger that was so apparent from the beginning.

Martha thought about the sad reality of parents setting the wrong example for their children, infecting them with an uneducated and narrowminded view of disabled children and adults. She knew that there had to be many disabled children who began life, as Bo had, full of life with high expectations. They began life feeling on top of the world, only to be beaten down to the point of feeling like an outsider, the object of ridicule as a child and pitied as an adult.

Yes, poor little Bo Bozell had struggled through his first few years of grade school just like Martha had been remembering that very morning. He had tried in vain to keep up with the other normal children in the class. The teachers, aware of his hearing problem, always placed him in the front of the class. They meant well by doing so, but this only heightened his feelings of inadequacy. Children could be so cruel at that age. Simple little miscues could set off simple little minds. Pronouncing the word "friend" as "fiend" was all it ever took for the other children to point and giggle at the outsider who had to sit in the front of the class.

After four years of enduring such torture, that visionary, thoughtful fourth-grade teacher whom Martha had been thinking about earlier, as she sat by her unconscious son, recommended to Henry and Martha that they consider sending their son to the school in Omaha for the hearing impaired. It was a difficult decision for Bo's parents to make because they wouldn't get to see their youngest son except on weekends. As Martha had been remembering earlier, Henry would never know how hard all that had been on her back then.

After some painful soul-searching, they sent their son away to be with children who shared his perception of life. It turned out to be a good decision. After two years of learning to study without the full benefit of one of his senses, Bo returned to Plattsmouth Junior High School. He now had the skills that enabled him to compete with classmates who had no idea what it took for him to at least appear to be normal except for the hearing aids that he wore in each of his ears. He had mastered the skill of lip-reading. No one other than those in the same predicament could understand how challenging it was to be able to heighten the sense of sight to appear relatively normal in day-to-day living.

Finally, in the eighth grade, Bo was introduced to wrestling in physical education class. It was a blessing. He finally found something that he was good at. He wasn't just good—he was damned good. Bo had always demonstrated a lot of natural athletic ability. Along with that, he had started out life with a fearless attitude, not easily intimidated by anyone or anything. So it really shouldn't have been any big surprise that he had taken to wrestling like a duck took to water. He annihilated everyone in his class, regardless of their weight. The gym teacher was an assistant wrestling coach for the high school varsity team. He knew talent when he saw it.

It wasn't long before Bo was asked to come and practice with the high school team. It became embarrassing for high school wrestlers to get their ass kicked by an eighth grader. Word soon got around school that Bo was not only someone to not be made fun of or pitied but also someone to be looked up to because of his physical prowess. Bo quickly went from being pitied to being admired. Shallow young minds can, at times, be very predictable in the teenage years. All he had to prove was that he could kick some ass to be accepted by his peers.

Unfortunately, Bo got too caught up with his newfound fame. He decided that wrestling was his ticket to glory. He forgot about all the commonsense things that he learned at the Nebraska School for the Deaf. Bo only got by in the classroom in his eighth-grade and freshman years because the teachers knew about both his strengths and his weaknesses. Maybe his disability disguised his lack of effort when it came to preparation for his school assignments. His newfound safe world came crashing down on him the night he foolishly tried to walk in a bus that was skating on a frozen highway.

In one moment, Bo went once again from being on top of the world to a person of pity. Wrestling had been his savior—and now it was gone. How could he now make sense of his purpose in life? He would have to start all over again. As Bo lay in his hospital bed, he wasn't thinking about feeling lucky to be alive. Instead, he was feeling sorry for himself. *What am 1 any good at other than wrestling? It just isn't fair.*

A week had passed since the bus accident. Bo had received a lot of visitors during the past week while recovering in the hospital. Leonard, especially, had made it a point to come up and see Bo every night. Despite constant reassurances from Martha, his brother, and even Bo, he seemed to be racked with guilt over the bus accident. Everyone in the family had become as worried about Leonard's state of mind as they were about Bo's recovery from his fall. Had it not been for Leonard's attempted suicide several years earlier, the family probably wouldn't have been as worried as they were now.

Leonard was the youngest of three boys born to Claude and Marie Bozell. Claude and Marie had emigrated from France after World War I, having joined a cousin who was able to help Claude land his first job in one of the beefpacking plants in South Omaha. They finally saved up enough money to allow Claude to begin tenant farming southwest of Plattsmouth. Claude's sudden death from a heart attack in 1939 left the three boys—Henry, Stanley, and Leonard—to work the farm along with their mother, Marie.

Marie then a suffered a stroke less than a year after her husband died. Maybe she was trying to join her husband in the afterlife. Fortunately or unfortunately, depending on one's point of view, she only got herself halfway there. After her stroke, Marie was a little scary to look at. She was left with a lazy left eye as she dragged her half-paralyzed body around the farmhouse. Marie had stringy gray hair and a habitual sullen expression. She had always been a strong-willed and oftentimes a very stubborn woman, but the stroke had taken her overall attitude to a whole new level of despair and distrust.

Henry had already left the farm by then, having inherited his body shop business from his bachelor boss who retired and moved to Florida. Henry and Stanley both served in the military during World War II. Henry served out his time as a gunnery instructor in Puerto Rico while Stanley was on a supply ship in the North Atlantic. Stanley left for the mountains of Colorado after returning from the war. That just left Leonard, the youngest son, as the only one left on the farm to care for his ailing mother while trying to scratch out a living as a tenant farmer like his father had done.

Leonard had a limited relationship in high school with a classmate named Ida Carlson. They had lost touch for the first couple of years after graduation. He was in town doing some grocery shopping for his mother one day when he encountered Ida, who was working for her father at his IGA Grocery Store in Plattsmouth during the summer. He was totally smitten with her that day as the blossom had totally bloomed since he had last seen her on graduation day.

They began a whirlwind romance that culminated with a small wedding toward the end of that summer. In hindsight, Ida probably should have spent more time around her new mother-in-law before agreeing to become a farm wife to Leonard and a maidservant to Marie.

Marie Bozell constantly berated Ida, the insults always flying out of the right corner of her half-dead mouth. She seemed to always find fault in everything her young daughter-in-law did, whether it be cooking, housekeeping, or laundry. Ida finally couldn't take it anymore, moving back in with her parents and immediately filing for divorce. It was only a few months later that she married Sam Goldstein, meeting him at Sam's pharmacy when she had come by one day to talk to Martha.

To say that Leonard took her leaving hard would be an understatement. Only ten months after Ida had left him, his mother fell down the stairs in their farmhouse while he was out working the fields. She was dead before he found her that day, all twisted up with her neck broken.

Of course, he blamed himself for her untimely demise, even though it was his mother who had been too stubborn to move to the downstairs bedroom after her stroke. It was such a sad irony that the obstacle to his happiness with Ida had been removed only a few weeks after she had married Sam. Ida had gone away, but Leonard never stopped loving her, just like he never stopped loving his mother, even though her stroke had taken away her willingness to return his love.

He knew how much Ida had hated living with her parents before marrying him, so he had surmised that her quick marriage to Sam Goldstein probably had as much to do with getting away from her parents as it did her love for Sam. His theory was somewhat solidified when Martha had mentioned to him that Ida's parents, especially her father, continued to treat her like a helpless child, demanding that she live by their strict rules, even though she was a grown woman.

Leonard totally lost it on the day of his mother's funeral. He was a big teddy bear of a man, and the tragic events that had piled up on him in less than a year's time had finally taken their toll. Luckily, Henry—knowing the fragile state of mind of his brother—had sensed that something was wrong. Leonard's sudden disappearance and absence from the meal served after the funeral had Henry thinking the worst. He made it out to the farm in time to cut his brother down as Leonard was trying to hang himself from a tree on a hill in the pasture. It was the same tree that Leonard and Ida had stood under on the summer night that he had gotten up the courage to ask for her hand in marriage.

The suicide attempt was kept secret. Henry had driven his brother straight to a hospital in Omaha. It was there that Leonard had met Alice, his wife of twenty-three years. She was a night-shift nurse in the psychiatric ward. It was Alice who helped Leonard the most in healing his heart. While Leonard was in the hospital, Henry had a farm sale, selling off all the antiquated farm machinery, as well as the remaining livestock. He persuaded Leonard to come to work for him at his body shop, knowing that there were too many painful reminders out on the old farm for his brother to bear anymore.

A nurse was wheeling Bo out of the emergency door to the hospital while Martha walked alongside him. Bo waved goodbye to Leonard, who was pulling out of the parking lot and heading back to work at the body shop. It was a sunny, unseasonably warm, and calm day, and the snow was melting away quickly. The curved concrete driveway and sidewalk were cleared and dry, and the snowdrifts created by the plowed and shoveled snow were shrinking into the grass. The sun felt warm to the skin, and there was a fresh smell in the air. It was a sign that it would be spring soon.

The big dog was sitting next to the entrance, just as he was the first night Bo was brought in. Martha had a pickup truck pulled up close to the rear entrance so her son didn't have to walk so far. When the dog saw that it was finally Bo, he sat up, with his tail wagging vigorously. Bo glanced at the bullmastiff. "This is the dog that was in my room."

"That's impossible, son. He was outside the whole time," Martha explained.

"Oh well, it doesn't matter," Bo mumbled.

"What did you say, honey?"

"Nothing. I'm just glad to get out of here."

The dog slowly padded over and laid his head on his lap. Bo immediately felt the weight of the big head and could feel the dog's hot breath blowing between his legs. Some warm drool started seeping through his jeans and into the skin near his crotch. It was uncomfortable to look down at the dog for very long as he was wearing a neck brace that restricted his motion.

The young nurse who had wheeled Bo up to the truck leaned forward and spoke softly next to his left ear. "Okay, Bo, end of the line. You can get up now. It's time to go home."

Bo looked up at the nurse and smiled. "Good. If I'd sat here much longer, I was going to ask if you could go get me a towel so I could dry myself off." Bo slowly rose from the chair, causing the dog to back up a bit. Dog's big brown eyes looked sad as he longingly looked at his new master, a look that said he'd made a bad first impression. Bo looked down at the big wet spot on the front of his jeans. "We're not stopping anywhere on the way home, are we, Ma?"

Martha smiled as she looked down at the wet spots on her son's jeans. "No, we're heading straight home."

Bo had a perplexed look on his face as he looked at the nurse. "Don't people who are discharged normally leave through the front entrance?"

"We made an exception in your case. We figured it was the only way this dog would be assured that you weren't inside the hospital anymore." The nurse smiled as she turned her head, looking back at the closest lamppost and the emergency room entrance door in the background. "He's been here waiting for you by that lamppost and staring at that door for over a week now, except for the couple of times that your dad took him back to your house. He was back within an hour both times. To be honest with you, the whole staff is kind of going to miss him. He never barked or bothered anybody. He just sat here and stared at the door. We all started taking turns bringing him food scraps."

Martha reached out and shook hands with the nurse. "My family can't thank you all enough for your kindness and consideration."

"No thanks necessary, Mrs. BozelL It was a pleasure." The nurse looked at the bullmastiff. "It looks like you've found yourself a very loyal dog, Bo."

Bo smiled back at the nurse as he carefully climbed into the passenger seat of the truck. "I still can't believe Pop said we could keep him."

Martha grinned back at her son. "I think it was more a matter of not figuring out how to get rid of him ... in your father's case."

Just as Martha had finished her comment to Bo, the dog jumped up into the back of the truck bed. Martha closed the passenger door for her son, walked around to the driver's door, and got in. The dog moved to the front of the truck bed and flopped down on his belly, but he was still big enough to be staring at the back of the boy's head through the rear window when he raised his head up. Martha started the engine, and they pulled away as the nurse rolled the empty wheelchair back toward the emergency entrance.

It was late afternoon in the Bozell kitchen. Bo was sitting at the kitchen table with a glass of milk while looking through some pictures. The dog was sitting near him. His mother was busy preparing the evening meal.

Bo had mentioned to his mother after he had walked into the kitchen that the smell of her home-cooked food made him feel especially happy to finally be home. She had just smiled back at her son, taking his comment as a compliment, before they both fell silent for a few minutes.

Bo finally quit shuffling through the pictures and glanced at his mother at the kitchen counter. "Man, I am so glad I don't have to eat that slop they serve at the hospital anymore. I always knew you were a good cook, Ma. 1 just want ya to know that 1 appreciate your cooking even more, now that I have something really bad to compare it with."

Martha got a funny look on her face. "Well, thank you, son ... 1 think." She interrupted Bo's pleasant thoughts of food. "Maybe you should take the dog outside before your father gets home. I can tell you right now he's not going to be too keen on letting this big dog stay inside the house."

Being all too familiar with his father's household rules, Bo had to have known this was coming. "Ah, Ma, just because Rex always had to stay outside doesn't mean this guy has to. He's been a good dog, and he hasn't gotten into anything since we got home. He seems like he's really smart."

"Well, he *did* know enough to pull you out of the way of that oncoming car," Martha replied. She went back to what she had been doing without asking again for her youngest son to remove the dog from the house.

Bo glanced up from the pictures he was looking at. "So you say you ran an ad in the newspaper while I was in the hospital?"

Martha turned her head back toward her son as she removed an onion from the refrigerator. "Yes, we did, but nobody called or came over to claim him. My guess is he was eating someone out of house and home, and they're glad he's found a new owner."

Bo looked back at the big dog as he continued to lie quietly on the floor next to the kitchen table. "Well, whatever the reason, I'm glad he's mine now. Right, boy?"

The bullmastiff lifted his head off the floor and looked straight at Bo. His brown eyes were very penetrating and friendly. "Woof!" he responded, his tail wagging vigorously, leaving no doubt that he was pleased to be a new member of the Bozell family. Of course, he hadn't spent much time with Henry yet. His overall take on the situation was certainly subject to change.

Bo began to carry on a conversation with the mystery dog. "I guess the next thing is to figure out what your name's gonna be."

The bullmastiff stared at Bo as if he was looking right through him.

Bo scratched his head as he looked up toward the ceiling. "Let's see . . . hmmm . . . how about. . . Goliath?"

The big dog immediately dropped down flat on his belly with his chin resting on the linoleum floor. He crossed his front paws over his head and moaned.

"Ma, will you look at that? I think he's trying to tell me he doesn't like that name."

Martha stopped cutting up the onion in time to see that the dog had his paws crossed over his head. "Well, I've never seen him do that before. You may be right, Bo."

Bo looked back down at the dog. "Okay, you win. It won't be Goliath." The dog immediately removed his paws from atop his head and sat back up, his tail wagging back and forth across the linoleum floor.

Bo placed his right hand under his chin while his eyes looked upward for inspiration. He drummed the table with the fingers of his left hand. "All right then, how about. . . Maximillion?"

The dog once again flopped flat on the floor and covered his head with his front paws while moaning in a soft, guttural tone.

"So, you don't like that name either, huh?" The boy resumed drumming the kitchen table as he watched the dog remove his paws from over his head but stayed sprawled out on the floor. "I know. I'll start at the beginning of the alphabet, and you can let me know when I come up with a name that'll suit you."

The dog rose back off the floor and into a sitting position once again.

Bo resumed his conversation with the dog while Martha continued to prepare the evening meal. "Okay then, let's see . . . the letter a . . . hmmm. How about. . . Ace?"

The mastiff rose on all fours, his tail wagging so vigorously that it was making a "wop-wop" sound against a kitchen cabinet nearby. "Woof!"

Bo must have had no doubt in his mind now about what name would suit his newfound furry friend. "All right then, good choice. Ace it is."

Meanwhile, Ace was thinking as he rolled his big brown eyes upward, *I get really frustrated sometimes trying to communicate with these humans without being able to talk. You know that, don't you?*

Martha had been taking it all in with an astonished look on her face. She felt that her life, for the most part, had been reasonably ordinary. What she had just observed seemed very out of the ordinary, just like when Bo had claimed that the dog was in his hospital room. She dismissed any thoughts other than what she had just observed herself. "Ya know, son, I'm beginning to think you're right about this dog being pretty smart." Martha finally let out a deep sigh. "So what did you think of the pictures we took at your brother's going- away party?"

"Looked like everybody was having a good time," answered Bo.

Martha moved forward with the new topic, putting aside her new uneasiness concerning this dog that seemed to understand the English language quite well. "It helped knowing you were going to be okay. I'm sorry you had to miss it."

Bo shrugged. "Yeah, me too. At least Ben came up to the hospital for a while before he left."

Martha walked over and placed her arm around her son. "He's always been very protective of you, Bo. He was really worried about you, just like everyone else in the family."

Just then, she and Bo heard the engine sound of the family sedan as it pulled into the driveway in the back. She and Henry had switched vehicles that day with the anticipation that the dog would be returning from the hospital with their son. The car door slammed as Martha went over to the window and watched her husband, Henry, pull the double door up before walking into their garage.

The double garage sat in the back of the lot next to the alley and faced west while the Bozells' two-story house on their corner lot faced north. It was an older neighborhood not too far from the downtown area, and the Bozell house had been one of the first homes built there. It had a big front porch with a half wall that was stucco with a wide wooden ledge and some strategically placed support beams, all painted white to match the rest of the house.

"I don't know why your father doesn't just fess up to sneaking a cigarette out in the garage after he gets home from work. He keeps telling me it has to do with that special paintjob he's doing out there on Sidney's motorcycle, but he's not fooling me. You can smell the smoke all over him when he walks in the door. Oh well, at least he's cut way down, and he doesn't smoke in the house anymore."

A few minutes passed before the back door finally opened, and Henry walked in, looking very fatigued from his long day of laboring at his body shop. His once thick blond hair was much thinner now, and he was getting quite gray around the temples. Apparently, he had driven home with the windows down in the car, attempting to hide the smoke smell, because his thinning hair looked windblown.

Martha noticed how windblown her husband's hair was, but she made no comment about it to Henry. Unseasonably warmer weather had arrived that morning, so a lot of people were probably driving around with their windows open. Martha didn't comment about Henry's hair because she already knew that the cigarette smoked in the garage was probably the second one Henry had "hotboxed" down to the filter since he had left his shop. She also knew that he never smoked at the shop because her son John would rat on him. The whole family had been bugging him to quit. Unfortunately, as most everyone knows, such a decision to quit must ultimately be made by the addicted. And Martha knew that poor Henry still enjoyed an occasional smoke too much to be able to give up the nasty habit entirely.

He was dressed in his dark blue work clothes and looked even more tired than normal. He smelled of stale tobacco, perspiration, and fresh paint. The sweat and paint was visible—the smoke smell was not. Henry had always stayed clean shaven through the years after listening to some of his employees complain about how hard it was to scrub dried paint out of their mustaches or beards. However, he had grown a five o'clock shadow by then, having shaven last at five o'clock that morning. No one could ever accuse Henry of not being an early riser.

As soon as he had closed the door, he glanced at the bullmastiff lying on the kitchen floor next to Bo. Henry seemed to direct his full attention to his son, but Bo could tell that his dad was eyeing Ace out of the corner of his eye. Ace was already hoping that Henry wouldn't stay long in the kitchen before he left to go clean up. The strong smell that had begun to overwhelm the pleasant cooking smell the moment Henry had walked into the room was already irritating his nostrils.

"Hello, dear. How is Sidney's paint job coming along?" inquired Martha.

"Uh, it's coming along great, just great," Henry answered with his back to Martha as he was facing Bo. "Welcome home, son. Judging by the time Leonard got back to the shop today, they must have released you shortly after the lunch hour, huh?"

"Yeah, they discharged me early in the afternoon."

Henry finally looked directly down at the dog. "Has he been in the house the whole time?"

"No, not the whole time," Bo calmly replied while thinking about his mother's earlier warning. *Ma is right. It's gonna be a tough sell to get Ace house privileges.*

Henry walked over and placed his lunch pail on the kitchen counter. He was still facing the counter as he peered out of one of the kitchen windows. "It's a good thing we still have the kennel in the back. I'm glad now that I didn't tear it out after Rex died."

Especially after his mother's earlier comment, Bo knew that this would be coming from his father. "Pop, does Ace have to stay in the kennel just because Rex had to?"

Henry finally turned around and looked at his youngest son. "Ace? Is that what you named him?"

Bo's eyebrows lifted, and his eyes widened as he grinned at his father. "Well, actually, he kinda named himself."

"Named himself?" Henry asked. "The dog named himself? Are ya sure you're over that concussion, son?"

"Don't make fun of the boy, Henry. He's telling you the truth," Martha interjected.

Henry looked at his wife with the same glare he had just given Bo. "Maybe 1 need to go outside and come back in again. Then we'll start all over. You're both tellin' me that the dog named himself?"

Martha decided that Henry needed a bit more detail before he thought he'd have to have them both committed. "You should have seen it, Henry. Bo would suggest a name, and Ace would let Bo know whether he liked it."

Henry just shook his head as he sat down next to Bo at the kitchen table. "Okay, whatever you say, but getting back to your previous question, the answer is yes."

Bo, who had been slouching a little, sat up straight in his chair, a look of excitement and anticipation on his face. "Yes, he can stay in the house?"

Henry quickly had Bo slouching in his chair again. "No. 1 meant yes, he has to stay in the kennel."

Ace lifted his chin off the floor and looked at Henry. The big dog made a low, moaning sound.

"Now look what you've done, Pop. You hurt his feelings."

Henry had just looked tired when he got home from work. Now he looked tired and exasperated. "Oh, for cryin' out loud, am 1 the only one around here who's noticed how much of a *moose* this dog is?" Ace let out another series of low moans.

"No, don't tell me 1 hurt his feelings again."

Ace rose and walked over to the back door, staring at it. The dog turned his head back toward Bo. "Woof!"

"You wanna go out, boy?"

Ace turned back toward the closed door and continued to stare at it. "Woof!"

Bo got up and opened the door for the eager dog. The mastiff quickly trotted through the opening, down the two steps, and into the backyard as Bo watched him from inside the screen door for a few seconds before he closed the inside door and sat back down at the kitchen table.

After pulling a cold beer out of the refrigerator and popping the top, Henry had walked back and sat down at the kitchen table himself. He started shuffling through the pictures from Ben's going-away party. "There, you see, that settles it," he said as he continued to look through the photographs, stopping long enough to gulp down part of his beer before looking at the next picture.

A few more seconds had passed until they heard Ace barking outside the back door. Bo got up and let the dog in while Henry was gulping down the last of his first beer. The boy paused and looked through the screen door before closing the inside door and returning to his kitchen chair next to his father. Meanwhile, the dog padded over to the corner of the kitchen and plopped back down. "Ace just did number two in the backyard. Pop, maybe that was his way of telling you he can be trusted in the house."

"Woof!" The dog had quickly confirmed what Bo was contending with his father.

Henry glanced up from looking at the pictures. "I think you're reading too much into his barking and toilet needs, son. After all, he's just a dog."

The big sulking mastiff looked at Henry and dropped his chin flat on the floor. He moaned a little bit in a low, guttural tone. He looked up at Henry with the most pathetic-looking, sad droopy brown eyes. "You hurt his feelings again, Pop."

Henry rose from his chair and walked over to the refrigerator. He opened the door, leaned in, and pulled out another can of beer. "Oh, for cryin' out loud, he stays out in the kennel tonight, and that's that. I'm not out to win a dog popularity contest. He's too big to be an inside dog. I don't know which would be worse, the slobber puddles on the kitchen floor or the dog hair all over the carpeting and furniture."

Ace continued to keep his chin on the floor while moaning some more after Henry's remarks, especially since his recent trek outside was as much to get a breath of fresh air as it was to prove anything to Henry.

After taking another significant slurp out of his second beer, Henry let out a big belch. Ace seemed to moan in protest at Henry's bad manners. "Henry!" Martha scolded. "How many times have I told you not to guzzle your beer? You do this every time. It's downright disgusting, and you know it."

"Woof!"

"That's it! That's it! Take him outside, Bo. It's bad enough having your mother chastise me, let alone this mangy mutt!" Henry's face had turned all red, and the veins in his neck were popping out as he glared at Ace over in the corner.

While Bo grudgingly rose from his chair to open the back door, Martha walked over next to her husband, glaring at Henry in much the same way he had just been glaring at the dog. "Well?"

"Well what, Mother?" Henry asked back as he looked up at his obviously irritated wife.

Martha didn't answer him while Ace slowly rose and padded over to the back door that Bo was holding open for him. Both boy and dog dejectedly left the kitchen and stepped out onto the back porch before taking the two steps down to the backyard sidewalk that led to the garage and adjoining dog kennel in the back of the lot.

"Oh. *Excuse me,* " he finally mumbled before looking back down at the top picture in the pile on the table.

Martha wheeled around and headed back over to the kitchen sink, saying a few of her own mumbled words about her husband as she stepped away. "Belittling our nice docile new dog and then belching in the kitchen a minute later. I'm thinking maybe there ought to be someone sleeping in the doghouse tonight."

"It's not a doghouse, *Mother.*"

"Whatever."

As Ace obediently followed his new master down the back sidewalk to the dog kennel, a dark blue Ford Galaxy rounded the comer and slowly passed by. Bo was too bummed out that he had to put his new dog in the kennel to notice who was in the Galaxy. Once the car had finally cruised past the garage at the back of the lot, it accelerated, squealing its tires, before it finally slowed slightly to make a right turn at the corner of the next block. The two young men in the car were finishing their brief conversation. "I can't believe we drove all the way to Plattsmouth just to see where Bozell lives."

"Don't sweat it, Larry. It was my gas."

"You mean it was your dad's gas, don't you?"

"Don't get technical with me. Besides, I didn't twist your arm to come along, ya know."

"I just don't see why you're so obsessed with Bozell. I mean, he's not even wrestling anymore. The state tournament's next weekend, and you've already beaten everybody you're going to face."

"You just don't get it, do you, Larry? I didn't beat Bozell! That cocky deafmute son of a bitch is gonna pay someday!"

Bo was sleeping soundly alone in his room later that evening. Everything was quiet. The bedroom window was slightly open as it continued to be an unseasonably warm evening for late winter. The weatherman had been right for a change. Bo's alarm clock was on his nightstand next to his bed. It showed that it was midnight.

The silence of the night was suddenly disturbed with the loud, booming bark of a bullmastiff that apparently was determined to change the balance of power in the Bozell household. It was unmistakably Ace with his series of low, deep "woof!" There was a short pause and then more barking.

Just as Bo woke up enough to start struggling out of bed with his neck brace on, Henry entered his son's room in a hurry. His father's face was red with anger, and his thinning hair stuck out in all directions as if his midnight rage had called his hair to attention. "Get that big lummox in here before he wakes up the whole neighborhood! If he hadn't saved your life that night, he'd be lookin' for a new home across the river in Iowa by now!"

Bo began putting on his bathrobe and sliding into his slippers, too sleepy to be intimidated by Henry's midnight temper tantrum. "Whatever you say, Pop," he replied through a big yawn.

Henry turned around and headed for the door. "Try to get back to bed as soon as you can. You've got school tomorrow, you know."

Ace continued to bark as Bo followed his father out of the bedroom.

Bo was up early for his first day back at school. Apparently being nervous and somewhat apprehensive, he opted for only toast and orange juice for breakfast. Martha had noticed that he seemed to be taking his time getting ready. He had just come back downstairs and walked toward the front door when a horn honked in front of the Bozell house. Bo peered out through the partially opened curtains of the front door window. His friend Jerry was sitting in his car with the engine running as the blue-white exhaust fumes visibly shot out from behind the car and spiraled up into the crisp morning air.

Martha spoke to her son softly, trying to be supportive but not too pushy, while her son had his back to her in the living room. "Go ahead, son. It'll be okay, you'll see."

Bo turned his head and looked back at his mother. He had a nervous smile on his face as he opened the front door to leave. He closed the door behind him and walked down the sidewalk toward the front curb where Jerry was waiting in his car. He took a temporary detour around the front comer of the house, finally stopping and looking at Ace, who was back in the dog run. "Bye, buddy! See you after school!" he yelled as he wheeled around and headed back to the front curb.

Bo acknowledged Jerry with a brief wave while he walked up to the passenger door. Before he opened the car door, he stopped and stared at the house across the street and three houses down as he clutched his schoolbooks against his left hip. Martha was watching from the front door. Their quiet, well- kept neighborhood had really changed a lot in the past few years. Many of their older neighbors who had taken so much pride in their manicured lawns, trimmed hedges, and lush gardens had either moved away or passed away.

Old Mrs. Duffy, a good neighbor for many years, had a beautiful flower garden every spring and summer that was the envy of the neighborhood. The flower garden was gone now, just like Mrs. Duffy, rest her soul. The new owners had unsuccessfully planted grass seed in the same spot where she had once labored in the hot summer sun for hours on end. What was once a lush garden was now an unsightly patch of weeds. Bo still had faint fond memories of that sweet old lady in her wide-brimmed straw hat and assortment of bright- colored summer dresses. Many of the younger families who had moved into the old neighborhood were obviously not as caring or meticulous as their predecessors had been about their lawns and homes.

The house and yard that Bo was staring at across the street, however, was by far the most run-down property on either side of the whole block. Bo stared for several seconds and seemed to be deep in thought. He looks hypnotized, Martha was thinking. Following his glance and stare, she suddenly understood. Martha hadn't heard anything herself that morning from inside the house, but apparently, Bo—even with his hearing problems— had heard something unsettling coming from the rental house as he walked to Jerry's car.

Watching her son staring quietly at the house across the street and so serious in thought, Martha felt badly for Bo. He feels it, and he knows, she thought. Bo was a good boy and had a good heart. She hated the fact that some of the ugliness of the world was so close at hand, an ugliness that was firmly planted across the street not more than two hundred feet from the Bozell front door.

Randy Whitfield grew up in North Omaha. He briefly played football in his sophomore year of high school before getting kicked off the team for underage drinking. He had shown some promise as a tailback on offense and a safety on defense. He was solidly built but small, nothing but muscle and bone, and he had some speed.

It was his desire for speed, as in speeding cars, that had become his new obsession during his last two years of high school, which continued after he graduated while he worked construction in the past year. He was lucky he had gotten away with his drag racing for so long without any major incident. It wasn't that there weren't any incidents before then. It was just that this brash young man with a fast car had been lucky enough to not get caught.

He unfortunately had no father figure in his life. His parents had divorced when he was in early grade school. His father eventually left town, taking his younger brother with him. Randy stayed behind with his mother.

On a late Saturday night in early October, he was driving down Omaha's main drag—Dodge Street—with a couple of his buddies who were still in their late teens while Randy was close to celebrating his twentieth birthday in a few days. Regardless, none of them were of legal drinking age. They were celebrating his drag-racing victories from a little earlier in the evening. There was a stretch of seldom traveled highway north of Omaha that had become a Saturday night meeting place for young men with fast cars.

Maybe it was a badly needed diversion for some of the boys, many of whom came from broken homes like Randy. Some of the boys had elder siblings serving overseas in the escalating war in Vietnam. A few of them had inherited their fast cars from their elder brothers who had been suddenly plucked from civilian life after drawing a low number in the annual draft lottery.

Randy had a girlfriend named Brenda, who had always accompanied him to the illegal weekend drag-racing events the year before, but the unexpected birth of Trevor, their son, had changed all that. Brenda had dropped out of college in her freshman year and spent most of her time caring for little Trevor, fortunate that her parents had embraced their grandchild and allowed both her and her baby boy to still live with them.

Even though Randy had not shown any interest in marrying or even supporting Brenda and their son in a place of their own, Brenda's parents allowed Randy to come over sometimes so he could spend some time with his infant son. He appreciated the fact that they tried to hide their contempt, but it was obvious to Randy that Brenda's parents didn't like him very much. He understood that they allowed him to come over only because, like it or not, he was the father of their grandson.

Of course, Randy didn't help his own cause any by racing around Omaha in a souped-up '62 red Chevy Impala with a modified Corvette transmission. On that Saturday night, he had one buddy in the back while his closest friend, Jake, was riding shotgun. There were still two full beers lying on the floor at the feet of Steve in the back seat. They had already tossed their other empty cans out of the window shortly after reaching the city limits.

Randy waited for the red light to change at the Forty-Second Street intersection as he was heading west on Dodge Street. A black Dodge Charger with Kansas license plates was revving up its engine in the lane next to them. Randy took a drag on his cigarette before he looked in his rearview mirror. Seeing no other cars approaching from behind, he revved his engine as well.

There were a couple of cars in both opposite eastbound lanes traveling toward them several blocks ahead, but neither one was a cop. The driver of the Charger was alone. He looked at Randy and nodded.

"You're not gonna chance dragging that idiot here on Dodge, are you, Randy?" Jake asked him with obvious alarm in his voice.

Randy glanced at his friend. "Nah. I'll gun it when the light changes and then shut it down after second gear. Maybe our newfound friend will keep screaming ahead, so we can get him introduced to the local cops by the time he hits the Fiftieth Street intersection." He took one last drag from his spent cigarette before tossing it out his window.

Steve tried to point out something to Randy from the back seat, but the light changed before he got the chance. The squealing of car tires drowned out Steve's voice. A small dust cloud arose when both drivers reacted to the green light with their right foot buried to the gas pedal. The smell of burning rubber and the roar of high-powered engines were overwhelming during the first half block as both Randy and the driver in the Charger were struggling to keep their accelerating cars in their own lanes.

Then something unexpected happened. The Charger was just slightly behind the Impala in the other lane when a loud pop came from the Dodge Charger engine, accompanied by a loud backfire out of the its dual exhaust pipes. White smoke started to seep out of the seams of the front hood of the car. The out-of-towner had just blown his engine.

Randy was so stunned by this sudden turn of events that he didn't shut down his own car until he had already slammed the transmission into third gear. His previous plan to only go a block at high speed had quickly turned into two blocks before he caught himself. He started tapping his brakes, looking in his rearview mirror as the Charger limped around a comer onto a side street.

Before Randy took his eyes off his rearview mirror, he saw the flashing red light of a fast-approaching patrol car. *Damn hills here in Omaha. He must have been back there, hidden behind a hill, when we left the Forty-Second Street stoplight,* Randy thought in disgust.

Steve finally could be heard from the back seat. "Randy! I think we're in big trouble, man! There's still two full cans of beer back here on the floor." "Son of a bitch, Steve! Why didn't you tell me earlier! 1 thought it was all out of the car!" yelled Randy. He stomped down on the gas pedal, waiting for the right time to slam it up to fourth gear.

"I tried to tell you!" Steve yelled back, barely heard over the roar of the engine as the Impala was, at least temporarily, putting some distance between itself and the patrol car in pursuit.

In just a matter of seconds after Randy had slammed his floor shift into fifth gear, Steve tried to lean forward and look at the speedometer. He saw that the needle was somewhere between 120 and 130 miles an hour before he was bounced into the ceiling, smashing the top of his head into the inside roof of the car after they had just crested a hill.

Randy looked once again into his rearview mirror. He saw the head of a big slobbery dog. Steve was almost being bounced out of the right rear window at the time. All Randy had to do was blink, and then the dog was gone. *What the hell was that?* he asked himself. He let the moment go as he directed his attention to the matter at hand.

"We've got to get the hell off Dodge Street and throw that damn beer out the window!" Randy excitedly yelled to his frightened passengers. The sound of other police sirens could be heard in the distance. "They've probably radioed every cop in town by now." He hit the brakes and downshifted to fourth gear. The car fishtailed as he tried to decelerate as quickly as possible. He finally was able to downshift to third gear as he continued pumping the brakes. There were flashing lights in all directions, except to the north, as Randy negotiated a hard right turn onto SixtySecond Street; his right tires lifted off the pavement temporarily until he regained control as they now were traveling north. Steve tossed the two beers from the car, and they landed in some bushes of someone's front yard.

Randy was just about to accelerate again as he was crossing through the first intersection of the street one block north of Dodge Street. The next thing the three boys knew, they were in a car that was spinning like a top. A police car with two officers on board had rammed into the right rear fender of the Impala that was headed north as their car crossed through the intersection, coming from the east. The patrolmen later said they were planning on turning left on Sixty- Second to get to Dodge Street so they could join in the chase.

It was a miracle that the Impala didn't flip. Instead, it spun around several times until it ended up in someone's front yard, facing the opposite direction it had been traveling just seconds before. The police cruiser had smashed into a utility pole, the front end wrapped around it, with steam pouring out of the exposed, crushed engine compartment.

The officers looked shaken but managed to force their way out of the jammed passenger door. The three young men were still dizzy and disoriented when the two officers approached them with guns drawn. One officer yanked the driver's side door open. "Everyone! Get out of the car! Real slow now! Keep your hands where I can see them!"

While the three dazed teenagers slowly slid out of the driver's side of the car, the other officer quickly came around from the passenger side to join his partner. "Now face the car and place your hands on top. Spread your legs and lean forward."

Randy, leaning over his badly damaged car, getting frisked by one of the two excited officers, looked at Walt, who was waiting his turn to be patted down. "Don't worry, Walt. I was the one driving," he whispered.

"Shut up, punk, and keep your face looking forward," the young officer sternly warned Randy as he continued to pat him down.

Randy had been right about what he had said to Walt that night before they were hauled off to jail. The police never found the beer, so no charges were filed against Walt and Steve. The prosecutor made up for that, however, when he threw the book at Randy.

Randy was almost certain he was going to do some significant jail time until the judge surprisingly gave him another alternative. He could either go to jail or enlist in the army. It really wasn't that hard of a choice to make. Randy couldn't afford to go to college after he graduated from high school. Besides that, he had no desire to go to college anyway.

Randy had been getting tired lately of only being able to see his son when Brenda's parents allowed it, so he had a new plan to find the best job he could and hoped that he would make enough money to help support Brenda and their son. Ironically, he had gotten a high number in the draft lottery on his nineteenth birthday and probably would have been able to avoid military service had it not been for the choice given to him by the judge so he could avoid jail time.

The day before he was scheduled to leave, he sold his still damaged car to one of his racing buddies. He was booked on a chartered plane with other raw recruits destined for San Diego Marine Corps Boot Camp.

He had been standing in a long line at the downtown recruitment center. Every seventh recruit was told he was going into the marines instead of the army. Randy would have been perfectly content to be sent to an army boot camp. He kind of shook his head and smiled when he ended up being a lucky seven.

The next day, he said his tearful goodbye to Brenda and Trevor at the airport. His mother was noticeably absent. Mrs. Whitfield never even came to his hearing, nor did she make any attempt to say goodbye to him when he flew out of Omaha for San Diego. His mother and he, despite the fact she had been left behind to raise him by herself, had never really been that close as mother and son. She was always working two jobs, leaving her son alone at a young age to shift for himself. The car chase and subsequent arrest must have been the straw that broke the camel's back.

He had only been in Vietnam for a couple of weeks when he learned that Brenda's father had been transferred to a position in Philadelphia, Pennsylvania, with Brenda and his son having no other option but to move with them. He was saddened by the news. The only family he had left in Omaha now was his estranged mother, who hadn't talked to him since his arrest.

The only thing that kept him going day after day in the jungles of 'Nam was the belief that Brenda and Trevor would hopefully someday come back to Omaha. That belief was reinforced by Brenda's constant letters that said she would indeed come to him with their son when he made it back safe and sound. They could be a real family, like he'd never really experienced before in his life, at least not any moment he could really remember.

Whitfield's one-year tour of duty in Vietnam was cut short by three months when he dove for cover from an incoming grenade, only to learn too late that there was a steep drop behind the big rock he had dived over to save his own life. When one of his buddies looked down at Randy lying on a ledge below, his fellow soldiers saw him grimace at the sight of Randy's legs bent at unnatural angles. Randy would always remember that first morning when he woke up in the VA hospital in Omaha. His flight from California hadn't arrived at Offutt Air Force Base in Bellevue, Nebraska, until very late the night before. After being transported by ambulance from Offutt to the VA hospital, they had wheeled him in on a stretcher and placed him in a room with little fanfare.

He had been a little disappointed and saddened when no one he knew was there to greet him. He was told that his mother had been informed about his pending arrival. He had held out hope that she might be there, even though she had never answered any of his letters over the past nine months.

Fortunately for Randy, standing in front of him that very next morning when he opened his eyes was Brenda, holding a blond-haired toddler in her arms who looked a lot like him, distinctive blond hair and all. There was no mistaking that Trevor was his son. A tear trickled down Randy's right cheek as Brenda placed their son down on the edge of the bed so little Trevor could get a hug from his daddy. During the time that Randy had spent in Vietnam, he had matured, spending his downtime thinking about his son and how lucky he was to be his father.

Of course, the rendezvous at the hospital came at a cost. When Brenda abruptly and without warning announced that Randy had been badly wounded and was being flown back home, her parents must have known what was coming next as they forbade her to leave. But Brenda was over twenty years old by then. Her parents had to have known that they couldn't legally force her to stay, so they switched to plan B, requesting that she leave little Trevor behind with them.

Over the past few months, their grandson had constantly demonstrated to them that he was a special little boy who deserved to be where his thirst for learning could be nurtured. It was apparent to Brenda that they had quickly evolved into even prouder grandparents than before, seemingly only wanting what was best for their gifted grandson, constantly buying him developmental learning toys that she could not afford. She knew that they obviously couldn't bear to see him taken away from them so abruptly and to such a relatively distant place. It was close to a twoday drive.

When Brenda promptly told her parents that Trevor would not be left behind, she watched them turn bitter and vicious. As her mother finally broke down in tears, her father gave her an ultimatum. He had said that if she left with their grandson, she would never be welcomed back into their home ever again. His dare didn't work. Brenda packed up everything she could on such short notice and left with Trevor that very night in the used yellow Volkswagen van she had purchased a few months earlier.

Brenda got a little help from one of her old girlfriends in Omaha while Randy slowly recovered in the hospital from his injuries. Her old high school friend Judy let her stay in her one-bedroom apartment until Randy finally was discharged from the hospital. Randy had enough military pay left to enable the three of them to get a cheap apartment in the same complex that Judy lived in.

Once Randy was willing and able, he applied for several jobs in and around Omaha. It didn't hurt for employers to know that he was a war veteran in search of a badly needed job. It wasn't long before he had the job at the railroad machinist shop in Plattsmouth. Since their only mode of transportation was the old van, they decided to try to find a rental house in the same town. That way, Randy wouldn't have to put so many miles on their only vehicle. Not only that but they also discovered they could rent a house in a small town for about the same amount of money they were spending for a small apartment in Omaha.

The first few months that Randy, Brenda, and Trevor spent in the Bozell neighborhood were relatively quiet and uneventful. Then the pain slowly began to increase in Randy's legs, left hip, and lower back. Degenerative arthritis was slowly eating away at cartilage in several joints and in his lower back. Before he was forced to give up his job with the railroad, Randy had already started consuming large quantities of beer to go with the pain pills he was taking every day. He got tired of feeling bloated all the time from the beer, so he started buying bottles of whiskey as well.

Then he put in a call to one of his old buddies in North Omaha. Randy had been yearning for some of that Thai stick stuff that he used to smoke in 'Nam. His old buddy Bud Dahlke didn't disappoint. He started to become a regular visitor to Randy's house in Plattsmouth, much to the obvious disappointment of Brenda.

She always stayed in the back bedroom with little Trevor when Bud was around. She told Randy that she constantly worried that some wellmeaning neighbor was going to come to the front door someday, only to be literally bowled over by the strong marijuana smell hanging in the living room air. Randy and Brenda were both cigarette smokers, though, and he always lit incense when he and Bud were smoking. Since Randy believed that most of the local Plattsmouth people were naive when it came to marijuana smell, he hoped that they would logically assume that it was just bad, cheap incense, assuming, of course, that they even knew what incense was.

The combination of drugs and alcohol started to take its toll not only on Randy but also on his relationship with his son and Brenda. Brenda had practically begged him to finally marry her shortly after he got out of the hospital. For some reason, Randy had been against the idea of getting married right away. He kept telling Brenda that he wanted to prove he could be a good provider before they finally would legitimize their relationship.

Brenda finally quit asking after they had lived in Plattsmouth for several months. The neighbors started hearing Randy yell at her daily and nightly, which could explain why she had finally stopped asking him. Finally, the yelling turned into some occasional physical abuse, not against Trevor though. Even in his druginduced, drunken stupor, Randy never laid a hand on his son. Even at the tender young age of four, it was apparent that Trevor was increasingly becoming painfully aware of his parents' problems. He always ran to his room and covered his head with his pillow when his daddy started yelling at his mommy.

That was what was happening in the morning of Bo Bozell's first day back at school. Brenda and Randy had gotten into a shouting match before she left for work that day. It was so loud that even Bo could hear it as he approached Jerry's car in front of the Bozell house. He knew that was why Ace had started barking from his kennel.

The small rental house where increasingly loud voices could often be heard well into the night was across the street and three houses down to the east from the Bozell household. Martha was saddened and sorry that Mary McGovern's children had decided to keep the house as rental property after the sudden death of their mother three years earlier. Martha had been told by one of the other neighbors that a couple (with a small child) from Omaha had snapped up the rental property shortly after it had been listed. Some initial conversations by the young couple with next-door neighbors revealed that they weren't married, but the little boy, Trevor, was their son. The young couple's names were Randy Whitfield and Brenda Rogers.

Martha learned through Rita Landon, a next-door neighbor to the young couple with the illegitimate child, that Randy had been diagnosed with degenerative arthritis in his back, left hip, and legs—a condition that had been brought on from the injuries he suffered over in Vietnam. He had completed his recovery in the Omaha VA Hospital from two ruptured and two other herniated disks in his lower back, a broken pelvis, and multiple breaks in both legs. Rita had explained at the time that it was the job as a machinist at a railroad repair shop in town that originally brought Randy, his girlfriend, and his son to Plattsmouth. No one else in town knew about his Purple Heart and other ribbons he had earned while fighting for his country.

Randy arrived with a noticeable limp. It gradually became more pronounced along with the accompanying facial sneer as Randy Whitfield tried his best to ignore the pain with every labored step he took. Within a little over a year, he had to give up his job and go on military-assisted disability.

The combination of prescription drugs, illegal drugs, and alcohol had Randy spinning out of control. Within the past couple of years, he had been downright scary to be around. No one seemed surprised when he started getting into trouble with the law. He had found himself with too much time on his hands as he sulked at home while Brenda toiled long hours working at and commuting to and from a meatpacking plant in South Omaha. It finally reached the point that Brenda felt she couldn't leave her son alone all day with Randy, so she started leaving him with her next-door neighbor Rita Landon while she was away at work. Rita, having developed quite a fondness for the boy, didn't hesitate when Brenda asked her if she could babysit her son.

Brenda peeked out between the curtains while she slipped into her canvas sneakers that had been sitting on a welcome mat placed in the front door. She winced when she saw Bo standing outside his friend's car, staring at their house. At least she had already taken Trevor over to Rita's house for the day, sparing her son from being a witness to yet another outburst of anger by his father. She let the curtains fall before wheeling around to face Randy again. "Now look what you've done, you drunken fool! Even that boy from across the street with a hearing problem just heard your last tirade!"

Randy Whitfield flopped back down on the sofa. His head and neck swiveled around on his shoulders in a counterclockwise direction while his eyeballs rolled up half out of sight. There was drool glistening from the comer of his mouth and dropping onto the left side of his chin as he sat there with nothing on but his underwear. "I don't give a rat's ass what the neighbors think! Do you really think I give a shit what anybody else thinks anymore?"

Brenda just stood there for a few seconds, looking at her boyfriend with a blank look on her face. She finally let out a deep sigh. "No, I guess you really don't, do you?" She realized that the drunken father of her child probably hadn't even heard her rhetorical question as she passed by him on her way to the kitchen to get her purse because his eyes were now closed, and she could hear him snoring already.

That same night after Bo's first day back at school, Brenda got home late from work. Trevor was already asleep for the night. For only the second time in the several months since she had taken the job at the packing plant, she had met some coworkers at a South Omaha bar again on her way home from work. It must have been the nasty argument and shouting match that morning before she got out the door, so loud that even Bo had heard them before getting into Jerry's car. She was still very upset with Randy. It didn't take much coaxing from her friends at work to get her to agree to stop for a few beers that night.

Her friends acted really surprised when she so quickly agreed to meet them at the bar after work. Brenda had previously turned them down so many times that they hadn't even thought to ask her to join them in several months. She got really drunk that night at the bar. She hardly ever drank alcohol, so after three or four beers and a couple of shots, her friends could tell that she was really buzzed up. Her closest friend at work, Roberta, called her husband to come and help get her home to Plattsmouth.

The only other time that Brenda had joined her friends at the bar, she had only one beer and was home much earlier, finding Randy passed out on the sofa. He didn't even know she had been late getting home. This time, Randy was drunk but not passed out. He had been peeking out the window every few minutes when he finally saw the van pull into the driveway.

A large Hispanic man got out of the driver's seat of the VW and handed the keys to a totally tipsy Brenda, who had staggered out of the passenger side of the van and was leaning against the front windshield.

The man had his back to the house as he was saying something to Randy's girlfriend. Another car pulled into the driveway behind the van. The man, who had been blocking Randy's view of Brenda, then walked to the other car and got into the driver's side. The headlights prevented Randy from seeing who else was in the old car as it backed out of the driveway and sped off down the street.

Brenda half-staggered and half-crawled to the front door. She finally made it to the door and flung open the screen door first, falling on her butt with her back to the inside door. She reached up and grabbed the doorknob, twisting and pulling herself up into a standing position, before boldly opening the door and walking through as if nothing was wrong.

She was abruptly greeted with a fist to her face as she staggered through the open doorway.

She woke up the next morning on the couch. She struggled to get up using only her left arm for leverage as she pushed against her aching forehead with her right hand. She stumbled past a mirror in the living room, noticing that her right eye was swollen and bruised. There was a note on the kitchen counter. It was from Randy. She didn't read it before quickening her pace into Trevor's room, only to find his empty bed, and she saw that his winter coat wasn't hanging on the peg on the back of his closet door.

She finished checking the rest of the house before finally reading Randy's note. It read,

Brenda,

I think it's time for you to move out. At least for a while. You can take the van and go stay with Judy again for a while in Omaha. I'm keeping Trevor with me. I went and got him from Rita a couple of hours after you were supposed to be home last night. A son belongs with his father. Besides, it 'll be crowded enough in Judy's apartment with just the two of you. Don't worry about Trevor. I would never hurt my son in any way. If things get too rough for me some days or nights, I'll ask Rita to take him until I'm feeling better. Don't involve the cops in this. It would only make matters worse.

Randy

Most young mothers would never leave their child behind in such a situation, but Brenda was weak and vulnerable. Not only that but she also was still tormented by guilt. She had a short affair while living in Philadelphia with her parents while Randy was over in Vietnam. Her little fling didn't last very long, but it was long enough to still be having an influence on her decision-making abilities. She had never confessed to Randy about the affair after he returned from Vietnam, especially after being witness to his growing anger as the months progressed after his return. She somehow rationalized that leaving Trevor behind with Randy was payback for her sins, so she left as Randy had requested.

The previous night while Brenda was in the South Omaha bar with her coworkers, getting snookered, the Bozells were seated around the kitchen table, eating supper after Bo's first day back at school. Ace was in the backyard. They were having one of Henry's favorite meals—steak, salad, beans, and baked potatoes. Henry finished chewing on a piece of his steak. "How was your first day back at school, son?"

Bo looked at Henry, a piece of baked potato stuck to his fork that hadn't found its way to his mouth yet. "Oh, okay ... I guess. Everybody kept coming up to me and asking me how I felt."

"Did you get asked if you were going to be able to wrestle again?" asked Martha.

Bo turned and glared at his mother; the veins on his neck started sticking out as his face suddenly reddened. "I really don't want to talk about that. In fact, I don't ever want to talk about wrestling *ever* again. Understand?"

Martha seemed to be avoiding Bo's glare as she looked down at her plate of food. "I'm sorry I brought it up. If you don't want to talk about it, I *do* understand."

From outside the back door came the sound of barking. Ace barked two or three times, paused, and then barked some more. It was obvious that he wanted to come inside. Henry glanced briefly at the door before resuming eating. "Just ignore him. He'll give up eventually."

Having outlasted her youngest son's glare, Martha finally glanced at her husband. "Like he did last night, Henry?"

Ace continued to bark out on the back porch. His repeated barking seemed to be getting louder each time he started up again. Henry glared back at Martha, reminding her of where her son had acquired the Bozell glare. "This is different. I don't want that big mutt salivating around the kitchen table. I want to eat in peace."

Henry's constant berating of Ace was starting to worry Bo. He was afraid that his father's insults were an early warning that his newfound friendship with this special dog, who had saved his life, might be short lived. "I think you're underestimating Ace, Pop. I checked with the neighbors when I got home from school. They said he was quiet all day, barely a peep out of him. I had a little talk with him this morning before I put him in the kennel."

Henry chuckled. "Oh, you did, did you? And just what did you tell him?"

Bo seemed to ignore his father's cynical response. "I told him that daytime was different, that he had to stay in the kennel while we were all gone for the day. 1 told him that I had to go to school and that he couldn't come with me."

Henry resumed eating, but he tried to continue talking as he was chewing a piece of his steak, an unmannerly practice that had always irritated Martha. "And what makes you think he understood what you said?"

Ace was still barking from outside the kitchen door.

"Well, he looked me right in the eye when I was done, and then he barked one time. Then he followed me out to the kennel, and when 1 opened the gate, he went right in and sat down."

Ace was still barking. The constant barking had to be getting on Henry's nerves at that point. Martha would be the first to attest to the fact that two characteristics that would have to be excluded from Henry's list of strong points would be patience and tolerance. "Oh, all right, let him in so we can finish eating without having to listen to that the whole time. But I'm warning you, son, he better be good, or out the door he goes."

Bo rose from the table to let Ace into the kitchen. "Yes, Pop, he'll be good. You'll see."

Henry continued to consume his evening meal while Martha lay down her fork, anticipating the encounter that was soon to begin. Bo opened the back door, and Ace came trotting into the kitchen. Bo looked down at his mastiff as he closed the door. "Pop said you could join us."

The kitchen table had four chairs around it. There was one empty chair left as Bo sat back down to finish his meal. Ace promptly went around to that fourth chair, taking his left paw and pulling on the back leg until the chair slid back from the table enough for him to hop up into it. Henry was too busy cutting his meat and hadn't yet seen where the big dog had sat down. Martha looked at Ace with an astonished look on her face. Her mouth opened and froze, rendering her temporarily speechless.

Ace's eyes got wide when he saw that they were eating steak. The smell was overwhelming to him. His tongue rolled around outside his mouth and then back in, dropping drool on the table top. He closed his eyes for a second, imagining himself grabbing the serving plate of tasty steak in his mouth and hightailing it to a safe place where he could devour every tiny morsel into oblivion.

Henry finally glanced up to see where Ace was sitting. The master of the house had a look of disbelief. "No, get down! Bo didn't mean you could join us at the table!"

Ace moaned a bit before jumping down off the chair.

Bo pointed over to the corner of the kitchen as he looked at the dog. "Ace, go sit over in the corner and be a good boy. I promised Pop you'd behave."

The mastiff slowly padded over to the corner of the kitchen, turned around, and sat down, crossing his paws in front of him on the linoleum floor. He stared up at Henry's back, which was now blocking his angle of view of the mother lode that was on the serving plate on the table, still sending out a strong olfactory signal for any canine's carnivorous delight. Meanwhile, Bo hastily reached over and wiped up the drool with his napkin while Henry was turned and watching Ace take a seat on the floor. "That's better. Now you just sit there and be quiet. Show Pop what a good boy you can be."

The Bozells continued to finish their evening meal while the slightly confused dog finally flopped down with his chin on his outstretched front paws. Bo was sitting where he could see Ace, but Henry and Martha's backs were to the dog. Martha was relieved that things seemed to be back to normal—or at least normal for the Bozell household. "Were you busy at the shop today, dear?"

"Of course, we were busy, Mother. We're always busy. We still have a backlog from that recent ice storm." Henry took another couple of bites of steak and chewed them up before the supper table's silence was broken—a brief silence in Martha's opinion, more attributable to her cooking than Henry being at a loss for words. "How were things at the drugstore?"

Bo glanced at Ace and saw that he was starting to inch forward, dragging his belly on the floor while moving one front paw and then the other front paw a little bit at a time. Bo cleared his throat real loud while he made eye contact with Ace.

Ace immediately retreated to where he was lying originally, thinking how torturous it was to be in the same room with such a sweet smell that he wasn't going to have the opportunity to taste—at least for now anyway.

"It was kind of slow at the drugstore today," Martha replied. "I was able to get some extra cleaning done—you know, dusting shelves and things like that." She looked at her son. "What's the matter, Bo? Are you getting a sore throat or something?"

Bo answered his mother in a croaky voice, "No, I just have a little frog in my throat. I'm fine." He took a big slug of milk from his glass before glancing back at Ace again.

Martha must have accepted her son's explanation for his sudden outburst because she abruptly changed the subject. "You better take Ace to your room and get started on your homework as soon as we're done eating."

Henry apparently either accepted or missed Martha's remark about where the dog could go in the house once Bo had finished his evening meal. "Your mother's right, son. I'm sure you've got a lot of catching up to do."

Bo wiped his mouth with his napkin, not remembering that he had wiped up Ace's drool with it earlier. He grimaced before moving the napkin around for a dry area to wipe off his food-stained and now gooey face. "Nothin' I can't handle. I'll be caught up in no time."

"From what your mother's been telling me, you weren't keeping up very well when you were in school," said Henry.

Bo threw his wadded-up napkin onto his plate. "Ah, what difference does it make now anyway? I'm never going to be able to afford college, so what's the point?"

Martha stopped eating and stared at her son. "The point is getting a good education is more important now than it ever was. Do you want to face the possibility of working a manual labor job for the rest of your life, with the uncertainty of how well your body's going to hold up as you get older?"

Bo rolled his eyes as he leaned back and stretched. "Yeah, yeah, I hear what you're saying. I'll try to start hittin' the books a little harder from now on. I promise."

Martha corrected her son's bad grammar, making her point stronger. "That should have been 'I'll try to start "hitting" the books,' not 'hittin" the books."

Ace piped up from his corner spot in the kitchen. "Woof!"

Bo rolled his eyes while giving his new dog a dirty look. It was bad enough being ganged up on by his two parents, but now a four-legged slobbering animal had sided against him. It was a good thing it didn't really matter to Ace because he wasn't winning any points with his new master anyway. "Hey, you stay out of this. Whose side are you on anyway?"

Henry started chuckling as he looked at Ace. "For once, I agree with the dog. Now get going on your homework."

Bo slid his chair out from the table and stomped out of the room with a scowl on his face.

As her son left the room, Martha looked at Henry. "I need to run to the store and get some more milk and bread after I get the dishes done. Can you think of anything else we need?"

Henry was still looking at Ace, who was quietly sitting out of the way in the comer of the kitchen. "I was going to suggest a muzzle, but I'll give you- knowwho a reprieve for now."

Ace knew exactly what Henry was referring to—and he thanked him out loud. "Woof!" All the while, he was thinking, *He thinks he's so funny. If he only knew.*

Bo was leaning over his desk, working on a book report. One small desk lamp was on, illuminating the shuffle of papers and textbooks piled on top next to where he was busy writing. He continued to write as he made a comment to his dog, assuming the bullmastiff was still sitting behind him. "Well, Ace, are you going to be a good boy again tomorrow while I'm at school?" With no obvious response from the dog, Bo shifted his whole body around since he couldn't twist his neck. He discovered that his new dog was not in his bedroom. "Ace, where did you go, boy? Ace?"

When the dog didn't appear in the doorway, Bo got up from his desk and left the room to search for him. He hurriedly walked down the staircase to the first floor and passed by the entrance to the living room as he moved down the hallway. He noticed that his father was asleep in his recliner, with part of the evening newspaper spread across his chest.

As he quickly approached the open doorway to the kitchen, Ace came trotting out, seemingly grinning from ear to ear; but when he saw Bo, he dropped down and started moving forward by dragging his belly across the hallway floor. When he reached Bo's feet, he stopped and crossed his paws over his head.

Bo looked down at him and whispered, "All right, Ace, what did you do? You got into something in the kitchen, didn't ya?"

The mastiff moaned a little bit, still cowering in front of his new master.

Bo moved past him and hurried into the kitchen, with the dog following him at a safe distance. As he entered the room, he immediately saw what Ace had done. There was garbage spread out all over the throw rug. The garbage pail, which was nearly full, was now almost empty. Next to the garbage on the throw rug were the steak bones from the evening meal. Bo could see that Ace had finished chewing off the leftover meat from the bones. The throw rug was a good two feet from the garbage pail, so it was obvious to Bo that Ace was at least trying to be as neat as he could be under the circumstances.

He turned around and looked at his distraught dog, who had followed him into the kitchen. "What are you trying to do?" he asked before pausing for an answer that he surely knew would never come. "You're going to get yourself banished from the house for good if you keep doing stuff like this."

Ace looked up at Bo and moaned a little bit, thinking all the while, *the temptation of the steak bones has distracted me from my mission. I know that someone else besides Bo isn't very happy with me right now. I would have to make amends for succumbing to temptation. It doesn't matter that I am a dog. I know what my mission is, and it certainly doesn't have anything to do with getting into the garbage.*

It was obvious to Bo that Ace was feeling sorry for what he'd done. He gently patted the pathetic-looking dog on top of his massive head. "We need to get this cleaned up pronto."

Bo went over to the back door and looked out of the window. He saw that Martha had just returned home and was removing a couple of grocery sacks from the trunk of the family car. Bo wheeled around from the window and hurried back to the throw rug. "Oh crap, oh crap, gotta hurry."

Bo rushed over to the throw rug. He grabbed it on each end and let the contents fall into the middle. As he was trying to carry the rug with the garbage inside, an empty can of beans dropped onto the linoleum floor. Bo flinched from the loud noise caused by the dropped can, worrying that the sound might have awakened his sleeping father. He placed the rug on top of the garbage pail and tilted the contents back into it. As he was doing that, Ace trotted over to the empty bean can and grabbed it in his mouth. As soon as Bo had dumped the garbage back into the pail, the big dog was next to him, dropping the bean can into the garbage as well.

Bo threw the rug back down where it was before. Meanwhile, an observant Ace had noticed that there was some bean juice that had dribbled onto the floor when the can had dropped out of the rug. He quickly licked it up in one big slurp. As Bo finished making sure the throw rug was spread out flat, Ace came over and started moving his right paw back and forth across it, like using a broom to clear away any last particles. Bo flattened the rug back out again with his foot. "That's good enough. Now you get back to my room, you *bad boy.*"

As Ace was running out of the kitchen, both Henry and Martha entered at the same time. Martha came in through the back door from outside, and Henry entered from the inner hallway. Ace hurried by Henry so fast that he almost knocked him over. "Whoa, slow down, King Kong." Henry then directed his attention to his youngest son. "What's all the commotion in here? Something woke me up."

Bo tried to look calm. He had almost broken into a sweat as a result of his rapid clean-up effort. "You sure you weren't just dreaming, Pop? I just came in to get a glass of milk, that's all."

"Then why was Ace in such a hurry to get out of the kitchen?"

Bo shrugged. "I don't know? Ya want me to go ask him?"

"Don't get smart with me, young man."

Bo always knew when he'd gone too far. "Sorry, Pop. Something must have spooked him."

Martha seemed to have bought into Bo's excuse. "Maybe I scared the dog, Henry. I did come through the door rather suddenly." She always had blinders on when it came to her youngest son. Martha had always trusted Bo explicitly, regardless of evidence during or after incidents throughout the years that should have eroded that trust, at least a little bit anyway.

Henry scratched his head and yawned. "You know what, I think I'll just go back to reading the paper." He turned and left the kitchen while Martha started to put the groceries away.

Bo opened the refrigerator door and reached in for the little bit of milk that was left in the oldest container. "You might try holding the paper a little bit farther from your face this time, Pop!"

Martha giggled to herself, wondering if her husband would come back to the kitchen again. Within a few seconds, she heard the footrest on Henry's recliner pop back open. She knew her wiseacre son had gotten away with that one. Martha watched as Bo closed the refrigerator door, drank the last of the milk right out of the milk container, and tossed it into the garbage. It was the only time that he or Henry could get away with not using a glass, if Martha was watching them, that is.

Before Bo could leave the kitchen, Martha thought of something he could do for her as she pointedly sniffed the air. "Son, would you please take out the garbage for me. I just noticed that it smells bad in here. We probably should have emptied it after we were done eating tonight. It seems like the whole kitchen smells like garbage."

Bo didn't hesitate or complain. He quickly grabbed the garbage pail and headed for the back door. Martha didn't even notice that it was one of the few times that Bo had responded so quickly to one of her chore requests.

A ce came trotting out of the back door with Bo close behind in the early morning of the next day after the kitchen trash caper. Martha was over in the driveway, straining over the hood of the family car, scraping ice off the windshield with the engine running. Exhaust fumes spiraled into the air before being carried off by a northern morning breeze. The mastiff reached the closed gate of the dog run and waited for Bo.

It's was a good-sized dog run that connected with the garage that was set far back in the backyard near the alley. There was a doggy door inside the dog run that allowed a dog to enter part of the garage if he wanted to. The dog run had very high fencing, making it impossible for Ace to jump or to climb over the fence.

Bo opened the gate, and Ace padded through the opening. As Bo secured the gate, the dog turned around and faced Bo, his tail wagging back and forth. "You almost blew it last night. You know that, don't you, Ace?"

"Woof!"

"The only thing that saved us is when you dropped all the garbage on the rug." He looked intently into the mastiff's eyes, apparently searching for and finding an answer. "You did that on purpose, didn't you?"

"Woof!"

Bo leaned down so that he was close to Ace's slobbery face. He was not a stupid boy. He'd already witnessed enough of Ace's behavior to know that he and his family were now in the possession of a special dog. Bo was thinking about the fact that "special" and "strange" both started with the same letter. The word "strange" had almost completed his thoughts until the word "special" had crowded it out at the last second.

Obviously, there was a fine line in how Ace was affecting Bo. He wondered if his parents were already starting to feel that way too. And if not, how soon would it be before it was unanimous? "I'll make you a deal. From now on, when we have steak bones, I'll save them for you. In return, you promise never to get into the garbage again. Have we got a deal?"

"Woof!"

"How do I know you're telling me the truth?"

Ace sat his butt down on the concrete floor and lifted his right paw.

"Does that mean you want to shake on it?"

"Woof!"

Bo reopened the gate, reached in, and shook Ace's paw. He looked into the big dog's eyes. They seemed so penetrating to Bo, like Ace was looking right through him. He had to look away after a few seconds because it was starting to scare him.

Ace was thinking, *Jeez, what a hassle this is, just to get through to these people. Anybody who says a dog's life is great is clueless when it comes to understanding how dependent we are on humans. The only bit of redemption comes from the fact that they clean up our poop—a small price to pay for forcing us to constantly poop in public in front of You and anyone else who happens to be looking out their window or walking by at the time. That's why I usually go when it's dark out. And what about that neighbor dog I saw eating his? How disgusting! I'll have to have a little talk with him about that. It only reinforces the stereotype that humans have about us being an inferior species.*

Martha had finished scraping the ice from the car windows and looked at Bo and Ace as they finished making their pact with each other. "Come on, Bo! I don't want you being late for school!"

The boy walked hurriedly toward the car, but he turned partially around so he could see Ace inside the dog run. "Have a good day, buddy. I'll see you tonight, okay?"

The big bullmastiff lifted one paw.

Bo turned around and headed for the car as Martha began to enter on the driver's side. He looked at his mother as he opened the passenger door.

"Did you get my books and notebook?"

"Yes! They're in the back seat!"

Students were filing into the history class midmorning. Bo was sitting in the desk that was second from the front in the last aisle near the windows. Sarah was sitting in front of him in the first row.

Sarah was a pretty petite blonde who was a cheerleader. In fact, she was wearing her cheerleader outfit because of a basketball game to be played that night. She had been absent from school the day before, so this was his first encounter with her since he had returned after getting discharged from the hospital. Bo was opening his notebook and history book, getting ready for the start of class. Sarah turned around in her chair, her long straight blond hair brushing Bo's cheek as she looked into Bo's eyes. "Welcome back, Bo. How are you doing?"

Sarah staring at him was making Bo feel uncomfortable. He looked down at his textbook to avoid eye contact. "I'm doing okay."

His short response must have done little to deter Sarah. "I'm so sorry to hear that you can't wrestle anymore."

He immediately became angry that Sarah had so quickly brought up the subject of wrestling, something that he had been trying to put out of his mind once and for all. He tried as best as he could not to show his sudden contempt toward her for bringing up such a sore subject with him. He was wishing that he could have gotten this encounter over with the day before, when he had first returned to school. Here we go again, he thought. How many others in school were going to make it obvious that they were probably more concerned that the wrestling team was now without its best wrestler than about his personal injury and loss? He finally looked back up at her. "Yeah, well, I really don't want to talk about that."

Bo had always been keenly aware about how Sarah had always seemed more into herself than anyone else, so he wasn't surprised when she failed to notice how his eyes were piercing into her like darts. "Oh, sure, I understand."

Bo was thinking of the word "bimbo" in his head. This was one of the pretty little girls who used to laugh at him during the early grade school years. "But you can still cheer for me if you want to," he answered.

"Huh?" was all that Sarah could manage to say before the teacher had walked into the classroom.

The teacher, Miss Krenkle, walked over to her desk in the front of the room and called the class to order. Miss Krenkle had short wavy gray hair, wore Coke bottle glasses, and was heavyset in appearance. She was also near retirement. The faculty, particularly the younger teachers, knew she was a good and knowledgeable teacher, but she was often the butt of jokes behind her back. Many of her students always acted intimidated by her intelligence, so they must have made fun of her appearance to better cope with the situation. Miss Krenkle was only guilty of not being born with beautiful looks. Other than that, she was a wealth of information that delivered it for forty years with a passion.

Just the other day, as the principal was discussing with the vice principal her pending retirement, he had remarked, "God help us if the Miss Krenkle's of the world have faded away with the innocent times that faded away with her."

One time a couple of the boys in the class who had a reputation for pulling pranks put a couple of tacks on her chair before she arrived. She finally sat down in her chair, not grimacing or saying anything, not even "ouch." The entire class was aware of the prank. Everyone was amazed that she apparently couldn't feel the tacks in her rear end.

When she got up again and was facing the blackboard, the two tack heads were noticeably stuck in each cheek of her butt. It was obvious to the class that she couldn't figure out why she kept hearing snickers every time she turned her back to the class while writing on the blackboard. The only thing anyone could figure out later was that she must have been wearing the thickest girdle on the planet. If she ever eventually found or noticed the tacks, no one—at least in her sophomore history class—ever heard about the discovery. Somebody had suggested that some other teacher in the hallway or in the teacher's lounge might have told her later. How does anyone, male or female, gracefully and with tact (no pun intended) tell someone else that they unknowingly have two tacks stuck in their butt?

"Good morning, class. Are we ready to discuss the ramifications of our entry into World War I today?" No one answered her. A few whispers were heard throughout the room. "Very well then. Let us begin. Who would like to tell us why the United States was drawn into the war?"

As Miss Krenkle finished her last sentence, Bo glanced to his left and looked out of the row of windows. Sitting right outside the window was Ace. The big dog was just sitting there, staring at him. He was totally taken off guard to see his dog staring at him from the window when he knew he had left him secured inside the dog run at home.

"Mr. Bozell, would you like to tell us?"

Bo turned his body toward Miss Krenkle and then once again looked out of the window. Ace was not there anymore. He was startled by both the dog's appearance and the fact that he had just been called on by the teacher.

"What? What did you say?"

Miss Krenkle did not look amused by Bo's lack of attention. "I see you are your normal attentive self again today, Mr. Bozell. Are we disturbing you?"

Bo was clearly flustered. "Yes—I mean, no. I'm sorry, Miss Krenkle. Can I be excused for a minute?"

Miss Krenkle looked like she was becoming very annoyed by now. This probably was not what she anticipated when she walked into the room, fully prepared to enter into a stimulating discussion with her class about the epic period of the First World War. "Excused, Mr. Bozell? We're just getting started."

Bo got up from his desk and walked up to Miss Krenkle. He leaned over and whispered to her, "I really, really have to go to the bathroom."

Miss Krenkle whispered back into Bo's ear, "Why didn't you go before class?"

He reacted as quickly to Miss Krenkle's question as he would to his wrestling opponent who was trying to get the upper hand on him. "I did. It's these pain pills the doctor's got me on." He looked intently and seemingly innocently into Miss Krenkle's eyes after his quick explanation, sensing that she was satisfied with his answer even before her reply.

"Very well. You are excused, but please hurry back."

Bo quickly headed for the door as he completed his deception. "1 will, Miss Krenkle. I will." He didn't have a problem with lying if it didn't really hurt anyone else. Besides, he was raised in the church. He never thought of it as lying. Bo was just bending the truth sometimes if it served the common cause. He always had a rationale for a common cause to exist between him and the person he was deceiving. The other person just wasn't aware of it at the time.

He opened and closed the classroom door and made a beeline for the nearest exit. Mr. Hellerman—the biology teacher, a four-eyed, bow-tied midget of a man—came around the corner of an adjoining hallway. His distinctive aftershave announced his arrival before he had even rounded the corner into view. It allowed Bo to slow his pace upon seeing him, trying to act nonchalant until Hellerman and his aftershave were out of sight and out of smell.

He then quickened his pace once again and hit the double-door exit on a dead run. He hurriedly walked around the corner of the building and peered down the side of the school where he had seen Ace. Bo saw no one. He walked around the building as much as he dared without walking in front of the outside of his own classroom, but his dog was nowhere to be found. As Bo was walking back into the high school, he asked himself, "Did 1 really see Ace outside the window, or do I just need to get off these pain pills?"

His neck was throbbing by the time he turned the handle on his history classroom door. The pain was reminding him that he really wasn't ready yet to run anywhere for any reason, at least not until his neck brace was removed so he would know for sure what he was going to be dealing with for the rest of his life. He tried to put on a happy face before walking into the classroom, ignoring as best as he could the intense pain in his neck. He made a mental note before sliding back into his chair near the window. *Hallucinations or no hallucinations, I'm takin' another pain pill as soon as class is over.*

A car pulled up into the back driveway of the Bozells' yard. Bo's high school friend Jerry was once again dropping him off from school. Bo got out of the car on the passenger side, with his notebook and books tucked under his arm. "Thanks for the lift, Jerry."

Jerry nodded as Bo got out of his car. "Anytime, Bo." Bo had started to walk toward the dog run before Jerry remembered he had meant to ask his friend something earlier, apparently reminded by the surroundings in which the gift had been given originally. "Bo! How do you like the microscope set so far!"

As Bo kept walking away, he rationalized that Jerry would soon remember that it was quite possible that he hadn't heard him, a ploy he had probably used much too often. The fact of the matter was Bo hadn't even looked at the microscope set Jerry had given him. He knew his geek science friend had meant well, but Bo had no desire to replace his love for wrestling with something as boring as science.

His last pair of new hearing aids he had just acquired was markedly better. If someone shouted at him from out of his line of vision, Bo could still hear the person's remarks most of the time, depending on his or her pitch. His total dependence on lip-reading had been alleviated somewhat, a welcome improvement. He knew it was wrong to use his disability for clever deception, and he had thought about discontinuing the practice on several occasions. The problem was it was just too easy.

Bo continued to walk away, waiting to hear the car accelerating away. He knew the next time Jerry would ask him the same question, he'd be better prepared with an answer. Jerry just rolled his eyes, put his old Chevy into reverse, and backed out of the driveway as Bo walked around the corner of the garage.

Ace was sitting inside the dog run. As soon as he saw Bo, he let out a loud woof. The big dog raised his butt off the concrete and started wagging his tail. "Hi, buddy. You ready to get out of there for a while?"

Ace got very excited. His wagging tail made music like a wind chime on the gate's fence post. "Woof!"

Bo opened the gate to the dog run and let the big mastiff out. He closed the gate and started to walk toward the house with Ace right beside him. Unexpectedly, Bo stopped in his tracks and turned around before walking back to the garage and over to the side door. He reached into his pocket and pulled out some keys, unlocking the door and entering the garage, with Ace following him. He turned on a light switch inside the door and peered at the corner of the garage. In the back left corner was the same type of high fencing that the dog run had on the outside. It was a small area in the corner of the garage that the dog could get into from the doggy door if the weather got bad or if it got too cold outside. There was a gate on the inside as well, but it seemed to be securely fastened shut. Bo just stood there for a few seconds, staring at this inner part of the dog run. He looked down at Ace, who was patiently sitting by his side, wagging his tail with a vengeance. "Just checking something, buddy."

Ace knew what his new master was checking. His curiosity had almost gotten him caught. At a minimum, he had aroused a suspicion that probably shouldn't have been aroused yet. Bo turned around and shut the light off as he exited the door, with the dog following close behind.

Bo had just finished his supper. He grabbed a plastic bag from under the kitchen sink and headed for the garage. With the big dog following at his heels, he told the bullmastiff what he was doing. "Time to clean up the backyard, buddy." He unlocked the garage door and found a metal bucket in the corner by some of the other yard tools. Bo lined the metal bucket with the plastic bag and grabbed one of the shovels that were hanging on hooks along the far wall. He headed out to the backyard to do his first stint of pooper-scooper duty.

After he got out into the middle of the backyard, he began to look around for piles of doggy doo-doo. He figured ahead of time that it wouldn't be like the challenging Easter egg hunts he remembered as a small child. After all, Ace wasn't a small dog, so he anticipated that the excrement would be easy to find. He looked at his dog.

Ace seemed to be acting like he was embarrassed or something. He looked down at the ground with his tail between his legs and his ears tucked down.

Bo scanned the yard from left to right as he stood in front of the garage. He spotted the pile that Ace had deposited the day he had been discharged from the hospital—the pile that he had used as an example to his father concerning his new dog's trustworthiness in the house. After scooping that up, he looked around the yard for the other piles of poop that he knew had to be somewhere in the yard. He couldn't see one single additional pile. Before he decided to take off walking around the yard to find the rest of Ace's "treasures," he looked at his new dog and asked a simple question as a joke. "I don't suppose you could just show me where they are, could you?"

"Woof!"

"Well, where are they then?"

Ace padded over to the line of bushes that ran along part of the middle of the backyard next to the clothesline. He abruptly stopped at the end of the bushes and stared straight ahead like a hunting dog pointing to its prey.

Bo rounded the corner of the bushes and stopped dead in his tracks. He looked dumbfounded. There, in a straight line almost hidden from view, laid all of Ace's number twos. They were deposited as close to the bushes as possible, suggesting that the dog had backed up as far as he could into the bushes without scratching his heinie.

"I ... 1 can't believe it," the boy mumbled. He looked at Ace, who had started moaning before turning around and padding away from the "scene of the crime."

"I'd tell somebody else about this, but who'd believe it?" he said to himself as he began scooping up the piles into his bucket.

Bo was lying on his bed, reading a Spider-Man comic book. The bullmastiff was lying on the floor near his bed. Martha yelled at Bo from an adjoining bedroom in the house, "Bo! Are you doing your homework?" "Yes, Mother!" he yelled back.

Martha probed for more detail, not that she didn't trust her youngest son, but she was experienced, having been tested through the years by two elder sons who had educated her, each in their own way, with their subtle techniques of delay or deception. "What subject?"

He didn't hesitate for even a second before he responded, "Science!"

Ace groaned as he looked over with glaring big brown eyes and a frown on his slobbery face at his new master. Bo, unaware that a judgmental canine was staring at him, continued to read his Spider-Man comic book. The big dog finally got up and padded over to the bed, placing his chin on the edge. The boy ignored Ace, which was no easy task considering that the dog was drooling all over his bedspread. Finally, Bo gave up and looked at the mammoth head that was staring at him over his bed. "What is it, Ace? Do you need to go outside?"

Ace backed away, went over to where he was lying before, and sat down. This time, he didn't lie down; but instead, he parked his butt on the floor and continued to stare back at the boy. Bo was too preoccupied to notice at first. Finally, he picked up on the stare-down from out of the corner of his eye. He looked at the intent, insistent canine. "If you don't have to go outside, then what do you want, Ace?"

The dog didn't answer. He just continued to sit perfectly still and stare. Bo buried his head in the comic book again and finally responded to his furry friend's silence. "Suit yourself." He continued to read his comic book and ignored the big dog for another couple of minutes.

Suddenly, Ace got up and padded quickly to his bedside. He unexpectedly grabbed the comic book out of Bo's hands with his mouth and ran out of the bedroom with it. The boy was surprised and startled by his dog's bold sudden move. "Hey, you thief! Come back here with that!"

Bo hurried out into the hallway, but Ace was nowhere to be found. Martha yelled again from the other bedroom, "What's going on, Bo?"

Bo stopped in his tracks in the hallway. He tried to defuse Martha's concern since he had other more pressing problems at hand. "Nothing! Just getting ready to let Ace out, that's all!"

The bullmastiff reappeared from the top of the stairs at the other end of the hallway and was trotting toward Bo. He didn't have the comic book in his mouth anymore. He defiantly returned to his new master, seemingly unafraid of rebuke and retribution.

"What's the big idea, Ace? Why did you do that?"

The mastiff trotted by Bo and back into the bedroom. He immediately went over to Bo's stack of books, grabbed the top textbook off the stack with his mouth, and brought it to him.

"Okay, 1 get it." Bo went over to his desk and turned on the lamp, sitting down with the textbook in front of him, wiping off the dog saliva from the hardback cover. He glanced at Ace, who was sitting back down now. "1 expect you to bring that comic book back when I'm done with my homework."

His new dog reassured him that he would do just that. "Woof!"

Bo kept looking at Ace before beginning to read his textbook. "You know, you'd make a great hall monitor at school."

The big dog proudly lifted his head even higher.

Bo shook his head and began to read as he concluded his conversation with a dog that was starting to have a very scary new influence on his life. "I was just kidding, Ace. Don't get your hopes up."

It was almost bedtime, and Bo was lying in bed under the covers, trying to read what was left of his Spider-Man comic book, which had been in mint condition before Ace had stolen it out of his hands with his mouth. He had finished his homework to the dog's satisfaction, and then the comic book was returned using the same method of transportation as before. Ace was lying on the floor next to the bed. All the goo had already been wiped off the outer cover with a hand towel from the bathroom that Bo had hung back up for some other unsuspecting family member to use.

As he was turning the last few pages that were stuck together like a rain- soaked newspaper, he looked over with a scowl on his face at the big dog that was lying there peacefully by his side. "The next time you decide to swipe something away from me, 1 wish you'd at least use your paw instead of your jaw. 1 had a perfect collection going until you decided to gum up the works with your slobbery getaway."

Ace let out a low moan and closed his eyes as he was lying on his right side on the bedroom floor. He was rationalizing his actions, lost in his thoughts. *Come on, Bo, think. You should know that I don't have an opposing thumb on my paws. And even if I did somehow manage to carry away the comic book clutched between my chest and paw, how hard would it have been trying to make my getaway on three legs? It was the unfortunate (for you) obvious choice. It came down to four paws versus three paws. I think the choice was obvious. Besides, if you were doing your homework, I wouldn 't have ruined your stupid comic book in the first place, now woidd I?*

Bo, unaware that his dog was lying there thinking thoughts normally reserved for humans, finally placed the comic book down on the dresser next to his bed and reached for the lamp to shut it off. "Good night, Ace."

The big dog didn't respond to Bo's final comment of the night. He continued to lie motionless on the floor, seemingly already in deep slumber. He must have been so tired that he fell asleep right next to the bed that night instead of closer to the window, where he could have eventually felt an early morning breeze. His new master shut off the light and rolled over to go to sleep. Bo tossed and turned a little bit before getting comfortable, and then he fell sound asleep, totally exhausted from such a stressful and confusing day.

It was late evening as an elderly black couple, tending to their liquor store in North Omaha, were going about their nightly duties before closing for the night. The husband was behind the front counter, digging around, looking for something on a lower shelf, while his wife was in the back room doing some paperwork. The wife shouted to her husband in the front of the store, "George! It's almost eleven o'clock! Are you gonna lock the front door now?"

The husband had heard this "last call" many times through the years. "In a minute, Izzy!" George yelled back.

Izzy offered more incentive to call it quits for the night. "I have to get up early tomorrow and babysit Candice!"

"Oh yeah, I forgot!" George yelled back.

Candice was their little granddaughter. Their only daughter, Sherlyn, had given birth to Candice almost three months ago. Sherlyn wasn't married. She probably would have been married by now, but her husbandto-be, Ed, was still over in Vietnam, finishing up his one-year tour of duty. The wedding plans were all arranged for Ed's return. All he had to do was make it back home, having survived his year in hell.

Sherlyn had moved back in with her parents when Ed had left for the war. It was only a matter of a few weeks before they knew that Ed had unknowingly left a "going-away present" on his last night in Omaha before leaving. Sherlyn had mailed off her first letter to Ed since getting the news from her doctor. She had hoped that it would be happy news for him. His letter back to her hadn't disappointed her as she had feared it might. He had said he was very excited that he was going to be a father.

He also said that the news had given him even greater incentive to make it back in one piece.

It was several months later, and he was only days now from fulfilling that promise. He had just called a couple of days ago that he was still safe and sound and eager to get on the plane that would take him out of harm's way.

It probably wasn't so much that George was getting forgetful as it was the difficulty in remembering his daughter's work schedule at the Safeway Grocery Store, where Sherlyn had gone back to work after having the baby. It worked out well that Izzy could babysit her granddaughter in the daytime and then help George at night at the liquor store when Sherlyn was home from work. They had discussed the possibility, but they had never seriously considered having their daughter work at the store. North Omaha was a predominantly poor black community, and many of the young men, unable to get a college deferment or lacking the right connections with government officials who could pull some strings, either had been drafted into the military or were roaming the streets without a job.

There were convicted felons in North Omaha who had served their time in the Nebraska State Penitentiary. Such men, who were thrust back into their neighborhoods, had an uphill battle to right their ships. They somehow had to ignore the "professional criminal degree" that they had earned while in prison, striking out in a new positive direction without any true direction from anyone. All the odds for success weighed heavily against them. They couldn't escape their jungle any more than their brothers could over in 'Nam.

Young black men in North Omaha had few choices in life back in the late sixties. The choice, at a very young age, was to stay the course—as Martin Luther King had preached in front of young ears with minds that were searching for answers—or, as a more destructive alternative, to strike out without reason or thought, letting hatred feed their souls. Heroin and cocaine addicts needed quick cash, and liquor stores were often seen as easy targets. Sure, there were still many fine law-abiding young black men in North Omaha, but there were many who were not, and that was what made the area a potentially dangerous place to work and live in.

Just then, the front door opened, causing the bell above the door to ring as an apparent late customer had come into the store. George was still hunched over behind the counter, having not made eye contact yet with the late-arriving customer. "I'll be right with you. You're lucky you came in when ya did. We were just about to close."

He hadn't looked up at the customer yet, but the young man responded just the same, "What do ya mean we?"

George rose from behind the counter. "My wife an' . . . He stopped short of finishing his sentence as he was now staring down the barrel of a sawed-off shotgun. He looked both frightened and mad at himself for being so careless at that time of night. The armed robber was wearing a dark blue ski mask and dressed in dark clothes. George had a justifiably scared look on his face, and his eyes were bugging out. "Izzy! Get out the back—now!"

The robber cocked his shotgun and reaimed it directly at George's face. "Don't go anywhere, lady, or your man here is a dead man! Come out to the front—now!"

Izzy came hurriedly out from the back room. She was trembling. The fear she must have been feeling was written all over her face. In the years that George and Izzy had owned the liquor store, this wasn't the first time they had been held up, but that didn't seem to make it any less terrifying when it happened.

Izzy spoke to the robber as the masked assailant kept his sawedoff shotgun trained on George while also trying to watch Izzy as she approached the front counter. "Please don't hurt my husband! You can have all the money!"

"Shut up, bitch, and get over here next to your man!"

She hurriedly walked up to George and joined him, undoubtedly knowing at that point that no amount of pleading was going the help them get out of the predicament they were now in.

"Keep your hands up where I can see them! You! Old man! Open the register!"

George's hands were shaking, but he managed to somehow get the register open.

The robber reached into a coat pocket and tossed a small burlap sack onto the counter. "Fill it up!" George grabbed the bag and emptied everything from the register into it while the young robber intermittently glanced at the front door, out the front windows, and then back at George and Izzy. His right foot tapped incessantly on the store's old parquet floor. He glanced down at his wristwatch and checked the time before looking back up at George and Izzy. "Now toss it here, old man!"

George tossed the bag to the robber as he and his wife continued to stay frozen in place behind the counter. The robber shook the bag up and down a couple of times with his free hand. "This feels pretty light, old man! I'm bettin' the old lady here was countin' more in the back!"

Izzy started to cry. She held her hands, cupped in front of her as if she was at a Sunday prayer breakfast at their Baptist church. "No, sir! That's all of it! I swear!"

The young thug, hiding behind his ski mask, seemed unconvinced. "I don't believe you, Grandma! Nice and easy now, I want you both to move to the back room."

"Please! She's tellin' ya the truth!" George pleaded.

"Shut up, old man! Now both of you! Move it!"

The thief was suddenly startled by the loud, unmistakable sound of breaking glass. A big dog came crashing through the right front window of the liquor store. Glass was flying everywhere as the dog was coming too fast for the armed robber to react. By the time the stunned assailant had begun to move his sawed- off shotgun in its direction, the snarling dog was on him.

The ferocious big beast was growling and spewing spit as he leaped onto the robber. The dog grabbed the thug's gun arm in his mouth as the shotgun fired off into the ceiling. Plaster and debris came raining down on them. The robber dropped the shotgun to the floor as the momentum of the big bullmastiffs weight and speed spilled him onto his back. The wild dog was snarling and slobbering into the intruder's face as George quickly came around the counter, holding his own .38 revolver in his right hand. George picked up the shotgun with his free hand as he pointed his revolver at the assailant.

The big dog could see that George had his handgun trained on the punk, who was still stunned from the surprise attack. He finally moved off to the side of the young thug while still snarling. George yelled at his wife, who had fallen behind the counter. "Izzy! Call the police!"

She got to her feet, wheeled around, and headed to the back of the counter. Izzy picked up a phone that was hidden from view, half-gagging from the strong smell of gunpowder. As she started to dial the phone, a police siren was already blaring from a distance. Someone nearby must have heard the gunshot and had apparently already called the police. The big dog turned, ran to the front of the store, and leaped back through the broken window, disappearing into the night.

Bo's alarm clock went off. The alarm had a buzzer as well as a strobe light that was flashing on and off. He rolled over and shut it off, rolling back over the other way again and trying to fall back asleep. Ace was lying on the floor next to his bed between the bed and the outside window.

Martha opened Bo's door enough to flip the light switch on. "Time to get up for school!"

Bo slid his head under the pillow to avoid the bright light that Martha had just inflicted on him. His voice was muffled as his head was still partially under the pillow. "Yes, Ma. I'm getting up."

He finally sat up in bed and looked at Ace as he stretched his arms over his head. The dog was lying with his belly on the floor, and his front paws were stretched out in front of him. Bo noticed some dark red streaks in a few places on Ace's front paws. "Come here, buddy. Let's have a look at those paws."

Ace sat up, but he didn't move from his spot. He just moaned a little bit and sat still.

"Ace, I said come here, boy. I won't hurt you. Now come here." The dog finally padded slowly over to the side of the bed.

"Come on, put one of your paws up here."

Ace finally put his right paw up on the edge of the bed. With both of his hands, Bo lifted the paw to examine it more closely. He looked surprised when he surmised that the red streaks were possible bloodstains. He observed that there was, indeed, dried blood, but he also noticed that there were a few small shards of glass in Ace's paw that were stuck between his claws. Bo's eyes got wide when he found the shards of glass. "Holy cow,

Ace! What did you get into last night? 1 didn't notice this before we went to bed. Let's head for the bathroom and get you cleaned up."

Bo slid out of bed after gently putting the dog's paw back down. Ace removed his right paw from on top of the edge of the bed and slowly padded behind his new master. He was limping a little bit when the puzzled and still sleepy boy turned back toward him while they were both leaving the bedroom. "Then I'm gonna do a little inspection of the house."

Henry was sitting in his recliner, watching the world news on television the following evening after the attempted liquor store holdup in North Omaha. Bo was lying on the sofa, and Ace was sitting next to him on the floor. The news was showing footage of the war in Vietnam as a war correspondent was finishing talking in the background.

"How was school today, son?" asked Henry without taking his eyes off the television screen.

"Oh, okay, I guess," answered Bo.

Henry seemed intent on watching the news broadcast. He was leaning forward on the edge of his chair with his feet flat on the floor. Normally, as everyone else in the family would attest to, he would have flipped the release handle on the side, and his feet would have been dangling off the edge of the footrest shortly after he had sat down.

"Seems like you watch the evening news more often now, Pop," Bo finally chimed in.

Henry glanced away from the television for a second as Walter Cronkite continued his evening presentation to the country. "Yeah, I guess I have been, haven't 1?" said Henry before turning his full attention back to Walter on the television.

"Are you hoping you might see Ben?"

Henry didn't answer his youngest son at first. He continued to stare at the television screen like he was in a trance or something. "Yeah, kinda silly, 1 guess, considering how many troops are over there. But you never know. This could be the night that I see my son again . . . and know for sure . . . that he's still alive."

Bo sat silently for a few seconds, staring at the television set with his dad. "You worry about him a lot, don't you, Pop?"

Henry finally took his eyes off the television again and looked at the baby of the family. Bo could have sworn that there was a tear or two in his father's eyes. "He's my son, Bo. 1 worry about you and John too." Henry kept watching the news some more before looking once again at Bo. "That reminds me. What were you doing this morning before I went to work? 1 noticed you had Ace in the bathroom with you for quite a while, and then you were roamin' around all over the house like you were looking for something. What was that all about?"

Bo looked into his father's questioning eyes. "I'm startin' to teach Ace how to use the toilet so I don't have to let him out all the time."

Henry gave Bo a dirty look and acted like he was about to speak when Bo beat him to the punch.

"1 know. I'm bein' a smart-ass again. The truth is I was cleaning some mud out of his paws. Then I checked around the house to make sure he didn't track it in anywhere else."

Even if Henry didn't buy Bo's story, he didn't let it show. "That's good, boy. You know he's your responsibility. I'm not gonna put up with no funny business from him."

Ace moaned from his spot in front of the sofa.

The latter part of the national news shifted to a far less serious subject. There was a story about a socialite gathering of teenage daughters and sons of influential Washington bureaucrats. Bo watched the footage of the gathering, seemingly intrigued by the pomp and circumstance of it all. He looked at his father as the piece was ending. "Pop, do you think people like that enjoy life more than we do? Is life more interesting to them than it is to us?"

Henry looked at Bo and smiled. "Son, I've always felt that life is what you make of it. Do those rich and powerful people have more fun than we do? Maybe, maybe not. It's all in how you look at life. I'm gonna guess that not all those young people you just saw on TV are overly happy. In fact, some of them could be downright suicidal. Having fame and fortune doesn't guarantee happiness. What one would consider as elite is all in the eyes of the beholder. It all depends on what your definition of 'elite' is. Does it involve knowing how to recognize and respect who has the most expensive clothes and jewelry on? Is it being aware of the best places to eat in London or knowing who was thought to be the best seventeenth century English poet?"

"Huh?"

"Never mind. You know how much I read at night." Henry paused while looking at the bookshelf near the fireplace. "1 think all one has to do to put the whole thing in perspective is to remember that some of the greatest people in history who walked this earth came from humble beginnings and then remained humble for the rest of their lives."

Bo looked back at his father and grinned. "Yeah, I understand what you mean by that, Pop. I can think of a couple of examples. The first one who comes to mind was just a simple carpenter."

Henry laughed out loud. "I think you've got it, boy. I think you've got it."

In customary Bozell fashion, Martha yelled at Bo from the kitchen, interrupting some apparent quality time between father and son. "Bo! Come and set the table, please! Dinner's almost ready!"

Bo rolled up off the sofa and left the living room, with Ace trotting along close behind as the world news was over, and there was a commercial on television. Henry continued to sit in his recliner as the local news came on.

The news anchor began his evening presentation, supposedly reading from his notes in front of him on his desk, all the while looking more often directly into the camera as well as the teleprompter, unseen to viewers, which was scrolling his lines in sync with his smooth delivery. "Our lead story tonight involves a foiled holdup at a North Omaha liquor store last night. What is so interesting about this story is the accounts given by the owners of G&l Liquor on Ames Avenue. According to them, a dog is being credited with overpowering the shotgun wielding robber."

Before Henry was able to listen to more of the story, Martha yelled out from the kitchen. "Henry! Would you please come and take out the garbage while Bo is finishing setting the table!"

Martha's yelling at Henry distracted him from hearing the rest of the local news story. Henry immediately reacted to Martha's request, got out of his recliner, and left the living room. "I'm on my way, Mother!"

Such a quick response was rare for Henry. Martha had perfected her skills in getting what she wanted through the years. She knew that Henry always had less incentive to take out the trash after the meal than before the meal. Martha had always insisted that Henry not dump all the chores onto the boys through the years. She had convinced him that he must sometimes lead by example. Such a philosophy had always worked wonders for Martha. She suspected that her husband, on the other hand, had never really seen the value in it.

The Bozell family was sitting around the kitchen table, eating their evening meal. Ace was lying down over in the comer, watching them, his chin resting on his front paws on the floor. Martha picked up a half-empty serving plate of roast beef. "More roast beef, Henry?" "Yeah, I'll have a little more," replied Henry.

Martha passed the plate over to Henry, who dished some more onto his plate.

Henry finally looked at his youngest boy. "You want some more, son?"

Bo shook his head. "No thanks. I've had enough."

Bo's father put the plate down. He grabbed the ketchup bottle, dumping some more ketchup onto his replenished pile of roast beef before stabbing back into it, quickly bringing a forkful up to his mouth like he hadn't eaten for a week. Martha had long ago given up on trying to teach her husband to eat slower and to look up from his plate more often between bites. It was a good thing for Henry that he had other endearing qualities about him because this clearly wasn't one of them.

Henry put another big piece of meat in his mouth from the end of his fork and chewed it into submission. He finally looked up from his feast. "There was something on the local news tonight about a dog preventing a robbery at a liquor store in North Omaha. At least somebody owns a dog that earns his keep." Henry turned his head around and looked at Ace. The dog immediately moaned, got up, turned around, and faced the wall as he lay back down.

Bo was acutely aware of his dad's taunting of his dog. "Pop, you hur—" Henry interrupted Bo before he could finish his sentence. "I know. I hurt his feelings again. He sure is sensitive for as big as he is." Henry turned back around and stabbed another bite of roast beef onto his fork.

Ace continued to groan with his back turned to the family. Bo attempted to mend fences between his father and the big newcomer to the family. "He didn't mean it, Ace."

"Yes, I did."

Martha, watching this "table tennis" at her kitchen table, had seen and heard enough. "Henry, stop being so mean to Ace. Are you forgetting what this dog did for our son?"

Henry must have realized that he had taken his sarcasm too far. He nodded. "Yeah, I know. You're right, Mother. Okay, I apologize."

Ace got up and turned around to face the family again before plopping back down. It was obvious that the dog didn't seem to hold a grudge. The fact that he so quickly accepted Henry's apology spoke volumes about his temperament, not to mention his intelligence.

Henry had already turned back around and missed the fact that Ace had accepted his apology. "Oh, I almost forgot to tell you, Martha. Stanley's going to be staying with us tomorrow night. He's on his way to a coin collector convention in Des Moines."

Bo dropped his fork and pinched his nose with his thumb and index finger. "Oh no, not stinky Uncle Stanley."

Martha again had to play disciplinarian but this time to her son instead of her cranky old husband. "Bo, shame on you. Is that any way to talk about one of your father's brothers?"

"Yes, son. Show more respect," added Henry.

Bo fanned his open hand back and forth in front of his face as he apologized. "Sorry, Pop. It's just that, every time he stays, it takes a couple of days after he's gone before the odor goes away." He picked his fork back up off the table and resumed eating.

Martha decided she needed to stick up for Stanley, regardless of the fact that she too had haunting memories from Stanley's previous visits. "Bo, your uncle Stanley's been a bachelor all his life. He's never had a woman around to help him with his personal hygiene."

"Can't you set him up with one of your widow friends or somethin'?" asked Bo.

Martha shook her head as she looked at Henry and then back at her son. "I'm afraid it's too late for that, Bo."

Bo looked confused. "What do you mean?"

"Your uncle Stanley's too set in his ways now, and so are my friends." Bo tried to act like he understood so his mother would think of him as more of a man now instead of being her youngest baby boy. "Oh, yeah. I guess I know what you mean. Well, I'm done. Gotta go to the bathroom." Bo got up from the table and left the kitchen. Ace had apparently chosen not to follow his young master this time because he stayed in his sleepy position on the kitchen floor after Bo had left the room.

Having finished her dinner as well, Martha got up and started to clear the table as Henry was still finishing his second helping of roast beef. She began to run water in the kitchen sink before starting to put food away in the refrigerator. "Sorry to leave you sitting there by yourself, Henry, but if your brother's coming tomorrow night, I've got a lot to get done tonight before I go to bed."

Henry continued to chew a big piece of roast beef and answered Martha in a garbled tone, "That's okay, Mother. You go right ahead."

Martha, having corrected Henry so many times throughout their years of marriage but to no avail, chose to ignore Henry's latest bad manner episode of talking with his mouth full. "Henry, when you're done eating, would you mind getting my rubber gloves from the laundry room in the basement while I finish putting away these leftovers?"

Henry was down to his last few bites of roast beef as he looked up from his plate. "Sure, Mother, I'll get them for you in a couple of minutes."

While Henry was answering his wife, Ace had gotten up and quietly padded out of the kitchen through the other door that led to the basement. A few more seconds passed before Ace came trotting back into the kitchen with the rubber gloves stuck in his mouth. Instead of going directly to Martha, he made a pass around the kitchen table by Henry, holding his head high as he trotted around the table just like one of those trained show horses. Ace finally took the gloves up to Martha, and she removed them from his mouth. The whole time since the dog had arrived with the gloves, Henry had stopped in mid-chew, with his mouth gaping open.

"Why, thank you, Ace. What a good boy you are," Martha said as she patted him on top of his huge head before turning back toward the sink. She turned on the faucet and held the gloves under scalding hot water before putting them on. Having accomplished his mini-mission and his intent, Ace proudly trotted out of the room, presumably to find Bo.

Henry finally started eating again as he looked at Martha, who was putting on the rubber gloves so she could begin to wash the dishes. "I'm guessin' that had something to do with my comment earlier about earning his keep around here." Henry let out a deep sigh, muffling an unexpected belch before finishing his thoughts. "That dog ain't normal, Mother."

Martha returned a curious look at her husband. "I've noticed that too, Henry."

It was late afternoon in Lincoln, the site of the Nebraska State High School Wrestling Tournament. The first round of the event was nearing completion. There were four mats placed in a square on the coliseum floor. At the state tournament, four different matches were usually always underway at the same time. Which mat a wrestler would wrestle on depended on how big his school enrollment was. Class A was made up of all the schools with the most student enrollment. Therefore, all the class A school matches were held on the same mat, class B had their own mat, and so on.

Getting ready to wrestle on the class C mat was Matt Duncan of Papillion. The crowd's noise was deafening, especially since there were still some matches underway on two of the other four mats at that moment. Duncan was limbering up and stretching on the edge of the mat. His opponent was from Fullerton, a small town located in southwest central Nebraska. With Bo out of commission, his replacement from Plattsmouth in the heavyweight division didn't even make it out of district competition.

Bo's closest friend from the wrestling team, Tommy, had managed to win in the district, only to lose in the first round of the state tournament earlier in the day. He had stuck around, though, to offer his support to Darren, a Plattsmouth wrestler who had just won his opening day match in the weight division just below the heavyweights. As Tommy sat in the bleachers, watching Duncan and the Fullerton heavyweight finally square off at the beginning of their match, he had a forlorn look on his face, like he was reflecting on his friend not being there. He commented to Bo on the bus ride home from Papillion after the dual meet that he was certain that his friend and teammate would be able to beat Duncan again. Unfortunately, Bo would never get that chance.

The match between the two class C heavyweights was slow in developing. The Fullerton heavyweight was every bit as big as Duncan was. But he was carrying too much weight around his belly, which seemed to make his movements slow and laborious. He was a big ol' freckle-faced redheaded farm boy, and he was already sweating like a pig just a few seconds into the first period of the match.

Both wrestlers began trying to grab the other behind the neck as they circled around. Duncan was the first to succeed as he obviously was the quicker of the two, an advantage he didn't often have in other matches during the year. Once he had a grip on the neck, he pulled down hard, getting the farm boy to bend forward enough to throw him off balance for a second. That was all the time Duncan needed to slip around behind him and get him in a bear hug. Then he tried to lift him off the floor so he could throw him to the mat. He failed as the fat farm boy was just too heavy to outmuscle. The first period ended without either wrestler scoring a point.

The beginning of the second period started off much faster, with Duncan scoring quickly by escaping from his opponent. After his escape, he managed to get the obviously tiring redhead from Fullerton facedown on the mat with a barely legal tripping maneuver. Duncan's fat foe looked like he was gassed at that point. Once he had his heavier opponent down, Duncan began his attempt to get the big boy rolled over onto his back so he could get the pin and end the match early. The Fullerton farm boy seemed to be grimacing in pain once Duncan was able to pin one of the boy's arms behind his back and exert some leverage.

Within several more seconds of sweaty struggle, it appeared that Duncan was going to have one hell of a hard time getting this big fat old farm boy onto his back. But then just like that, the Fullerton wrestler let out a loud yelp. The referee must have immediately seen the reason for the scream as he ruled the match over and ordered Duncan to get off his opponent. The crowd saw it now too, letting out a collective gasp. The farm boy's left shoulder was grotesquely popped out of its socket. He had dislocated his left shoulder. Either that or Duncan had dislocated it for him.

Duncan was bouncing around the mat in victory, beaming from ear to ear while the Fullerton wrestler was beginning to receive medical attention from a distinguished-looking middle-aged man who had come running from the bleachers once he and the crowd could see what had happened. Duncan's mom kept staring at where the fallen Fullerton boy sat before saying something to her husband. His father finally shouted at his son, "For god's sake, Matt, go over and see if he's all right!"

Duncan apparently could tell that his father was trying to tell him something. He cupped his hand behind his right ear while giving his father a questioning look.

"I said go check on your opponent to see if he's okay!"

"Oh yeah!" he yelled back. Then he walked over and bent down in front of the Fullerton wrestler.

Tommy could tell that Duncan was saying something to the Fullerton heavyweight. The hurting farm boy reacted by looking back up at Matt Duncan with a dirty look on his face. The man who was tending to the injured wrestler appeared to say something to Duncan. Matt Duncan then wheeled around and trotted back toward his coach and Papillion teammates on the edge of the mat.

Tommy was just getting ready to leave the coliseum when Duncan came walking by, heading up the pack of Papillion wrestlers who were headed to the locker room while their coach was visiting with the referee. "Hey, aren't you one of Bozell's friends?" Duncan asked after stopping in his tracks and looking up into the bleachers, dabbing a white towel against his sweaty cheek.

"Maybe. What's it to ya?" replied Tommy.

"You go back to Plattsmouth and tell your chickenshit buddy what you just saw here this afternoon. You tell him for me that I'm not done with him yet."

"What do you mean by that?"

"Just do it!"

"Yeah, I'll tell him, all right. I'll also tell him he was right about you!"

"Right about me? What was he right about?"

"That you're an asshole, Duncan!"

Duncan tried to storm up the bleachers after Tommy before several of his teammates held on to him and coaxed him to head to the locker room and forget about going after Bo's friend and former teammate. Tommy's face had turned all red as he finally stood up to leave. Duncan turned around one last time and looked up at him again. "You tell him for me, punk. You hear me?"

Tommy just rolled his eyes before he started his descent down the center aisle of the bleachers while Duncan and his teammates finally disappeared through the doorway that led to the locker rooms.

It was early evening on the day after Ace had paraded around the kitchen table for Henry and Martha. Standing on the porch was Uncle Stanley. He was dressed in khaki pants and shirt, white socks, black work shoes, dark brown jacket, and cream-colored ball cap. Tucked under his arm was a small traveling bag that contained his razor and shaving cream. Parked in front of the house was his faded old white Econoline Chevy van. Stanley rang the doorbell. Within a few seconds, Henry answered the door. "Hello, Stanley. Right on time, I see."

Stanley removed his cap, revealing his round hairless head before wiping some sweat from his brow with his coat sleeve. He put his sweatstained cap back on. "Hello, Henry. How's my favorite elder brother doing?"

"Uh, Stanley, I'm your only elder brother."

"Doesn't matter," answered Stanley. "Well, are you going to let me in or leave me standing here on your front porch all night?"

Henry quickly opened the screen door. "Oh, sorry. Come in. Come in." Stanley stepped inside the front door into the living room, not seeing his brother half-gagging behind him after he had passed by. Martha appeared through the doorway and walked up to greet Henry's bachelor brother. She extended her right arm, and the two of them shook hands. For many other members of the family, Martha would always give them a big hug upon greeting them. Stanley was not one of those family members. "How are you, Stanley?"

"Doing okay, I guess. Worse than some and better than some. Wouldn't do any good to complain anyway."

Martha could have mouthed the words with Stanley as he had said them. Stanley had always been very predictable when it came to verbal exchanges with him after long absences. Martha motioned with her arm toward one of their living room chairs. "Please sit down and relax. It'll just be a few minutes, and supper will be ready."

Henry started to sit back down in his recliner as his younger brother took a seat in a high-back padded chair next to him. Stanley was still clutching his small overnight bag. "Henry, why don't you take Stanley's stuff to the upstairs guest room?" asked Martha.

Henry had just plopped back down into his comfortable recliner as Martha had completed her request, worded cleverly as a question. He had another suggestion. "Bo! Come and get your uncle Stanley's stuff!"

"He's in the backyard, Henry," said Martha. She wore a look of disappointment on her face.

"Ace! Come here, boy! Ace!" Henry called out.

Martha was getting perturbed with Henry's laziness. "Henry, I'm sure your brother doesn't want his cap and coat all slobbered over. Besides, Ace is in the backyard with Bo, getting fed."

Henry finally struggled back up as Stanley stood up and took off his jacket and cap, handing them to Henry along with his small bag before sitting back down and asking the obvious questions. "Who is Ace? Did you get another dog, Henry?"

Henry turned his head back around as he was leaving the living room with Stanley's stuff. "1 wouldn't say we got him, but he's here now just the same."

Stanley looked confused—something that seemed to be happening a lot lately in the Bozell household. "What do you mean by that, Henry?"

Henry didn't answer Stanley as he left the room. "It's a long story, Stanley," answered Martha. "We'll tell you all about it while we're having supper."

A few minutes later, Martha had the last of the food on the table. "Henry! Stanley! Supper's ready!" After yelling at her husband and his brother, Martha walked over to the back door and opened it. "Bo! Supper's ready!" Henry and Stanley entered the kitchen and took their seats. Bo hadn't come in yet.

Henry finally broke the silence as he placed his napkin on his lap. "So, Stanley, the last couple of times you've passed through, you've asked to stay with us instead of Leonard and Alice."

Stanley kept looking at Martha like he didn't even hear what his brother had said. Henry was just about to say something further when his brother suddenly turned his head in his direction and finally looked at him. "Yeah, this time, Leonard said they were repainting their guest room."

Martha looked puzzled by Stanley's remark. "I just talked to Alice a couple of nights ago, and she didn't mention anything about doing any painting."

Henry looked at Martha with a cross look on his face, lowering his eyebrows. Stanley couldn't see the stern look that Henry was giving Martha. "Uh, Martha, you know how it is when Alice gets a wild hair and wants to do something right now." Henry winked a couple of times at her.

Martha finally understood what was going on. "Oh, yeah, you're right, Henry. I guess I forgot about that."

Stanley either didn't catch onto the deception or really didn't care. Only Stanley knew the answer to that mental mystery. "I didn't want to impose on you two twice in a row, so I even called John, but he said he and Melanie had to go to little Stephanie's piano recital tonight. Boy, they sure are starting 'em out young these days. Isn't Stephanie only about five years old now?"

Martha took the lead in dealing with Stanley's tricky questions. "Well, actually, she'll be six in six more months, Stanley. Our little granddaughter seems to be ahead of her age group in many areas."

"What's her piano teacher's name? Would it be anyone I would remember?"

Martha mentally stumbled with that one. "Her name? Uh, I'm not sure what it is. Do you know, Henry?"

"I didn't even know she was taking piano lessons," replied Henry while drooling over all the food on the table.

Martha was still fiddling in the cupboards so Stanley couldn't see her face. She looked sternly back at Henry like he had been looking at her only a minute before.

"Oh, Henry, you are the forgetful one, aren't you? Don't you remember when they were over here last Christmas talking about it?" Henry let out a big sigh while smacking his forehead with the palm of his hand. "Oh, yeah, now I remember. You're right, Martha."

Martha walked over to the back door again, opened it, and yelled at Bo a second time. "Bo! Would you please hurry up and get in here! We're waiting on you!"

Her son finally came through the door with Ace close behind him. The dog looked at Stanley and tilted his head to the side. "Hi, Uncle Stanley. It's nice to see you again," said Bo, hoping he sounded genuine.

"Hello, Bo. Your dad told me about your accident. So how much longer do you have to wear that neck brace?"

"The doctor said for at least another three weeks," replied Bo, who was still standing and looking at Ace, who had wasted little time in padding to his spot over in the corner of the kitchen.

Stanley, following Bo's lead, also looked at the dog. "So this is Ace, huh? He's a big one."

Henry started chuckling. "Yeah, he's got a big brain too. Don't you, Ace?"

Ace ignored Henry and stayed in his corner.

"Ace, come over and shake hands with my brother."

Martha, who might have been aware that a dog's sense of smell is superior to a human's, tried to get Ace off the hook. "Stanley just washed his hands for supper, Henry."

"No, I didn't," Stanley quickly replied.

Henry either didn't know or remember about a dog's superior olfactory capabilities or was still trying to torment Ace whenever he had the chance.

"Come on, Ace, say hello to Stanley," Henry commanded the reluctant dog.

The poor dog slowly got up and went over to Stanley. As Ace got closer to Henry's brother, he started sniffing him. Before he had gotten right in front of Stanley, Ace started backing up. "What's the matter, Ace? Where's your manners?" asked Henry. The dog backed up, turned around, and went back to his comer.

"He's just acting shy, Uncle Stanley," offered Bo.

"A big dog like him acting shy?" asked Stanley.

Henry looked like he had become very amused about the whole situation by now. "Oh yeah, he's real sensitive sometimes."

Ace sat down in his corner for a few seconds and then got up, went over to the back door, and stared at it. He finally turned his head around and barked.

"You want to go back outside?" asked Bo.

"Woof!"

The boy got up from the dinner table and let Ace out of the back door. Bo was getting pretty good at this game by now. You'd think that he, Henry, and Martha had had a strategy session before Stanley had arrived. "He probably ate too much or something," said Bo as he sat back down at the supper table.

"So, Stanley, how's your television repair business doing?" Henry asked.

"Oh, not too bad, except some people seem a bit standoffish at times," answered Stanley.

Supper was long over with, and Bo was studying at his desk. His big dog was lying behind him. Finally, Ace got up and barked. "All right, Ace, just hold on for a minute. Let me finish this paragraph."

As Bo continued to read, the mastiff got up and padded out into the hallway. Bo finished his reading and realized that Ace had already left the room. He slowly rose from his chair and entered the darkened hallway. He saw that his dog had just come out of the guest bedroom that Stanley was sleeping in and had headed down the hallway in front of him. He watched him descend the stairway to the first floor.

Bo stopped at Stanley's doorway and peered in. The room was dark, and he could hear Uncle Stanley snoring in his bed. He closed the door so that it was slightly ajar again. When he reached the back door in the kitchen, Ace was standing there, staring at the door, waiting to be let out. Bo rubbed his eyes and yawned before letting out his bullmastiff one last time for the night. He didn't bother to turn on a light as he watched Ace pad down the back stairs and disappear into the darkness of the backyard.

Stanley sauntered into the kitchen as Henry was sitting at the table, drinking a cup of coffee, while Martha was preparing breakfast. Henry's brother was all dressed except he didn't have any socks or shoes on. Other than that, he had the same clothes on that he had the night before. "Good morning, Stanley. Ready to get an early start, I see," said Henry.

Stanley stretched a little before he answered his brother, "Yeah, except I can't seem to find my socks this morning. 1 could have sworn I left them hanging over the footboard."

Martha had a quick solution probably because she was counting down the final minutes before she could start fumigating the house. "1 know you're in a hurry to get on the road, Stanley, so I'll just get a pair of Henry's socks for you."

Henry must have understood why Martha was so quick to give away a pair of his socks to his brother. "Yeah, take a pair of my socks, Stanley. Oh, and, Stanley, don't worry about giving them back later. You can just keep them."

"Mighty nice of you, big brother," Stanley answered.

Martha stopped short of leaving the room and wheeled around before reaching the doorway. "Oh, by the way, did you find the extra bath towel I left for you in the upstairs bathroom, Stanley?"

Stanley took a sip of black coffee that Martha had just placed in front of him. "Yup, didn't use it though, Martha. Just had time for a quick shave this morning."

Martha hurried out of the kitchen, but she kept talking to Stanley as she left the room. "Well, let me go get those socks for you. Come on,

Stanley. We'll have you fixed up in no time." Stanley followed Martha out of the kitchen.

Bo and Ace had conveniently slept in that morning while his uncle finished having breakfast with Henry and Martha.

Stanley walked out of the front door of the house and onto the front porch, clutching his little shaving kit bag. Henry was standing in the doorway. "Thanks again for putting me up for the night, Henry."

Henry shook his head back and forth as he looked back at his younger brother. "You don't have to thank me, Stanley. That's what family is all about."

Stinky Stanley stepped off the porch and headed down the sidewalk to his van. Henry opened the front door and walked out onto the porch. As Stanley stepped in front of his van to walk over to the driver's side, he stopped dead in his tracks. There, hanging over his front bumper, were his missing socks. Stanley got a surprised and disappointed look on his face. "Henry! Would you come over here for a minute?"

After Stanley's summons, Henry walked down the sidewalk toward his younger brother with an inquisitive expression on his face. "What is it, Stanley? Is something wrong?"

Stanley bent over and reached down. He straightened back up and lifted the socks from the bumper to show Henry. "Yes, there's something wrong! Is this all about family too, Henry? If my socks smelled that bad, why didn't you just say something?"

Henry finally walked all the way up to his brother, something he had probably hoped to avoid. His face looked sincere enough as he gently placed a hand on his obviously irate brother's shoulder. "Honest, Stanley! I didn't have anything to do with this!"

Stanley looked really upset and agitated at that point. His face and ears had turned all red, and his squinty eyes, which the family had always thought looked a lot like Roy Rogers's, were wide open for a change. "Well, if it wasn't you, it must have been Bo because I know Martha wouldn't think of insulting me like this!"

Henry looked down at the front bumper of his brother's van while pinching the bridge of his nose. "Actually, Stanley, I'm thinkin' it probably wasn't Bo either."

Stanley just stood there for a few seconds and looked at Henry with a quizzical look on his face before removing his ball cap and rubbing his balding head with his right hand. "Well, that doesn't leave anybody else, except. . . the *dog?*" He slapped his cap back on with such a force that his red-rimmed ears were temporarily pinned against his temples and hidden from view. He lifted the front of the bill with his left hand until his ears popped back out, looking even redder than before along the edges.

"I'm afraid so, Stanley. Ace doesn't seem to be no normal dog. He's a smart one. He is."

Stanley still didn't appear fully convinced. "You're telling me your dog took my socks and brought them out here and put them on my front bumper?"

Henry must have fought it real hard, but in the end, his face betrayed him with a grin. "Actually, when you think about it, it was kinda considerate of him . . . to make sure you found 'em this morning before you drove away."

Stanley hurriedly walked around, got into his van in a huff, and rolled down his window. "Going on the assumption that it was maybe your dog who did it, Henry, 'considerate' is not the word that I'm thinking of right now."

Henry followed his brother around to the driver's door. "I'm sorry, Stanley.

I'll have a word with Ace when I get back inside."

His brother stuck his head slightly out of his window as he pulled away from the curb. "Yes, you do that, Henry. You do *just* that!"

Randall Whitfield, called Randy by his buddies, was wallowing in self-pity after Brenda had been gone for several weeks. He tried to convince himself that it was all justified—his decisions and his actions. Yet that still sane part of him said that he had made a big mistake. It had been wrong to chase Brenda away as he did. The darker other side of him said that the bitch had to go. She didn't respect him or understand him anymore. His views and thoughts would flipflop pretty much hourly.

Out of boredom and self-destructiveness, the darker side of him told him to call Bud. He woke Bud up when he called in the early afternoon. He didn't stop to wonder why Bud was still asleep when it was almost two o'clock on a Friday afternoon. Maybe Bud was worse off than he was. "Birds of a feather flock together" as the old saying went.

Bud was probably one of the first white boys to experiment with drugs in the whole city of Omaha back in the midsixties. He was ahead of his time. Or maybe you could say he was a head before his time. Regardless, Randy had had the good fortune, or possibly the misfortune, of crossing paths with Bud because of their mutual obsession with fast cars.

Randy was immediately drawn to Bud not just because of their shared fascination with speed but also because Bud was already twenty-one and was willing and able to buy booze for Randy and his high school buddies. Even before Randy's flight from the law that night, Bud had offered him a joint; but at the time, Randy had turned the marijuana down. Apparently, it took scaring the crap out of him halfway around the world in the middle of an insane war before Randy finally decided he needed something a little more powerful than Schlitz Malt Liquor. Before Randy had hung up the phone, Bud had alluded to something new he had that he wanted Randy to try. He promised it would set him free in a way that the *Thai sticks* and *Mexican gold* could never do. With that in mind, Randy asked Bud to wait until early evening before coming over so he could arrange to have Trevor spend the night with the next-door neighbors.

Trevor was an innocent and undeserving victim of his father's inability to cope with life without having to resort to alcohol and drugs. It was always the children who suffered the most when parents didn't know or care how to be good parents. And Brenda really wasn't that much more of a good parent than Randy was, not having the courage to find and take her son back the very same day that she had found Randy's note on the kitchen table. Having a bad hangover certainly wasn't an excuse. Being afraid of Randy wasn't a valid excuse either. In their own way, both of Trevor's parents had abandoned him— Brenda by being physically absent, Randy by being mentally absent.

Trevor was forced to literally fend for himself, save for a few reprieves when he was able to spend time with Rita and her children, their nextdoor neighbors. When he was with Rita, he could just be a child again. He savored those moments. Having to act like an adult in a small boy's body was not something he had willingly volunteered for.

Even at a very early age, it was obvious to everyone that little Trevor was a gifted child. He was quick to talk and quick to walk. Walking before he was even eight months of age had its consequences, though, as Trevor turned out a bit bowlegged. He wore out a lot of little tennis shoes in short order, not so much because he was always on the go, seeking new stimuli to quench his thirst for learning. It was because the outside bottom heels were worn down to the exposed innersole before the inside bottoms were barely broken in.

Brenda's parents appeared to be more knowledgeable than their own daughter when it came to their understanding that their grandson had the potential for greatness someday. She seemed to be always more focused on salvaging her relationship with Randy. That was why it must have pained them even more to see him being taken away from them. They told their daughter that they could ensure that Trevor would not only be truly loved and cared for but also be nurtured in the most stimulant environment possible.

It would forever remain a mystery within the family about how Trevor had inherited what was already an obvious IQ that was up in the genius range. Brenda's parents had never inquired that much about the history of Randy's side of the family. They didn't know that Randy's mother had been adopted. She had been the illegitimate child of a brushed-aside affair involving one of the greatest thinkers thus far known to mankind. The adoption papers were sealed and confidential, so even Randy's own mother knew nothing of her origin. The passing down of genes would forever remain a mystery of life as well, with notable traits and talents sometimes skipping over two or three generations before reemerging with a vengeance.

No one had any way of knowing how important it was that Trevor should experience a reasonably happy childhood. To grow up otherwise could create the possibility that the next great evil genius was now on the planet, capable of wreaking havoc on the entire world someday. Trevor might someday come up with something more positively profound than the theory of relativity, or he could end up developing something more destructive than the atomic bomb. Everyone, at some point, experiences a crossroads in their life where they must make a choice between good and evil. Thankfully, Trevor was probably still too young to be contemplating that choice.

His young mind was being thoroughly tested as of late though. It was bad enough that he had to bear witness to his parents' constant quarreling over the past couple of years. Now to be abandoned by his mother and stuck with a drunk and a dope addict for a father was starting to test his young fortitude to the limit. He didn't act like an angry little boy, but he certainly didn't seem to be a happy child either.

He kept telling Rita how much he still loved his mommy and daddy very much. He told her he desperately wanted his daddy to get better so his mommy would come back to him and they could be a family again. He said he missed his mommy a little more every day. "Why did she have to leave me?" he would ask. It was a question that he kept asking Rita with increasing regularity.

With his daddy's downward spiral into spaced-out oblivion, he seemed to be quite resourceful for a little boy who hadn't even started going to school yet. It was obvious by his actions that he must have figured out that it was often up to him to get things done around the house both for himself and his drunken, drugged-out father.

He must have remembered well when watching his mommy fix dinner in the kitchen every night. With the help of a stool, he was able to duplicate her previous efforts to some degree. It would take him a lot longer than it took his mommy, but he was able to open cans of beans or com with the can opener he found in a kitchen drawer and then heat them up on the stove in a saucepan.

Thankfully for a sleeping Randy, Trevor apparently remembered the precise setting Brenda had had the gas stove set at and how important it was to keep a close eye on it while the food was being warmed or cooked. The little guy never took his eyes off the food heating up on the stove until he had carefully removed it to the counter. Brenda had implanted the danger of fire in her son long before she had left him. He also figured out how to boil hot dogs on the stove. Trevor probably would have been content with potato chips and cookies, so it was obvious that he cooked the meals for his daddy.

Randy was usually sleeping it off when such a meal was prepared. Little Trevor would rouse him enough to get him to eat, usually after pulling his legs down off the sofa to get him up into a sitting position. His daddy's eyes would always be bloodshot, a fact that was barely discernable as he forced his eyelids open to no more than slits, like Venetian blinds positioned to allow in only the faintest of light in a room. He would slurp down the beans or corn with a big spoon right out of the pan and then gobble down a couple of hot dogs, minus the buns, before flopping back down and passing out again. When he was sober later and noticed the missing food, he would have to draw on his drunken memory of having eaten the night before on the sofa. He always assumed that he must have fixed the meal for him and his son himself. He just couldn't remember doing it.

On chillier evenings before Trevor would take the empty pan and spoon back to the kitchen, he always threw a blanket over his daddy and pulled it down over Randy's bare feet. Then he would go back to the kitchen, where he had left a plate of food for himself, and would eat alone at the kitchen table, sitting on a tall stool so he could reach everything. Once he was finished, he would stand on another stool at the kitchen sink and wash the dirty dishes.

Most evenings after supper, while his daddy was snoring loudly on the sofa, he would change into his pajamas before turning on the television and sitting crosslegged directly in front of it, keeping the volume low but discernable. Unfortunately, there wasn't an adult watching to tell him he was sitting too close. His eyes would remain glued to the TV, save for an occasional potty break, as he continually sat no more than a couple of feet from the screen. Trevor's vocabulary was increasing at a rapid rate as he watched adult shows each evening. His mind must have been like a vast sponge, soaking in everything he possibly could.

After brushing his teeth and crawling into bed, he would sometimes make the mistake of using the wrong word in a sentence when talking to his teddy bear, Freddy, before falling asleep, but being wrong seemed to be rare for little Trevor. He usually got it right. He usually got everything right the first time. If only his poor daddy could get it right someday, then maybe little Trevor's mommy would come back home.

When Bud arrived in his black and loud Mustang, Randy was lighting some incense, having just returned from dropping Trevor off with Rita Landon, his nextdoor neighbor. Bud knocked once and then came in without waiting for Randy to greet him at the door. They locked hands with thumbs up to greet each other.

Bud didn't look so good that night, even to Randy. His long stringy black hair looked greasier than it normally did, and he had about a four-day growth of beard. His deep-set brown eyes looked wild with excitement. Randy had never seen Bud look quite that way before probably because he had never seen him when he was tripping on LSD.

Bud helped himself to a beer in the fridge while Randy loaded his marijuana bong with the last of what he'd bought from Bud the week before. After they shared the bong until the room was a mixture of incense and blown-out smoke, Bud fumbled in his blue jean jacket until he produced a bag of weed for sale. Randy paid for it with what was left of what would have been the rent money. They proceeded to smoke some of the new stuff while listening to "Purple Haze" and other songs on the recently released album by Jimi Hendrix on Randy's stereo.

Bud turned to Randy with a suddenly serious look on his face. "I've been meaning to ask you something. You were strictly a beer man before you went over to 'Nam. What made you decide to take up the weed?" Randy thought about Bud's question for a few seconds before he answered, "Well, over in 'Nam, there were three different groups of guys in most every platoon. There were the stoners, the alkies, and the idiots. The idiots had the highest mortality rate. Our theory was that they never did figure out when to duck or when to hop over that foreign-looking object in the grass. The rest of us, on the other hand, always gave that a lot of serious thought."

Finally, Randy lit up another cigarette and took a big sip out of his can of beer. "Actually, Bud, there was another group over in 'Nam. They were the guys that always seemed to have their heads on straight. Some were lifers, and some were drafted in. I never could figure out how they always seemed so calm under fire. I asked one guy once how he kept his sanity even though he didn't drink or smoke. He said he just kept repeating the same words over and over in his head when he had to. Though I walk through the shadow of the valley of death, I shall fear no evil 'cause the Lord is with me. I never did understand how being religious could have helped that much. I can't say I don't believe in God, but I can't say I do either. It's always seemed more like something man must have made up because of his fear of the unknown. And the biggest unknown in life is what happens to us once our life is over with. I think it was the fear of death, plain and simple, that created God in the mind of man." Randy took another drag on his cigarette. "Do you believe in God, Bud?"

"Whoa. What got ya on that subject, Randy, my man? Politics and religion are two areas I normally steer clear of," said Bud as he looked away into the candle flame on the coffee table.

"1 don't know. I guess you just got me to thinking. 'Nam was a ninemonth nightmare for me. There was a lot I didn't understand about the war, and there was a lot I didn't understand about the guys I fought with." Randy took another sip of beer. "So, Bud, what were you talking about over the phone? What ya got for me now?"

Bud Dahlke pulled his jacket open and reached into his front shirt pocket, pulling out a small prescription drug bottle. But Bud's little bottle had been devoid of anything legal in it for quite some time. He popped open the cap and carefully tipped the bottle over the open palm of his other hand, tapping the side with his finger until a tiny, little purple square of paper dropped out.

Randy looked on in amazement. "You've gotta be kidding me. That's it? It doesn't even look like a pill. I have to swallow a little purple piece of paper?"

"Randy, my man, I'm sure you've heard the old saying 'It's not the quantity that counts. It's the quality.' Well, this little baby will keep you going strong for a good ten hours or more. You're right. It is made with paper or something like that, and then you cut it into little squares, kinda like a pan of brownies, except a lot smaller."

"What do you feel like on this stuff?"

"It makes you see things you don't normally see. It makes you feel things you don't normally feel."

"This is acid, isn't it, Bud? I've heard about this stuff."

Bud didn't answer Randy's rhetorical question as he carefully deposited the little sticky square sheet down on the coffee table with the tip of his index finger before lighting up a cigarette of his own.

"How much do 1 owe you for this?" Randy asked as he touched the sheet with his own finger, the sticky purple square attaching to his fingertip like a piece of metal to a magnet. He raised it to his mouth and deposited it on his tongue without giving it a second thought, washing it down with a swig of beer. It was so small that he couldn't even feel it as it traveled down his throat in search of a target audience, a mind-blowing minisurfboard on a wave of beer ridden by an invisible dark rider—a rider of truth or a rider of terror. The powerful drug LSD fueled a fire in the mind that snaked along the boundaries of truth and tragedy.

"This one's a free sample. If you like it, I can get you some more. Then we'll talk money," Bud replied as he exhaled a big puff of blue-white smoke into the air.

Bud surprised Randy by telling him that he planned on staying around just long enough to make sure Randy wasn't going to freak out on the stuff. Bud had never seen it firsthand, but he told Randy about a friend from California who had told him about a guy who got so paranoid on it that he hammered scrap wood from his garage all over the inside of his windows and doors of his rental house. Then he lit a candle in every room and sat totally naked in his bathtub for the next ten hours. He rocked back and forth, clutching a hatchet in one hand and gripping a fully loaded .44 Magnum handgun in the other, while the candles burned out in every room. The bathtub apparently served the dual purpose of providing protection in the event of an unlikely earthquake or other such surprise and containing his outgoing urine when he had to pee a few times.

The guy was lucky he didn't burn the place down or blow his fool head off. It was not what could be characterized as a Timothy Leary-type mental enrichment. Well, Randy was still fully clothed and had only one candle burning in his living room, not boarding up a single window, but he did turn out all the lights in the house.

Bud finally stood up slowly and stretched a little bit. He turned around and put his jacket back on, which he had tossed over the back of a chair earlier.

"You're really not leaving me here like this, are you?" Randy asked as he was making big circles with his cigarette in front of him. The yelloworange circles made by the glow of his lit cigarette would hang in the air in front of him for what seemed like several seconds. Bud had previously referred to the hallucination as trailers, only a small part of the psychedelic experience.

"Sorry, my friend, it's time for me to go," Bud said in a somberly tone as he stood over Randy, shaking and stretching his arms out inside his jacket sleeves apparently to make sure he'd be comfortable on his somewhat challenging long drive home.

"Are you sure you can drive?"

"I got here, didn't I? Sure, I can drive. It's the stoplights at the intersections, the oncoming headlights, and the headlights in my rearview mirror that challenge me the most. Other than that, it should be a nice trip, if you know what I mean. I think I'll take the back roads as much as possible and wear my sunglasses. It's not like I got somebody waiting for me when I get home," Bud rationalized as he headed for the front door.

Bud was turning the handle on the front door when Randy said his last words of the evening to him. "I hope you keep coming back, buddy, 'cause if you don't, I might have to rob a drugstore or something."

Bud turned around, grinning. "Don't worry, compadre, I'll be back as many times as you've got money on the table." With that, Bud walked through the door, closing it tightly behind him.

Randy was still sitting on his sofa, staring at his candle burning in front of him on the coffee table. Bud Dahlke had been gone for several hours.

It was close to three o'clock in the morning. A Moody Blues album had long ago reached the end of side two. Randy was leaning back on the sofa, watching the ceiling, which was dancing a jig from the flickering candle on the coffee table. He finally leaned forward and grabbed his marijuana bong.

A song from the last album was replaying over and over in Randy's head. He didn't have to put on another album. The music in his head was every bit as intense and haunting. "To lose the love I've known" was a particularly striking set of lyrics that Randy put on auto rewind in his mind that early morning. He picked up his lighter and toked the last of a bud in his bong. The gurgling sound from the water in the bong sounded like a tidal wave to Randy's sensitive ears. He held the smoke in long enough that only a faint cloud of smoke was finally exhaled from his aching lungs.

It was a bit of a waste of his money that he was still smoking marijuana while he was tripping on LSD because the intensity of the LSD high was totally overshadowing any effects from the marijuana, the beer, the whiskey, and even Randy's pain pills. Oops. Did I say pain pills? Even in Randy's extremely elevated state of mind, he was starting to kick himself for taking something that was totally counteracting the partial relief he got from the prescription pain pills. His sciatic nerve down his left leg was acting up big time. There was a lightning storm of nerve neurons popping like flashbulbs in his left calf. He had fought off cramping in his left hamstring several times already that night, and his left foot seemed even more numb than normal. He had that familiar feeling that an unseen demon was pulling an unseen cord out of the bottom of his foot, starting from his lower back down to his left buttocks and then through the entire length of his left leg.

The only thing that was taking his mind off the pain down his leg that night was the pain in his heart. The song lyrics kept resonating in his head as he stared into the flickering candle, thinking deeply about Brenda and all that they had shared together.

Suddenly, he saw the huge head and body of a giant dog appear behind the flame. He quickly rubbed his eyes and slowly reopened them. The big face of the dog with penetrating huge brown eyes was still staring over the fire at him. "You're not real, big dog. Go away," he said out loud.

I'm hallucinating, he thought. "Go away, big dog."

The big dog suddenly vanished as quickly as he had appeared. Randy breathed a big sigh of relief. I don't think I ever want to do this shit ever again, he thought. That seemed almost too real.

In the blink of an eye, the huge dog was back. But this time, he was a little off to the right and a little bit closer to Randy, no longer directly behind the fire. The big dog's eyes seemed like they were almost glowing this time. It was like there was a bright light beaming from behind the whites of the monster canine's eyes. "You're not real. You're not real," Randy stammered in a shaky, scared voice.

Then the dog started to look like it was almost smiling. Randy got really scared when he finally realized that he could feel the dog's hot breath against the flush of his cheek. He fell back into the back cushions of the sofa as far as he could press his back, bumping the back of his head on the wall.

The big dog (which wasn't real) lunged to the right and forward and chomped down with his massive jaws onto the top of the bong. He started chewing and chewing downward until the entire soft plastic bong had totally disappeared inside his mouth. Then the (imaginary) dog made a big gulping sound and took a step back before vanishing into thin air again.

Before Randy had had a chance to really grasp what had just happened, he heard barking coming from his front yard. He sprang from the sofa and ran to the locked front door. Peering out between the curtains of the door's window, he saw the dog standing in the yard, staring at the front door. Randy slowly opened the inside door and stood inside of the screen door, staring back at the big (bullmastiff) dog. "What do you want from me? Who are you? What are you?" Randy pleaded for an answer.

The dog turned and trotted to the east side of the yard on the front sidewalk before turning back around and facing Randy. "Woof!"

"Hush! You'll wake up the neighborhood," he pleaded to the imaginary dog, which had just allowed some imaginary drool to splash onto the sidewalk from his big imaginary, blubbering jaws.

The big dog turned away again and padded a few more steps to the east, stopping on the front sidewalk of Rita and David's house before turning back around to once more face Randy.

"You want me to follow you, don't you?"

"Woof!"

Randy grabbed his jacket off a chair near the front door and opened the screen door, stepping out onto the porch while the dog, once again, turned around and trotted away to the east down the sidewalk. He walked out of his yard and followed the dog at a safe distance as a full moon kept drifting behind and out of clouds, constantly changing the shadows of the night. There was a gusty wind that sent a chill through Randy's body and made him walk a little faster to warm up as he buttoned up his jacket and turned the collar up around his neck.

When he walked faster, the dog trotted faster ahead of him, the dog's butt being easy to follow, even if the distance separating the two became greater at times. A few other dogs that were guarding their masters' yards barked briefly as dog and then man passed by on the front sidewalk. An occasional bedroom light would go on and then be turned back off after the curtains had stirred long enough to satisfy a light sleeper's curiosity. The dog had led him several blocks from home.

As luck would have it, the graveyard shift police cruiser was patrolling the other side of town at the time. It would have been hard for Randy to explain to the cop why he was taking a walk at almost three-thirty in the morning, especially after he would have undoubtedly had a flashlight shone into his wild dilated eyes, revealing his nervous demeanor. He undoubtedly would have looked like he had done something wrong.

A set of headlights did suddenly come around a corner two blocks ahead and pass by a trembling Randy, who had quickly hidden behind a tree. It was an old pickup truck that putted on by. He looked down the sidewalk. The imaginary dog must have hidden too. He was nowhere in sight for a few seconds before he materialized again on the sidewalk, about fifty feet ahead of Randy.

The moon peeked out again for a few seconds, revealing the dog in more detail now, too much detail to be a figment of the imagination or an apparition inspired by Randy's drug-induced night of neurosis. He just kept following the big dog on foot in the early morning before dawn. After the long walk, the big dog led him into a city park, all the way to the far comer. The bullmastiff finally stopped in front of a big marker of some kind.

The light from the early morning moon was momentarily obscured behind a massive moving cloud when Randy finally caught up with the dog, sitting silently in front of the marker. The granite marker was bigger than a tombstone, and it had a lot of lettering chiseled into it that couldn't be read in the dark. A gusty early morning wind continued to blow through the surrounding trees, making them dance and sing for their lone spaced-out spectator.

Randy had to know. He slowly and gently bent over and touched the back of the dog. He felt warm fur before the dog vanished from under his hand. He lost his balance and fell into the grass where the mastiff had just been sitting a split second before.

The cloud moved on, and the full moon revealed itself once again in the early morning sky. Darkness turned to partial light. The full moon's glow made the stone marker look like it had a spotlight shining on it. Randy sat up and stared up at the marker.

The Jaycees had donated the granite marker back in 1965 to the city of Plattsmouth. He read the top line: "The Ten Commandments." He knew about such rules to live by, but he'd never been in a church in his life. He'd never read any part of a Christian Bible before. He read all the words on the entire marker over and over as he sat in front of it, contemplating God's ten rules to live by. Then he thought about the dog that had led him there in the middle of the night.

He began to weep uncontrollably for several minutes. He finally realized that everything he had experienced ever since the dog had appeared in his living room that night was real and that the ten rules were real rules to live by. The mysterious dog with unexplainable powers had led him to a crossroads in his life that early morning.

As he cried, looking up on top of the granite marker, he knew that his path in life had suddenly taken a life-changing detour. He vowed right then and there that he would live the rest of his life in a different way. The sudden transformation of Randy that early morning seemed to be a miracle. Only time would tell if it were indeed a miracle or just a bump in the road for Randy Whitfield.

Ironically, almost thirty-five years later, the ACLU would file a lawsuit on behalf of an atheist who would find the marker to be offensive. At last word, the mayor of Plattsmouth had vowed to fight the removal of the marker all the way to the Supreme Court if necessary. It was good that Ace was there for Randy that early morning in the year 1969. It was a shame that he wasn't there thirty-five years later when the atheist became offended by the contents of the marker on city property. Maybe Ace got to retire eventually. He was certainly deserving of a rest, at least for a while. If he did come back again someday, the marker might be gone by then. It was like a person whom you'd see every day who was slowly losing weight, and you didn't really notice just how much had been lost until most of it was gone.

Randy made it safely back home that night without Ace's guidance. He got lost a few times, but it was a small town, and it was only a matter of time before he found familiar houses on the edge of his neighborhood. He probably was able to make it home much sooner by opting to hide behind some bushes rather than ask the passing cop in his patrol car for directions.

Bo had been tossing and turning in his bed earlier in the night. He had finally given up and turned his light back on to read one of his textbooks. He was normally a sound sleeper, but recent events at school and at home were weighing heavily on his mind. He still had his hearing aids in when he had finally fallen asleep again, having let the book drop to the floor next to his bed.

He was suddenly awakened by the sound of crunching coming from the floor near his bed. He slowly opened his eyes. The first thing he noticed while lying on his right side was that his normally closed bedroom door was wide open. He rolled over onto his left side and looked down at the floor.

Ace was lying there, crunching on the last of a pile of potato chips that had been scattered all over the floor. The empty, ripped-open bag was lying next to him. There were also three empty peanut bag wrappers (which Martha always bought for Henry to go along with his evening beer) scattered all over the floor, obviously not having been opened with care.

Bo's eyes opened wider. He couldn't believe it. Ace had promised him after the close call with the steak bones in the kitchen garbage that he wouldn't get into anything in the kitchen anymore. Bo threw off the covers and slid out of bed.

Ace stopped eating the last pile of potato chips on the floor and looked up at Bo, who was standing over him. The big dog had a pathetic look on his face, and his eyes looked bloodshot to Bo. "Ace, what do you think you're doing? You know better than this," he scolded.

Ace just moaned in response while staring at what remained of the potato chips.

"Go ahead. You might as well finish them off. It's not like anybody else is going to want them now," said Bo.

He didn't have to say it twice. Ace resumed munching on the last of the chips.

"Don't we feed you enough for crying out loud?" he asked as if he expected his dog to answer him. Ace finished off the chips and quickly trotted out of the door.

Bo slid out of bed and reached the open doorway in time to see his badbehaving dog enter the upstairs bathroom. He heard the toilet lid hit the front of the water tank before listening to some loud slurping for several seconds. The bullmastiff finally came back into the bedroom with water still dripping from his jowls. He slowly padded over to his normal spot on the floor near the window before lying down and closing his eyes.

Bo closed his bedroom door before picking up the empty, ripped-open peanut wrappers and the shredded potato chip bag. He deposited them in his garbage can next to his desk before crawling back into bed and turning off the light. "We'll talk more about this in the morning, Ace, you bad dog." Bo then attempted to fall asleep again, hoping he would remember not to let his dog lick his face first thing in the morning.

Ace wasn't asleep yet. He had just been admonished and was trying to justify his actions. *What about the good deed 1 did by scaring Randy and then leading him to Your rules? What? Yeah, but You put that type of plant here on Earth. What do You mean it's been genetically altered by man? I don't know what that means. I'm just a dog, remember? Why did I get so hungry? They call it the munchies? No, don't worry, I won't ever do that again. That water in Randy's smoking device was some really nasty-tasting stuff. Leaving the marker when 1 did wasn't just for dramatic effect. I needed a drink of water and something to eat. What I swallowed wasn't even fit for a dog. Oh, and by the way, I think I must have swallowed a small metal bowl. Do You think that maybe You could ease the pain a little bit for me tomorrow when 1 'm getting rid of it in the backyard, if You know what I mean? What do You mean You'll think about it?*

Students were filing into the classroom before the start of class at Plattsmouth High School. Bo came walking into the classroom along with all the other students for sophomore English class. Everyone had finally taken his or her seat. Bo was sitting near the front of the class. The teacher entered and was standing next to her desk at the front of the room. Bo was no longer wearing his neck brace.

The teacher, Mrs. Watson, cleared her throat quite loud, signaling for all the chatter to subside. "Good morning, class. 1 know you were all expecting to tackle the proper use of prepositional phrases this morning. However, we're going to deviate from our normal schedule today. We have spent this entire semester learning how to communicate better both verbally and with the written word. The special guests that I have invited here today will be demonstrating an effective alternative approach to communication. A dear friend of mine, whom I have known for many years, is a teacher at the Iowa School for the Deaf. She has graciously accepted my invitation to come here today to give you some insight into what it is like to communicate using sign language, as well as the fine art of lip-reading, something one of your own classmates is very familiar with. Isn't that right, Bo?"

Bo got a little red in the face and unconsciously slouched down in his seat more, not answering Mrs. Watson.

"I'm sorry, Bo. I didn't mean to embarrass you. I'm sure that most of you are aware that Bo has a partial hearing loss. But with the use of his hearing aids and his ability to read lips, we tend not to notice. Bo must deal with something every second of every day that the rest of us tend to take for granted. Therefore, by bringing my friend and one of her star pupils here today, I felt that we could all gain some insight and appreciation for those who are hearing impaired."

Mrs. Watson walked over to the door and signaled for her guests to come in. An attractive middle-aged blond woman and a beautiful petite young red- haired girl entered the classroom. Mrs. Watson continued, "Class, I would like you to meet Jean Janssen and one of her students, Bonnie Gifford. Jean has been a teacher at Iowa School for the Deaf for the past eight years, and Bonnie is a sophomore at the school."

Bonnie greeted the class by using sign language. Jean Janssen could speak, but her speech sounded a lot like Bo's, a little distorted. Because of this, she must speak slowly so she could be understood more easily. As with Bo, pronunciation of some words was difficult for Jean. "Good morning, class. My student Bonnie has also just told you 'good morning' and that she is glad to be here today."

Bo turned around to Jerry. "I knew that."

Jean Janssen continued, "Bonnie must rely almost exclusively on the use of sign language to communicate. I, on the other hand, still have enough hearing retention to enable me to bridge the gap between the world of the hearing impaired and the world of the hearing. This morning, Bonnie and 1 will take you through the sign language alphabet, as well as some of the hand signals we use that would be comparable to shorthand dictation, the business language shortcut that some of you may be familiar with."

Bo didn't realize that he had been staring at Bonnie ever since she and her teacher had walked into the classroom. He had never seen, or perhaps never had noticed, any girl prettier than she was. She stood up there so assured of herself. What had made him realize that he had been staring at her, probably with a goofy smile on his face, was that she had shyly smiled back at him. It snapped him out of the trance he had been in, but he couldn't seem to take his eyes off her. She seemed so different from anyone he had ever seen before.

It was not that Bo had not been interested in girls; it was that they had never been a priority to him. Ever since he had reached puberty, he had always had wrestling in his life. Among school, the homework attached to that, wrestling practice, and the matches he attended, he had found very little time for much else.

Smiling to himself, he realized that he was pretty interested in this girl. He decided that he was going to have to find a way to get to know her better and soon. She was watching him from the corner of her eyes, smiling at him while Mrs. Watson was talking to the class. Well, he thought, *she seems to be interested in me too. We 'll have to see about this after class.*

Bo turned around to Jerry and whispered to him, "After class, you go on to the cafeteria without me. I want to try to speak with Bonnie."

Jerry smiled at his friend and whispered back to Bo, "Can't blame you there, Bo. She's drop-dead gorgeous."

The presentation was finally over, and everyone in the English class was filing out of the classroom, including Bo and Jerry. However, Bo stepped out of the room and then stopped just outside the door, waiting. It was exactly noon now. Finally, Mrs. Watson, Mrs. Janssen, and Bonnie came walking out of the classroom and into the hallway. Bo's voice was stuck in his throat, but he finally managed to speak. "Mrs. Janssen, I was wondering if I could speak briefly with Bonnie, that is, if she doesn't mind."

Mrs. Janssen glanced over questionably at Bonnie, who was smiling. Bonnie signed to her teacher. "No, Bonnie doesn't mind," she replied.

Bo began to grin before he answered back, "I know. 1 understand what she says. That's why I wanted to talk with her."

You can understand me? Bonnie signed to Bo with a smile. Bo smiled back broadly, signing back that he could understand her completely.

Jean Janssen looked at Bo and then glanced at Mrs. Watson. "Oh, you are the young man that Margaret has told me about."

Margaret Watson nodded at her friend and smiled. "Yes, Jean, this is Bo Bozell. Bo too has a hearing loss."

Mrs. Janssen looked thoughtfully at Bo as he stood nervously, shifting his weight from foot to foot in front of her and Bonnie. "Where did you learn sign language, Bo?" asked Jean.

"I spent two years of grade school at the Nebraska School for the Deaf."

"Oh, of course, I know some colleagues who teach there," Jean answered with a broadening smile on her face.

"Jean, Bonnie, and 1 were just going down to the cafeteria for lunch before they leave to drive back to Iowa, Bo," explained Margaret. "Why don't you escort Bonnie? Jean and I have some catching up to do."

Yes! thought Bo. Everything was working out better than he had hoped it would.

Jean looked at Bonnie with a smile on her face. Is that okay with you, Bonnie? she signed to her. Bonnie nodded back to her with a faint smile on her face.

Mrs. Watson and Mrs. Janssen walked off together down the hallway, leaving Bo and Bonnie to stare at each other for what seemed like an hour to Bo before he caught himself, knowing that he needed to say something, anything, to break the silence. Then Bo realized how ironic his thoughts were since Bonnie was, to the casual observer, a very silent person. "Would you rather communicate by signing, or is it okay to just talk to you by speaking?"

Bonnie smiled and replied by signing that she was very good at lip-reading.

"Oh, you read lips that well, huh? Well, that's probably good 'cause my signing is a little rusty. I can understand the signs better than I can give them," Bo responded.

Bonnie signed that she agreed with his confession, smiling big.

Bo suddenly got a little flushed in his face before he answered her, "That bad, huh? I sure hope that I didn't accidentally offend you in any way."

Bonnie replied in sign language, once again, that he had been doing okay and that she hadn't wanted to slap him . . . yet.

"No, you haven't slapped me yet. Maybe we had better head on down to the cafeteria, where there will be more witnesses."

Bonnie laughed silently at Bo's last remark. The two started down the hallway as a few other students were walking back and forth around them. They were seemingly in their own little world.

Bo and Bonnie were sitting off to themselves, alone at a table in the cafeteria. Their food was gone from their trays, and they seemed engulfed in conversation. Bo's friend Jerry and another male student were sitting close by the young couple. Mrs. Watson and Mrs. Janssen were talking up a storm over in an area for faculty only. Most of the other students in the cafeteria were busy talking to one another at their separate tables. The room was a bit noisy from all the constant chatter.

Jerry and the other boy were sitting at the other end of the table across from Bonnie and Bo. "So who's the cute deaf-mute sitting with Bo?" the other boy asked as he stared at Bonnie.

Jerry was a very close friend of Bo's and, because of that fact, surely understood the difficulty of what Bo dealt with every day. "Ron, I don't think that they like being called deaf-mutes."

"Why not? That's what they are, aren't they?" Ron asked in a very matter - offact tone.

"I think it's just as insulting to them as if I were to call you a moron, you moron," Jerry angrily answered.

"Hey, you don't have to get all bent out of shape with me. We can at least hear," Ron countered.

"Isn't that ironic? Because, right now, I wish I couldn't," Jerry mumbled as he looked back at Bo and Bonnie.

The young couple seemed to be oblivious that they were being talked about. At least to Bo, it was as if they were on their own little island with no one else in view. "So your folks bought a house near the Iowa School for the Deaf when you were five years old?" asked Bo.

Bonnie signed yes to his question.

Bo was enthralled with Bonnie and her sweet, gentle disposition. He pressed on with more questions as if he couldn't get enough knowledge about her. "They didn't want you to have to stay in the dorms, huh?"

Bonnie shook her head in a negative response and signed that Bo was incorrect in his assumption.

"So you think that, since you are their only child, their concern for you taking care of yourself was affecting their decision?" Bo asked.

Suddenly, that smile he had quickly fallen in love with vanished from her face, replaced by a frown. Bo could sense what Bonnie was thinking. He hesitated before speaking again, but when he spoke, it was from his own experience and the comfort that came from knowing that truly good parents' love was unconditional. "1 think you have to go with the thought that even if you had other sisters or brothers, they loved you too much to see you only on weekends."

A tear ran down Bonnie's cheek as her frown fell away, giving way to that smile—that smile that had so enraptured Bo from the first moment their eyes had met, really met, for the first time. Bonnie hesitated and seemed to ponder Bo's words for a few seconds. Then she suddenly and hurriedly began signing a new message to Bo. She told Bo about her love for dogs and that her parents had given her an older dog, rescued from a puppy mill, when she was only three years old. She told Bo that her parents must have known how attached she was to that dog by the time she was old enough to start school and how hard it would have been on her to only see her dog on weekends.

He smiled at her, and when she was done, he asked more thoughtful questions. "They knew how attached you were to the dog that they had given you when you were just three? So you think it was a combination of factors that they chose to sell their home and move so you wouldn't have to live on campus and only be home on weekends?"

She looked into his eyes and then nodded quickly in agreement.

"Well, maybe so, but the bottom line is that they loved you, so much so that they sold their house and your dad found a different job just for you." Bonnie Gifford signed a quick response to Bo's last remark.

"Of course, I'm sweet," Bo replied with a laugh. "And 1 love dogs too."

Bo and Bonnie resumed staring into each other's eyes without speaking as it must not have been necessary at that point. They were both apparently in the same place mentally.

She must have finally realized how much time had passed while they were just gazing at each other, which was a good thing because Bo was in la-la land and really hadn't noticed. Bonnie signed out a question to Bo. *If you love dogs, do you have one?*

"Yes, I have a dog. His name is Ace. We think he's a bullmastiff," Bo told her. Bonnie smiled with seemingly renewed interest and told him, I have a boxer now, and her name is Lucy.

Bo repeated this statement, and Bonnie nodded her approval that he was reading her correctly. Bo was now thinking that Bonnie had innocently given him the perfect excuse for him to see her again. At that point, he had been desperately searching for such an excuse. With a huge smile on his face, he not so innocently stated, "You know what, I've got a wild idea. Maybe our two dogs could meet each other." Bonnie nodded in approval.

Bo had just graduated from la-la land to never-never land. Yes, it sure seemed like things were working out the way that Bo had hoped for. Bo's mind was racing at that point. When, where, and how? was swirling around in his brain like a quickly approaching hurricane. He immediately came up with a good plan. Bo suddenly realized that the plan was there all along. He was now in eye of the storm, where it was calm, and everything fell into place. Things he knew about before meeting Bonnie had been blocked as he had focused all his nervous energy in trying to impress her, but now pertinent information had resurfaced just in time to help him. "There's a school dance on Friday night. Maybe you could bring Lucy, and my folks could watch the dogs while we're at the dance," he suddenly blurted out.

Bonnie looked at Bo with sadness as she responded in sign language.

"You don't drive, huh." He hesitated for a few seconds while he drummed his fingers on top of the table while glancing up at the ceiling. Finally, he looked at Bonnie with a smile and a solution in mind. "I know. Maybe my folks will let me use our pickup truck, and I could come and pick you and Lucy up. I just got my driver's license a couple of weeks ago."

Bonnie seemed to contemplate Bo's solution and then signed her concern at the distance that Bo would have to drive to pick her up and then bring her back home.

"Ah, heck, it wouldn't be that much driving," Bo told her. "Isn't it only about a forty-minute drive from here?"

Bonnie nodded at him. After a little hesitation, Bonnie asked Bo if it would be okay if she came with a couple of her friends and if they picked him up instead.

"Sure, that would work too," he slowly answered. "There's no reason you couldn't come with your friends from school."

At that point, as far as Bo was concerned, seeing Bonnie again in any capacity was a great thing. Still smiling at her, Bo asked her, "Hey, do you think you could still bring your dog along to meet Ace?"

Seeing the huge grin on Bo's face, Bonnie nodded and put on the sweetest smile that Bo had ever seen. He was glad his knees were hidden from view under the table so she couldn't see them knocking together from an uncontrollable twitch, the onset of which occurred when she had offered a solution to their driving dilemma.

Henry was sitting in his recliner alone in the living room, watching television. It was finally Friday night, with the workweek almost over for Henry. When you owned your own business, the workweek wasn't over on Friday night, but it was almost over for Henry. A half day on Saturday spent at his body shop, and then Henry could finally vegetate until Monday morning.

Martha passed by in the hallway and caught Henry's eye. "Martha, are you sure you can't cancel out on Alice? After all, it's just a bridge game."

Martha appeared in the entryway from the hallway, holding a laundry basket filled with her husband's dirty work clothes. "Now, Henry, you know we all get together once a month and play bridge."

Henry took a sip of his beer he was caressing and then sneered at his wife of thirty years. "Bridge, my butt! It's just an excuse for all you mother hens to get together and gossip."

Martha thumbed her nose at her predictable husband. "You're just trying to make me feel guilty for not staying home and helping you watch the dogs while Bo and his new friend are at the dance."

Henry seemed undaunted by his wife's candid comments. "Well, why does she have to bring her mutt along to meet our mutt anyway?"

The mental match of wits was on—the ball was in Martha's court, and it was her turn to return serve. "Because our son asked her to. Besides, I think it's kinda cute."

"It's not going to be very cute if those two dogs fight the entire time that I'm left alone with them." Henry had unknowingly revealed to Martha with his last comment that, once again, he had failed to pay attention to details when they were first presented to him, and Martha was aptly ready to pound it down his throat.

"Henry, what's the name of the dog that Bo's friend is bringing to meet Ace?"

Henry looked puzzled and seemed to try in vain to think of the dog's name before giving up. "I don't know. I'm lucky to remember the girl's name."

Martha then asked a perfectly legitimate and seemingly innocent question. "And what is her name?"

"Didn't Bo say her name was Bunny?"

"No, it's Bonnie, and her dog's name is Lucy. Now what does that tell you, Henry?"

Henry just kept staring at the television before answering, "It tells me I've got a lot more to worry about now than just fighting. Please stay home, Martha."

Martha felt no pity for her whiny husband at that point. "Oh, big baby, you'll be just fine." She turned around and headed back down the hallway with the basket of dirty clothes while Henry was left alone in the living room again, mumbling to himself.

He finally turned off the television and picked up the sports section of the Friday newspaper, which was sitting on the end table next to his recliner. Henry reached down and flipped the handle on the side of his chair, causing the footrest to pop up into place as he leaned back into more of a reclining position. It was his favorite position—still upright enough to hold and read the paper but reclined enough to unburden his aching feet and full belly after another mouthwatering Martha-made meal.

Henry had finally opened the sports section to page 2 when the front door bell chime interrupted his reading. He lowered his newspaper and looked at the front door. Instead of getting up out of his comfortable recliner and answering the door, he glanced at the entrance to the hallway. "Mother! Are you going to get the door?"

Several seconds passed. The doorbell rang again. "Will you get it, Henry? I'm tied up back here!" Martha yelled back to Henry from another room.

"Well, who did that to you?"

"What did you say, dear?" Martha asked while changing her clothes in the back bedroom.

Henry let out a deep sigh before lowering his footrest and slowly hoisting himself out of his cozy recliner. "Never mind! I'll get it!" He hurriedly stepped to the front door, reaching up to smooth out his tousled hair before turning the doorknob.

Standing on the front porch was Bonnie with her dog, Lucy, next to her. A teenage boy and girl were waiting in an old gray Plymouth sedan that was parked in front of the house, with the engine idling. The boy was driving the car, and the girl was in the front passenger seat.

Henry smiled broadly at Bonnie and her boxer as he held the door open for them. "Well, hello there. Come in, come in," he said as he gave her the onceover, starting at the top of her head and down to her toes and then up again to finally resume eye contact (nothing obvious about Henry).

Bonnie smiled back at Bo's father and then stepped through the doorway, with Lucy following closely behind. After closing the door, he left them standing just inside the doorway as he walked through the entrance to the hallway and to the foot of the staircase before shouting up to his youngest son, who apparently was still upstairs. "Bo! Your friend is here!"

Bonnie stood there shifting her weight from side to side as her dog stayed glued to her pant leg. This part of the evening was probably the hardest for Bonnie. It was a situation that she undoubtedly had little, if any, experience in.

Bo yelled back down to his father from his bedroom, "Be right there, Pop!"

After hearing his son's response, Henry wheeled around and walked back over to the other side of the living room before sitting down in his recliner again. "He'll be right with you." Just like Bonnie's inexperience, Henry must not have had any experience with girls picking up his sons on first dates because he didn't think to offer her a seat. He plopped back down in his recliner while Bonnie continued to stand, with her dog sitting next to her near the front door of the living room. "Nicelooking dog you got there," Henry finally said in a loud, booming voice to break the silence. Bonnie just smiled back.

Lucy, Bonnie's female boxer, had sat down so close to her that she probably could feel the female canine's weight against her leg as the shy dog looked around the room, not moving from Bonnie's side. She had a little look of worry and uncertainty on her boxer face. She was a very cute dog. Lucy had beautiful eyes, pretty white paws, and patchy white face that accentuated her short silky brown fur, which covered the rest of her muscular frame. It was all in the eyes of the beholder, but this dog could beg food off a beggar if she had to. She was that cute.

Bo finally hurried down the stairs and walked into the living room from the hallway, with Ace right behind him. As soon as the two dogs saw each other, the timid boxer arose from her sitting position and moved behind Bonnie, peeking around her just enough for her head to be seen. At the same time, Ace got behind Bo and peeked around him just like Lucy was doing, except for the fact that it was like a cow trying to hide behind a fence post. Henry started chuckling as he looked at Ace. "This ought to be an interesting evening, huh, Romeo?"

When Bo and his entourage finally arrived, the school dance in the Plattsmouth High School Gym was already underway. Bo entered through the open gym doors with Bonnie by his side. Behind them were Bonnie's two friends from the Iowa School for the Deaf.

On the surface, Marvin and Tanya looked like a mismatched pair. He had lilywhite skin and short blond hair and was very skinny, wearing Coke-bottle glasses that seemed to make his eyes bug out. The girl, Tanya, looked like she could be of Indian descent. She was dark skinned and a little overweight, with long straight black hair that almost reached down to the small of her back. The only apparent commonality was the fact that both were wearing a pair of hearing aids in each of their ears. Bonnie had told Bo that her two friends were not dating each other. She also told him that they had really connected during their first year together at the school and that they had pretty much been inseparable from that time forward.

As the four walked into the dance, many eyes were on them as Bo and Bonnie presented the appearance of a strikingly attractive couple in contrast to Marvin and Tonya. Pretty much everyone at the dance, including Bo and his new friends, were dressed casually in blue jeans, cotton shirts, jackets, and either cowboy boots or tennis shoes. The young band was playing a fast tune.

Ron, the boy who had been sitting with Bo's close friend Jerry earlier in the week in the cafeteria, was huddled near a group of girls, chatting with Bruce, another acquaintance. "Hey, check out the deaf-mute babe that Bo was with in the cafeteria this week. Maybe she could teach me some sign language too."

Bruce glanced back at Ron. "Sure, why don't you go ask Bo if that's okay with him?"

Ron just kept staring at Bonnie. "Yeah, I just might do that."

Bo and his new friends kept walking through the crowd until they reached an open spot off the dance floor area and near some tables where some of the teenagers were seated. There were quite a few couples as well as just girls dancing together out on the dance floor. The music was loud. The band was pretty good for a local group of teenagers themselves. Bonnie was communicating with Marvin and Tanya using sign language, and they were signing back to her as Bo looked on.

Ron shot his mouth off again to Bruce, and luckily for Ron, Bo didn't hear him. "Looks like she brought a couple of more just like her."

"I don't know, Ron. One of them looks like a guy to me," Bruce deadpanned in response.

"You know what I mean," Ron shot back.

Bruce was starting to look frustrated. "Man, what do you have against deaf people?"

Ron looked at Bruce with a blank stare. How appropriate that it was a blank stare since Ron was demonstrating with almost every spoken word that the lights were on, but nobody was home. "Nothin' really. I just can't understand why they would want to come to a dance. I mean, they probably can't even hear the music."

Bruce stared back at Ron with cold eyes. "Maybe they just enjoy being around other people."

Ron apparently still hadn't picked up on the fact that he really wasn't having a conversation with an understanding friend. "Why would you enjoy being around other people if you couldn't understand what they were saying?"

"Maybe they understand more than you think they do."

Ron must have run out of material by then because a one-word response was all that he could muster. "Whatever," he concluded.

Back to where Bo and his entourage were standing, the two young girls were signing back and forth to each other with rapid-fire hand signals. Bonnie took off her jacket and handed it to Tanya, tossing her purse on the nearest chair. She looked at Bo, smiling, and then signed to him as she helped him off with his jacket before handing it to Tanya.

The new arrivals were getting plenty of attention from the groups of teenagers around them. Bonnie grabbed Bo's hand and began pulling him onto the dance floor. "You want to dance already?" he protested. "But we just got here." He was being tugged along away from the table.

Meanwhile, back in the Bozell living room, Henry looked comfortable in his recliner while reading the newspaper. Ace and Lucy were sitting on the floor in front of Henry, staring at him. The television wasn't on anymore, so it was very quiet. Martha had been gone for some time, so it was just Henry and the dogs.

Henry finally lifted the newspaper above the level of his head and saw that the two dogs were just sitting there side by side, staring at him. "You two must be really bored to be sitting there watching my every move," he said before lowering the newspaper back down and resuming his reading.

After about a minute, Henry's reading was abruptly disturbed as Ace had gotten up and moved forward a couple of steps before burrowing his big head under the newspaper in his lap. The bullmastiff stared up at him with sad, pleading eyes before starting to whine. Henry looked down into those pleading big brown eyes. "What do you want now? You're slobbering all over me, you big ox! Now back off. I just let you two out a few minutes ago."

Ace immediately backed away from Henry and walked over and stared at the empty fireplace. He proceeded to pad over to a pile of logs that were sitting in an oval-shaped tin near the fireplace and grabbed the top log by biting down on a twig that was still sticking out of the side of the eighteen-inch chopped wood. He carried the log in his teeth over to the fireplace and dropped it in.

Henry looked mildly surprised as he watched the determined dog begin to load up the fireplace with or without his help. "Big knucklehead. You've been here how many weeks now? During some of the colder nights of March and April, and now you want me to start a fire in the fireplace for you?"

Ace walked back over to Lucy and looked at her, then at the fireplace again, and finally back at Henry.

"Oh, 1 get it. You want to impress old Lucy Liu here, don't ya?"

"Woof!" *Sometimes the old man isn't as dense as he looks,* thought Ace.

Back at the high school gymnasium, Bo and Bonnie were dancing on the edge of the dance floor. Bonnie had her back to the band. The band was playing "Good Vibrations" by the Beach Boys. She was really moving to the music. People nearby were all watching her and Bo. Most of the other teenagers, being predominantly boys, who were nearby at the time had their eyes trained more specifically on Bonnie. She was strikingly beautiful and was demonstrating that she certainly knew how to dance. Bo was getting some looks as well from some of his female classmates, even though when it came to a sense of rhythm, he obviously had none as he was bobbing when he should have been weaving. The attention-drawing couple's gaze was firmly fixed on each other, totally oblivious to the eyes that were currently trained on them, as they smiled back and forth at each other on the dance floor.

As soon as the band stopped playing, Bonnie was the first one to stop dancing. When Bo and everyone else had stopped as well and the band was getting ready to play another song, he playfully pleaded with his new female friend, "You're wearing me out, Bonnie. Can't we take a little break?"

She nodded yes, so the two of them began to walk over to where Marvin and Tanya were sitting at their table. They passed right in front of Ron and Bruce. Ron tapped Bo on the shoulder after Bonnie had already passed by him. "Bo, how did she know when to stop dancing?"

Bo just stared at Ron for a few seconds with much the same cold, steely eyes that his friend Bruce's eyes had looked an hour earlier. "Uh, Ron, isn't it obvious? Good vibrations" was all that Bo answered as a sly grin appeared on his face before giving way to the cold stare again.

Ron looked puzzled. "Huh? Oh, I get it," he finally managed to say.

Bo walked away from Ron to catch up with Bonnie before abruptly stopping and wheeling around. "Do you, Ron? Do you really get it?" he asked before turning back around and walking away.

Ron looked like he'd just had the wind knocked out of him. "1 don't think Bo liked my question very much."

Bruce was chuckling to himself as he watched Bo sit down next to Bonnie at their table. "Oh yeah? What gave you your first clue?"

Meanwhile, back at the ranch, Henry was still reading his newspaper. Ace and Lucy were sitting next to each other in front of a blazing fire in the fireplace. The two dogs were at a reasonably safe distance from the fire. Ace decided to creep forward a little bit before looking back at Lucy. Lucy followed Ace's lead and crept forward too until she was even with him again. Henry finally lowered the newspaper, seeing how dangerously close the dogs were to the fireplace. "Ace! You and your sweetie are gettin' too close to that fire! Now back it up a little bit!"

The mischievous mastiff let out a few moans and then arose, with Lucy following suit, before the two dogs padded back a few feet, turning around to the fire once again and sitting back down.

"That's better. I don't want our guest getting her fur singed. Mother would have my hide if that happened." Henry went back to his reading as the two dogs stared at the fire from a safer distance now.

Back at the dance, Bo and Bonnie were dancing in a crowd of couples on the dance floor to a slow song. The band was playing "Sound of Silence" by Simon and Garfunkel. As they slow-danced, Bo signed the lyrics in front of Bonnie's face. She was smiling back at him. "Now you see why 1 especially wanted us to dance to this song?" Bo gently asked.

Bonnie nodded as she gazed into Bo's eyes. The mutually enamored young couple continued to hold each other tightly, slowly turning in circles, while Bo made sure that his legally deaf date now knew some of the poignant lyrics to "Sound of Silence."

As soon as the song was over, she gave Bo a soft kiss on the cheek before they left the dance floor. He was taken off guard by Bonnie's tender gesture. His face turned a little red with embarrassment, but inside, Bo felt a sense of excitement. His heart started pounding faster, and his knees suddenly felt weak.

The lead singer of the young band grabbed onto his microphone again. "We're gonna take a short break, and then we'll get back to some rockin' and rollin' for you, so stick around, everybody."

Bo turned to Bonnie as they started to walk back to the table area. "I have to use the restroom."

She understandingly nodded and continued walking back over to Marvin and Tanya as Bo headed for the men's room. With the band not playing now, there were various conversations going on around the gym.

Bonnie sat down with her deaf friends, and they immediately started communicating in sign language with one another. They conversed back and forth for a few minutes. Bonnie thanked Marvin once again for driving, and she thanked Tanya for coming along as well. She asked them both if they were having a good time.

Finally, Bonnie said something that made Marvin laugh out loud. His laugh had a very loud, guttural, screechy sound since what little speech he had was pretty much undecipherable to most people. When you combined the screechy sounds coming out of Marvin's mouth with his overall appearance (his Cokebottle glasses and skinny physique), he had easily and immediately attracted a lot of attention in the gym. Marvin signed back to Bonnie and then laughed again.

Ron and Bruce were watching Marvin's antics when Bo had returned from the restroom and was within earshot of what Ron was saying at the time. "Doesn't this deaf geek know how ridiculous he sounds?" Ron asked Bruce.

Within a couple of seconds, Bo was in Ron's face like a marine drill instructor facing down a raw recruit. "Some of us can still hear," he managed to say through clenched teeth.

Ron looked suddenly afraid. "Bo ... I... I didn't mean to—"

"You didn't mean to be mean! Is that what you were going to say, Ron?" Bo barked back, having interrupted him in midsentence, unintentionally spitting in his face.

"No ... I didn't mean to offend anyone," Ron stammered back.

Bo stood nose to nose with Ron for a few seconds before answering. The veins in his neck were popping out all over the place, and his face had reddened with rage. His was the spitting image of his father, like the first night Ace was allowed back into the Bozell house after the mastiff's midnight temper tantrum. "Offended? No, we aren't offended! We know who we are! Do you know who you are, Ron?" Bo unexpectedly wheeled around and walked away before Ron had a chance to answer him, which was a good thing because Ron wasn't going to undo the damage, no matter what he would have said at that point.

Back at the Bozell house, Henry was still reading his newspaper. It was peacefully quiet, save for the sound of the firewood crackling in the fireplace. He read the newspaper from front page to back page every night. Henry was a very slow reader. He often would stop and grab a red pen that he kept on the end table next to his chair, circling specific articles, so reading the newspaper took up a good deal of his time each evening.

In the basement were stacks and stacks of newspapers, most of which had at least two or three articles circled in red ink. Some were so old that the paper had turned yellow with age. Despite Martha's occasional nagging about the fire hazard that the stacks of paper presented, they remained nonetheless. Martha sometimes had to bite her lip and remind herself that she would take a pack rat over an alcoholic or abusive husband any day.

Ace and Lucy were sitting at a safe distance from the fire. Once again, Ace crept forward, closer to the fireplace. Lucy crept forward too. The canine turned his head around and looked back at Henry, seeing that he was too engrossed in his reading to notice that he and Lucy had gotten closer to the fire once again. The persistent dog then crawled up real close to the fire, and Lucy crawled up beside him, apparently trusting his judgment unquestionably.

Suddenly, an ember from the fire popped out onto Ace's back. The startled dog jumped up, howling, and scared Lucy, who dashed out of the room like a greyhound chasing the fake rabbit out of the starting gate. Henry threw the newspaper aside and rushed to the aid of Ace. The mastiff quickly shook the hot ember off his back.

Henry grabbed the small fireplace shovel and scooped the still burning ember up off the partial tile floor where it had luckily landed instead of on the surrounding living room carpeting. He tossed it back into the fire before rubbing Ace's back where the ember had been. He could smell the singed fur. Finally looking over to see where Lucy had gone, he saw her frightened face peeking around the corner of the entryway to the hallway. He continued to rub Ace's back. "Well, Romeo, you really impressed your guest now, didn't you?"

As Ace moaned, Henry walked over to the fireplace. He leaned down and slid the metal mesh screen across to the center in front of the fire from both sides. "Maybe next time you'll listen to me. And maybe next time I'll remember to slide this screen across after I start the fire for you." Henry chuckled as he looked at the very humiliated dog. He had no way of knowing how close he came to a bite in the ass by an upset bullmastiff with that last comment. He should have thanked the Lord literally that Ace got talked out of it at the last second.

The old man was still chuckling as he walked back over to his recliner and sat down. Lucy was still peeking around the comer of the entryway to the hallway. Ace, having learned a lesson the hard way, sat back down at a safe distance from the fireplace this time, not necessarily trusting the mesh screen for protection. Henry looked at Lucy before he resumed reading his newspaper. "It's safe to come back in now, Lucy Liu."

The scared boxer slowly and hesitantly padded back into the room and sat down next to her embarrassed first date. She started to lick his back where the hot ember had landed. "Ahh, playin' the sympathy card. You are the clever one, aren't you, Ace?" Henry said as he relocated the article in the newspaper that he had been reading before the mastiff mayhem.

Just then, Martha came through the front door. "Well, how did it go, Henry?"

Henry looked away from his newspaper, and Martha could see that he was grinning from ear to ear. "Oh, I'd have to say that there's a real hot romance in the works here, Mother."

"Isn't that cute? She's licking him on the back!" Martha exclaimed.

Henry apparently couldn't contain himself anymore as he busted out laughing. "What's so funny, Henry?"

Bo glanced around the high school parking lot as he and his new friends left the dance and were heading to Marvin's car. He was holding Bonnie's hand as the two of them walked behind Marvin and Tanya. What a great night it had been so far for Bo. Even though his thoughts were filled with warmth and excitement as his first date with Bonnie would soon be coming to an end, he noticed some people sitting in a car that was parked in the next row behind Marvin's car.

It was too dark to tell who was in the car or what kind of car it was because, for some reason, the parking lot lights weren't on that evening. It struck Bo as being odd that the lights weren't working on a night when a school dance was going on. He didn't give much thought to the other car, though, as it was not uncommon for high school students to sit in their parked cars at night. He wasn't naive. He knew what things could be transpiring inside the car, despite the fact that the local police would cruise by regularly on such a night with an event going on. Maybe it was just a couple making out before heading home.

As he and Bonnie approached the right rear passenger door, Bo stepped forward and tried to open the car door for his date as he had done earlier in the evening. The door was unlocked, but it was sticking just like when he had tried it earlier. As Bonnie had done before, she gave it a quick kick, and it sprung open, with Bo still pulling on the door handle. He almost fell to the ground when it suddenly popped open. Bonnie chuckled as she slid across the seat while Bo was mumbling, "He really needs to get that fixed." He had to slam the door three times before it finally latched closed.

After Marvin shut his driver's door and started the engine, Bo watched him as he glanced at Tanya, then to the back seat at Bonnie, and finally at him to make sure everyone had their doors closed before putting the car into gear. It was at that moment that a loud thud could be felt by everyone in the car as a full can of beer careened off the trunk of Marvin's old Plymouth. "Whoa!" yelled Bo before looking back through the rear window.

At that point, little skinny Marvin popped the column shift into drive and stomped on the accelerator. The old Plymouth had a good-sized engine in it, which bellowed to life, with the tires squealing and laying down some rubber on the parking lot concrete. Everyone's head snapped back as the old Plymouth fishtailed a little bit before an obviously frightened-looking Marvin regained control of the car just before they hit the parking lot exit that led to the city side street that passed by the front of the school. He barely made the turn out into the street as the right wheels left the pavement for a brief second.

As Bo looked back through the rear window again, he saw the car that had been behind them squeal out from its parking spot as the car's headlights came on just before it slid around the turn into the street. He looked at Bonnie. She looked relatively calm for someone who was in a suddenly speeding car being chased by another. As she looked searchingly into his eyes, he shouted over the sound of the engine noise, "Why did he just take off like that?"

Bonnie quickly used sign language to answer him.

Bo shook his head before answering back, "I said 'whoa,' not 'go.'" She signed a fairly long response as the Plymouth continued to fly down the street with the other car in hot pursuit. Bo's take on what she said was that Marvin was very excitable and that he probably would have peeled out and taken off anyway, regardless of what he had understood Bo to say.

They raced through an intersection. Everyone in the car was lifted out of his or her seat as the old Plymouth hit a dip at high speed. Bo looked behind him in time to see the other car's headlights bounce up and down in the same intersection that Marvin's car had just literally flown through a couple of seconds earlier. "Tell him to pull over! I'm not afraid of whoever's in that car!" Bo yelled over to Bonnie.

Bonnie just kept looking ahead. She must not have heard him. Bo grabbed

Bonnie by the arm. "1 said tell him to pull over! Pull over!" Bonnie still didn't look at Bo as he finally let go of her arm.

No one in the car, not even Bonnie, seemed to understand what he was saying. Maybe during the heat of the moment, Bo had forgotten that they were all legally deaf. Tanya kept looking straight ahead, never looking at Marvin or into the back seat. Bonnie just kept staring straight ahead as Marvin tightly gripped the steering wheel, with his foot buried to the floorboard on the gas pedal.

Marvin began to hit the brakes a few times and was able to get his runaway Plymouth to slow down just enough for him to negotiate a lefthand turn onto another street. When Marvin steered the car into the turn, Bo got slammed up against the inside of the car door. The door suddenly popped open and flung Bo out of the speeding car. He didn't have time to grab Bonnie or anything else in the back seat before he found himself rolling backward, end over end, along the concrete surface. No . . . please . . . not again, he was thinking as he just kept rolling over and over.

Bo finally jerked upright in bed in a cold sweat, realizing it had all been just a bad dream. He must have been talking in his sleep during his nightmare because Ace was awake and staring at him in front of the moonlit bedroom window. "Wow, Ace, that was just too, too real!"

He flopped back down on his back and rolled over on his side before fluffing up his pillow and trying to go back to sleep, realizing that the nightmare was full of symbolism. Bo was no expert on interpreting dreams, but he had to know that his previous fall out of the school bus weeks before must have had a lasting effect on his understanding that life can be full of unexpected twists and turns that had the capability of changing one's life forever in a mere instant.

As Bo closed his eyes, he dreamily thought about how the evening really had ended, with he and Bonnie sharing an embrace and a good-night kiss on his front porch before his new friends had departed for home. The only detail of his bad dream that had been real was Marvin's stuck car door that Bonnie had to

open for him. Thankfully, there had been no car chase and no fall out of the car on the way home.

Ace moaned a little bit, still feeling some pain from where the hot ember had landed on his back earlier in the evening, before he closed his eyes and repositioned himself on the throw rug next to his master's bed.

Bo pulled into a parking spot on the campus of Iowa School for the Deaf. It was early evening. He had his father's pickup truck, and Ace was riding shotgun. "I think this is about where Bonnie said she'd meet us."

Ace just stared at Bo with a look that said, Well, okay, if you say so, as some drool splashed onto the plastic-covered bench seat.

Marvin's old Plymouth sedan came around the corner and pulled into the parking spot next to Bo and Ace. Tanya was in the front seat with Marvin, and Bonnie and Lucy were in the back. Bo smiled and waved at everyone in the adjoining car before opening his truck door and stepping out.

Before he closed his door, Ace came bounding out of it. He immediately jumped up on Marvin's car, so he was staring into the face of Lucy, who had her head sticking out of the left rear window. "Ace! Get down!" yelled Bo.

Ace dropped back down to the pavement before everyone got out of Marvin's car. Bonnie signed a hello to Bo before reaching out and giving him a little hug. "So now are you going to tell me what we're doing here?" asked Bo.

Marvin and Tanya had already walked away, heading in the direction of one of the bigger buildings on campus. Bonnie smiled at Bo before going into a long signing session with him. After about a minute of signing to Bo, she stopped and waited for his reply.

"You and your friends do this every week? Wow, so how long have you been doing it?"

Bonnie signed a quick reply as her dog, Lucy, had already started to pad away in the direction of Marvin and Tanya, with Ace right next to her. "For the last six months now? I think that's great. I must say I'm pretty impressed."

Bonnie gave a quick reply as a very serious expression crossed her face.

"No, I didn't mean it that way. I know you're not doing it to impress anyone.

In fact, I'm going to guess that hardly anyone even knows about it, right?" Bonnie nodded in the affirmative as she grabbed Bo's hand and pulled him off in the same direction as the others, who seemed to be heading to the back entrance of a building that had a strong food smell emanating from it.

Marvin's old Plymouth was driving down a winding gravel road that led to the banks of the Missouri River. Lucy was sitting in between Marvin and Tanya in the front seat while Ace was taking up a lot of room in the back seat between Bo and Bonnie. As they got close to the river, cottonwood trees now surrounded them on both sides of the road. The sun was starting to set as they finally came to a stop about fifty feet from the Iowa side of the riverbank. After Marvin got out of the driver's door, he walked to the back of his car and opened the trunk.

Everyone had gotten out of the car now, and the four teenagers were, one by one, reaching into the trunk and pulling out a box. Bonnie took the lead and began walking on a winding, narrow dirt path toward the river.

They all emerged from the path, which was surrounded by trees, and walked into a small clearing just a few feet from the river. There was a couple of makeshift old tents set up on the other side of the clearing close to where the tree line ended. Two men were sitting on logs around a small campfire that was burning brightly as the evening sky slowly darkened, with the sun no longer visible on the west horizon.

The men both looked to be in their forties or fifties. They both had scraggly beards and wild-looking hair, and their clothes were old, soiled, and tattered. They both looked up with smiles on their faces as the teenagers and the two dogs approached them. "Bonnie, I don't know what Milt and I would do without you and your friends' help lately," the first man said as he slowly stood up.

Bonnie placed her box down in the sand and immediately walked over to hug the man who had just spoken. They hugged each other for several seconds as the others put down their boxes next to the one that Bonnie had already placed near the fire. Meanwhile, Ace and Lucy had run off to the edge of the riverbank together as the man named Milt had already reached into one of the boxes, pulled out a fried chicken leg, and began to ravenously eat the chicken off the bone.

While Bonnie finally pulled away from the man's hug, he kissed her on the check. Bo looked surprised by the level of affection between this man and his new girlfriend. Even though he remained silent, Bonnie can apparently tell that he was a little disturbed. She signed for a few seconds in front of Bo. "Oh, you didn't tell me that part on the way here. Now it makes more sense," Bo answered.

The man who had just finished hugging and kissing Bonnie looked at Bo. "She's telling you the truth, son. I am Bonnie's uncle."

Bonnie signed to the man and then motioned for the others to follow her back to the car.

"Sorry you can't stay longer, but I understand. Looks like you've got just enough time to make it back on the trail before it's really dark out," Bonnie's uncle remarked.

Bonnie whistled for Lucy as she and the others disappeared down the darkened trail. Lucy turned and trotted toward the trail with Ace right behind her.

The teenagers and dogs were back in the car as Marvin stepped down on the gas pedal, and the old Plymouth made its way down the winding gravel road away from the Missouri River. This time, Ace was sitting in the back seat next to the open rear window, with his big head sticking out and his ears pinned back from the wind against his face. Bonnie was sitting in the middle with Bo on her left.

"Your dad has a pretty good job. You live in a nice house near the school. What happened to his brother? Why is he homeless?" asked Bo.

Bonnie signed for quite a while in response to Bo's questions as they made their way back to the Iowa School for the Deaf.

"Yeah, it sounds like your uncle Charlie has had some tough breaks in life. You're right, there are some similarities with my uncle Leonard. I guess the big difference is the fact that my uncle Leonard has my aunt Alice to lean on."

Bonnie nodded with a faraway look on her face as she turned her head slightly and looked back toward the river briefly before looking back into the eyes of Bo.

"You mean to tell me that your dad doesn't know his own brother is living down here by the river in a tent?"

Bonnie solemnly nodded yes to Bo's last question. "But why? Why doesn't he want him to know?" Bonnie signed her response for the next few seconds.

"But they're brothers for god's sake. I come from a family where we're always there for one another, no matter what has happened."

Bonnie grabbed hold of Bo's hand and smiled at him. She signed with her other free hand in front of the moonlit rear window so Bo can see her message better in the darkening car.

"Long story or not, I'm a good listener, and we've got a good ten minutes before we'll be back at your campus."

She gripped his hand more intently before finally letting go to free up both of her hands so she can begin telling Bo the whole tragic story of her homeless uncle Charlie.

O nly the first lieutenant, an Irishman from Queens named O'Hare, and the sergeant, a Puerto Rican named Carlos, knew the exact coordinates of their location. For Ben Bozell and his new best buddy—Danny, a young black man from South Chicago—it really didn't matter. They were somewhere smack-dab in the middle of Vietnam. Packs, night-vision scopes, flak jackets, guns, and ammo were all scattered around a small clearing, giving some semblance of a temporary camp that was further removed from a bigger camp several miles away.

Ben and Danny were sitting together, eating their evening meal of C rations. With the enemy potentially close by, no fires were lit. Marines never ate hot food when they were out in the field on night recon duty. The two marines were eating their nonheated C rations while some of their other buddies were doing the same nearby.

Their temporary camp was well hidden on the edge of a cave nestled among the trees and tall grass of a minor mountain in the area. Besides being well hidden, the location was obviously on higher ground, giving the sentry (of what was now a nine-man platoon) a clear view of the countryside below and to the sides. Predictably, a helicopter would fly overhead at regular intervals. The hum of the huge propellers provided the comforting sound of knowing that backup was close at hand. It was like a homeless man who was able to stay at a shelter for one night, and the constant hum of the cheap window air conditioner reminded him that, at least for this one night, he was safe falling asleep. But what every man remembered, if he remembered nothing else, years after he was safely removed from the nightmare was the acrid smell of burnt jet fuel, burnt flesh, and spent gunpowder that drifted into the air for miles. It was the smell of war and the smell of death that would cling to a soldier's soul forever.

The marines periodically swatted at the many flying insects that were a constant pain in the butt. Every insect, from a gnat to a horsefly, was bigger than anything they had ever encountered back home in the good old US of A. Ben (sandy hair with a muscular build) sat with his shirt off, having allowed the remaining sunlight to bake his bare back in warmth. No one had his helmet on. Danny (a little taller but just as muscular and very handsome and very black) was still wearing his drab-green T-shirt that was sweat soaked. They both were wearing their jungle fatigue pants just like the rest of the platoon.

It was obvious that this was just a temporary camp because none of the young marines had shaved for a few days. Besides Ben and Danny, who were corporals, there were the first lieutenant, the sergeant, a lance corporal, and four other privates. There were four other black men in the platoon besides Danny, and they were all privates. Three of them sat together off to themselves. The other, the platoon's current radioman, sat huddled with the first lieutenant at a higher point of the ridge, just outside the mouth of the cave. It would be getting dark soon, and their graveyard shift would be getting underway once again. In military jargon, it was called night recon duty. Recon was short for "reconnaissance." Somebody had to get a fix on the enemy position.

Ben was just finishing up something that tasted like minced ham, but he couldn't be certain. He finally looked at Danny. "So have you decided which law school you're going to try for once you finish your bachelor's degree?"

Danny shook his head no. "As long as it's accredited, I really don't care. I figure my GI Bill money is going to run out shortly into my first year of law school, so I can't be too choosy."

A tropical bird chortled in the distance as they continued to sit and eat. "You seem so driven that you know what you want to do with your life once we get the hell out of this place," said Ben.

"My mama made me promise that I'd become a lawyer. She expects me to figure out a way to get my elder brother out of prison someday. We know he's innocent. I've just got to figure out a way to prove it," Danny answered.

Ben looked stunned. "You never told me before that that's why you want to be a lawyer. You never told me you had a brother in prison before."

Danny took another mouthful of food before answering Ben. "Yeah, well, it's not something I feel like broadcasting to the world, you know. Besides, 1 feel kind of weird tonight. I decided it was time to finally tell you more about me. We've gone through a lot together these past few weeks. I guess I finally trust you."

"Wow, I feel honored... I guess." Ben took a sip of water out of his canteen before looking around the area and then back at Danny. "So what happened? Or would you rather not talk about it?" he asked in a hushed tone.

"He was just in the wrong place at the wrong time. Hell, where I grew up, you were always in the wrong place at the wrong time. It's still true, you know. A whole lot of hateful white people are scattered all over this planet that still think we all look alike. They can't see into our hearts and into our souls. They only see the color of our skin, and they make the conscious decision to look no further. We're all suspects ... every day of our lives, man." Danny then glanced at the three black marines who were huddled together nearby.

A year or two earlier, Ben probably wouldn't have really understood what his friend was talking about. But he had gotten an education in the military. It was a dose of prejudicial reality that had saddened him at first. He hadn't been brought up that way. "Yeah, it was a kind of culture shock for me when I first joined the marines. Even though my hometown was only a few miles from Omaha, I never even talked to a black person, let alone be friends with one, until 1 finally left Plattsmouth. I guess I led a sheltered life. I had no idea what life must have been like growing up black in a big city like Chicago."

"Ben, you still don't know half of it. You don't know how hard it was for me to find my place. 1 had a voracious appetite for reading. I'm sure you've figured out by now that I'm more articulate than my brothers are over there." Danny once again looked at the other three black marines huddled together. "It wasn't cool to be smart in school."

An early evening breeze picked up and started to blow the tall grass to the downwind side near where the two young Marine Corps corporals sat in the small clearing. Danny had finished his C rations and pulled a pack of menthol Kools and his lighter out of his pants pocket. He cupped his hands around the cigarette as he lit it with his Zippo lighter, returning the cigarette pack and lighter to his right pants pocket before exhaling for the first time.

"Danny, what does 'voracious' mean? It sounds like it might be a word I'd use to describe my little brother, Bo," Ben finally asked.

"Is your little brother obsessed with anything? Because that's what it basically means."

"Yeah, my little brother was obsessed with wrestling until he got hurt and had to give it up."

Danny exhaled another stream of smoke from his lungs as he looked up at the darkening sky. "Too bad. I couldn't imagine not ever being able to read again." He took another deep drag on his cigarette before looking back into Ben's eyes. "I was obsessed with reading, everything I could get my hands on. Reading about faraway places helped keep my mind off the reality of my own world, a crazy world, crawling with gangs, pimps, prostitutes, thieves, thugs, and addicts on almost every corner of my neighborhood," Danny replied.

"Jesus, I can't even begin to imagine what that was like for you, Danny. I'm glad you made it through that time."

Danny looked around him for a few seconds before looking back at Ben. "Yup, lucky me. I survived all that so I could be in this tropical paradise."

Ben finally finished eating. "Can I bum one of your smokes, man?" he asked Danny.

"Hell no. It's bad enough that I was stupid enough to pick up the habit again myself. I won't be a party to you getting hooked too. If I ever got to meet your mama and she knew I was to blame for you smokin', after what you've told me about her, she'd probably slap me in the face."

"My mom has always been a strong-willed woman, but she'd probably be more likely to greet you with a big hug just knowing that you were my friend, and you helped me get home."

Danny chuckled. "1 know. I was just shittin' ya. You're my naive white boy friend from *Leave It to Beaver land*."

"Very funny," Ben answered. He unscrewed the cap off his canteen again before taking another sip of water. He finally looked back at his fellow marine. "Danny, you keep changing the subject. You never did tell me why your brother's in prison."

Danny looked away and took another drag on his cigarette. "He was accused of mugging a young couple who were walking home from a latenight movie in Downtown Chicago. The husband had refused to hand over his wallet and was nearly beaten to death. To make matters worse, the husband was the son of a popular white councilman for the downtown district where the mugging went down. When he was finally released from the hospital, the guy and his wife picked my brother out of a lineup at the cop station. My brother got called in because he was on their list of usual suspects but only because he got busted before trying to steal some food for Mama and my younger brother and me.

"My elder brother had just moved into his own apartment a few months before the mugging. He told the cops he was home alone that night, so he had no alibi. It was just circumstantial evidence, but it was enough to get him convicted. I know he didn't do it. He was too busy trying to help the family once my daddy died. Even though he had moved into his own crib, he was still giving Mama money every week. 1 know my brother well enough to know that he could never do what he was convicted of doing. It's just not in him. I will find a way to prove his innocence someday. You just wait and see."

Ben put his T-shirt back on as he sat on the ground next to Danny. "I'd never bet against you, my friend. I'm sure you'll succeed someday. You know what, though, I don't think your daddy would be too proud and pleased seeing you sucking on that fag, seeing as how you said he died of lung cancer."

Danny finally snuffed out his cigarette on a rock nearby. "Ah hell, Bozell. Who was just trying to bum one off me a couple of minutes ago?"

Ben shook his finger back at Danny. "See how crazy this place makes you? One minute you're thinking how bad it is for you, and the next minute it still seems like the only logical thing to do."

The sergeant passed by just then. "Okay, boys. Time to start saddling up. We got work to do."

Everyone in the platoon started to put their jungle fatigue shirts back on, followed by their 782 gear and their all-important flak jackets, helmets, and other gear for the mission.

Danny looked at Ben. "Was your old man in the service?"

Ben shouldered his M16 before answering, "Yeah. He was a gunnery instructor in Puerto Rico during World War II. He wanted to go to Europe, but they told him he was such a good instructor they decided he was more valuable teaching instead of fighting. Probably a good thing though. I might not be standing *here* today otherwise. God, what am I saying? I'd rather not be standing here right now for any logical reason." Danny got a funny look on his face. "Listen, Ben, if something happens to me, promise me you'll go see my mama for me when you get back. Would you do that for me?"

Ben wheeled around, stepped in front of Danny, and put a hand on his shoulder. "Will you stop talkin' that way? What's the matter with you?"

Danny shrugged as the platoon started walking forward. "I don't know. I just feel weird tonight. Promise me you'll go see her, Ben."

Ben kept holding on to Danny's shoulder as they both quit walking. The rest of the platoon was getting a few feet ahead of them by now as they brought up the rear. "I tell you what. First, we'll stop and see my mom, and then we'll both fly up to Chicago and see your mom," Ben answered.

The sergeant, several feet ahead of them by now, looked over his shoulder as he was walking away. "Come on, you guys. You can settle your little domestic dispute when we get back."

It was three days after Ben and Danny had gotten to know each other a little better before their most recent night recon mission over in 'Nam. Sophomore history class was in session at Plattsmouth High School. Bo was sitting in the second seat from the front behind Sarah, the cheerleader, in the row of desks next to the windows. Another girl, Julie Applebee—who had short brunette hair, was a little overweight, and wore glasses—was sitting in the front seat of the middle row. Julie was speaking to the class, having volunteered her opinion regarding the subject of the United States military's role in the Vietnam "conflict." Bo was staring out of the window and didn't appear to be paying attention.

"We must continue to help the South Vietnamese people. They have a right to be free just as we are free. In conclusion, I think it is very important for the United States to remain in Vietnam and stop the spread of communism."

There was a brief silence in the classroom. Miss Krenkle must have picked up on Bo's seemingly inattentiveness when Julie Applebee had been speaking. "Mr. Bozell, why don't you tell the class what you know about this subject?" Miss Krenkle said as the brief silence was broken. "Do you agree with Miss Applebee that the United States is playing an important role in stopping the threat of communism in Southeast Asia?"

Bo continued to stare out the window.

"Mr. Bozell!"

Bo finally turned his head back in the direction of Miss Krenkle. "Yes" was his one-word reply.

"Yes, you do agree?"

"Yes, I heard you." There were some giggles from some of Bo's classmates.

"No, I don't agree," Bo finally answered.

"And why is that, Mr. Bozell?" Miss Krenkle asked in an exasperated tone.

Bo looked out of the window again as the silence seemed to be making everyone a bit nervous and uncomfortable.

"Mr. Bozell, would you please share your knowledge with the rest of the class?"

Bo finally turned back around in the direction of Miss Krenkle, knowing he was probably on the verge of getting kicked out of her class and sent to the principal's office. He finally began to speak, slowly and softly at first. "The Vietnamese endured over a hundred years of colonial imperialism by the French. And more recently, they suffered the 'double yoke' of French rule in the South and Japanese rule in the North during World War II. Most Vietnamese view Americans now no differently from the way they viewed the French . . . as unwanted capitalist imperialists. What's more, there's no sense of a unified country. Most Vietnamese only care about what's happening to their own families and their surrounding village. It's primarily a country of rural peasants who know nothing nor care nothing about democracy. The South Vietnamese leadership, both politically and militarily, is weak and corrupt. Americans will never be able to win over the masses into the American way of thinking, just as the French failed before us."

The class, including Miss Krenkle, was in stunned silence. You could have heard a pin drop.

Bo continued, "The domino theory—that if South Vietnam falls to communism, the other Southeast Asian countries will fall as well—is seriously flawed. History doesn't support such a theory. The buildup of our troops under the Johnson presidency was due to this American cowboy thinking that just because all Asians look alike, they must act alike as well. You combine that flawed thinking with his paranoia of being known as the president who lost the Vietnam War, and you've got a big problem. So no, I don't think we should be in Vietnam."

No one said anything after Bo finished speaking, including Miss Krenkle. After a few more seconds of silence, Miss Krenkle—who looked to be in a state of shock from Bo's surprise oratory—finally came up with a relevant followup question. "How is it that you seem to be so surprisingly well read on this subject, Bo?"

Bo hesitated before speaking as he gathered his thoughts. His eyes began to turn red, but he managed to fight back his tears. "Julie Applebee comes from a family of all girls, and her father is too old to serve in Vietnam. She doesn't understand the personal sacrifice that comes from this unwinnable war."

Miss Krenkle must have finally realized what Bo was talking about. Ben Bozell had also been one of her students a few years earlier. "Are you talking about your elder brother, Bo?"

"Yes," Bo replied. "We were told two days ago that he's missing in action. Since then, I decided to find out what he got himself into."

"What sources of material did you find to formulate your opinion on this subject, Bo?"

"I started by driving to Omaha and doing some research at the downtown library, and then I stopped at some bookstores. After that, I came back to town and visited a couple of neighbors who were over there."

Miss Krenkle's expression clearly showed a respect for Bo that he had never seen before. "You pursued your research using a very balanced approach, Bo. I'm impressed with your ingenuity."

Bo didn't really care at that point whether she was impressed or not. His teacher's praise or the attention he was getting at the time neither embarrassed nor invigorated him. His entire focus was on understanding why his brother was put in that situation in the first place. "None of that matters right now, Miss Krenkle. All that matters is that they find my brother alive. 1 wish he hadn't had to go over there. He shouldn't have had to go. 1 know we've fought wars that had to be fought, and someday, we'll probably have to fight another war that needs to be fought. I just don't think this war is one of them."

The classroom continued to be dead silent. Everyone seemed speechless and dumbfounded about how intelligently Bo had presented his case, especially since he didn't even seem to be paying attention when Julie Applebee was speaking.

"Bo, I'm sure I speak for the rest of the class in expressing our concern for your brother. This must be a very difficult time for you and your family," Miss Krenkle finally replied.

The bell rang, suggesting that the class time had expired. The students began to rise from their chairs while gathering up their books, allowing

Miss Krenkle time to make a final comment. "Today concludes our spring semester before your final exam on Thursday. Class dismissed."

It was late afternoon as a car pulled up in the back driveway at the Bozell house. Jerry, Bo's friend, was dropping him off from school again. He looked at Bo in the passenger seat after putting the gearshift in park with the engine idling. "That was really awesome what you said in history class today."

Bo shrugged as he looked back at his longtime friend. "Thanks, but I didn't say it to impress anybody. It's just how I feel."

"Bo, I don't have a brother that's in a war zone. But you know, I do have a sister who's away at college on the East Coast. I couldn't imagine us receiving a phone call someday that she was missing. I'm trying to understand, at least a little bit, what you and your family must be going through right now."

"Thanks for your concern, Jerry," Bo somberly replied.

Jerry moved the gearshift from park into reverse. He looked back at Bo, who was staring forward. "Listen, if you ever need somebody to talk to, I'm here for you."

Bo continued to stare through the windshield, seemingly a million miles away or at least halfway around the world anyway. "I know you are, Jerry. Thanks for the lift."

After rubbing his tired-looking eyes, Bo grabbed his books and got out of the car. Jerry gave a final wave before backing out of the driveway, speeding down the street, and turning right at the first intersection.

As Bo cradled his books under his arm, he walked over to the dog run to let Ace out. When he walked over to the gate, he could see that Ace wasn't in the outside portion of the kennel. "Ace! Come on out, boy!" Ace didn't come out through the doggy door after Bo had called for him. Bo stood there for a few more seconds, staring at the dog run. "Come on, Ace! It's too nice outside to be cooped up in the garage!"

After a few more seconds without his dog appearing through the doggy door from the garage, he went over to the side entrance, pulled his keys out of his pocket, unlocked the door, and entered the garage. He flipped on the light switch on the left just inside the door. Bo's jaw dropped when he saw that Ace wasn't in the kennel at all. He dropped his books in a heap on the garage floor. *Oh no,* he thought, wheeling around and running out of the garage.

He stopped in the backyard and yelled at the top of his lungs, "Ace!" Then he ran to the front yard and stopped to yell again as he looked all around him. He was starting to look panic stricken. "Ace! Where are you, boy?"

A little later that night, Bo, Henry, and Martha were finishing supper. The boy looked completely dejected as he moved his food around his plate with his empty fork. He had hardly touched his food. His parents didn't look much better. "Come on, Bo, you need to eat something," Martha urged her son.

"1 can't help it. First, Ben, and now Ace is missing. It's just too much," he replied, looking about as downtrodden as his mother had ever seen him.

"You drove around in the pickup for over an hour, son. It's a small town. You did all you could do for now," Henry said in sympathetic tone.

"No, I haven't done enough. That's why I called Bonnie," Bo answered.

Now no one was eating. There was a long silence as everyone stared into space around the dinner table. "You don't think Ace could have tried to find Lucy, do you?" Henry asked before finally forking a piece of his meat to resume eating.

Bo looked at his father and shook his head. "No, of course not. Lucy rode in the car. There wouldn't have been any scent trail to follow. Besides, it's too far away." He forlornly looked at the comer spot in the kitchen where Ace had always positioned himself during the evening meal.

They sat in silence for a minute before their son revealed that he had arranged a search party. He knew it was a long shot, but it was the best he could come up with for now. "What I thought we could try is for Lucy to see if she could follow Ace's scent out of the yard. They should be over within the next hour. We're going to give it a try."

Martha let out a deep sigh. "Just don't get your hopes up too high, son," she softly said. "Remember how Ace came into your life. Maybe he came for a reason, and now he's left for a reason."

Bo apparently couldn't hold back the tears anymore. "I don't want to even think that way right now. We'll find him, just like they're going to find Ben. You'll see."

Martha, so moved by her youngest son's emotions, couldn't stop her own tears from flowing. "I hope you're right, Bo. I know 1 pray for that. . . all the time."

"Ben and Ace are tough, Ma. I know I'm going to see them both again. 1 just know it," Bo said, with his voice rising.

"Bo's right, Mother. We have to keep the faith," said Henry.

The tears were running down Martha's cheeks in constant streams now. "Faith is all 1 have right now. I just hope it's enough," Martha choked out between sobs. Henry got up from his chair and walked over behind his wife, leaning down and giving her a hug.

B o was on the front porch in the early evening. He was leaning against the railing that surrounded the perimeter of the porch. Marvin's car rounded the comer and pulled up to the curb in front of the house. He and Tanya were in the front seat, and Bonnie and Lucy were in the back. They all got out of the car and walked up to Bo, who had stepped off the porch to greet them in the front yard.

Bonnie approached Bo with Lucy at her side. She used sign language to tell him how sorry she felt for him that both Ben and Ace were missing. She reached out and gave him a big hug. Bo looked into Bonnie's eyes after letting go from the embrace. "Thank you, and thank you all for coming."

Bonnie flashed a comforting brief smile at him before turning and using sign language to confirm to Marvin and Tanya what Bo had just said. Both of Bonnie's friends nodded back at Bo and smiled sympathetically.

Bo began to explain his game plan to the others. "Well, I guess the first thing to do is to take Lucy to Ace's kennel."

They all walked to the dog run. Bonnie squatted down and held Lucy's chin in one hand while signing to her dog with the other hand. The female boxer was only capable of understanding just a handful of hearing-impaired signals, but what she could understand made it seem very impressive to the casual observer. The boxer's beautiful young master stood back up, and Lucy immediately started sniffing around the dog run. Bonnie then looked at Bo and communicated to him in sign language.

Bo nodded. "I know she's not a bloodhound, but it's worth a try just the same," he answered.

Lucy sniffed all around the backyard while all four of the teenagers watched. The boxer went around to the front yard and sniffed all around the perimeter. Everyone followed her to the front yard. Lucy trotted back into the backyard and up to the dog run as everyone, once again, followed her. Bo looked at Bonnie. "Would Lucy have followed Ace's scent out of the yard and kept going?"

Bonnie signed an affirmative to Bo.

"You think so, huh. Well, this looks like a dead end. I've got another place we can try," Bo said as he started to walk away. He used sign language with Marvin, who nodded, and they all started to walk to his car. Lucy finally quit sniffing around the dog run and ran to catch up with the others after Bonnie had put her fingers to her lips and whistled for her dog, one of the few audible sounds she was capable of. They all piled into Marvin's car and drove away.

A few minutes later, they pulled into the high school parking lot, and everyone piled out of the car. They walked from the edge of the parking lot and into the grass next to the school. Bo led the way, motioning for everyone to follow him. They walked around the corner of the building and followed him until he stopped outside his history classroom. "Ace's scent might be around here," he told the others.

Bonnie stooped down and used sign language again with Lucy. Her boxer walked over to the window that was next to where Bo's seat had been inside the classroom. Lucy sniffed around on the ground for a little while.

Bonnie turned to Bo and used sign language.

"1 guess she can't pick up his scent?" he asked.

Bonnie shook her head no to Bo.

Bo couldn't hide his disappointment. He looked like he'd just had the wind knocked right out of him. He looked up at the darkening sky for several seconds. "Well, if you all don't mind, I'd like to ride around town for a little while."

Bonnie used sign language with Marvin. He nodded yes to her, and they all headed for his car. They drove all over Plattsmouth and then circled around the town on all the surrounding gravel roads. They saw several dogs, but it was never Ace.

Bo got all excited as they had turned from the last gravel road onto the paved highway that would take them back into town. There was a big dog that had just run up through the ditch and was heading into a cornfield. But as they got closer, everyone could see that it was some sort of mixedbreed dog, looking more like a Great Dane but stockier.

Marvin's car finally pulled up to the curb in front of Bo's house. It was starting to get dark. Bo and Bonnie got out of the back seat while the others waited patiently in the car for her to return after walking Bo to his front door. She walked with her obviously dejected new boyfriend side by side until they had slowly strolled up to the front porch steps and were standing together at the front door.

Bo turned to her before opening the screen door. "Thanks again for coming. I'm going to ask my mom to place an ad in the newspaper tomorrow. Maybe someone's seen him and will call." Bonnie nodded in agreement.

"Well, I better get going. I've still got two final exams to cram for." Bo started to turn away from her, and he reached for the door handle.

She grabbed his shoulder and gently pulled him toward her so that he was facing her again. She reached out to him, throwing her arms up over his shoulders and giving him a big long hug. Bo started to tear up. He blinked a few times, trying to will away his tears as he looked over her shoulder, feeling her warm and tender embrace and smelling the sweet smell of her perfume.

Bonnie finally released her grip on him, turned, and walked off the porch toward Marvin's car. After she had gotten back into the car and they were pulling away from the curb, Bo stood on the porch and waved to everyone. They all waved back before the car disappeared around the comer. He stood there a few seconds longer, scanning the neighborhood one last time before wiping his eyes with the back of his hand and opening the screen door, disappearing into the house.

The ride back to the Iowa School for the Deaf could only be described as a very solemn drive that night. It was always normally quiet unless Marvin was blasting his car radio, but no one seemed to be in the mood for head-thumping music on the drive home that evening. Bonnie sat in the back seat, slowly stroking Lucy's head, as they made their way to the highway that led back to Omaha and eventually to Council Bluffs. She had tears in her eyes not just for Bo because of Ace's disappearance but apparently also for more selfish reasons. She tapped on Tanya's shoulder soon after they had turned onto the highway for the ride home. She told her friend in sign language that she had come ever so close to telling Bo that she loved him.

Marvin was watching the road, but he wanted to know what Bonnie and Tanya were discussing. Tanya politely signed to him that it was a girl thing, just between her and Bonnie.

Bonnie poured her heart out to Tanya, telling her all the things that were on her mind as the old Plymouth rumbled down the highway as darkness fell.

She told Tanya that she couldn't believe that she had almost said those words to him. After all, she was only sixteen. She had only known Bo for just a few weeks. Her parents would have a cow if they knew that she was falling in love with a young man already. Bonnie's parents had consistently choreographed her life for as long as she could remember, and she told her friend that such thoughts about Bo didn't coincide with the finale that her parents had in mind for her.

She was remembering some of the first questions out of their mouths when she had come home from school that day, all excited about having met Bo. "Does he also have a hearing impairment? What does his father do for a living? Is he planning on going to college?" Tanya giggled as she watched her close friend mimic her parents.

Bonnie went on to say that when they finally met Bo for the first time, the questions continued in rapid-fire succession, some being questions that had been asked of her initially that she hadn't had an answer to at the time. Bo had charmed them both and, at least for now, had won them over.

Part of their acceptance may have had to do with the fact that Bo had only a partial hearing loss that enabled him to fluently converse both orally and with sign language if necessary. They probably would have been less accepting of the budding relationship had Bo either been totally deaf as she was or, worse yet, had perfect hearing. If Bo heard perfectly and didn't know or understand sign language, they probably would have perceived too huge of a gap in his ability to truly understand and appreciate their daughter.

After Bonnie's prediction of what her parents' reaction could have been, depending on Bo's ability to hear or not hear, Tanya signed back that maybe Bonnie was selling her parents short. Bonnie politely replied that she knew her parents well and that she was still convinced that their behavior, when meeting Bo, would have been lukewarm at best had Bo had perfect hearing.

As the car traveled through the darkening night back to Iowa, Bonnie finished her sign language conversation with Tanya by telling her that she would not reveal her true feelings to either Bo or her parents for a long time to come. She couldn't bear the thought of being forbidden to see him again, a consequence that was sure to result if she were to make her true feelings known. Tanya, who had always been a supportive and understanding friend, told Bonnie that she was very mature for her age and that such maturity would serve her well as she put her heart on hold for a while.

Bo was kneeling in the first pew of Saint Mary's Catholic Church near the altar. In a spur of the moment, he had decided to stop at the church after excusing himself from the supper table and going for a drive in Henry's pickup truck. The conversation during dinner had been very limited that night, only consisting in a short question-and-answer period concerning Bo's last two final exams he had taken earlier in the day.

An elderly woman appeared from the left of the altar before kneeling and moving her hand up and down with the sign of the cross. She slowly rose before silently passing in front of Bo.

There was a statue of Mother Mary off to the right side of the altar and another statue of Christ on the cross prominently displayed high above the center of the altar attached to the back wall just below a huge stained glass window depicting the Last Supper.

The church was old but beautiful. The altar and entrance areas had exquisite marble flooring, and there was lush deep-red carpeting down the center and side aisles of the pews. The handcrafted woodwork on the sides of the dark mahogany pews was obviously completed not just by a skilled craftsman but also by a true artist.

Bo continued to kneel, with his hands together in front of him resting on his forehead. A priest finally appeared near the altar and looked over in his direction. The priest was old and a bit hunched over with pale skin and an unruly mop of thinning gray hair. His deep-set hazel eyes looked warm and caring. He had on a black shirt with the white clerical collar, a rumbled-looking pair of black trousers, and black dress shoes that looked like they could use some polish.

Bo wasn't aware that the priest was there. The sanctity and solitude of such a holy place began to draw out of the troubled teenager his inner emotions as the boy's tears began to flow uncontrollably. He seemed to be deep in prayer and deep in despair as he began to sob loud enough for the priest to hear him.

The old priest walked over to him. "I don't mean to disturb you, but I just wanted you to know that I'm here for you if you need someone to talk to."

Bo looked embarrassed and tried to hide his deep emotions as he stood up. He wiped his eyes with his fingers as he rose, taking in a deep breath before answering the priest, "Thank you, Father, but all I really wanted to do was to come and pray for my brother."

The priest had a curious look on his face after listening to his comments. "Is your brother hurt?" he asked.

"No, he's missing in action in Vietnam." Bo uncontrollably sobbed in reply. The priest's face took on a look of genuine grave concern. He looked deeply into Bo's troubled red-rimmed eyes as he placed a comforting warm right hand on Bo's shoulder. "You do have a heavy burden. But you came to the right place. God will surely hear your prayers," the priest answered.

"I don't know, Father. I just don't know anymore," Bo said as he lowered his head, breaking away from the old priest's gaze.

The priest maintained his right hand on the troubled teen's shoulder before gently lifting Bo's chin so they were once again looking into each other's eyes. "God works in mysterious ways. Your faith is being tested right now. God's plan isn't always so clear at first. You must be patient and have faith that God is watching over your brother."

The boy continued to look into the old priest's eyes after the priest had lowered his hand from under his chin. "I'll try, Father. I'll try." Bo turned and slowly walked down the center aisle toward the front door. His footsteps were silent in the thick carpeting.

The priest stood and watched him as he was leaving. He finally called out to Bo, breaking the eerie, reverent silence of the sanctuary as the church was temporarily empty except for the two of them. "I've never seen you here before. Will you be back this weekend?"

Bo turned back toward the priest before he opened one of the two doors. "Probably not, Father. I'm not Catholic. My church was locked up right now. I figured a church is a church. Ya know what I mean."

The priest's face broke out into a grin. "Yes, I know what you mean. A church is a church. You're always welcome here, son."

As Bo pushed open the heavy door, it was made known that the goldplated hinges apparently needed lubrication. The resulting creaking sound as the door swung open echoed off the old sanctuary walls. He turned his head back one last time toward the priest before stepping through the door.

"Thanks, Father."

The second that Ace materialized behind Ben in the jungle, he could sense the fear in Bo's elder brother. The mastiff was sure that Ben hadn't yet detected his presence, so he knew that Ben's fear was probably being felt long before he had arrived on the scene. Ace realized within a few seconds of arriving that Vietnam was going to be the hardest part of his overall mission, both physically and psychologically.

Ace had been debriefed by the Big Guy Himself before arriving. He had never been sent directly into a war zone before. As part of his debriefing, he was made aware that there were other dogs from America there as well— the hundreds of military dogs that were serving their country and risking death, just like their twolegged masters.

Even as he arrived at night, he was immediately aware of how stiflingly hot and muggy it was. His respect for the other dogs that he knew were there was heightened upon dealing with the heat and humidity for the first few minutes. He felt sad for the dogs of war. After all, they had nothing whatsoever to do with the decisions that were made by humans who had forced them into such dangerous servitude. It wasn't their fault that human beings couldn't get along with one another. Packs of dogs had never waged major wars against another. Oh sure, a dog might get into a fight with another dog once in while over food or a territorial dispute, but it was seldom, if ever, an organized group effort. There was something to be said for simplicity of thought.

Knowing that Ben probably wasn't in a very calm state of mind anyway, Ace didn't want to scare him even more by materializing right next to him. He had to take a few strides toward Ben from behind him before being at his side, finally getting close enough to be literally leaning into him. Since he couldn't speak to Ben, Ace went about making him feel comfortable with his presence by using body language and some subdued but effective face licking. After receiving a couple of sloppy kisses, Ben had to know that he wasn't just hallucinating. He also had to know at that point that it was a four-legged friend, not a foe.

The other reason why the bullmastiff materialized a few feet from behind was to prevent Ben from having any awareness that he had special powers. He didn't want to chance Bo's elder brother developing a false sense of security. Ben was going to have to put forth a lot of effort on his own to get back to his base camp. More importantly, just because Ace was with him now didn't guarantee that he would make it back safely. Ace couldn't stop a bullet from killing him or Ben. He would stop a bullet for Ben by stepping between him and the would-be assassin, but then he would be dead (for a while) and no more help to Bo's brother at that point.

Ben started to talk to him shortly after he arrived. "Where did you come from, boy? Are you lost from your unit too?" It was kind of funny in a way because Ben started to talk to him like he was another human being, capable of understanding his every word. What Ben didn't know was that Ace could indeed comprehend his every word.

It was a bit challenging for Ace not to react to Ben's words every time in a totally understanding way for fear of freaking him out that he was in the company of someone (or something) very different and possibly scary. It was important that he play out his role as rescuer dog and nothing more than that. He had been making a few mistakes now and then back in Plattsmouth, but this was another matter. There wasn't any wiggle room for mistakes in the jungles of Vietnam. It was a time to draw on all the powers of the Holy Spirit to survive.

The first task at hand was to take Ben's empty canteen and find water. He found a stream a short distance away. He was glad that he had the cover of darkness because of his size. It wasn't going to be easy not being seen in broad daylight. Ace knew he was the Mack Truck of dogs. He was wishing he had the power to temporarily transform himself into a small terrier when the need arose.

Ben left the cap off the canteen, not worried about the possibility of Ace spilling some of the contents on the way back. Even in the dark, Ace could tell by the smell that the water he had found probably wasn't the most sanitary in the world, but he was confident that Ben wasn't going to dump it out and send him back out in search of something fresher. When he came back with the canteen, it was still full all the way to the top, a feat that didn't go unnoticed by his stranded, tired, and torn marine. "Good boy. You must have been really careful. What a good boy you are!" Before Ben took the canteen from Ace, he hugged the big dog as the canteen still hung by its straps in the mastiffs mouth.

It was obvious to Ace that Ben must have been worried that he might not come back (or make it back). Ben aggressively patted Ace on top of his head a few times before he finally grabbed hold of the canteen. Holding it with both of his trembling hands, he tilted it up over his head and took several gulps before coming up for air. If he thought that it tasted funny, he certainly didn't mention it to his new friend.

Ben informed Ace that they would wait until the next night before leaving the area where the dog had found him. He started to refer to Ace as Buddy, which was fine with Ace. At least he hadn't initially come up with some stupid name like his younger brother had a few weeks before. With Ace's help, Ben wanted to look for Danny before leaving. He knew his friend was dead, but he wanted to see if he could bury his remains before moving on. He told Buddy that he couldn't bear the thought of his friend's corpse being exposed to the elements indefinitely. He would have expected that Danny would have felt the same way had it been him who had stepped on the land mine.

Early the next morning at the break of dawn, Ace could finally see the extent of damage to the left foot and leg of Bo's elder brother. Ben had been dangerously close to Danny when his fellow corporal had tripped the mine and blown himself up, fulfilling the prophecy that must have been stuck in his head as they had left at dusk on patrol that fateful night. Ben's left boot was nowhere to be found. His foot looked like a bloody mushy mess, and there were other less serious-looking wounds along his left leg and side. It must have been a sad irony to Ben that it was his buddy's body that had taken the brunt of the blow, a powerful explosion of deadly, lethal shrapnel.

Ace found a branch that Ben was able to fashion into a walking stick. They found Danny's body about thirty feet away. Ace had known by the smell that the corpse was close by. And even though Ben's olfactory sense was inferior to Ace's, he also had to know. Both man and dog were respectful and solemn when they came on the body or what was left of it. Ben dropped to his knees and wept openly while Ace sat quietly by his side. The young marine suddenly looked up at the early morning sky. "Why, Lord? Why Danny? He was a good man! He had so much to live for!" Bo's brother then fell silent for a few minutes as he looked down on the body, his chest heaving in and out as tears continued to stream down his dirty, sunburned cheeks. He finally folded his hands, closed his eyes, and bowed his head.

While Ben said a prayer and his final goodbye to his friend, Ace quickly dug a shallow grave. It was Ace who dragged the remains of the body into the grave and then covered Danny over with loose dirt, using his front paws with rapid precision as he threw the dirt through his hind legs behind him. He even took a chance that Ben might become wise to his true intelligence when he found two sticks and some twine and brought it back to Ben, who sat staring down next to the freshly dug grave. Ben just looked up at him with a blank stare, seemingly in shock, before tying the twine around the two sticks in the shape of a cross. Either Ben's mind was elsewhere or it didn't really matter at that point that a dog seemed to understand the concept of the need for a cross on the grave.

After a few more minutes of mourning and quiet reflection, man and dog made their way back to their original hiding spot. Ben stayed well hidden in the brush throughout the daylight hours. Ace ventured out a couple of times for more water and to bring back some nuts and berries, which Ben wolfed down without questioning the possibility of them being poisonous.

A North Vietnamese patrol passed by within twenty feet of their hiding place in the midafternoon. As the patrol moved on by, Ace was just as scared as Ben was. They huddled together side by side, neither one making the least bit of a sound. Even with a bothersome fly that was buzzing around their faces at the time, neither man nor dog moved a muscle, not even a twitch. Only when the patrol was totally out of sight did they both breathe normally again, at least normal for being stranded out in the middle of enemy territory with thoughts of being potentially captured or killed.

The first night that they started to make their way back to Ben's base camp went off without a hitch. They passed by a couple of enemy campsites but always at a safe distance. Ace was able to make Ben understand that he needed to follow the dog's lead in such regard, allowing the dog's superior sense of smell to warn them of any possible danger.

It was a slow and tedious trip through the jungle at night, especially dealing with Ben's bum leg. The walking stick helped a lot, but there were times when they were struggling their way through thick mud and shallow water. Ben would have never made it through those barriers on his own. Sometimes his bad leg would literally get stuck in the mud, and he would have to hand the end of his walking stick or his rifle to Ace, who would chomp down on the other end and pull Ben along, sometimes only moving a few feet in an hour.

They found a new hiding place when daylight came again. Both man and dog had to endure the sweltering heat and the wicked sun that was beating down on them as they rested in some tall grass at the base of a hill. The second night of slow travel was even more difficult than the first. There was more mud and treacherous swampland to somehow trudge through one arduous step at a time.

Then the worst thing that could have happened transpired. They stumbled on an enemy camp. Ben was becoming too weak to try to evade the camp by half a football field's distance, which would have been the totally safe thing to do. Every yard gained toward their destination had become hard earned and precious, so Ben apparently decided to take the chance that he and Ace could slither on by without being detected.

There were three young Vietnamese men sitting around a low barely lit campfire. Ben scanned the area around the three soldiers. Ace sensed what his companion was thinking. Because of his debriefing, he expected to see other soldiers present, maybe sleeping, but there weren't any. He surmised that, like Ben, maybe they had somehow been separated from the rest of their squad.

As the two evening travelers were carefully and slowly treading their way around the unexpected barrier to their path toward safety, Ace couldn't help but listen to the enemy soldiers' conversation. Because of who the dog was and what he was, he could listen to them, while Ben didn't have a clue what was being said. One of the young soldiers had some pictures of home that he was holding close to the fire so his two other companions could see. He was telling them that one was a picture of his wife and the other was of his wife and two daughters. He told his fellow soldiers that he hadn't seen them for over a year. He said how he longed to be with them again, to be able to someday resume his life with his loving family.

Ace was struck by the young man's sentimental meandering. He thought about the fact that this young man had loved ones, just like Ben did, praying and hoping that their brave soldiers would someday return to them safe and sound. He thought about the fact that if Ben and this young man could really understand each other, understanding what each had at stake, it would be much harder to kill each other.

The whole tragedy of war was weighing heavily on Ace's mind when Ben stepped on a large twig that cracked in two under his weight. He and Ben stopped dead in their tracks and didn't move a muscle. The men around the campfire jumped up and grabbed their rifles, looking in the direction of the sound. At that moment, Ace couldn't be concerned with Ben's reaction to observing his disappearing act. He disappeared next to Ben and reappeared on the opposite side of the camp but still hidden from view behind a line of trees. "Woof! Woof!"

Ace had already reappeared next to Ben before the enemy soldiers had reacted to the barking with mild laughter, placing their rifles aside and sitting back down around the fire. Ace was counting on the fact that they would think an echo of the sound had made it seem like it was coming from the opposite direction. His quickly devised plan worked to perfection.

He was relieved for several reasons. He knew that Ben still had his gun and was prepared to use it if necessary. After listening to the enemy soldier's heartfelt desire to see his family again, he was tom by the fact that one of two families would more than likely be eventually grieving the death of their loved one if Ben would have been forced into firing his weapon. He was relieved that, at least for that moment, both young men still had a chance to someday see the people who gave meaning to their lives, a longing that had to be quickly put aside during the heat of battle.

Ace didn't think that these three enemy soldiers were likely to make it back home, however. For one thing, they shouldn't have built a fire, regardless of how small it was. They had failed to have at least one man standing out of sight as sentry, and they were uncharacteristically loud. He had been debriefed that both the Vietcong and the North Vietnamese regular army were resourceful and sneaky. None of the three soldiers they had avoided a battle with had struck him as matching that previous description. Maybe they were just tired—tired of war and tired of being paranoid for every waking second of their forced existence over the past year or more.

Once they were safely beyond earshot of that last enemy camp, Ben sat down and asked his new mysterious friend to sit down with him. He got into Ace's face at that point. "You know I saw what you did back there. How did you do that? Or more importantly, who are you?"

Ace looked back into Ben's eyes and starting whimpering and whining. The big dog then licked Ben's face before rising and starting to pad his way in the direction of where they were heading before Ben had stopped to talk to him. He could hear Ben mumbling to himself from behind. "Maybe I was just hallucinating," he heard him say as Ben strained to keep up with him on the solid mud-caked path that they had happened on only seconds before. Ace veered off from the path, knowing as Ben did that it wasn't a safe place to be unless you were a full squad with maximum firepower.

As they got closer to Ben's base camp, the enemy was nowhere to be found. It was good that they didn't encounter anyone else from the other side before making it back. It had been hard enough struggling through the dense jungle. Ace could tell that Ben's body was totally spent by the time the base camp had finally come into view. His bad foot was swollen so severely that even Ace couldn't bring himself to look at it.

Once the big dog was sure that Bo's elder brother was safe, he bolted away and disappeared in the thick underbrush. Ben stood reflectively for a couple of minutes, leaning on his walking stick before softly calling out the password that would prevent a friendly fire incident. He had gone through too much to ironically end up dead at the hands of other American soldiers.

As he was helped the last few yards by a fellow marine standing guard duty, Ben was mumbling to himself about whether he would ever see the mysterious savior dog again, which he undoubtedly owed his life to. "What are you talking about? What dog?" the sentry asked.

"Nothing. Never mind. 1 must have been hallucinating," Ben calmly replied.

As Ace ran through the underbrush before returning home, he was smiling, relishing the part of his missions тнat he enjoyed the most, the homecoming and the reunion.

Martha had just returned from visiting Ida in the hospital. Ida had been diagnosed a few months ago with pancreatic cancer. She had put up a good fight until the past couple of weeks. Unfortunately and predictably, the deadly cancer was finally winning out. She had gone back into the hospital several days ago, no doubt realizing that the end was now near.

Martha noticed that Bo was back from wherever he had gone to after supper. The pickup truck was back in the driveway, and a light was on in his second- floor bedroom as she walked up the sidewalk to the back door. Walking down the hallway from the kitchen, she passed by the entryway leading into the living room, where she saw that Henry was alone, having fallen asleep in his recliner while reading a book that was still lying open in his lap. She put her purse away in their bedroom and then returned to the kitchen, fixing a cup of hot tea before sitting down at the table with a troubled look on her face.

Ida didn't look very good. She had lost so much weight from what was a tiny frame to begin with. It was obvious that the pancreatic cancer was slowly killing her. The doctors had told Sam some time ago that there was nothing more they could do for his wife other than try to minimize her pain and suffering during her final days.

Sam wasn't at the hospital while Martha was visiting. It was just her and Ida in the room together. For most of the time that Martha sat in the chair, Ida just laid there with her eyes closed. Occasionally, her face would grimace from an unannounced jolt of pain. She finally opened her eyes and looked at Martha with a forced smile on her face. What Ida had finally said was being replayed in Martha's mind as she sat, sipping her cup of tea.

Ida had made a request—a request that Martha wasn't sure if she could accommodate. She had already chosen not to burden this dying woman, who was once her sister-in-law, with news that her son was missing in a war zone halfway around the world. But Ida's request bore a bigger burden and wasn't as clear cut and easy as the decision to withhold information from her about Ben.

Martha sat there, staring at the back door, as the pros and cons of whether she should do what Ida had asked her to do kept swimming around in her head. She glanced at the empty corner of the kitchen where Ace had laid in so many previous evenings while she had sipped her tea in quiet solitude. Finally, she slid out of her chair and walked over to the wall phone near the door. She grabbed the handpiece in one hand while dialing the number on the rotary phone. It was a number she had dialed many times before.

She walked back over to the kitchen table and sat down in her chair as the spiral phone cord was stretched to its limit from the wall. The phone rang so many times that she was about to give up, until finally it was picked up on the other end. "Hello," said the voice.

"Leonard, is Alice home?"

"No, she's working."

"She wants to see you, Leonard," Martha blurted out.

"Who is this?"

"What's the matter with you, Leonard? Don't you recognize your own sisterin-law's voice?"

"Oh, yeah. What do you want, Martha?"

"Ida wants to see you. She wants you to come up to the hospital."

There was a long silence. Martha was contemplating repeating her last sentence again.

"1... 1 don't think that would be a good idea," he finally replied.

"Listen, Leonard, I know you're probably having a tough time with all this. 1 wouldn't blame you if you chose not to go, but it seems to be very important to Ida. I at least think you should consider it. Okay?"

There was another long silence, until Martha asked again, "Okay, Leonard?"

"Yeah, okay. I'll think about it," he finally answered.

"I think Alice would understand if you went," Martha added.

There was more silence from Leonard's end. Martha was about ready to end the conversation and hang up. "Have you heard any more news about Ben?" Leonard asked, breaking the silence.

"No, not yet. But I'll be sure to let you and Alice know just as soon as we get news."

"What about Bo? How's he doing?"

"He's doing okay, Leonard."

"I'm going to hang up now." Then the phone went click as Leonard had hung up on Martha.

My, that went well, Martha thought sarcastically as she got up and returned the handpiece of the phone to the hook on the wall, secondguessing herself at that point for having made the call. I don't think Leonard's never gotten over his part in the bus accident. And now Ben is missing in action, and Ida is dying. How much more can the poor man take?

Visiting hours were almost over at the hospital. Ida was awake and staring at the closed door to her room. She had asked one of the nurses to help her apply some makeup after Martha had left. Questions and thoughts must have been running over and over in her mind as she longingly stared at the door.

Then the door came open, and Leonard stepped into the room. He stayed standing just inside the doorway. Ida smiled at him as she lay with her head and shoulders propped up on her pillows. "Leonard, you did come," she said in a very weak voice.

"Hello, Ida," he said in greeting as he tried to force a smile while still standing a little slouched over near the door.

"Please come and sit down next to my bed. It's okay, Leonard. I just have a few things I want to say to you."

Leonard hesitantly walked up closer and sat down in the same chair that Martha had sat in earlier in the evening. He was shocked at how frail Ida looked. The makeup had helped some, but it couldn't hide her sunken cheekbones, and her once beautiful blond hair was partly gray and stringy. Her eyes looked full of fear.

Ida seemed to look deeply into Leonard's eyes before she spoke. "Henry told me years ago what you tried to do on the day of your mother's funeral."

Leonard's eyes started to well up with tears as he looked longingly into Ida's eyes. He used his thumb to rub away the streams that began running uncontrollably down his cheeks while he remained solemnly silent.

Ida went on with her recollection of the past. "We were at a summer picnic that Sam had arranged for his employees. Henry might have had a couple of more beers than he should have that day. While Martha was busy talking with Sam and the others were playing horseshoes, Henry asked me to go for a walk with him. He told me everything that day."

The sudden change of expression on Leonard's face showed that he knew immediately what she meant by everything.

"Leonard, it was never your fault. You tried every way possible to make it work. I was the weak one. I was the one who gave up and went home to Daddy and Mommy with my tail between my legs. Maybe I was just too immature to handle it at the time. Even so, it was never your fault, Leonard, never your fault. And if I had found the strength to stand up to your mother on my own, I might never have left. Your mother might not have died when she did if I had stayed. Maybe God is punishing me now. I don't know. Maybe it's just my time to go."

The door to the room swung open again, and Sam walked in. Leonard looked at Sam while trying to wipe away his tears with his right hand. He got up to leave. "No, Leonard. You don't have to go. Please stay. I just stopped in to say goodnight. It's okay," Sam said in a reassuring tone. He went over and kissed his wife on the forehead before turning and leaving the room.

Leonard sat back down and looked at Ida. "No .. . you're wrong, Ida. It was my fault. I was her son. It was up to me to stand up to my own mother. Besides, I should have never put you in that position in the first place. It was too much to ask of anyone. God is not punishing you. He's punishing me because I failed you in your time of need."

Ida started to cry. She tried to speak between sobs. "Oh, Leonard ... my sweet Leonard ... 1 wish things had turned out differently for us. Don't get me wrong. I love Sam very much. He's been good to me all these years. It's just that. . . that... I have my regrets in life. I wanted you to know how I felt . . . before it was too late. And I wanted you to know that you shouldn't ever blame yourself. . . for my leaving ... or your mother's death."

Leonard leaned over and lay his head down in Ida's lap. He started to sob softly as she stroked the back of his head with her hand.

"It's going to be okay, Leonard. You're going to be okay."

Leonard laid there for a few minutes with his head in Ida's lap until the public address system announced for the second time that visiting hours were over. He had noticed that Ida had stopped stroking the back of his head. He looked at her with tearstained eyes as he gently placed her hand back by her side. She was sleeping peacefully when he walked quietly across the room before turning and looking at her one last time. He opened the door, having said his last goodbye to the woman of his dreams, the first woman whom he had ever loved.

o was still sleeping. It was early the next morning after he had said his prayers the night before at the Catholic church. Quite unexpectedly, Bo was getting his face washed by a familiar very big sloppy, warm tongue. He opened his eyes, not yet believing who was staring him in the face. A very muddy Ace was back. The still sleepy boy's eyes widened with excitement as he looked eyeball to eyeball with his beloved dog. "Ace! Where have you been, boy?"

Ace backed up a little bit and plopped his muddy butt down on the hardwood floor as Bo sat up in bed. The surprised boy wiped away the slobber from his face with his hand. He finally noticed how incredibly muddy his mastiff was. He started petting Ace on the head. The big dog's tail was wagging back and forth across the floor, leaving a cone-shaped outline of mud on the previously clean hardwood floor.

Even though Bo had already felt his dog's soft fur and had wiped away some doggy drool, he was hoping it wasn't all just a dream. "How did you get in here, Ace? I can't believe you're back. Man, you really need a bath." He could feel his whole body percolating with warmth that had only been felt once before— when Bonnie had first kissed him tenderly on the cheek at the high school dance.

His mother, Martha, interrupted his unexpected, joyful reunion as she jogged down the hallway toward his room, shouting at the top of her lungs, "Bo! Wake up! I have wonderful news!" Martha rapped loudly on his bedroom door.

"Come in, Mother!"

Martha started talking excitedly as she opened the door until she saw Ace. "They found your brother! They . ... when did he show up?" Martha stood there looking both profoundly happy and a little confused.

"They found Ben? When? Where?" Bo asked in rapid succession.

"All they could tell me so far was that your brother made it back to his base camp. He's been injured, but he's alive. He's alive!" Martha exclaimed.

The sudden mood swing that he was experiencing within a period of less than twelve hours was emotionally overwhelming but delightfully welcome. Bo had a look of relief and joy written all over his face as he spoke without looking at his equally emotionally charged mother. "Thank you, Father. You were right."

Martha didn't seem to have a clue what or who he was talking about or to whom. "Are you still half asleep? I'm your mother, son."

Bo realized that he was confusing his mother. "I know who you are, Ma. I was talking about someone else."

Martha had just gone through a multitude of emotions and surprises in the last few minutes. She answered, but she was on automatic pilot at that point. "Oh. I think I understand. Isn't it wonderful, Bo? I've never been so relieved and so happy in my entire life."

Bo couldn't help but feel a strong sense of compassion for his mother. Yes, he felt the warm glow of relief and satisfaction for himself, but it paled in comparison to seeing his mother at peace with life once again. "Me too, Ma, me too" was all that he could say.

Martha appeared to be calming down a little bit now. She took a couple of deep breaths as she stared at the big muddy dog before looking back at her son. "When did Ace come back? Did you hear him barking outside or something?"

Bo slid out of bed, so he was sitting on the edge. "No, he just woke me up before you came in."

Martha looked bewildered. She looked back at Ace, who was sitting near the bed, still covered in mud. "Well, how did he get into your room?"

Bo shrugged. "I don't know. I thought you or Pop let him in."

"Your father left for the shop over an hour ago. And I wouldn't have let Ace in if I'd seen how much of a muddy mess he was."

The cold, hard facts that were presenting themselves to Martha's racing mind must have set the wondering wheels in motion. "Wait a minute. I didn't see any mud in the hallway or kitchen. The only muddy paw prints are on your bedroom floor. How is that possible?"

Bo looked at Ace and then back at his mother. "I don't know, Ma, but someone just told me last night that God works in mysterious ways."

"Who told you that? What are you talking about?"

Bo kept staring at his muddy dog sitting patiently near his bed, his tail still swishing back and forth across the hardwood floor.

"Son, I asked you a question. Who told you that?"

"Never mind. I'll explain later."

Still sitting on the edge of his bed, Bo reached over and picked up his hearing aids, which were sitting next to his alarm clock on the nightstand. After placing them in his ears, he looked back at his mother. "Ma, I want to know more about Ben."

Martha looked a bit exhausted, so she plopped down on her son's bed. "You better get Ace cleaned up first, and then I'll tell you what I know while you're having some breakfast."

Bo stood up next to his bed as Ace just sat there, still wagging his tail and looking very glad to be home. Martha's youngest son looked back at his mother. "Have you told Pop, John, and Uncle Leonard yet?"

"I called the shop before coming to tell you. I could hear them whooping it up and hollering in the background as your father passed along the good news," Martha answered as she continued to look at Ace.

Bo sat back down next to his mother on the edge of the bed. "You sure I'm not dreaming, Ma? I mean, Ben and Ace turn up at the same time. This is just too good to be true."

Martha turned her head and looked into his eyes. "It is all a bit overwhelming. I still don't understand how Ace could have ended up back in your bedroom this morning. His disappearance and then suddenly showing up again in your bedroom—it has me totally baffled. 1 know he's not a ghost because I've watched him eat and do 'the other' in the backyard."

"What are you trying to say, Ma?"

Martha seemed to be deep in thought as she looked back at the mastiff, which continued to sit on the bedroom floor with his tail wagging. "I don't know. I just don't know. It's got me spooked, that's all."

They both fell silent for a few seconds as they continued to sit and look at the dog. "So what do you want to do about it?" Bo finally asked.

"What can we do? I guess he's just a special dog, and we'll have to leave it at that for now. Just get him cleaned up while I get some breakfast going for you," Martha finally answered. She finally got up to leave. "Scrambled eggs and bacon sound okay?"

"Woof!"

Martha started to leave the bedroom. "I wasn't talking to you, Ace," she said over her shoulder as she disappeared into the upstairs hallway.

Bo led Ace into the upstairs bathroom as he watched the top of his mother's head disappear down the stairway to the first floor. He told Ace to hop into the tub. The big dog obeyed immediately without complaint, although he didn't exactly hop into the tub. It was more of a slow and calculated stepping into the tub.

Bo pulled out a couple of big bath towels from the bathroom closet. He then grabbed the showerhead that was attached to the tub faucet with his right hand while using his left hand to turn the hot-and-cold knobs to specific degrees that would produce the perfect blend of warm water. He proceeded to move the end of the showerhead back and forth along Ace's back. Any dog lover who can recognize whether his or her dog was smiling can appreciate the look that was on Ace's face at that moment. It really was a more complex look than just smiling. It was more of a combined look of relief, happiness, and "a job well done" feeling.

Once Bo had scrubbed all the mud off while Ace was on all fours, he asked the dog to lift one paw at a time behind him so he could rinse off his paws. What Bo discovered under the first paw sent him back in his mind to the morning that he had found broken shards of glass between his paws. But this time, it was much worse. There were thorns stuck in Ace's paw pads, lots of them. And they weren't all the same in thickness and texture either. There were even parts of leaves that had been impaled between the paw pad and the thorn or stem or whatever it was. Bo was certainly no botanist, but it was easy for him to tell that Ace must have gone on quite a long trip while he was gone because he seemed to have a little bit of everything stuck in his paws.

Bo was in awe that his big dog had even been able to still walk. He remembered how his gentle dog had gingerly stepped into the tub. No wonder, Bo was thinking. He felt bad for his new loyal friend—a friend that he thought he had lost forever until just a few minutes ago.

Martha was frying the bacon in the skillet when Bo dashed into the room, going straight to the "junk drawer" and extracting an old pair of needle-nose pliers. "What are you doing, Bo?" she asked as she looked at him intently.

"I'm still cleaning Ace up," he said over his shoulder as he hurriedly left the room.

"With pliers?" he heard her ask as he made a beeline for the stairway that led up to the upstairs bathroom.

Several minutes later, Bo was standing in the kitchen, peering at Ace through the screen door. It was the beginning of June now, so the inside door was wide open to let in a refreshing morning breeze. Bo was watching his obviously hungry dog wolf down his dry dog food.

Martha finished preparing his breakfast at the counter, brought it over to the table, and sat down next to where he would sit. "Breakfast is ready. Come and sit down before it gets cold."

Bo turned around and walked to the kitchen table, taking his seat next to his mother. "Wherever Ace was, he must not have gotten much to eat. He's eating like there's no tomorrow," he said. The boy finally dug into his breakfast as Martha sipped on a cup of coffee.

"Why did you need the pliers, Bo?" she asked after lowering her cup to the table.

"He had a few thorns in his paws—no, not a few, quite a few actually."

"Oh my. I wonder where he's been. Was there a lot of blood when you pulled out the thorns?"

Bo got a funny look on his face. He turned back toward the screen door and watched as Ace continued to wolf down his supersized bowl of dog food. He finally looked back at Martha. "There was hardly any blood after I pulled out the thorns. Within seconds, the blood stopped flowing every time."

Martha looked surprised. "What do you mean?"

"I'm telling you, there were a whole bunch of puncture wounds that looked deep and wide in his paws that just seemed to close up and stop bleeding right after I yanked the thorns out with the pliers."

"Come on, son. After what you've just told me about the thorns, there had to be more blood than that, and I can't believe that the puncture wounds could have closed up so quickly."

"Ma, I know you think it sounds a little crazy, but I saw it with my own eyes."

Martha just shook her head and turned her attention back to the frying bacon. Her son's breakfast had been prepared first. Now she was fixing her own. She finished up with the bacon, dropping them onto a couple of paper towels folded together. She proceeded to break two eggs on the edge of the skillet, dropping them in, one big sizzle at a time, before she broke the yokes with her spatula and whipped up the eggs into a duller color of yellow. She finally turned her head back in her son's direction and looked at him longingly. "I'm happy for you that he's back, son. I know how much he means to you."

Mother and son continued to reflect on all the morning's events as they sat in silence for a few minutes as Bo gobbled down his scrambled eggs with bacon. Finally, Bo broke the long silence. "Well . . "Well what?" Martha asked.

"Are you going to tell me more about Ben or not?"

Martha rubbed her face with her open hand. "I'm sorry, my mind's been racing a million miles an hour this morning." She smiled at her youngest son, apparently appreciating the fact that she really did have something to smile about again. "Yes, getting back to Ben, it was a marine officer who called and talked to me. He couldn't go into much detail other than to tell me that Ben finally made it back to his base camp after he went missing from an overnight patrol for almost a week. His left foot and leg are badly injured, so they've taken him by helicopter to a medical facility. He assured me it wasn't life threatening and that, as soon as they knew more, they would be calling again."

"That's it? That's all they told you?"

"Well, at least we know he's alive and not a prisoner of war or something," Martha replied.

"Yeah, I guess you're right. We know he's okay, and that's the main thing. So how long do you think it will be before we get more news?"

"He couldn't tell me when we would be getting a call again." She went back to drinking her cup of coffee as her son finished his breakfast. Apparently, both mother and son were emotionally spent about the surprise safe return of son, brother, and devoted dog.

The topic of conversation changed abruptly to a much lighter subject. "So now that school's over, what did your father say about you working at the shop again this summer? He hasn't said anything about it to me," said Martha. "Pop said I could sleep in this morning and take it easy today, but he's expecting me back at the shop first thing tomorrow morning. Boy, I can't wait to be the shop gofer again this year," he sarcastically replied.

Martha glanced at her youngest son with a sympathetic look. "Now that you have your driver's license, maybe your father will let you drive the tow truck once in a while this summer."

Bo rolled his eyes as he finished off his last piece of toast and jam. "I'm not holdin' my breath that's gonna happen." He finished gulping down his glass of orange juice as Martha got up and went to the kitchen sink to wash up the dirty dishes and the oily skillet.

Finally, Ace started barking from the dog run to let his young master know that he was done eating and wanted to come inside the house. Bo got up from the kitchen table and walked out through the door to the backyard. He let Ace out of the dog run, and the big dog followed him back into the house; his tail was wagging back and forth all the way into the door. His very tired-looking dog lay down in the corner of the kitchen and started to take a nap as Bo sat back down at the kitchen table.

"Ma, you know what you were saying earlier about Ace? Well, something strange happened several weeks ago, and I didn't say anything to you and Pop because I was afraid that you'd make me get rid of him."

Martha turned around from the kitchen sink and gave Bo a reassuring look. "Son, you don't need to worry about that happening, not unless Ace suddenly got vicious and hurt someone or something. I mean, he saved your life. We'll never be able to repay him for that." Apparently, it finally registered with Martha what her son had just said. "So tell me what happened."

Bo looked at Ace in the corner and then back at his mother, who was still standing in front of the kitchen sink. She turned her head and was staring at him before he continued with his story. "It was just a normal night. Ace slept next to my bed, just like he always does. But when I woke up the next morning, I noticed he had some dried blood and pieces of glass stuck in his paws. After I got him cleaned up, I checked all over the house, but I couldn't find anything he could have gotten into. It was really weird."

Martha turned her head back around, looking into the sink of sudsy water and dishes that she had her hands immersed in as she scrubbed a plate with her dishcloth. "Are you sure he wasn't like that when you two went to bed the night before?" she asked with her back to Bo.

"No way, I would have noticed."

"Hrnmrn, kind of similar to what just happened this morning, isn't it?" she commented as she turned and faced her son again. This was a difficult moment for Martha because the whole aspect of it was totally new territory for her. Supernatural events hadn't ever been anything that she had even had to think about before. Fortunately, her upbringing and her lifelong open-mindedness took over her thought processes when push came to shove, guiding her into the unknown.

"That's why 1 thought I better finally tell you about the other time," Bo answered. "And there's more weird stuff. The second day I was back at school, 1 thought 1 saw Ace staring at me through the classroom window. The teacher distracted me, and when I looked again, he was gone. Ma, 1 locked him in the dog run that day. There's no way he could have gotten out and then back in, unless . . ."

Martha interrupted Bo's trancelike thoughts. "Unless what, Bo?"

"You don't want to know what I'm thinking, Ma."

Martha looked into his eyes as she had so many times before. "I already know, son. I already know." She went back to doing her dishes in the sink for a couple of more minutes before resuming her conversation with her son. She spoke with her back turned as she kept scrubbing the dishes. "I think it's time for Ace to go to the vet and get checked out. In fact, I wasn't thinking. We should have done that right after you got out of the hospital. I'll call Carol's assistant before I go to work this morning and see how soon we can get him in."

Bo understood that Ace probably should be checked for fleas and ticks and stuff like that, but he still looked a little puzzled. "How is having Ace checked over by Doc Lange going to help us figure out how he seems to be able to get in and out of the house without any help?"

Martha shrugged after her son's legitimate question. "I don't know. It's the only thing I can think of doing right now. Besides, he probably needs to get some shots or something."

Ace had been lying motionless with his back to Bo and Martha, but as soon as Martha brought up the word "shots," he let out a long low, moaning sound. Bo turned around in his chair and looked at the big dog in the corner of the kitchen. "Hey, I thought you were sleeping."

In the following afternoon, Ace found himself sitting on one of Carol Lange's examining tables. Bo was standing close by as Carol was finishing her initial examination. "Well, Doc, what do you think so far?"

Carol was in the middle of examining Ace's teeth and jaws. She answered Bo as she had the dog's mouth wide open. The big dog had been an accommodating model patient so far. "He seems like he's pretty healthy, Bo. I'd guess he's only about two or three years old. There is one odd thing I've determined though."

Bo's expression suddenly turned sour. "What's that, Doc?"

Carol Lange finally let Ace close his mouth. "This dog has one of the slowest resting heart rates of any animal I've ever examined."

Bo knew from one of his science classes that that was usually a good thing. His sour expression turned into a smiling face. "Wow, I knew there was something special about him."

Carol gently patted Ace on top of his head before she turned and walked over to one of the cupboards on the wall above a long counter area.

The big dog continued to sit passively on the examining table.

"So now what?" Bo asked.

"Going on the assumption that he may never have had any of his shots, I'm giving him a rabies and heartworm injection before you take him home." She had her back to Ace and Bo as she prepared the two shots. She left one of the needles on the counter and turned around so that Ace could see she had a needle in her hand when she approached him. "Okay, big fella, you've been a perfect patient so far. Just a couple of little shots here, and you can be on your way."

When Ace realized what was finally about to happen, he rose and began to bark as he jumped off the table. He knocked over a tray that clanged to the floor and headed for the door, which was partially open. Carol was obviously startled by this sudden turn of events as she was almost bowled over by the rampaging mastiff as he hurried by her. Bo was just standing there with his mouth hanging open, taken completely off guard by Ace's sudden unpredictable behavior.

Ace swiftly reached the door, inching his big nose into the partial opening. The door flew open all the way, banging into the wall stop and bouncing back to being partway closed again. The big dog ran down the hallway, woofing all the way, with Carol and Bo giving chase. The sound of other dogs barking in response to Ace's outburst could be heard throughout the entire veterinary clinic once her previous model patient had begun his unannounced escape from big bad Carol Lange. "Ace! Come back, boy! Doc's not gonna hurt you! Ace!" Bo yelled down the hallway.

A few minutes later, Ace was back on the examining table. Bo was gently stroking him on the head. Dr. Lange was not in the room. "You just caused quite a ruckus around here. You realize that, don't you?"

"Woof!"

"No, don't speak, no more barking till we're outa here." He removed his hand from the top of his dog's head. "Now have 1 ever done anything to hurt you before?"

Ace threw his head back and forth sideways as he moaned a little bit.

"No, 1 haven't, have I? Now I'm tellin' ya that Doc Lange is not going to hurt you. All she's gonna do is give you a couple of little shots that you need so you won't get sick someday. So don't be such a big wussy and take your medicine like a man—I mean, dog. Oh, you know what I mean." Bo leaned in and got eyeball to eyeball with his dog. "So do I have your promise that you'll let the doc do what she's gotta do when she gets back in here?" Ace raised his paw in front of his young master, extending it toward him. Bo extended his right hand and grabbed the big extended paw, and they shook on it. "That's better. I knew you'd finally come to your senses."

Carol Lange came walking back into the room, with her assistant following her. The assistant, Mindy, closed the door tightly behind her. The look on Dr. Lange's face revealed her apparent surprise at seeing how calm Ace seemed to be now, such a short time since being a major pain in her clinic. "Is this the same dog that caused such havoc only minutes ago? The same dog that trashed my waiting room and scared the daylights out of Mrs. Parker and her pet poodle?"

Bo cracked a smile. "He's okay with getting the shots now, Doc. I just had to have a little heart-to-heart talk with him, that's all."

"Are you sure, Bo? We do have other methods of giving him the shots if we have to."

Bo's smile evaporated into a look of solemn seriousness. "Nah. Trust me, Doc. He'll let you give him the shots now."

Dr. Lange walked back over to the counter area to get the first needle injection.

"Okay, Bo, I'll trust your judgment. Mindy, you can go back to the front desk now." Mindy slowly turned and left the examining room, taking one last anxious glance over her shoulder at the big bullmastiff before she closed the door tightly behind her.

Carol turned back around and walked very slowly over to Ace. This time, he sat perfectly still while she gave him the first shot and then the second, only flinching slightly each time. Bo stood next to Ace and stroked him on his head as the vet administered the two shots. Carol turned back around to dispose of the needles. "I don't know what you said to him, Bo, but I'm thinking I should hire you."

Bo started to blush. "Thanks, Doc, but it really doesn't have anything to do with my talents. It was Ace who made the decision to cooperate. I don't have any magical touch when it comes to other animals."

Carol continued talking with her back to Bo and his dog. "So Ace is a smart one, huh? Okay, Ace, you can go home now." The bullmastiff immediately jumped down off the examining table and trotted over to the door, staring at it as Bo caught up with him. Carol turned around to see that the big dog was waiting at the door. "You understood what I just said to you, didn't you, Ace?" Carol said, smiling at the dog.

"Woof!"

Bo gave Ace a little slap to his butt. "Hey, I said no barking until we're outside, remember?" The disciplined dog moaned a little bit as Bo opened the door for him, and they both disappeared through the doorway.

As they were leaving, Ace was having another conversation in his mind. *It wasn't that I was afraid of getting stuck with the needles. I just thought, you know, that I wouldn't be able to travel places anymore if I needed to. What? You would have warned me ahead of time? Well, now You tell me. Uh, no disrespect, of course.*

S am Goldstein was still tossing and turning in bed. It was well after eleven o'clock on a Sunday evening. It had been a few hours since he had left the hospital. His wife, Ida—thanks to a strong sedative—was finally sleeping peacefully when he had gently kissed her forehead and slipped out of her room. Sam made a comment at the nurses' station that he was always relieved for his suffering wife when she could finally sleep again for a few hours at most. It was the only time she could escape the constant pain that accompanied her battle with the deadly cancer.

He was seemingly startled as the ringing of his bedside phone broke the dead silence and the predictable loneliness that permeated the bedroom that he had shared with Ida for over twenty-five years of marriage. On the line was Sgt. Bill Bradford of the Plattsmouth Police Department. "Sam, I'm sorry to have to be the bearer of bad news, especially when I can only imagine what you and Ida are going through right now."

"What is it, Bill?"

"It's your pharmacy. It's apparently been burglarized. Doug discovered it on his eleven o'clock rounds."

"How bad is it?"

"We're not sure yet. You better get down here as soon as you can."

Sam threw the covers off and swung around, sliding his bare feet into his slippers on the floor next to the bed as he still held the phone to his ear. "I'll be there as soon as I can," he said before placing the handset back down onto the mount, disconnecting the call. He put on his eyeglasses, which were folded up on the nightstand next to the bed; stood up; and started unbuttoning his pajama top.

Two police cruisers were parked in front of the pharmacy as Sam swung into the parking lot in his blue Buick and parked in the first stall just around the comer from the front door. Sergeant Bradford was standing by the door as Sam approached him. "Where's Doug?" Sam asked.

"He's inside. Would you disarm your perimeter alarm and unlock the front door for me, please?" Sergeant Bradford asked of Sam, who was standing in front of him by then.

Sam had a puzzled look on his face. "But how did he get inside? How come the alarm didn't go off?"

"You'll see once we're inside," Bradford replied.

Sam disarmed the alarm and unlocked the front door. He entered first, followed by Bradford. Doug was standing in the back with his flashlight illuminating the darkness until Sam switched on all the lights. It wasn't immediately obvious that anything was missing as Sam and Sergeant Bradford walked to the back of the pharmacy. Sam Goldstein looked at Doug. "How did you get in here?"

"The same way the burglar did, Sam," Officer Doug Richey replied. "He came up through the trapdoor from your cellar. You must have forgotten to latch it. Once he broke the padlocked latch on your outside cellar doors, it was easy entry for him into the upstairs. The wood on your cellar doors has rotted. He must have used a crowbar or something to pry one side of the latch out of the wood. The lock is still on the latch, with the right side of the latch ripped loose. As soon as I saw that, I knew something was wrong."

"Damn it!" Sam exclaimed. "With all the rain we had this spring, I mighta known it was time to replace those doors again."

"Why wasn't the trapdoor latched, Sam?" Sergeant Bradford asked as he stared at the open trapdoor.

"Remember the tornado warning we had late this afternoon? We locked the front door, and we all went down into the cellar until we heard on the radio that the storm had passed. I was the last one up. It's my fault. The phone was ringing when I stepped out of the hole. Everyone else was already outside, looking at the sky. I let the trapdoor back down before I took the call because 1 didn't want one of my employees falling through the hole after coming back in from outside. After I took the call, I must have forgotten to slide the dead bolt back in place."

Officer Richey and Sergeant Bradford just looked at each other and shook their heads. "Sam, you've got bars on the back windows. You've got alarm foil on your front windows and magnets on your front and back doors. You left yourself vulnerable by not keeping those cellar doors alarmed," Bradford said as he looked at Sam with a sympathetic expression.

"Yes, yes, I know that, Bill. Don't you remember meeting me down here in the middle of the night several times over the past few years because some animal must have walked across the cellar doors, breaking the contact on the magnets and setting off the alarm? It just became a big nuisance, so I had the alarm company come out and disconnect it. While they were here working on the cellar doors, 1 got to thinking that instead of just disconnecting it, 1 should have them rewire it and move the alarm to the trapdoor, but they had already left by the time I went outside to tell them. Then I kept forgetting to call the Omaha office to have them come back out again. Besides, I figured nobody was going to be able to get through the trapdoor with the dead bolt lock on the top side anyway," Sam offered in his defense. "By the way, you said 'burglar' as in one person. How do you know there was only one?"

"Because we found only one set of fresh boot prints in the muddy ground outside the cellar doors and on the mud-caked steps leading down into the cellar," Officer Richey answered.

Sergeant Bradford looked like he was getting tired. His shift should have been over by now. He probably saw himself at home, having that first can of cold beer in front of the television, while his wife of twenty years would be snoring in the back bedroom. "Well, look around thoroughly, Sam, and tell us what you think is missing. Don't touch anything though. We'll be dusting for fingerprints later. So far, all Doug's noticed is some stuff knocked off the shelves in the last aisle by the pharmacy counter. Kind of weird, but your wall clock got knocked off the wall as well. The time on the clock reads 10:13 p.m. before it was disconnected from the wall socket."

Sam briskly walked up and down the aisles in front of the pharmacy. After walking along the last aisle, where some toiletry articles and the clock were lying on the floor, Sam headed to the back room. Before Bill and Doug could catch up with him, they heard Sam call out, "Oh no!

There's a whole shelf full of drugs missing back here!" Sam was staring at the empty shelf when Bill and Doug finally joined him.

"What kind of drugs were on that shelf, Sam?" Sergeant Bradford asked.

"ft was all our prescription pain medication. Whoever did this must have known exactly what they were looking for. They would have had to have some medical knowledge to be able to read the labels and know what was worth taking," Sam replied.

"Any estimate on the dollar amount, Sam?" asked Bradford.

Sam took off his eyeglasses with one hand and reached up and scratched the top of his bald head with the other while Bill and Doug waited for his reply. "Hard to say until Martha and I go over the inventory sheets tomorrow morning." He rubbed his eyes before putting his glasses back on.

"Pretty daring for someone to do this at that time of the evening. Most store burglaries occur in the wee hours of the morning," said Officer Richey. "I wonder if the burglar knew that we don't make our first rounds of the downtown businesses until eleven."

Sergeant Bradford looked at Richey. "It would appear to me that whoever did this was familiar with our procedures. I think it might be time to change our schedule around a bit so we're not so predictable from now on." He then turned his attention back to Sam. "You close at six on Sundays, don't you?" asked Bradford.

"Yeah, six on Sundays and nine every other day of the week."

"You don't usually work on Sundays yourself, do you, Sam?"

"No, usually, it's Rick and Terri filling the prescriptions on Sundays. Terri's been sick the last couple of days, so I worked this weekend for her. Damn the luck. I know Terri would have remembered to make sure the trapdoor was locked up again. Or even if Martha had been here, she always makes sure stuff like that gets done. Unfortunately, Martha doesn't normally work on weekends," Sam said. He continued to stare at the empty shelf.

"Now, Sam, no point in beating yourself up over this. It could have happened to anyone. Besides, I'm sure you've got a lot on your mind lately," Bradford said as he placed his hand on Sam's shoulder.

"Yeah, you're right about that, Bill. I've got a lot on my mind lately, too much, in fact."

It had been two days since the burglary at Sam's Pharmacy. There had been a front-page article in the local paper, as well as an article in the local section of the Omaha newspaper. It was the first time that the pharmacy had ever been broken into. Besides the details of the burglary, several longtime residents of Plattsmouth had been quoted about their concerns over criminal elements infecting a town that had remained relatively crimefree until recently.

People who used to not even bother to lock their doors at night were sadly awakened to the fact that Plattsmouth wasn't the sleepy little safe haven it used to be. Unfortunately, the times were changing. In recent years, there had been an influx of people from larger cities such as nearby Omaha. To many of the longtime residents of Plattsmouth, these newcomers were not always welcomed with open arms. The burglary had only heightened their fear and distrust of anyone who wasn't born and raised in Plattsmouth.

Randy Whitfield would have been one of the first people whom these longtime residents would mention as an example of someone who should have never moved to town. When Randy; his girlfriend, Brenda; and their little boy, Trevor, first moved into the neighborhood across the street from the Bozells, everything seemed normal enough about them other than the fact that they weren't married. Randy had a pretty good job to begin with, while Brenda initially stayed home to care for their son. Then that dramatic change had occurred in Randy. Only Rita and David next door, and Martha because of recent conversations with Rita, knew that he hadn't been so scary to be around lately.

For the rest of the people in their neighborhood, no one seemed surprised when two police cruisers pulled into the driveway of his home late in the afternoon of the second day after the burglary. Randy was washing dishes in the kitchen, which was in the back of the house. The kitchen window above the sink overlooked the backyard. Randy was, at first, oblivious to the fact that he had visitors in his driveway. His son was over at the closest park, playing with Rita's kids as Rita looked after them.

Officer Doug Richey and another police officer exited their squad car, which had pulled in behind Sergeant Bradford's cruiser. Bradford was already out of his car as they approached. Bill Bradford was much taller than the two junior officers were. He towered over them both. "Doug, you cover the back door. Mike, I want you to stay off to the side of the front porch while I serve the search warrant." The two younger officers nodded as they took their positions.

Randy heard the loud knock at the front door. He dropped the pan he had been scrubbing back into the dishwater, turned, and dried his hands on the hand towel that was draped through the handle on the refrigerator. Before he left the kitchen, there was a second series of even louder knocks coming from the front door. The inside front door was open, so when Randy walked into the living room, he seemed surprised to see Sergeant Bradford standing on the front porch outside the screen door. He would have been even more surprised had he seen the other younger officer with his hand on his revolver off to the side of the porch.

Randy stopped when he reached the inside of the screen door. He knew who Bradford was. He was one of the officers who had come to the house on previous nights when their older neighbors to the west had called and complained about the noise when he and Brenda had been arguing.

"Randy Whitfield," Bradford declared as he stared through the screen door at Randy, revealing some papers that were in his left hand and were previously hidden from view behind his back.

"You know who I am, Bradford," Randy replied with a perplexed look on his face.

Sergeant Bradford continued as though he hadn't even heard what Randy had just said, "Randy Whitfield, 1 have a search warrant to search the premises of your property."

Randy's jaw dropped. He looked genuinely stunned. "Is this some kind of joke?"

"No joke, Whitfield. Please step out onto the porch and leave your hands where I can see them."

As Randy slowly opened the screen door and walked out onto the front porch, he could see some of the neighbors who happened to be home at the time standing out on their porches, trying to see what was going on. Two curious young boys on their bicycles had stopped at the front curb of his front yard. Randy finally became aware of the other officer who was standing in the driveway next to the porch because the young cop yelled at the two boys, "Move along, boys! Nothing to see here!"

The boys quickly pedaled away down the street, stopping and turning their bicycles around a few houses down the block so they could still observe an occurrence that used to be rare for the neighborhood. One of the boys turned to his friend. "I wonder what he did this time." The other boy just shrugged as they both kept their eyes trained on Randy's front porch.

Sergeant Bradford handed the search warrant to Randy to examine. He glanced at the warrant and then handed it back to Bradford. Randy was dressed in a white T-shirt and jeans with tennis shoes on. When it was obvious that he didn't have a weapon, the young officer off to the side of the porch took his hand off his bolstered gun. Bradford had such an imposing presence about him that no one who was unarmed would ever think that they could overpower him unless, of course, they were either crazy or incredibly stupid. Even though Randy had acted surprised, he still seemed relatively calm, and no one had ever accused him of being stupid— mean, yes but not stupid.

There were a couple of chairs on the front porch. Bradford motioned to them with a nod. "Why don't we both take a seat while Officer Richey and Officer Stapanek carry out the search?" Randy plopped down in the chair closest to the front door while Bradford sat down in the outside chair next to the side of the porch that was closest to the driveway. The long narrow driveway led to the single-car garage that was farther back in the lot.

At least twenty to thirty minutes had elapsed since Randy and Sergeant Bradford had sat down on the front porch. To Randy, it seemed more like two hours. There were several more neighbors milling around now and visible in the neighborhood. Two retired older men were standing and chatting with each other on each side of a low fence that separated their two yards across the street and a few houses down to the east.

It didn't appear that Sergeant Bradford had noticed them or any of the other curious onlookers since he and the other officers had arrived as most of his attention was obviously focused on Randy. They had talked briefly after they had first sat down, but for the past several minutes, they sat together in silence. "So when do you think your neighbor will be back with your son?" Bradford finally asked.

"Hard to say. I'm hoping not anytime soon though," Randy replied. Bradford must have known what Randy meant by that. He had often told his wife about observing the obvious embarrassment by a parent who was in trouble with the law in front of his children many times before. With what he knew about Randy's past, though, he probably was a little surprised that Randy would be thinking that way.

The front screen door opened, and Officer Stapanek stepped out onto the front porch, keeping his eyes trained on Randy the whole time. Before Sergeant Bradford could say anything to Stapanek, Officer Richey yelled for him from in front of the garage in the backyard, "Bill!"

Sergeant Bradford turned and slid his chair back far enough to lean his head back over the side of the porch and see Doug Richey standing there, holding up a big plastic bag in one hand and a pair of old cowboy boots in the other. Bradford looked back at Officer Stapanek, who was nodding yes. He then stood up and looked down at Randy, who had remained seated. "Okay, Whitfield, stand up and turn around. Face the wall and put your hands behind your back."

Randy might have been thinking that he was having a bad dream as Stapanek pulled his handcuffs off his belt and slapped them on his wrists as the side of his face was pressed up against the siding of his house on his own front porch. Sergeant Bradford then read Randy his rights before telling him, "You're under arrest, Whitfield."

While all this was going on, Rita had come walking up the sidewalk, returning from the park with Trevor and her own children. Officer Stapanek was leading Randy in handcuffs down the steps of the porch and toward the last patrol car in the driveway. Rita had a shocked look on her face. Her children were cowering close to her, obviously frightened by the police presence in the Whitfield front yard.

Little Trevor, on the other hand, seemed to show no fear as he bolted away from Rita and went running up to his father. Officer Stapanek held on to Randy's right arm as he escorted him ever closer to the rear left door of the squad car. "Daddy, Daddy!" little Trevor screamed. He kept running until he reached his father, wrapping himself around his left leg. Tears were streaming down his face as he held on to his father's leg for dear life.

This was just what Randy had hoped to avoid. His eyes became red and moist with emotion as he looked down at Trevor. "Go on, son. You need to go back over with Rita."

Little Trevor looked up at his father and then at the face of Officer Stapanek. "Please, please don't take my daddy away! He's all I got now!" he pleaded

Stapanek seemed at a loss for words. His superior and mentor, Sergeant Bradford, had to know that his junior officer had little experience in such matters. Stapanek looked at Bradford with a funny look on his face.

Bradford, acknowledging the young officer's silent pleading, yelled to Rita. He had immediately recognized her as a fellow parishioner from his church. "Mrs. Landon, would you please get over there and take the little boy?" Luckily, Rita's husband, David, had just pulled into the driveway next door. With a surprised look on his face, he came to the aid of his wife. He took charge of his children while his wife walked over and pried Trevor away from Randy's leg. The Landon children were crying. Rita literally did have to pry Trevor away from Randy, half-carrying and half-dragging him back over to David while Trevor kicked, screamed, and cried the whole time.

Over the sound of the screaming and crying, she managed to talk loud enough for David to hear her as she tried to hand Trevor off to him. David latched on to Trevor's upper right arm with his one free hand and held on.

"Take the children into the house while I go talk to the police," she said to her husband in a loud but calm voice.

By the time Rita returned to the Whitfield yard, Randy was sitting in the back seat of the second patrol car, with Officer Stapanek standing next to the car, letting out a deep sigh, and wiping some sweat from his brow. Sergeant Bradford was still standing on the Whitfield porch, facing Officer Richey, who had his back to Rita. Rita started talking to the two of them as she walked up the porch steps. "Can you at least tell me why he's been arrested?"

Richey turned around. He was wearing latex gloves and holding a white plastic bag in one hand and the pair of muddy cowboy boots in the other.

Bradford did the talking. "He's the prime suspect in the burglary of Sam's Pharmacy a couple of nights ago. We received anonymous tips that we should search the house and garage of Randy Whitfield. So we came this afternoon with a search warrant, and we found at least part of what we were looking for."

Rita shook her head as she looked pleadingly into the eyes of Sergeant Bradford. "No, I can't believe that Randy did it. He had quit drinking. He was attending meetings to help him stay clean and sober. 1 finally was starting to like him. He seemed like he was trying to finally turn his life around. It just doesn't make any sense."

Bradford shrugged. "I don't know what to tell you. It wouldn't be the first time that I've caught a crook whose family and friends thought the guy was innocent. Sometimes people like that can be a real con artist, especially around the people who think that they know them best. A lot of times, family and friends are the last ones to realize the truth."

"Well, I think you're wrong about this one," answered Rita.

"Mrs. Landon, I truly hope you're right, especially for the boy's sake, but I have to tell you, it doesn't look too good at this point."

Rita lowered her gaze and rubbed her brow before turning around and walking down the steps.

"Mrs. Landon, before you leave, I need to ask you a couple of questions." She stopped and wheeled back around at the foot of the porch steps, looking back up at Bradford.

He reached into his front shirt pocket of his uniform and pulled out a small notepad and pencil. "Do you know where Brenda Rogers is right now?"

Rita looked down at the sidewalk for a few seconds before looking back up at Bradford, who must have looked like a giant to her as he towered above her at the top of the steps. "No, I don't know. She was staying with a friend in Omaha. A while back, Randy came to pick up his son late the next Saturday morning after Trevor had stayed all night with us. He looked tired, but he seemed sober, and he was in the best mood I'd seen him in for a long time. He said he'd 'seen the light' the night before and that everything was going to be different from now on.

"He asked if he could use our phone. He said that the phone company must have shut his off earlier that morning. We sat around the kitchen table while he made a call to Brenda's friend Judy in Omaha, where Brenda had been staying. David and I watched as his good mood seemed to go away shortly into the conversation.

"Randy said that Judy had told him that Brenda had packed up and left two days earlier. He had asked this Judy where Brenda had gone, but she said that Brenda couldn't tell her for sure. She said that she thought that Brenda had become a bit depressed after getting laid off from the packing plant. She was having a hard time finding another job and apparently was feeling guilty that she thought she was starting to take advantage of her friend's generosity. Not feeling like she could call Randy, she decided to leave when she still had enough money for some gas and a few meals. Judy told Randy that she thought she may have gone back to her parents' house back east somewhere."

"What about the boy's grandparents? Do you know where they live or how we can get in touch with them?"

"No, I'm afraid not. I don't think Randy has talked to his parents in years. As for Brenda's parents, I think I heard Brenda say they live in Ohio or maybe Pennsylvania somewhere." Rita must have suddenly realized the significance of Sergeant Bradford's questions. "Oh no, what's going to happen to Trevor?"

"Well, in the short term, he'll have to be put in foster care," Bradford answered. "I was going to tell you that someone will be over this evening to pick him up. I was hoping that you and your husband could keep him at your house for the next couple of hours if need be. It's obvious that he knows you and trusts you."

Rita looked stunned as she stared back at Bradford without speaking for a few seconds. "Foster care? Brenda's son? No, that will never do. I've come to know him and love him as if he's my own. There must be another way," she emphatically replied.

Bradford put the notepad and pencil back into his shirt pocket. "Well, I suppose you could petition the court for temporary custody. But for now, he'll have to go to a foster family. I'm sorry, but that's the law."

Rita acted like she hadn't heard Bradford. She was looking at her house without saying a word.

"I tell you what, Mrs. Landon, we'll come back over tomorrow morning and unlock the house. After we're convinced that we're done with our investigation of the case in question, we'll see if we can find a phone number or an address somewhere in the house of one or both sets of grandparents. Maybe we can get you a little help here," Bradford suggested. "I hope we can, at least, find her parents' number," answered Rita. "I wish I could talk to her so she'd know it was okay to come home again. That boy needs his own mother, now more than ever before." She headed back to her house.

Sergeant Bradford locked up the Whitfield house while Officer Richey placed the incriminating, stolen drugs they had found into the trunk of the last patrol car. Richey got in on the front passenger side of the car, which contained a very sad and subdued-looking Randy Whitfield, staring forward through the mesh screen that separated the front and back seats of the black-and-white cruiser. Bradford ducked his head into the driver's seat of the front cruiser before slamming the door and starting the engine. Both squad cars backed out of the driveway, heading west toward the downtown police station.

The curious neighbors were starting to disperse and go back into their homes as the two patrol cars disappeared down the street. The curiosity wasn't restricted to just humans. Ace was standing next to the Bozell house when the two police cars passed by. He finally went around to the back door and woofed until the door swung open, and he was let in.

It was late the next morning after Randy Whitfield had been arrested. He was sitting in a small interrogation room in the Plattsmouth Police Department's downtown office and adjoining jail. Randy sat slouched in a chair. He was directly underneath a fluorescent light that was mounted in a false ceiling. Randy stared at one of the bare walls, remaining motionless.

Two of the other walls were also bare, including the wall with a door that had frosted glass in the top half with a thin mesh wire screen in it. The wall to his left had a huge inserted mirror in the middle. Randy had decided to face the bare wall. For starters, he had never been much into admiring himself in the mirror, especially not lately. He also wasn't stupid, knowing that the mirror surely was a way of being observed from the adjoining room. He was thinking about how his situation had become so surreal. It was like it was right out of the movies—complete with a twoway mirror.

He had finally sat up and started slouching forward, staring down at the floor in front of him, when he heard the door to his right creak open and slam shut. He looked up to see Sergeant Bradford towering over him. There were two other chairs around a small table that Randy sat at, but Bradford didn't take a seat in either one of them. On the table was a tape recorder. He just kept looking down at Randy until Randy looked back down at the floor again. "Okay, Randall, I think it's time we had a little talk," Bradford finally said.

Randy continued to look down at the floor. "It's Randy. I go by Randy," he softly replied.

"Very well. Randy it is," Bradford answered.

A few seconds of silence passed. "Randy, if we're going to have a talk, you need to look at me," Bradford said with a bit of an exasperated tone.

Randy didn't respond at first. Finally, he looked up and stared deeply into Bradford's equally penetrating eyes. "I'll look up when you finally take a seat so we can talk at the same level."

Bradford looked angry before he seemed to finally regain his composure. His frown disappeared in favor of a sly-looking grin. "All right, Randy, if it'll make you feel better, I'll sit down so we can get this hashed out." Bradford took a seat across the table from his prime suspect. He turned on the tape recorder. "I'm going to tell you once again, Mr. Randall 'Randy' Whitfield, that you may be represented by counsel at this time. Do you waive that right?

"Yeah, I do. I don't have anything to hide."

"Very well. Let us begin." Sergeant Bradford hesitated for a few seconds while it appeared that he was checking to make sure that the tape recorder was functioning properly. "Where were you on the night of May 25?"

"I fixed some dinner for my son. We ate. Then he played out in the yard for about an hour and a half before I took him over to my neighbor's house and walked to my eight o'clock meeting. The meeting got over about nine. I walked back home, picked Trevor back up around nine fifteen from my neighbor's house, and then put him to bed for the night. I watched a little TV and finally went to bed myself at about ten thirty."

"Can anyone collaborate your story that you never left the house after nine fifteen that night?"

"Probably not. Trevor was asleep by about ten o'clock. 1 was alone in the house with my kid all night."

Bradford stared into the tape recorder for a few seconds. Randy rubbed his chin with his left hand as he looked at the top of his adversary's head. Sergeant Bradford looked up and locked into the eyes of his captive audience. Neither man was blinking, let alone speaking.

Finally, Bradford let out a deep sigh. "Look, Randy, we found some of the stolen drugs from the pharmacy break-in on a shelf in your garage. We also found a pair of your boots nearby with red-caked mud on them. The pattern on the bottom of your boots matches the pattern left in the mud near the cellar doors of the pharmacy. The same boot prints were also found on the steps leading down into the cellar. The reddish mud on your boots is consistent with the color of the mud around the pharmacy. How do explain all that?"

Randy took a deep breath and then rubbed his eyes with his thumb and finger before pinching the bridge of his nose. "I don't know how the drugs ended up in my garage or who may have put them there. I haven't worn the boots you're talking about for several weeks. Somebody's trying to frame me for this. 1 don't know why. I'm sure I've made some enemies in the past couple of years."

Sergeant Bradford had a smirk on his face. "Come on, Randy, who could possibly want to frame you for this, all the while committing a felony?"

Randy just shook his head with a disgusted look on his face. "I don't know. How did you know to search my house and garage yesterday afternoon?"

Bradford didn't answer Randy at first, and when he spoke, he seemed to be choosing his words carefully. "We received an anonymous phone call."

Randy tried to hide the disgusting mood that was welling up inside him. "An anonymous call? You immediately got a search warrant to search my property because of one lousy phone call, and the lowlife wouldn't even give you his name?"

"1 never said it was a he."

"Well, I just assumed it had to be a man."

"That's quite a bit to assume, don't you think, Randy?"

"Not any different from you assuming it was me who broke into the pharmacy, don't you think, Sergeant Bradford?"

Bradford's sly grin quickly gave way to a stone face. "Since the first article about the burglary appeared in the newspaper, we received a second call, and this one wasn't anonymous. Do you know a Bud Dahlke, Randy?"

Randy tried to hide the alarm that he was feeling inside. He was dumbstruck that one of his old stoner buddies would have called the cops on him. "Yeah, 1 know him."

"He said he was over at your house a few weeks ago and that you said something about maybe having to rob a pharmacy."

Randy couldn't help but laugh to himself, even while knowing how much trouble he was in. "Did he tell you what we were doing when 1 said that?"

"No, he didn't."

"No, I didn't think so," Randy disgustedly replied. He dug his left thumb and index finger into his eyes again before continuing. "Look, it was just a joke. We got wasted that night, and I said it as a joke when he was leaving. I don't mind telling you this now because I've quit smoking pot, I've quit doing all illegal drugs, and I've given up the booze. I want Brenda back. 1 want to be there for Trevor as he grows up. When I made that stupid remark that night, I was just trying to be a smart-ass with my supposed friend. That's all it was, a joke."

Sergeant Bradford seemed to let Randy's last remarks soak in a little bit before he continued, "You know what, Randy, I have a different take on all this. I did a little checking of the pharmacy records. Most of the stolen drugs that we found in your garage are the same drugs that have been prescribed for your pain medication. I think that, assuming it's true that you supposedly gave up illegal drugs and alcohol, you now think you need more of your prescription drugs to keep you going. Since you can only fill your prescriptions once a month, you decided to steal a larger quantity so you could load up more without running out. I also found out that you're two months late on your rent payment. Stealing all those drugs from the pharmacy would kill two birds with one stone for you. You kept enough drugs for your own consumption and then sold the rest for cash."

Randy threw his head back and rolled his eyes, letting out a deep sigh. "Didn't I see on TV that Bud Dahlke got busted for dealin' pot and LSD in Douglas County a couple of weeks ago?"

Bradford didn't immediately answer as he avoided eye contact with Randy by looking down at the tape recorder, like he was checking to see if it was still running.

Randy continued, "Don't you see? Dahlke would say anything right now. He's just tryin' to save his own ass. I don't know for sure if it was Dahlke, but somebody set me up. 1 didn't do it."

Bradford finally looked back up and stared into Randy's eyes. "Is there anything else you have to say at this time, Randy?"

Randy thought for a few seconds. "Yeah, I have a question for you, Sergeant Bradford."

Bradford nodded and held the palm of his open right hand out toward Randy as a silent signal for him to ask away.

"Did you find any of my fingerprints anywhere around or in the pharmacy?"

"Gloves, Randy, gloves."

"Okay, why was I smart enough to wear gloves but dumb enough to leave a pair of my boots in my garage caked in the same-colored mud as what's around the pharmacy?"

"Probably because you didn't expect one of your pothead friends to fink on you," Bradford answered with a smug look on his face.

Randy opened the palms of his hands and pressed them against the sides of his face without answering.

"So who did you sell all the rest of the stolen drugs to, Randy? Sam's insurance company is going to be interested in knowing that piece of information."

Randy glared back at Bradford. "Have you not been listening to me at all?"

Bradford reached over and shut off the tape recorder. "1 think we're through for now. Your bond hearing is set for tomorrow morning. You got any rich relatives, Whitfield?"

"No, no one I would call anyway. What's going to happen to my son?"

Bradford's tough demeanor seemed to soften a bit after Randy's last question. "There's where you might not have to concern yourself, Randy, at least not in the short term. Your neighbor Rita Landon is petitioning the court for temporary custody."

Randy let out a big sigh and rubbed his open left hand across his face. "I'm lucky to have Rita and David as neighbors. I'm going to owe them big time when this nightmare is finally over."

Martha was at the front counter of Sam's Pharmacy, ringing up Doris Benson's purchases of hair dye, deodorant, and toothpaste. It was late afternoon on a Wednesday, the same day that Sergeant Bradford had interrogated Randy Whitfield at the police headquarters that morning. The bell over the front door jingled, announcing the arrival of another customer to the pharmacy. Martha handed Mrs. Benson her change from her twenty-dollar bill and dropped her receipt into the bag of purchases. "Have a nice day, Doris. Say hi to Ralph for me, will you?" Martha said with a bright smile on her face. Mrs. Benson smiled back and nodded as she turned to leave.

Martha watched Doris Benson walk out the front door and then turned her attention to the customer who had just walked in and was standing at the front side of the counter closest to the back side of the store. When she turned to see if she could help whoever it was, Henry was standing there in his work clothes, looking toward the back of the pharmacy where Rick was busy filling phoned-in prescriptions. "Henry, what are you doing here?"

"Oh, I was just curious to see how you were getting along here since the breakin the other night. By the way, when did you get rid of the soda counter?" Henry asked. He continued to scan the right side of the store that had rows of shelves filled with toiletry articles and other household needs. "Has it been that long since you were last in here, Henry? We took all that out over two years ago when Sam had the place remodeled."

"Oh yeah, I remember now you mentioned that at the time. I forgot," replied Henry. He could see that he was currently the only person in the pharmacy other than the employees. "Not very busy today?"

"Oh, we have been, off and on. It's probably the lull before the storm. A lot of customers will be stopping in soon to pick up their prescriptions on their way home from work."

Henry looked toward the back and then at his wife, who was still standing behind the front counter. "I don't see Sam back there. Is he gone right now?"

"He's up at the hospital again, sitting with Ida. He spends the late afternoons there with her every day, when it's usually slow here. He should be back any minute now."

Henry leaned back against the front part of the checkout counter and crossed his arms as he took an even closer look around the pharmacy. "It's hard to remember what this place looked like the day we first met here. I remember sitting over there where the soda fountain and counter used to be. Remember, Martha? It's where we first got to know each other. I can't believe how many years ago that was. It's downright scary how fast the years come and go. I guess it's true what they say about how time seems to speed up as you get older."

"You're starting to make me feel depressed with that kind of talk, Henry. Just be glad we're both still here to talk about it."

"Yeah, you're right, Mother. I usually don't give much thought to getting older." He unfolded his arms and turned back around toward his wife. "So have the police finished their investigation yet?"

"I don't know. They were back this morning for a while. Everyone who works for Sam had to be here at eight o'clock. They fingerprinted all of us so they would know if they found any fingerprints that were unaccounted for."

Henry's face gave away his apparent surprise to hear that his own wife had been fingerprinted. "Fingerprinted? You and everyone else got fingerprinted? That's just not right, Mother. That's an invasion of privacy," Henry almost shouted back at his wife.

"Hush, Henry. Hold it down. Rick or Susan might hear you," Martha said in a whisper as she held her right index finger in front of her lips.

"But, Martha, don't you understand? Your fingerprints will be on file from now on," Henry whispered back to his wife.

Martha just shook her head back and forth at her husband. "Dam, that ends my plans for holding up the bank next month."

"Very funny, Mother. You may make light of it, but I'm telling you, it's not right."

Martha leaned over the counter so she was nose to nose with Henry. "Think of it this way, dear, kind of like what we were just talking about earlier about how all the years have come and gone. I've never written or said anything in my life that would remain after I'm gone that would serve as a remembrance of me. This way, it will be on record, at least for a few years. Martha Klottenburg Bozell's fingerprints, left for posterity."

Henry got a disgusted look on his face. "That's just plain morbid, Mother," he finally said, snorting. Martha just smiled back at him without saying another word as she turned away and began to put a new register tape into the cash register while Henry turned his back to her and resumed leaning back against the front of the counter.

Henry finally broke the silence. "I was just curious. Did you lose any business this week because of the stolen drugs?"

"No, not really. We were restocked by early Monday afternoon. Sam has always had open credit terms with all our drug suppliers. If we're lucky, the insurance company will reimburse Sam before any invoices become due and payable," Martha explained. "Sam told me it all depends on whether the police investigation will lead to a recovery of the drugs or not. So far, I guess our neighbor Randy Whitfield is claiming his innocence, even though they caught him with some of the stolen drugs."

Martha couldn't see the scowl that had erupted on Henry's face as he still stood with his back to his wife. "He did it. You know he did. Everybody in the neighborhood thinks he did it except, I suppose, Rita and David," Henry loudly answered.

Martha often got embarrassed when Henry raised his voice in public, especially when he would do it when he was facing away from her, seemingly shouting to the world in a way that the words came back to her after circling the globe. Martha just shook her head, knowing from experience that it was easier at that point to be at least somewhat agreeable with her husband while offering a rational alternative explanation so he'd finally shut up for a while or at least speak more softly. She closed the register back up, having completed the changing of the register tape. She looked up at Henry, who had turned back around after declaring Whitfield guilty as charged. "You might be right, dear, but I've noticed a few things since the burglary that have me a bit puzzled. For one thing, I went out back and looked at the boot prints in the mud that were supposedly made by the burglar. The boot prints are quite deep. Randy Whitfield is a pretty skinny guy. I find it hard to believe that he would have sunk down into the mud that far. The young man is nothing but muscle and bone."

Henry chuckled. "I think you've been watching too many reruns of Perry Mason lately, Mother." The smile on Henry's face quickly gave way to a look of concern as he must have suddenly pondered the possible implications of his wife's last comment. "I hope you didn't express your theory to the Plattsmouth police."

"No, I didn't, dear. I'm sure they know a whole lot more about crime scene investigations than I do. I didn't want to embarrass myself."

Henry looked relieved. "Good, you made the right decision, Mother. They're the professionals. Let them handle it."

The sound of an approaching siren caused Henry and Martha to stop their conversation long enough to look toward the front windows of the pharmacy in time to watch an ambulance go by. Martha turned back to her husband. "If Randy Whitfield did do it, he's done an awfully good con job lately on Rita and David. Rita had been going on and on lately about how much Randy had changed, about how he was taking better care of himself and his son. She said he had been attending nightly meetings for weeks now, and she hadn't seen him drunk or all drugged up for quite some time. She said Randy and Trevor had been attending a different church every Sunday. Apparently, he's considering joining one eventually. Now does that sound like somebody who was planning on burglarizing the pharmacy?"

"You know what they say, Mother. 'A zebra never changes its stripes.' Or is it 'A leopard never changes its spots'? Oh well, it doesn't matter. You know what I mean, Martha."

"You and Sam seem to agree with each other on that take, Henry. He said the same thing when I had told him about the changes that Rita had observed in Randy lately. Unfortunately, Sam only remembers all the times that Randy came in here in the past. He was always crude and rude to Sam or anyone else who waited on him. Sam was at the hospital the last time he was in here to pick up his prescriptions. Randy was clean shaven, and his clothes were clean. But the biggest change I noticed was his attitude. He was polite and patient, a perfect gentleman in every way. It's mind boggling to think that he might have been planning the break-in the whole time. Maybe the politeness was just an act. But there's a few other things I've noticed around here that don't make a lot of sense to me."

The bell on the front door jingled again, announcing that someone had just entered the pharmacy.

"Oh, what's that, Mother?" Henry asked.

Martha looked at the front entrance as a scruffy-looking young darkhaired man had entered and was walking up to her at the register. "Never mind for now, Henry. I'll tell you later," she whispered to her husband.

Bud Dahlke was sitting on a barstool at the bar, staring at the front door. The interior of the bar was darkened. The only outside window and the front door were heavily tinted, giving the impression from the inside that it was always evening and time to drink and be merry. It was a neighborhood bar in South Omaha, not too far from the Omaha stockyards. The bar was beginning to fill up in the late afternoon as men and women from primarily the meatpacking plants were quenching their thirsts after a long hot day.

The name of the bar was O'Malley's, no doubt a recognizable name that the new owner, Ivan Bosiljevac, had left unchanged for a couple of good reasons, the most important of which was the heavy revenue day that happened once a year— St. Patrick's Day. Every night before that biggest holiday for the bar business, with the city's permission, of course, some of the Irish-sounding bars all over Omaha would have a huge green cloverleaf painted on the street in front of each bar. It served as a beacon, announcing that it was time, once again, to be Irish for one day, even if your name was Bosiljevac.

Finally, the person whom Bud had been waiting and watching for entered through the front door. She heard someone whistle and say, "Hubba- hubba." She strained to see where she was going, her eyes not adjusting to the dark yet. Bud didn't care much for whoever it was who had distastefully announced Susan's presence in the bar. He wasn't about to make an issue of it, though, unless he wanted to be beaten to a pulp by a bunch of redneck packing plant workers whose arms were generally bigger around than his legs.

Susan was an attractive-looking brunette who was fairly well endowed. She was used to being watched and mentally undressed in bars. In fact, she kind of liked it. It had never concerned her that she lived a double life. Sam had encouraged her and his other employees to attend church regularly on Sundays in Plattsmouth. He said it was good for business and that they were all ambassadors, giving a good impression to customers both inside and outside his pharmacy. Such effort meant more business and more revenue for Sam's Pharmacy and subsequently bigger pay raises for his employees. So Susan would party hardy at the bars on Saturday nights and then drag her tired body and aching head into church on Sundays if she wasn't scheduled to work.

She had first met Bud at a gas station on the outskirts of Plattsmouth. They were both getting their cars filled up at the same set of pumps. Bud was on his way back to Omaha at the time, and Susan had just gotten off work at the pharmacy.

As she walked up to Bud, he grabbed his can of beer off the top of the bar and motioned toward an empty booth over in the back corner. "Let's go sit over there. It'll be more private."

"What about me?"

"Huh?"

"Aren't you going to buy me a beer first?"

Bud got a funny look on his face. "Oh yeah, right. Sorry, I wasn't thinking." He turned back toward the bar as the male bartender was approaching from the other end. "Give me another one for the lady here. And you might as well open another one for me now too."

"You got it," the burly, heavily tattooed bartender answered as he turned and opened one of the cooler doors behind the bar and pulled out two more cans of beer while Bud fished out a sweat-soaked ten-dollar bill from his front blue jean pocket and laid it on the bar. The bartender turned back around and placed the two beers down before popping the tops and sliding them in the direction of Bud and Susan. He took the ten and walked over to the register.

Bud looked at Susan while he was waiting for his change. He handed her one of the two beers. "Why did you pick this place again to meet? Are you embarrassed to be seen with me around Plattsmouth or something?"

She looked back at him with a sheepish grin now planted on her face. "I can't believe you even asked me that. What a stupid question. What do you think? I didn't want to be seen with you around Plattsmouth even before you got busted."

He shook his head with a frown, some of his stringy black hair falling in front of his eyes. "Maybe that's why I'm still so attracted to you. You've always been so brutally honest with me."

The bartender brought back his change. Bud tipped a couple of quarters to him and stuffed the remaining bills back into his pants pocket. By then, Susan was already walking back to the empty booth that he had pointed out earlier. He sauntered over and slid into the booth on the opposite side of her. She was fishing around in her purse before pulling out a pack of cigarettes and a book of matches.

He reached up with his hand and unrolled his own pack from his left T - shirt sleeve. She lit her own cigarette and then held the burning match in front of Bud until he had leaned forward slightly and had his own cigarette burning.

Susan exhaled a stream of blue-white smoke from her mouth before taking a long sip of her cold can of beer. "1 thought you were in jail," she finally asked.

"I was until a few days ago. I talked my old man into putting up the bail. He said it was the last time he was ever going to help me again."

"Well, can you really blame him?"

"No, I guess not. I'm probably going to do some hard time this time. More than likely, 1'11 get sent to the state pen in Lincoln. Not really looking forward to hobnobbing with real criminals this time around—murderers, rapists, and such."

She frowned at him. "You should have thought about that before you decided to become a dope dealer."

He glared back at her after taking another drag on his cigarette. "You certainly didn't seem to mind when I was turning you onto the stuff for free."

"Well, I guess that's over now anyway. Isn't it, Bud?"

"Not if you don't want it to be. I've got a joint in the glove compartment of my car right now."

Susan got a surprised look on her face. "Are you insane? You get busted for dealing drugs. You're out on bail, and you're still driving around town with pot in your car?"

"Yup, that's about the size of it," he replied without the slightest trace of remorse in his expression. "Hey, you love it, and you know it. Otherwise, you wouldn't have hung out with me in the first place."

"That's where you're wrong this time, Bud. I met you here today so I could tell you in person that our relationship is over. I have a good reputation to maintain in Plattsmouth, and I can't afford to be hanging out with a convicted felon."

"I'm not a convicted felon yet."

"No, but you're going to be . . . real soon."

"Maybe not. Calling in and steering the Plattsmouth cops to my old buddy Randy might help my cause."

"Yeah, I wanted to ask you about that. Why call attention to yourself, and possibly me, after the cops had already received the first call? If I'd known you were going to do that, I wouldn't have told you."

"Because it normally takes two people to make an accusation before the cops will ask for a search warrant."

"You know he didn't do it. So why did you have to put me in possible jeopardy by talking to the cops?"

"'Cause I figured I didn't have anything to lose at this point."

"But I thought he was your friend."

"I don't have any friends. Judging by what you just told me a minute ago, you're not my friend either, are you, Susan?"

Susan took another sip of her beer and another drag on her cigarette before she looked intently into his eyes. "Bud, the pharmacy where I work at was burglarized. The last thing I need is for the cops and everyone else in Plattsmouth to know that you and I know each other. Can't you understand that?"

Bud looked back at her with a pathetic and somewhat understanding look. "Yeah, I guess I see your point. Oh well, it's too late now."

Henry was reading the evening newspaper in his recliner in the Bozell living room. Bo was lying on the sofa, watching television, while Ace was lying in front of him on the floor. Martha was gone, running some errands. "Hey, son, remind me to show this article in tonight's paper to your mother when she gets home," Henry said as he continued to hold the paper up in front of him.

"What article is that, Pop?"

"It's a follow-up story about the pharmacy burglary. It says that the insurance company is waiting for the outcome of Whitfield's trial before they compensate Sam for the stolen drugs. Kinda interesting. Maybe they think Whitfield will finally fess up to where the rest of the drugs are to get a lighter sentence."

"Maybe he didn't do it, Pop," Bo casually said as he kept looking at the television.

"Woof." Ace seemed to second Bo's belief.

Henry lowered the newspaper and looked at Bo and Ace. "You're both wrong. They caught him red handed. He did it. I know it was him," Henry said emphatically. "People like that never change, son. Just like your uncle Stanley will always be stinky, Randy Whitfield will always be a thief."

Martha had returned home. Henry had left while she was gone. Bo had told her that his dad had gone to pick something up at the shop. Then her youngest son scurried out the door, carrying an odd-shaped black case, saying that he was going over to Jerry's house to return the microscope and stuff that he had never used since his friend had loaned it to him a few months ago. So Martha was alone in the house for a while with only Ace for company.

She decided that it was a good time to get some laundry done. As she was loading the clothes washer in the basement, Ace came down the basement steps with part of the evening newspaper in his mouth. He dropped the rolled- up, soggy newspaper on top of her feet after padding up to her. "What is it, Ace?" she asked with a surprised look on her face before she bent down to pick up the paper. Ace sat down and watched her as she did, shaking a little drool off the edges as she straightened back up. She stared at him with a look of disgust over the present condition of a section of the newspaper, hoping that Henry had already read it. Ace moaned a bit to invoke sympathy.

Once she opened the paper all the way out, she spotted the article immediately. Henry had a habit of identifying articles he wanted Martha to read by circling them with a red ink pen. Martha proceeded to read the follow-up article about Sam's Pharmacy. Then she read it a little slower and more carefully a second time. She folded the newspaper over a couple of times and then laid it on top of the dryer. She slowly turned, seemingly deep in thought, when she finally looked at Ace, who just kept sitting there, staring at her. "What? What, Ace? You think I'm supposed to know something more about all this or something? Well, I don't. Okay?" Wait a minute, she thought. Why am I defending myself to a dog for crying out loud?

"Ace, it seems like ever since you showed up here in Plattsmouth, some strange things have been happening. I don't really have an explanation for any of it. I'm a little confused right now. I need to think a few things through a bit more before I make any accusations that could turn out to be false. I'll come forward only when I'm convinced that I need to come forward. Okay? Fair enough, Ace?" Martha asked.

Ace tilted his head from side to side a couple of times before he turned and headed back up the basement steps, the wood creaking under him as the massive dog ascended the steps at a quicker pace than when he came down.

After Ace had gone upstairs, Martha grabbed the newspaper and unfolded it, reading the article again for a third time before resuming her work of loading the washer with some of Henry's filthy work clothes.

As she drove her van westward on Interstate 80, Brenda kept shaking her head back and forth as she tried to stay focused on the highway in front of her. She was tired after driving pretty much nonstop since she had left her parents' home in Philadelphia. Her fatigue was more the result of not sleeping well the night before than it was the long drive. She was still in Indiana, but she was only about thirty or forty miles from the Illinois border. The sun had set in front of her on the west horizon about an hour earlier.

She had wished she hadn't let her father talk her into getting the van serviced that morning as it delayed her departure until the early afternoon. The only thing that helped a little bit was the fact that she didn't have to contend with oncoming headlights. A wide ditch separated the eastbound and westbound traffic. The eastwest interstate system had been a welcome change from the two-lane highways that long-distance car and truck travelers had dealt with since the invention of the automobile. Occasionally, there would be a short section of uncompleted interstate forcing travelers back into a narrow two-lane highway, reminding older drivers of how it used to be.

Brenda still wasn't sure why she had gone back to her parents' house, especially without her son. She had been less than truthful when she had arrived at their front door two weeks ago. All she had said to her surprised parents was that Trevor and Randy were doing just fine. She told them it was just a spur-of- themoment decision to drive back and see them, that she had become suddenly obsessed with reestablishing their broken relationship. What she didn't tell them was that she had left Omaha several weeks earlier.

She was practically trembling when she rang her parents' doorbell, not knowing what kind of reception she would receive. Not surprisingly, it was an icy reception. It was her mother who had answered the door, not inviting her in initially. After an awkward silence, she finally told her daughter she could come into the house. She left Brenda sitting alone in the living room. Her father came home from an errand after she had been there for about five minutes. He walked past her in the living room without speaking, joining her mother in the kitchen. After about ten minutes, they both came back into the living room, sitting down across from her and waiting for her to explain what she was doing there.

Pretty much everything she proceeded to tell them was a lie. She made up a story that Trevor had a bad cold, and she and Randy thought it best that he should stay home this time. She told them that she couldn't wait any longer for Trevor to get over his cold, that she had to come and see them face-to-face immediately.

The truth was Brenda had run out of money on the road and had to take a job as a waitress at a truck stop for a month to have enough money to complete the trip back to Philadelphia. She had no idea how either her son or Randy had been doing for the past several weeks. She was having a hard time looking at herself in the mirror, what with all her lies and then putting on a happy face in front of her parents, who had finally softened their stance, allowing her to stay with them for a few days.

Brenda was washing up some dishes in the kitchen for her mother when the phone rang the day before. When her mother had yelled to her that it was Randy, a wet glass slipped from her grasp, smashing on the linoleum floor and sending shards of glass flying all over the kitchen. Brenda hurried to the phone, tiptoeing around the pieces of broken glass as she left the kitchen.

Randy had ranted on and on about what had happened to him a few weeks earlier. It was one of those good-news/bad-news types of phone calls. The good news was that Randy was a changed man. The bad news was that he was in jail, arrested for a crime that he didn't commit.

When Brenda's father got home, he found his daughter busily packing up her stuff for her return trip to Plattsmouth. The visit with her parents had gone well enough that they had eventually told her they felt like they'd like to come and visit their daughter, grandson, and soon-to-be son-in-law back in Nebraska. Since they had missed out this time on finally seeing their grandson again, they were already making plans to come back to Plattsmouth soon. Brenda was hoping for the best in her mind, so she didn't discourage her parents' talk of a Nebraska visit within the next few weeks. If Randy was still in jail by the time her parents came for a visit, she would tell them the truth then.

Even without having to endure oncoming headlights, Brenda had become so sleepy that she had caught herself nodding off a couple of times. She decided it was time to pull off at the next rest stop and try to sleep for a couple of hours before resuming her trip.

At least she was relieved to know that Trevor was safe and sound at Rita and David's house. Now all she had to figure out was how to get the bond money to bail Randy out of jail. She was excited and worried at the same time. She was excited about how different Randy had sounded over the phone, like he was upbeat and finally at peace with himself. It was unbelievable to her that he could have sounded that way, even after he had been falsely arrested. But she was worried that the real burglar wouldn't be found, leaving Randy to do some hard time that he didn't deserve. She knew with all her heart and all her common sense that Randy didn't do it. Randy had done a lot of bad things in his life, but being a thief wasn't one of them.

Besides the fact that Randy was in jail, she didn't know what to think about his wild story of a mystical dog. The dog had supposedly led him in the middle of the night to the Ten Commandments marker in the park before disappearing into thin air right in front of him. She had decided that Randy must have surely been hallucinating, but if that was what it took to make him a changed man, then she could accept that.

She was relieved when she finally saw the sign for the next rest stop up ahead. Brenda pulled the van into a parking spot that was a long walk to the restrooms so that, when she returned from using the bathroom, she wouldn't have car doors slamming near her as she tried to sleep in the back of the van. The parking spot for cars and small trucks ran parallel to the area for semitrucks and trailers. There was a sidewalk and narrow grassy strip that separated the two parking areas. A small park area was behind the restrooms, with picnic tables and a few charcoal grills interspersed on either side of a winding sidewalk that threaded its way through the middle of the elongated area of grass, small trees, and bushes. It was butted up against a vast cornfield, separated only by the farmer's barbed-wire fence.

Semi-tractor-trailers were parked back-to-back in a long row in the commercial parking area closest to the interstate. Not far from Brenda, sitting in the cab of his semi was a fat, scruffy-looking middle-aged man wearing a cowboy hat and sipping a cup of coffee as Brenda had pulled into her parking spot. He watched her as she got out of the driver's side of her van and walked around to the sliding side door, opening it up and apparently looking for something with a flashlight. He must have surmised from his angle of view that there wasn't anyone else in the van. The trucker watched her crawl around on her hands and knees all over the back of the van and then sit in the passenger seat for a minute before she got out and closed all the doors. She went to the restrooms alone, stopping briefly to drop some garbage into one of the closest trash receptacles that were spread out along the edge of the sidewalk that led to the restrooms.

As he watched her walk back to the van again, his later actions would confirm that he must have been trying to figure out if she was one of those hippie-type chicks he had seen for the past couple of years while traveling the country. She seemed to fit the stereotype. She had long straight hair, was wearing a bandanna, and was dressed in a tie-dyed T-shirt and faded blue jeans. What was more, she was driving an old van, the vehicle of choice those days for hippie-type kids.

He had told another trucker in the restroom that he wanted to get back on the interstate again, but he was too tired. Time was money, and the quicker he got his fully loaded trailer to Los Angeles, the quicker he could be picking up another load and heading back to the East Coast for yet another payday. He reached for the door handle to climb down from his cab when an old bum standing down below his driver's door interrupted him.

"Hey, buddy, can I hitch a ride with you for a while?" the old man asked. He stood just below the semi driver's open side window. With all his worldly possessions slung over his shoulder in a filthy cloth bag, he had a dirty, scruffy gray beard to match his matted hair that stood out in all directions under his sweatsoiled baseball cap. When he spoke, the truck driver could see his missing front teeth and yellowish smile. His dark brown shirt and khaki pants were torn and soiled. He had on an old pair of muddy, dirty tennis shoes with his big toe exposed on the left foot. His horrible body odor was wafting up into the open truck cab window.

The fat man up in the cab pulled a big red handkerchief out of his back pocket and held it up to his face. He finally removed the hankie from his face before looking down at the tramp. "Get lost, old man. It's against company policy to pick up hitchhikers."

The old man just kept standing there. "Come on, friend, you can bend the rules just this once for old Freddy here, can't ya?"

"I said get lost! What part of get lost do you not understand?"

"Okay, okay, you don't have to get all testy about it. I'll be on my way now. Sorry I bothered you," the old bum said as he walked away toward another semi.

The semi driver seemed to be really upset. He had tried to leave his rig after being fixated on Brenda's every move. The old man had probably detained him long enough for the young girl in the van to have time to leave the rest stop by now. So he looked pleasantly surprised when he saw that the old van was still parked in its stall when he finally looked back over in Brenda's direction after making sure the bum had kept walking away from his rig.

Brenda had curled up with a pillow in the back of the van. She was asleep almost as fast as her head had hit the pillow. The truck driver finally got out of his cab and approached the van. He walked around to the driver's side window, seeing that Brenda wasn't in the driver's seat. He tried to peer in toward the back of the van before knocking on the window.

"Hey, lady, you got any speed I can buy off ya?" he asked as he continued to tap on the window. He stopped tapping long enough to look at his rig, maybe making sure the bum hadn't come back. He turned back and faced the window again. Staring back at him was the biggest dog he had probably ever seen in his entire life. The dog's whole head fdled up the side window area.

"Woof! Woof! Woof!" the dog barked through the mostly closed window at the obviously startled trucker while showing his big teeth and snarling, looking like a big monster that could eat him. Some dog drool was already oozing down the inside of the closed part of the window.

The semi driver took off running for his rig, not stopping until he was back behind the wheel and pulling out of the rest stop. He had made it obvious that he had been looking for something that would help wake him up, and he had found it without it costing him a dime. He was just lucky he had already relieved himself a few minutes earlier before the van had showed up. Otherwise, he might have been changing into a dry pair of pants and underwear at the next available stop off the interstate. His ex-wife used to always tease him about his weak and excitable bladder, an embarrassing condition for a big burly truck driver.

Brenda had sat up in a startled state. Her vision was a bit blurry. Her muddled mind told her that a very loud dog's barking had just woken her up. It was so loud that it almost sounded like it was coming from right inside the van itself. She had thought she had seen a dark image of something quite big sitting in her driver's seat before rubbing her eyes to take another look. When she refocused, the dark image was gone.

She crawled forward and squeezed between the two front seats. What she found left her stunned. There was drool sliding down the inside of her driver's side window, ft was illuminated from the glow of a parking lot light nearby that was shining through the glass. She touched it ever so slightly to confirm its existence. The cab had the smell of a dog. Then she crawled back between the two front seats and finally found her flashlight in the back.

After she returned to the front seat area again, she flashed the beam of her flashlight onto her driver's seat. Sure enough, it had strands of dog hair on it. Brenda whirled around and plopped down in the front passenger seat. Oh my god, Randy wasn't hallucinating. There really is a mystical dog. I can't believe what just happened. I've got to get home as soon as I can. Nobody, except maybe Randy, is ever going to believe me. Brenda's fatigue had just been temporarily jolted aside with the adrenaline rush that occurred with the presence of the dog.

Brenda's thoughts were racing as she swung her legs up over the middle hump in the cab and positioned herself into the driver's seat, ready to speed out of the rest stop.

"You don't have to come back again, whoever or whatever you are. I'm okay now," she said aloud as she merged into the flow of traffic, heading east on Interstate 80. She would have rationalized that it was just a strange dream had it not been for the physical evidence that had been left behind on her window and seat.

As for the truck driver, he probably was able to drive another two hundred miles or more before fatigue set in again. A couple of short restroom breaks was all he would need. As he was driving over the speed limit, apparently trying to put some distance between himself and the rest stop, he was mumbling to himself out loud, trying to rationalize how such a scary huge dog could have been in the van without him noticing. He'd probably think twice before knocking on a hippie's van window again. "Those long-haired freaks are so unpredictable. So much for love and dope." (There was only one dope that night, and he had a receding hairline hidden under a cowboy hat, with a beer gut stretching out a T-shirt that read "America, love it or leave it.")

Martha was sitting in her straight-backed chair with her feet up on a stool as she read a romance novel in the living room. Her hair was in curlers, and she had on her favorite white quilted night coat with matching slippers. She was wearing her half-framed reading glasses, which were positioned a fair distance down on the bridge of her nose. A cup of tea sat on a coaster on the end table next to her.

It was past ten o'clock in the evening. She had woken up Henry and coaxed him to bed about fifteen minutes earlier after he had, once again, fallen asleep in his recliner. Bo was gone all evening, and Ace had been left in the dog run. Martha's quiet peace while relaxing with a good book was abruptly disturbed by the sound of the phone ringing right next to her on the small end table. Martha put her bookmark in place to mark her spot and quickly closed the book, placing it in her lap before reaching around to pick up the phone. "Hello."

"Martha, its Alice. Listen, Martha, you and I have known each other for quite a long time. I... I don't know how else to say this . . . other than . . . I'm very disappointed that you didn't talk to me first before telling Leonard about Ida's request. How could you not ask me before doing such a thing?"

Martha was stunned. In all the years that she had known her sister-in-law, Alice had never talked to her so bluntly before. She was speechless.

"Martha, are you still there?"

"Yes. I'm so sorry, Alice. I had no idea. You're right, I should have talked to you first. I just wasn't thinking."

There was a long silence that followed. All either woman could hear was the other one's breathing on the other end of the connection. This was new territory for such an old relationship. Alice finally broke the strained silence. "Martha, you know what profession I've been in for all these years. Did you not think that I might have not only a personal opinion but a professional opinion as well?"

"Alice, what's wrong? I don't think you would be asking me such a question if something hadn't happened. Is something wrong with Leonard?" Alice didn't answer. "Alice, tell me, please. Is something wrong?"

"Yes, something is wrong with Leonard. He seems to be regressing to the way he was when I first met him at the hospital. Oh, Martha, you have no idea what he went through. He overcame so much before. I can't stand to see him retreating into his shell . . . after all these years. It's just not fair," Alice blurted out before sobbing into the phone.

"You're right, Alice. You were certainly in a better position to know firsthand what Leonard went through in his recovery than anyone."

Neither woman spoke for a few seconds. Finally, Alice let out a big sigh. "Martha, I've never told anyone this before, but I had always secretly hoped that Ida would outlive Leonard. You see, I know Leonard probably better than anyone else on this earth, and I knew that if ever there came a time when Ida would pass away, Leonard would not be able to handle it well, not well at all. And now I know I was right. He's reliving all those old memories. He's feeling all over again all that old hurt. I can see it in his eyes, his sad, sad eyes. I know he never stopped loving her. In his mind, he's losing her all over again. I ask him questions, and most of the time, he acts like he didn't even hear me. And maybe he didn't hear me. He retreats into his own little world. I'm about ready to try to convince him that he needs to come back to my hospital again for a while. Didn't Henry know that something was wrong? Leonard hasn't gone to work for the past two days."

"Yes, he told me that Leonard had been acting strangely lately, but I had no idea it was that bad, Alice. Honest to God, I never would have told him that Ida wanted to see him if I'd known that it would affect him that much. I'm so sorry," Martha said as she started crying into the phone.

"Martha, please stop crying. I didn't mean to lay a guilt trip on you. Maybe it's partly my fault for not telling you and Henry sooner. Maybe then you would have known that it wasn't a good idea for Leonard to see Ida. Besides, some doctors I know might have suggested that he should see her so he could release some of his pent-up emotions. It's obvious to me now that they would have been wrong if such a suggestion had been made.

Leonard is a very fragile soul. I assume he probably always has been. Some people handle tragedy differently from others."

Alice's words seemed to comfort Martha enough that she finally quit crying. "I guess we've both had a lot on our minds lately, Alice. I've barely heard from Ben while he's been recovering in a military hospital. And . . . there's something else going on right now that is weighing heavily on my mind."

"What's that?" Alice asked.

"I... I can't tell you right now. It's a very sensitive situation. I need to come to a decision very soon. It's one of the hardest decisions that I've ever had to make in my entire life. It has to do with the pharmacy. That's all I can say right now." Martha quit talking, worrying that she might have said too much already.

"I'm sorry to hear that. I hope you're able to work things out," Alice answered. Martha quickly changed the subject back to her brother-in-law. "So when do you think you're going to try to get Leonard to the hospital?"

"The sooner, the better, 1 think. Tell Henry I'm going to try tomorrow morning, and I might need some reinforcements, if you know what 1 mean."

"I'll tell him first thing in the morning," Martha replied. "Try and get some sleep tonight. Call me in the morning, would you, please? It's Saturday, so I should be home all morning. I'll ask Henry if he can stay home too until we hear from you. Good night, Alice."

"Good night, Martha."

Martha reached over and placed the handset back on its base. She looked down at the book in her lap and placed it on the end table next to her before standing and switching off her reading lamp. She grabbed her empty cup of tea and walked toward the kitchen, wondering how late it would be before Bo would be home. He was once again over in Council Bluffs on a date to a drive-in movie with Bonnie. He had left Ace behind this time because Bonnie's parents were out of town and had taken Lucy with them.

Martha was reminding herself what a good boy Bo was. Not every son would readily admit that he was going over to his girlfriend's house while telling his mother that the girl's parents were out of town. She trusted him. She knew that a lot of other moms couldn't trust their sons the way she trusted Bo. Such thoughts made her realize that not everything was bad right now; plus, Ben would probably be home soon.

She had put her empty cup in the kitchen sink and had walked to the front door in the living room to make sure it was locked before heading for the bedroom. As she glanced out the window of the door while checking the dead bolt lock, she noticed Brenda's van pass by and pull into the driveway of the Whitfield house across the street and two houses down. Martha watched as Brenda got out of the driver's door and immediately walked in a hurry over to the front door of Rita and David's house.

In seeing Brenda return, Martha had finally made her decision. *I can't wait any longer. Tomorrow is going to be a tough day whether Leonard goes into the hospital or not. There's more I need to talk to Henry about in the morning than just Leonard. Lord, why does trouble come in bunches? Couldn't you spread things out a little bit from now on?*

Martha was worrying about what Saturday would bring as she looked up at the stars in the clear night sky through the open curtains of the window. There was a cool evening breeze, so some windows were open around the house. She heard Ace barking from the dog run in the backyard. The barking had started when the van had passed by, finally stopping after Brenda had entered the Landon house.

Rita and Brenda hugged each other long and hard just inside the front door of the Landon living room. "I missed you so much, Brenda. I'm so glad you're finally home."

"I missed you too. You have no idea how much. I'm sorry I didn't stay in touch. It was just that—"

"You don't have to explain anything to me. I understand. I really do."

Rita looked at her husband, David, who had gotten up from the sofa in front of the television. He was silently standing next to them. "David, honey, would you please go get Trevor? I think he's playing in Scotty's room right now."

David looked at Brenda with smiling eyes. "Don't I get a hug too?"

Brenda stepped forward and wrapped her arms around Rita's Prince Channing. "David, how can I ever thank you and Rita enough for taking such good care of my son?" With watery eyes, she planted her chin on David's left shoulder.

They pushed away from each other before David acknowledged the thank-you. "No thanks necessary. Your son is so doggone smart I feel like I'll have the privilege to someday say that I even knew him as a small child. I really get a kick out of some of the things that come out of his mouth. You're really going to be challenged in the coming years. You know that, don't you?"

Brenda looked at David and then at his wife. "Oh yeah, I know exactly what you're saying. I'm just glad I still have a chance to be a part of it."

Rita looked at her husband and furled her eyebrows. "Well, don't just stand there, honey. Go get him."

"Oh, sorry, right away." He wheeled around and headed for their son's bedroom.

Within seconds, little Trevor came running into the living room. "Mommy! Mommy! You're home!" he exclaimed before diving into the comfort of his mother's bosom.

Brenda had squatted down to his level before her little boy had excitedly bowled into her, almost knocking her onto her back. She must have been feeling the pressure of the impending floodgate of tears even before little Trevor had appeared in the doorway to the living room. Now the dam had broken, washing her little towhead's hair with tears of joy as she hugged him for dear life. "Oh, my son! My son! Mommy's never going to ever leave you again! I promise! Mommy's going to be here for you from now on!" Brenda took a deep breath and exhaled a shuddering series of sobs as she hugged her son.

When she spoke again, it was like all her emotions had just poured out of her with her last exhalation. What was left was a meek and mild mom who really needed a nap. "I'm so sorry. I'm so very sorry," she softly said into Trevor's listening ear. Brenda finally fell silent as she hugged her son for as long as it was going to take before she knew the moment was real and not just another dream that she would awaken from in a cold sweat.

Martha hurried up the steps from the basement when she heard the phone ringing. She finally reached the kitchen phone after the sixth ring. "Hello," Martha finally said after catching her breath.

"It's Alice, Martha. I'm really worried about Leonard. He left the house while I was back in the bedroom. His truck is gone. It's not like him to just suddenly leave without saying a word. He's always told me where he's going."

"I'm sure it's nothing, Alice. Maybe he just went to buy the newspaper or something."

"You don't understand, Martha. I can't just sit back and wait for him to come home at this point. I should have watched him more closely this morning. Now I'm not sure what to do."

"Have you called the shop to see if he might have gone there?" Martha asked.

"No . . . no, I haven't. Who's working this morning since Henry stayed home?"

"It's John who opened this morning. I'm not sure if anyone else came in."

"I'll call the shop and then call you right back," Alice said quickly before hanging up on Martha.

Martha walked into the living room to briefly tell Henry about Alice's first call before returning to the kitchen to stay by the phone. Within less than five minutes, the phone rang again. Alice sounded even more frantic this time. "Martha, John said Leonard stopped by the shop a few minutes ago. He told me he said good morning to Leonard, expecting to have a conversation with him, but I guess he barely acknowledged John before walking into the office. He said Leonard was in there for only a matter of seconds before he walked back out, carrying something in a paper sack and passing by him without saying a word."

"Just a minute, Alice. Let's get Henry on the line with us." Martha cupped her hand over the mouthpiece of the phone. Henry was sitting in his recliner, reading the Saturday morning paper. "Henry! Pick up the phone in the living room!" Martha shouted from the kitchen.

Henry tossed the newspaper aside before getting up and walking over to where the phone sat on the end table next to Martha's favorite chair. "Hello, Alice. What's going on?" he asked.

"I was just telling Martha that Leonard stopped at the shop a few minutes ago. He was in the office for less than a minute before he came walking back out, carrying a paper bag. He didn't say anything to John, not even 'hello' when he came in or 'goodbye' when he left. I'm very worried, Henry. What could he have gotten out of the office that he was apparently concealing in a sack when he left?"

It was a good thing that they were talking over the telephone and that Alice couldn't see Henry's face. He suddenly looked pale, and the concern was written all over his face. Apparently not wanting to unduly frighten Alice, Henry paused and took a deep breath before speaking again. "Listen, Alice, I'm sure it's nothing, but let me call John and talk to him for a couple of minutes, and then either I or Martha will get back in touch with you as soon as possible. Okay?"

"All right, Henry, I'll stay by the phone," she replied before hanging up.

Henry waited for Martha to hang up the phone in the kitchen before he frantically dialed the number to the shop. John must have been spraypainting a vehicle or something because the phone rang and rang. "Come on, son, pick up the phone, damn it." Henry listened to ring after ring while Martha walked into the living room to join him.

Finally, John answered the phone. "Bozell Body Shop. This is Jolin speaking."

"It's your father. I want you to go into the office and check in the back of the top left desk drawer. I want you to make sure that the .22 target pistol is still in the drawer. Hurry, son." Henry stood impatiently. He could hear his son's rapid footsteps on the concrete floor getting fainter and fainter as he ran from the phone that was on the far wall of the shop to the office on the other side of the building.

"Henry, you're not thinking what I think you're thinking, are you?" Martha asked in a frantic tone. Henry solemnly nodded yes to his wife as he waited with the phone in his hand.

Within a matter of seconds, John picked up the phone in the office, creating an echo in Henry's ear as he spoke. "It's not in the drawer, Dad. You want to tell me what's going on?"

"Holy shit, are you sure, son? Are you sure it's not in there?"

Martha's face took on the same extremely worried look as her husband's as she tried to speak, but Henry held his hand up to her like a traffic cop stopping traffic.

John finally said, "Yes, I'm sure. I've even been checking all the other drawers as we speak. It's not here." Just then, John must have figured out what Henry was so excited about concerning the pistol. "Oh crap, you don't think that's what Uncle Leonard had in the sack, do you?"

"That's exactly what I think, John. Is anyone else working this morning?"

"No, it's just me."

"Well, hurry up and shut everything off and lock up. I'll be by within five or ten minutes to pick you up," Henry said before slamming the phone down and hurrying for the master bedroom to get his billfold and keys.

He yelled over his left shoulder at his wife as he ran down the hallway to the bedroom, "Take the car and get over to Alice's just as fast as you can! Someone needs to be with her!"

Martha yelled back at Henry, "Should I wake up Bo? Maybe he and Ace can help look for Leonard!"

Henry was already heading back toward her as he answered, "No time for that now. Grab your keys and purse and get over to Alice and Leonard's house. You can call Bo from Alice's once you get over there." Henry ran for the back door as Martha hurried down the hallway.

Leonard was sitting in his pickup truck. The engine was shut off, and both windows were rolled down all the way. His truck was parked on the shoulder of a narrow gravel road between two cornfields. The only sounds were his labored breathing and the rustling of the short cornstalks on either side of him from an early morning breeze. The paper sack was sitting on the seat next to him.

He was staring forward through the windshield, not moving a muscle. He had been sitting there in a trancelike state for about ten minutes before he reached for the bag with his right hand. He lifted the bag and turned it upside down. The .22 long-nosed target pistol dropped onto the seat. He picked it up with his right hand before moving it into his left. He looked down at his stubby right index finger as he switched it to the other hand. Maybe he was reliving the memory of when he had lost most of the finger in a tractor accident as a boy, a mishap that had gotten him a deferment from serving in the military during World War II.

He held the gun up and away from his head so that the long barrel was pointing almost straight up toward the roof of the truck cab right inside the driver's side open window. His left index finger was sticking straight out, not yet curled around the trigger. He held the gun in that position for several minutes as he stared forward again. There was no sign of any vehicles coming from behind him or toward him.

His gloomy, trancelike state was suddenly interrupted by a dull thud that felt like something had bumped into the back of the truck's tailgate. It was enough of a feeling that his eyes darted over to his outside rearview mirrors, first looking into the mirror on the right and then the one closest to him on his left. He couldn't see anything. He stared straight ahead once again. He finally started to curl his finger around the trigger.

The next thing he knew, he felt a jolt on the driver's side of his truck, and the gun was jerked out of his hand but not before it discharged, sending a round into the air right outside the window. His empty left hand was instantly all gooey, and he could feel hot breath on the side of his face. He looked quickly to his left just long enough to see a big dog's head disappear from the open window.

The dog took off with the gun in his mouth, running in front of the pickup and down and up the shallow ditch to the right before dashing into the cornfield. The cornstalks were not very high yet as it was still early summer. The top of the dog's head and upper body remained visible while cornstalks were being trampled down along the path that the big dog took to get deeper into the field. "Ace?" he asked in a bewildered state. It wasn't more than a few seconds since the gun had been taken away from him, and the dog was getting farther and farther away from the truck.

In about a minute, Leonard couldn't even see the dog anymore. He was still looking to his right with a startled look on his face when Ace suddenly materialized on the passenger seat side of the truck cab. "Ace? Who are you, Ace?" Leonard asked as if expecting a verbal reply. Then he broke down and started to sob uncontrollably.

"Are you God, Ace?" he asked the dog between sobs while staring into Ace's big brown eyes.

Ace shook his head back and forth sideways in response to Leonard's question.

"Were you sent by God?" "Woof!" was Ace's reply.

"Why would God want to save someone like me?"

Ace lunged forward without warning and planted a sloppy kiss on Leonard's right cheek. Leonard looked surprised while wiping away the wetness from his cheek with his right hand. The mastiff shifted his massive body back toward the passenger door, giving Leonard a little space.

"It was all my fault. Ida might never have gotten sick if she had stayed on the farm. Mama might have lived longer if I hadn't had to leave her alone while I was working in the fields. I was weak. All I had to do was be more of a man back then. I failed Ida miserably."

As Leonard was staring into the big dog's eyes, the white of Ace's eyes became brighter white as if a lamp had been turned on inside his head. His pupils became dilated at the same time. Leonard sat mesmerized, like a person who had just fallen into a hypnotic state. He stared into Ace's eyes for several seconds as Ace stayed motionless, and Leonard did not speak. Finally, the whites of Ace's eyes became less bright, and his pupils became less dilated.

Leonard shook his head back and forth a couple of times, seemingly aware of his surroundings once again. He sat there in silence, staring straight ahead. He finally rubbed away some of the moisture from his eyes with his left thumb and finger before speaking to the dog. "Ida's going to a better place soon. What was meant to be was meant to be. How can Alice ever forgive me for such selfishness?"

Leonard turned the ignition key and started the pickup truck engine. "Well, do you want to ride back with me, or are you going to go back the same way you came?"

Ace appeared to get more comfortable in the passenger seat.

"Don't totally trust me yet, do you?" he asked the dog.

"Woof!" Ace replied while Leonard popped the clutch, and the truck jumped forward as he steered it back into the middle of the narrow gravel road and began the drive back into Plattsmouth.

"Can't blame you there, Ace or whatever your name really is," Leonard answered while keeping his eyes on the road.

Leonard stopped at the stop sign. His house was just around the comer to the left on the opposite side of the street. He saw Henry's truck parked out front, with Henry and John having a conversation with Alice in the front yard. They had just returned from searching to the north of town and were about to scour the south side of Plattsmouth. He watched them before making his left turn. "Well, Ace, I guess I have some explaining to do," he said before turning his head back toward the passenger seat.

Ace was gone. Leonard just shook his head before stepping on the gas and making the turn. "1 mighta known you'd take off before I got to the house," he said to the empty passenger seat.

He pulled up to a stop behind Henry's pickup. As he got out of the truck, Alice came running toward him, crying, while Henry and John stood near the front porch. She ran into Leonard's arms. "Oh, Leonard! I was worried sick! Where have you been?"

"You wouldn't believe me if I told you," Leonard answered, his chin resting on Alice's shoulder. He pulled away from her so he could look into her eyes.

"Alice, I want you to know that I love you very much, and I'm very sorry for the way I've been acting lately. Everything is going to be all right now."

Henry was washing his pickup truck in the driveway later that morning after leaving Leonard and Alice still embracing each other in their front yard. He had dropped John off at the shop before coming home. Martha came out the back door of the house just as he was finishing. "John called a few minutes ago. He said he found the gun sitting on the desk when he got back to the shop. He said that it had been fired once and that there was some mud stuck in the end of the barrel and some gooey stuff that looked like spit or something all over it."

Henry looked bewildered. "How could that be, Mother? Leonard said he fired it into the air once and then threw it out into the cornfield before coming back home. How could it be back in the shop already? And how could my brother seem like he's pretty much back to normal after he got home? I mean, we were planning on taking him to the hospital this morning. None of this makes any sense at all."

"Maybe it was a miracle, Henry. When miracles happen, things don't always make a lot of sense."

Henry looked at his wife like she was crazy. "There aren't any miracles in life, Mother. There isn't a Santa Claus. There isn't an Easter Bunny. And there aren't any miracles," he said while finishing wiping down the hood of the truck.

Martha was not surprised but nonetheless disappointed in hearing her husband's realistic view of the whole situation. "1 believe in miracles, Henry. 1 believe that it was a miracle that Bo survived his accident and that it was a miracle that Ben survived Vietnam."

"You keep on believing anything you want, Mother. I'd rather believe that there are logical explanations for everything. So right now, I'm trying to think of a logical explanation for why the gun is back in the shop and why Leonard seems to be okay now."

Martha knew, from all the years that she and Henry had been together, that it was pointless to try to change his thinking about accepting the notion that miracles really did happen, so she changed the subject. "Bo just got up about five minutes ago. Do you want to have a late breakfast with him now?"

Henry looked up from his buffing of the truck hood. "Just got up? It's almost ten o'clock in the morning. I swear, that boy can sleep longer than a bear in hibernation."

"He got home a little late last night," Martha replied.

"Don't tell me. He was out with Bonnie and her friends again last night, wasn't he?" said Henry as he started to walk toward the garage to put away his drying towel.

"Yes, he was. He must have been so tired he didn't even hear the phone ringing downstairs when 1 called him from Alice's house earlier. And poor Ace, he probably had to go potty a couple of hours ago."

The back door opened, and Ace came trotting out into the backyard. In seeing Henry and Martha standing in the back driveway, he quickly diverted his direction to behind the bushes that partially concealed the clothesline.

It was one hour later in the morning. Henry was sipping a cup of coffee at the kitchen table while Martha was finishing up some dishes in the kitchen sink. Bo and Ace had already left the kitchen. Martha turned from facing the sink and walked over and sat down with Henry at the kitchen table.

"So Bo's going over to Jerry's for a little while. That means we could take Ace along with us in the truck if we want to," said Henry.

"I really don't think that's necessary," Martha replied while rubbing her hands in front of her in a nervous manner. "Besides, I called Sergeant Bradford while you were washing your truck. I briefly told him about what you and 1 had discussed earlier. He said he would give me some time alone before pulling up and coming inside."

Henry shook his head. He was obviously concerned for his wife. "I don't know, Martha. I don't like this one little bit. I understand why you think you need to do it this way, but I still don't like it."

"Don't worry, dear, everything is going to be just fine. I tell you what, if it'll make you feel better, you can bring Ace along just in case. I don't see any harm in that, I guess," Martha said. She was trying to think rationally and remain calm, even though her heart was already beating faster in anticipation of the confrontation that would take place within the hour.

"Tell me again why the footprints in the mud made you suspicious," said Henry. "Bo came into the room, and you had to cut it short, remember?"

"Don't make fun of me again, but I did see that on an episode of Perry Mason. I also remember several years ago when the boys were little. I could always tell whether it was little Bo versus the older boys or the older boys instead of you. You all made different impressions in my garden when it was muddy. Bo's footprints were rather shallow, the other boys' prints were a little deeper, and yours was the deepest."

"I don't remember ever tracking through your garden like the boys did," said Henry.

Any other time, Martha might have smiled, but she just wasn't in the mood that day. "Yes, you did. When you mowed the lawn, you used to turn the mower around on the edge of the garden. You would sometimes leave deep footprints from where you turned around. You probably don't remember. You've had one of the boys do the mowing for so many years you've probably forgotten."

"Oh yeah, now I remember. You made me go back out and rake it smooth every time. Come to think of it, 1 think that's why I made one of the boys mow the lawn from then on," Henry answered, apparently trying to be funny so Martha wouldn't be as nervous about what was ahead of her that day. His attempt at dry humor wasn't working on his wife that morning though.

"Anyway," Martha continued, "1 figure Randy Whitfield doesn't weigh any more than a hundred and fifty pounds dripping wet. The person who left those prints in the mud had to weigh a good eighty to a hundred pounds more than that, judging by how deep the footprints were. It doesn't take a detective to figure that out."

"Well, the Plattsmouth police apparently didn't figure that out, Mother."

"I think that before they might have given that some thought, the prime suspect got dropped right into their laps because of the anonymous caller. Everything seemed to fit nice and neat, especially once they found some of the stolen drugs in Randy's garage. Maybe they did consider the depth of the footprints and decided that Randy might have been trying to jump over the muddy area and didn't clear it all the way. The difference between the police and me is the fact that 1 know some other things that make me think the person who stepped through the mud did it on purpose."

"Well, I guess it's time for you to call Sergeant Bradford, Mother. He's probably expecting your call by now. No, wait, you better hold off and not call Bradford until after Bo leaves. It's better if Bo doesn't know anything about this until it's over. If we leave now and take Ace with us, he might wonder what's going on."

Henry pulled up in front of Sam's Pharmacy, parking in one of the diagonal spots along the curb. He turned to Martha in the passenger seat. She was sitting there, almost trembling as she looked at the front of the pharmacy, not making a move yet to get out of the pickup truck. The sun was creating a glare on the large plateglass windows in front of the pharmacy, making it impossible to see inside. Ace was sitting patiently in the truck bed, looking through the back window of the cab.

Henry, concern etched on his face, turned to look at his wife. "You don't have to do it this way, you know."

"I know that. I could have taken the easy way out. 1 just felt like it needed to be done this way," Martha replied before turning her attention back to the front of the pharmacy. She finally grabbed for the door handle and opened the passenger door. "Well, 1 guess it's time to get this over with. Sergeant Bradford will be here soon."

Martha got out of the pickup and closed the door. She looked at Ace, who had moved over to her side of the truck, with his big head sticking out over the side of the truck bed. "You stay put, Ace," she said as she briefly petted him on top of his head.

As Martha entered through the front door, she saw that Sam was behind the front counter, rummaging through a shelf right below the register, while Rick was filling prescriptions in the back. Susan was busy stocking some shelves along the far wall. Sam was a big man like Leonard. Even bent over behind the counter, there was no mistaking that it was Sam. At this time, there weren't any customers in the pharmacy. Martha was relieved that she and Sam would be able to have a brief private conversation near the front of the store.

Sam glanced up with a surprised look on his face as he saw Martha walking toward him. "Martha, what brings you in here on your day off?" "We need to talk, Sam," answered a serious-looking Martha. She now stood on the customer side of the counter. Susan noticed Martha and gave a quick wave before resuming her stocking of the shelves. Martha was hoping that Susan would stay where she was, and luckily, she did.

Sam was standing straight up now behind the counter next to the register. Normally, Sam would have been smiling at Martha at that point. Maybe it was the way Martha had said We need to talk, Sam, that must have made him uneasy. He took off his glasses and rubbed his eyes.

They just looked at each other for several seconds before Martha finally broke the tense silence. "Why did you do it, Sam?"

Sam's expression on his face changed. Martha could tell that he was trying to act surprised, almost forcing a nervous smile, but his hands had begun to tremble, contradicting his faked facial expression. "Do what, Martha? 1 don't know what you're talking about," he said as he reached up and rubbed his brow with his trembling right hand.

"Why did you burglarize your own business?" Martha bluntly blurted out.

Sam looked like he'd just been kicked in the teeth, although his teeth were still intact. His jaw dropped, and he looked down at the floor. When he looked back up at Martha, his eyes had become red rimmed. It must have been quite a shock to his system upon hearing his dutiful longtime employee and good friend accuse him of something that would have seemed unimaginable only weeks before that moment.

"How . . . how did you figure it out?" Sam finally asked in a shaky voice. His cheeks suddenly turned beet red and began to sag. They both glanced at Susan, who was still busy working on the other side, and then they looked at the front door to see if anyone was coming into the pharmacy.

No one was coming in, but Ace had jumped out of the pickup bed, having ignored Henry's plea to remain in the truck. He was standing outside the window closest to the door, peering into the pharmacy. Sam must have recognized the dog, especially when he could see Henry sitting in the driver's seat of his pickup parked in front. "You didn't have to bring reinforcements, Martha. I would never do anything to harm you. You should know that."

"1 know, Sam. That's why I can't believe you tried to frame Randy Whitfield. What did he ever do to you?"

"He disrespected me, Martha. You weren't here the last time I had an encounter with him here at the pharmacy. He came in all in a tizzy. It was obvious he had been drinking and doing who knows what else. 1 didn't have his prescription ready, even though he had just called it in no more than ten minutes before that. He cursed at me right in front of Susan and another customer. The young man is scum, Martha. People like him never change," answered Sam, his voice rising and not as shaky as before.

"But why, Sam? Why jeopardize everything you've worked for? It just doesn't make any sense."

Sam let out a deep sigh and looked around his pharmacy, a business that he had built from the ground up, as his red-rimmed eyes scanned around the room. "I had a good run of success in my life. Now it's almost all over. More than likely, I'll be forced to sell my business . . . and Ida, the love of my life, will be gone soon . . . gone forever. I'll have to deal with her loss from behind bars . . . like a common criminal. Oh my god, from a successful businessman to a convicted felon, how did I manage to let my life steer so far off course, Martha?"

"Are you asking a rhetorical question, Sam?"

"I was in financial trouble. I'm a small business owner. You know how expensive health insurance is for people like Henry and me, with just a few employees. Ida's medical bills are already through the roof." Sam paused and glanced up at the ceiling for a few seconds before lowering his gaze once again. "Ah hell, it's more than that, Martha. I have a gambling problem. I lost a lot of money at the Aksarben horse races in Omaha last year, a lot of money. I was in danger of losing the business. I had to do something. Framing Randy Whitfield seemed to be the only answer. You unwittingly told me when 1 could be sure he wouldn't be home so I could search through his garage while he was at his nightly meeting. 1 drove by his house a few times first. 1 noticed a small door to his garage was always left open. I walked through from the alley. 1 didn't even have to break in. I thought I hit the jackpot when 1 found a pair of his boots out in his garage. I borrowed them the night before the burglary."

"The boots were too small for you, though, weren't they, Sam?" Martha asked.

"You must have slipped when you were walking down the steep cellar steps."

Sam got a scared look on his face, seemingly reliving that night in his mind before answering, "Yeah, the boots were a snug fit for me, but that's not what made me slip going down the stairs. After 1 had taken a couple of steps down, I felt a push against my back. It scared the hell out of me. I slid all the way down the rest of the way. I turned around to see who it was, and nobody was there. I hurried back up the steps and looked around. There wasn't a soul in sight. It scared me so much that I thought about scrapping my plan. I finally decided that it must have been my imagination. I took a few deep breaths before going back down into the cellar again."

Martha's face was inflamed with emotion. Her cheeks had turned a rosy red. "So that's what caused you to slip. It wasn't because the boots were too small after all. Interesting that I was able to find incriminating evidence but not for the same reason that I had thought I'd found."

"How did you figure all that out?" Sam inquired with a perplexed look on his face.

"Sam, you know I've always laundered the white smocks and towels in the washer and dryer in the back room. The day after the burglary, I was doing a load of the dirty smocks. There was dried red mud on the back of one of the smocks that had your name stenciled on the front. The only place around here where the mud is that red is back around the cellar door. So I went back there and looked at the footprints that the police had found. The prints looked pretty deep to me, like someone had to weigh a lot more than Randy Whitfield to make that deep of a print in the mud."

"Sounds like you've been wasting your talents all these years working for me," Sam answered. "I got so rattled after sliding down the cellar stairs

I wasn't thinking right after that. I was lucky I was able to finish the job, let alone remember to check the back of my smock before tossing it in the hamper. By then, my hands were shaking so badly it was everything I could do to get out of the building with the bag of drugs. It took me several tries just to get my key into the ignition of my car. Guess I flunked the course for clever crooks."

"Why did you wear your smock while you were breaking into you own business?" Martha asked.

"I figured if someone spotted me back there, they wouldn't be suspicious if they saw me in my white pharmacy smock. If someone had come along as I was about ready to break the padlock, 1 would have acted like I was repairing my own property and canceled the break-in until another night. But no one came along during the time that I was there. I knew the police wouldn't be by until eleven o'clock."

After Sam finished talking, he scanned around the pharmacy; the realization that he was busted must have really been starting to sink in by then. He reached up with his right hand and pinched at his runny nose. "Martha, you must have found more of a reason than what you've told me. You seemed to be so sure when you walked in here."

"I did. In all the years I've worked for you, Sam, you've never locked your desk before. Sometimes when I was doing paperwork, my pen would run out of ink. I always could find a spare pen in one of your desk drawers. I never told you that my first actual job lasted only a week with a locksmith that wanted to put a lip-lock on me. Before I finally hit him in the head with my purse and never went back, he showed off to me how easy it is to pick a lock if you know what you're doing.

"When I discovered that your desk was locked a few days ago, 1 finally got up the courage to pick the lock yesterday afternoon when you were up at the hospital. I didn't want to believe that you were capable of doing such a thing, but I didn't want to see Randy Whitfield go to prison for something he didn't do either. After finding the mud on the back of your smock, I was suspecting that you might have something to hide. I was right unfortunately. I also didn't buy your story that you forgot to lock the trapdoor after the tornado warning. You've always been so security conscious. I found one of the stolen drug bottles in the back of your top left drawer. The bottle was half empty."

"I've been giving Ida additional pain medication the past few days to help ease her pain even more. After I got the insurance money, I was going to slowly use up the rest of the stolen drugs while filling prescriptions over the next few months. I guess it was stupid of me to leave some in my desk drawer here at work. It never entered my mind that anyone would break into my locked desk, especially you, Martha." He was looking like he'd lost much more than his reputation and probably his business of thirty years.

Sergeant Bradford pulled up out front. Ace turned from outside the front window and trotted back over to the pickup truck bed, jumping back in as Bradford got out of his patrol car. Bradford nodded at Henry as he walked by on his way to the front door of the pharmacy.

Both Sam and Martha looked at the front door as Sergeant Bradford was about to enter. Henry must have said something to Bradford because he temporarily stopped and looked at the pickup truck before opening the door. "1 didn't tell him everything, Sam. I was hoping if you yourself confessed voluntarily, maybe the judge would go easier on you. I'm going to go tell Henry to go home. I'll stick around for now and make sure the pharmacy is taken care of after you leave."

"What about Rick and Susan? Oh Jesus, this is the most embarrassing moment of my entire life," Sam said as he took his glasses off and rubbed his eyes again before hastily putting them on.

"I'll talk to them for you. Don't worry, it's time for you to do the right thing now," Martha said reassuringly.

"Martha, please try and keep this news from Ida. She doesn't have to know about this," Sam pleaded. "I don't think she's very aware anymore of who's by her bedside. She's really gone downhill in the past couple of days. The doctors told me this morning that she probably doesn't have much time left. But if she does come around . . . and wants to know where I am . . . make something up . . . anything, I don't care, as long as . . . she doesn't know about what I've done. I couldn't live with myself if she were to know the truth. Help spare her that. Please, Martha." Sam looked thoroughly defeated. His cheeks were all flush, and his shoulders were drooping. His eyes were all red, and his glasses were now on crooked as he was leaning forward with his hands on the counter, his arms supporting his weight and possibly preventing him from passing out at that moment.

"I'll do the best I can, Sam. I'll stay by her side at the hospital as much as possible from now on," said Martha. She saw that Sergeant Bradford had come through the door. "1 better go outside now." She walked toward Bradford.

Sergeant Bradford and Martha exchanged solemn looks as they passed each other halfway between Sam and the front door. Martha opened the front door and walked out to talk to Henry while Bradford sauntered up to Sam at the front counter. "Bill, I have something to tell you," Sam said with a shaky voice. His troubled face and watery eyes were undoubtedly a look that Sergeant Bradford had never seen before.

Martha leaned against the driver's door of the pickup as she tried to look inside the pharmacy. "I hope I never have to go through anything like that again as long as I live."

Henry reached for the door handle. "Step back, Mother, so I can get out." "What are you doing, Henry? I told you to go on home," Martha said as she took a step back so Henry could get out of the truck.

"1 know. I just thought you might need a little hug right now," said Henry as he swung the door open, stepping out onto the street. Ace moved over and tried to lick Martha on the face from the edge of the truck bed, but she was out of range, oblivious of his attempt to help cheer her up, as she and Henry embraced next to the pickup truck. Martha was thinking about how lucky she was to have Henry as her husband—good old honest Henry. He wasn't the sharpest tack in the shed, but he had always been there for her through good times and bad.

Randy and Brenda were finishing up a steak dinner at a cheap steakhouse on the outskirts of Omaha. It was Saturday evening. They were celebrating Randy's release from jail that afternoon. Brenda hadn't been able to come up with the bond money. She had given up and was going to call her parents for the money, but when she had last visited Randy in jail and told him of her intentions, he was adamant that she not call them.

They were sitting at a small round table, one of many positioned together in the center of the dining area. The place was very busy with a wide variety of casually dressed patrons. There were couples, families, and a few people eating alone. Most of the tables were full as well as the booths that were lined along three of the four walls, with the kitchen, counter area, and bathrooms crammed in along the fourth wall at the back.

Large continuous plateglass windows were all along the walls with booths, only broken up by the front entrance area, where the hostess and cashier stood to the right of the door. The logo-emblazoned exterior tarp awnings that hung all around the three sides of the restaurant above the windows adequately contained the setting sun. The place was cheaply decorated with the old Wild West look, complete with wagon wheels mounted on the back wall and a cow's head mounted above the kitchen door.

"We should have brought Trevor along too. I feel guilty leaving him again with Rita and David," said Brenda.

"Oh, he'll be just fine," replied Randy as he snuffed out his cigarette in the ashtray. "I think Rita thought we should spend some time alone together tonight. I never realized until these past few weeks what good friends we have in her and David. And how about Martha Bozell? I can never thank her enough for coming forward like she did. I almost felt guilty accepting the fifty bucks from her. I'm sure she knew we couldn't afford to go out tonight without it. I only wish I could have taken you to a fancier place."

Brenda took the last bite of her baked potato, contemplating whether she had any room for dessert. She had mentioned to Randy a couple of minutes earlier that she was thinking that a dish of ice cream or piece of apple pie might be in order. She was beginning to enjoy herself, but Randy still had a lot to make up to her before she would truly trust and respect him again. She never could have imagined ever having a good time with him again as recently as a day earlier. She was looking at him with an air of skepticism. "I guess you really have changed, haven't you? You never noticed people's help and friendship before. As for the fifty dollars, I think Martha felt a little guilty for not saying something sooner. It probably was bothering her that you were stuck in jail for so long."

Randy looked back at Brenda with the most angelic expression on his face that she had undoubtedly never before seen or could have ever imagined seeing on her often troubled boyfriend's face. "I don't hold any grudges about that. I heard she's been working for Goldstein for close to, what, thirty years. I know it had to be more than just an owner-employee relationship. It must have been really hard for her to confront him like she did." Randy then stabbed into the last piece of steak on his plate. He pulled his Zippo lighter out of his pants pocket in anticipation of lighting up another cigarette once his food was gone.

"Randy, I've noticed you're smoking a lot more since I got home. Don't you think you ought to cut down a little bit?"

"Yeah, I probably should. But you've got to understand, Brenda. It's the only vice I've got left, just like all my new friends at the nightly meetings I go to. We drink so much coffee while we're there I have a hard time going to sleep some nights. It's like still getting wired but in a legal way. As for the smoking, we always crack a lot of windows during our meetings, but the cigarette smoke still hangs in the air like a thick fog. It's smokier than most of the bars I've ever been in. I guess it's a stupid rationale that by getting rid of one bad habit, we double up on the other one that's left. For some of the poor suckers I see in there, I don't get the impression they've found that serenity we always talk about while we're there. Don't get me wrong. The program has been a lifesaver for many alcoholics."

Randy paused and looked searchingly into her eyes. "I'm not miserable, Brenda. I've found serenity, a feeling of peace that I've never felt before in my life. I promise you, 1'll start cutting down from now on. Hell, I might even quit altogether someday. I know it's not good smoking so much in front of Trevor."

For the first time that evening, Brenda finally smiled at Randy from across the table. "You know what, Randy, you're starting to say all the things I've always dreamed of and wanted to hear from you ever since I fell in love with you back in high school. It's still going to take some time before 1 lose all the anger that I've felt toward you these past couple of years. This sudden change in you seems genuine, but it's still too soon to think that you can just erase the damage that was done to our relationship."

At that moment, she remembered her affair in Philadelphia when Randy was over in Vietnam. She knew she would never tell him, but she also knew it wasn't necessary to tell him to expunge any remaining guilt left over from that indiscretion. There seemed to have been enough poetic justice on both sides that had transpired since then to eliminate the need for true confessions.

Randy returned her earlier smile. "I love you, Brenda, very much. 1 don't blame you for being a bit skeptical at this point. I can only promise you that, in the coming months, I'm going to prove to you that this change is permanent." After chewing and swallowing his remaining piece of steak, Randy picked up his bottle of pop and held it in front of him. "I propose a toast," he said with a very serious expression emerging on his face.

Brenda picked up her bottle of beer and held it in front of her. She felt a little guilty drinking beer in front of Randy. She pondered how ironic it was that she was thinking that way, realizing that such a thought would never have even entered her mind just a few weeks ago.

Randy tapped his bottle of pop against Brenda's beer bottle. "To us. May we live together in happiness at least as many years as the Bozells have enjoyed together."

Brenda smiled as she took a sip of her beer as Randy drank his pop. She placed the bottle back down and looked intently into Randy's eyes.

"That's a good toast, Randy. But there is one major difference between us and the Bozells."

"They're older?" he asked.

"No, they're married, Randy. Martha and Henry Bozell are married," Brenda said emphatically.

"Well, I suppose we could do something about that," Randy mumbled nonchalantly as he looked up at the ceiling.

"Look at me, Randy Whitfield."

Randy lowered his gaze so he was looking at Brenda again.

"That had to be the lamest wedding proposal I've ever heard," said Brenda.

"Yeah, it was, wasn't it?" replied Randy with a sheepish grin.

"Randy, how can 1 be sure that this change in you is going to last?"

After listening to Brenda's question, Randy's expression changed from playful to serious. He looked deeply into her eyes. "I never really believed in God before. I've since heard and read that most of His faithful have never actually ever seen Him or felt His presence firsthand. Most of them believe on blind faith alone. You have no idea how special I feel that, for whatever reason, He singled me out—and I guess you as well—to know beyond blind faith that He really does exist."

Brenda returned Randy's luminous gaze, her brown eyes sparkling with delight as her sweet smile blossomed into full bloom. "You and I are lucky, Randy, and blessed. How many people can say they've seen, or at least heard, their guardian angel—and not just in a dream but also for real? Wow, I don't know what this all means. I mean, is one of us destined to do something significant for God? Who knows? Maybe it has something to do with Trevor. He's obviously very advanced in his thinking for a five-year-old.

"1 remember when he and 1 would have conversations when you were working late at the shop. It was during that first year after you got back from 'Nam, and we had moved to Plattsmouth. When we were done talking together, it would almost scare me when I realized I had been having an adult conversation with a little boy barely out of his diapers. I can't help but think there could be a connection. Let's face it, Randy, neither one of us has ever exhibited the potential for greatness. Do you think we'll ever be able to figure all this out?"

"I guess time will tell, Brend—" Randy's attempt to answer Brenda was interrupted. Before he could finish his last sentence, his chair was bumped into from behind, causing his head to bob forward and his stomach to be suddenly pressed into the side of the round table they were sitting at. Randy quickly slid his chair back and wheeled around in his seat. He was staring into a big fat belly that was covered only by a white T-shirt that was big enough to serve as a loose- fitting summer dress for Brenda. Randy was hurting his neck trying to look up high enough to see the big shaved head that was perched above this massive frame.

"Sorry, little man. Didn't mean to bump into ya when I got up," said the big trucker with tattoos all over his massive arms. His rig was parked out on the edge of the parking lot. He often told his wife that he would sometimes get tired of truck stop food and would venture a little off the interstate to get a better steak at a moderately priced steakhouse.

Randy stood up and turned to face the big man. The only trouble was he really wasn't facing him as he was still craning his neck, looking up at him. Randy looked like he was getting hot behind the collar. Here he was, minding his own business, having his victory dinner with the mother of his child, his wife-to-be, and some big dumb ass had to go and spoil the whole romantic and spiritual mood of the evening. "Who are you calling a little man, you big fat tub o' lard," Randy blurted out.

Brenda looked worried. She slid her chair back from the other side of the table and walked around next to her fiance of two minutes. "Randy, the man said he was sorry. What about your bad back? You can't risk it. This is all so childish."

Randy kept staring up at the big man. "He called me a little man. I was in the marines. I fought in 'Nam for god's sake."

The big guy's belly was still almost touching Randy in the chest. "You called me a big fat tub of lard, you little jarhead."

"Oh no, don't tell me you were a squid," Randy shot back. (Squid was a derogatory term for a guy in the navy and jarhead the equivalent for a man in the marines.)

People were looking up from other tables and whispering to one another as they observed the unusual confrontation. One of the waitresses must have alerted the manager on duty because he came scurrying over to try to calm the situation. "Do we have a problem here, gentlemen?" he asked in a low tone of voice.

With both men still locked in a stare, they responded to the manager, first Randy and then the big trucker. "No, no problem."

"No problem. I was finished anyway."

Even though neither man had quit staring at each other, the manager was apparently satisfied that blood would not be spilled on his shift. "Good, and thank you for coming to the Wagon Wheel," he said before retreating to the kitchen.

"Let's take this outside, big squid," Randy finally said, still looking up at the trucker after the manager had disappeared through the kitchen door.

Brenda rubbed her face with her hand in obvious frustration, wondering if Randy really had changed all that much. "Randy, please just let it go. It doesn't matter," she pleaded.

"Yeah, listen to her, shrimp. She's trying to save you a beatin' outside," the fat trucker said, practically spitting in Randy's face when he said the word shrimp.

Nothing apparently was going to cool Randy down at that point. "Let's go, fatso." Randy wheeled around and headed for the door.

Brenda looked like she didn't know what to do at that point. "Randy, give me the fifty so I can pay for our meal," she said. Randy turned back around and reached into his front blue jeans pocket and fished out the wad of two twenties and a ten-dollar bill to hand to her.

The trucker was throwing money on his table before waddling outside to give the little jarhead a lesson.

"Will you both not do anything until I get out there?" she naively asked of the two men, who looked like Mutt and Jeff as the big trucker followed Randy. She could hear them insulting each other all the way out the door.

"Squid."

"Jarhead."

"Squid."

"Jarhead."

Brenda hurried over to their waitress and asked for the check. She was torn. Even though she knew there probably wasn't much she could do to help Randy outside, she felt guilty thinking about the fact that their bill might be small enough that she could walk away with twenty, maybe thirty dollars. It is money that will come in real handy as we struggle to get back on our feet. No, I couldn't think that way. Run out the door and help Randy any way you can.

"Here's your check, miss," the waitress said as she handed the slip to Brenda, who was staring toward the front door.

The trucker's new blue jeans were making a swishing sound, like the sound a cricket made by rubbing his hind legs together, as the big man's fat legs rubbed together while walking directly behind Randy out of the front door. Randy could feel his hot, stinky breath beating down onto the top of his head. He expected common military courtesy that the big squid wouldn't sucker punch him before they had a chance to square off out in the parking lot.

He was luckily right in his assessment of the situation. The big man followed him out the door and around the corner of the building until they were in the most sparsely populated part of the lot near the trash dumpster. They looked at each other and then struck a defensive stance, both men raising their hands and making fists.

The big trucker must have been surprised that such a small man would dare to challenge him, ex-marine or no ex-marine. As they circled around, facing each other with fists clenched and at the ready, he asked, "What makes you think you even have a chance against me, jarhead?"

Randy grinned up at the big man. "He ought to be here any second," said Randy.

The trucker looked confused. "Who ought to be here? What are you talking about, jarhead?"

"My guardia—" Randy's response was cut short. Boom! The big man cut loose with a right jab that landed full force into Randy's left eye. Randy felt instant pain on the left side of his face as he lost his balance from the force of the blow and spun around, falling backward into the side of the trash dumpster. The side of his head bounced off the steel wall of the dumpster, and he slumped to the ground in a heap. Randy rolled over onto his back and made a half-hearted attempt to rise before falling back down and staring up at the evening sky. A lot of little black birds were flying around overhead.

Then the big man's fat face was moving down closer to the asphalt and coming into view, barely discernible behind the flying black birds. "What were you trying to say, jar—" said the trucker before being stopped in midsentence. Crash! Even in Randy's suddenly foggy state of mind, there was no mistaking the sound of glass shattering on the back of the big man's head.

And then something far worse happened. The fat man came down face first right on top of little Randy. The man's head landed a bit off to the side, but the big fat belly scored a direct hit on top of Randy's chest. Randy was gasping for air. He had never had the wind knocked out of him as badly as that moment, not even when he played football. He almost passed out.

The next thing he knew, the big limp body was being rolled off him. He looked up and saw Brenda staring down at him. "Are you all right? Can you get up and walk?" she asked.

He couldn't answer. He just stared up at her with a pathetic look on his face. Brenda finally reached down and grabbed Randy's arms, pulling him up into a sitting position. He was slowly beginning to get some air back into his lungs. It felt like maybe a rib or two might be broken or at least badly bruised.

Randy had an adrenaline rush or something and stumbled to his feet with Brenda's help. He draped his right arm around her neck as she was able to halflead and half-drag him over to the passenger door of the van. His left eye had swollen shut by the time she leaned him up against the side of the van and opened the door for him to slide into the passenger seat.

"Why didn't our guardian angel show up? Where's the big dog?" he mumbled as Brenda slammed the door before running around to the driver's side of the van to act out the role of the getaway driver while the fat man lay unconscious but still breathing next to the dumpster.

Brenda had first checked for the trucker's pulse and then kicked away the broken glass from the beer bottle after delivering the blow to the back of the big squid's head. When he came to, he wouldn't cut himself while struggling to get up. She had always been a very thoughtful person.

Randy must have passed out for a few minutes. He was being jostled around in his seat, and when his chin flopped down against his chest, he opened his one good eye and saw the oncoming cars and trucks and the highway up ahead. He tried to look out of his left eye, but he could only see well enough to make out the silhouette of Brenda in the driver's seat as she was concentrating on her driving. "Who hit the squid with the bottle? Was it you?" he asked as he tried to turn his head around far enough for his right eye to focus on Brenda.

"Yeah, it was me. I grabbed it off our table when I ran out the door," Brenda answered in a tone of voice that revealed an underlying irritation. "You have much to learn yet, Randy Whitfield. You could have easily avoided that fight back there. If you think I'm ever going to marry you, you're going to have to really change your ways. I think maybe God was testing you back there, and you failed the test big time."

"You think that's why the dog didn't show up?" Randy asked.

"That would be my guess. You weren't worthy of protection this time. If you had just accepted the man's apology, even in the way he offered it, turning the other cheek like the Bible says, we would still be sitting back there enjoying our dessert after the meal."

"Yeah, I suppose you're right."

"I know I'm right. And until you understand exactly why I'm right, I don't see a wedding ring on my finger anytime soon."

Randy was seemingly unaffected by her criticism. "Brenda, did you have to hit him in the head when he was leaning right over me? I don't know what hurts more, my eye or my chest."

. It was obvious that Brenda couldn't believe Randy was complaining about the deficiencies of her rescue effort. "Oh, so sorry. I guess I should have said, 'Excuse me, sir, but could you please move a little to the left or the right of my fiance before I smash this bottle into the back of your head?'"

Randy just snickered. He wasn't angry anymore, just very sore in two different places of his anatomy. "All right, I guess I deserved that. Thanks for helping me out back there."

"Don't mention it," she replied. "I just hope I didn't hurt that poor man too much." She kept her eyes on the road ahead.

Randy reached up with his left hand and turned the inside rearview mirror toward him so he could inspect the damage done to his face. "Oh Jesus, I look like shit," he said before turning the mirror back toward Brenda so she could readjust it for driving.

"Randy, remember what I said earlier about the fact that you still have a lot to learn about God. Well, you just said a word in the wrong context that is very offensive to the Lord."

"You mean I can't say the word shit anymore?" asked Randy.

Brenda briefly took her eyes off the road to look at Randy. "No, you lunkhead. You shouldn't take the name of the Lord in vain. It's disrespectful. When you said, 'Oh Jesus,' you used the word Jesus in a derogatory way. If you expect God to be in your corner from now on, you have to learn to treat Him with more respect."

"How come you know so much about God?" Randy asked. "You never talked about God with me before."

"I never thought you were ever interested in God before, so I never brought it up. I used to be the president of Luther League at St. Thomas Lutheran Church in Omaha back when I was in high school before I met you. I quit going to church as soon as I knew I was pregnant. It was embarrassing because I had had such a close relationship with the pastors, and they knew I wasn't married. I've really missed going to church these past few years. I'm so glad you want to go yourself now. This is all a good change for Trevor too. We need to get him baptized as soon as possible. Come to think of it, we need to get you baptized too."

"So that's something that's important if you believe in God?" Randy asked, sounding like a child learning new things for the first time.

"Yes, it's important, Randy. You'll learn everything in due time." They drove on in silence. The sun had almost disappeared entirely now on the west horizon. The oncoming headlights were becoming noticeably brighter against the backdrop of the darkening sky. "Brenda, pull off onto the shoulder of the road and stop for a minute," Randy suddenly requested.

Brenda looked worried as she glanced at Randy. "What's the matter? Are you getting sick?"

"No, not sick. Just need you to stop for a minute or two. There's something I need to do."

She looked into her rearview mirrors, making sure no one was right behind her before slowing down and pulling off onto the shoulder of the road. The van rolled to a stop, and Randy opened his door and looked at Brenda. "I want you to get out too." She had a perplexed look on her face but complied with Randy's request, opening her door. They both slid out of their seats, slamming their respective van doors and meeting up behind the van.

Randy suddenly dropped to one knee and gathered Brenda's hands in his. His expression turned very serious as he looked up at her. His left eye was swollen completely shut by now, and his left cheek was all red and puffy. He was starting to worry that maybe he could have picked a better time than that moment for what he was about to say, but then he let out a big sigh and just let it all go, blurting out, "Brenda Rogers, will you marry me?"

Just then, a semi-tractor-trailer rig came barreling by. The wind gust almost knocked Randy over as he was braced on one knee. He gathered himself, holding his ceremonial position.

"Yes, I'll marry you," she finally replied while looking intently down into his one remaining good right eye.

A red Mustang convertible full of teenage boys who had been driving in the opposite direction pulled off the road onto the shoulder directly across the highway from where the van was parked. The driver yelled out to them, "You folks need any help?"

Randy turned his head in their direction; the swollen left side of his face could easily be seen by the young occupants of the car. "Wow, lady! I don't know what he did to deserve that, but it looks like he's really sorry now!" the young driver yelled out.

The other young boys in the car cackled with laughter before the car pulled back onto the road and drove away. Randy finally stood up as the taillights from the departing car finally disappeared as it crested a hill and was gone. "Well, don't you want to jump in the van and chase after them, Randy? They just made fun of you."

"No, not really," he casually replied. "I wish it had been you who did this to my eye. I'll always have to live with the guilt, knowing that I hit you and hurt you before."

"Woof!"

They both looked at the row of trees that they had just driven by before stopping on the shoulder of the road. The trees formed what was referred to by farmers as a shelterbelt between cornfields, cutting down on soil erosion on windy days. Ace was standing by one of the larger trees. "Our guardian angel is back," Randy said as he smiled at his wife-to-be.

"That's Ace. I'm sure of it, Randy. That's the new Bozell family dog. They got him back in February or March, I think. You mean to tell me you never noticed him before over in the Bozell yard?"

Randy kept looking at Ace. "Since March, 1 either had my head in a fog or was in jail. No, 1 never noticed him across the street before. Are you sure it's the same dog?"

"Pretty sure."

"Well then, he's probably not just our guardian angel. He must be watching over the Bozells as well."

Then Ace suddenly vanished into thin air. They both just stared at each other for a few seconds, not saying a word. "Come on, Brenda, let's go home. I need to put an ice pack on this eye so I can get some of the swelling to go down before we go to church tomorrow morning. By the way, which church do you want to visit?"

"Why, a Lutheran church, of course," Brenda answered.

They both turned and walked back to the van. After slamming their doors and Brenda started the engine, Randy started chuckling. "I bet he beats us home."

Brenda checked her rearview mirrors before pulling back onto the road. She finally stepped on the gas pedal and steered the old van back onto the highway. "1'11 bet he already is home," she said with a grin as the van continued to pick up speed.

Randy stared at Brenda, looking a bit pathetic with one eye swollen shut. "Ya think it would look funny if I wore my sunglasses in church tomorrow?"

A car was sitting at a stoplight as traffic was traveling by on a main street in Downtown Plattsmouth. It was midafternoon on a sizzling hot June summer day. There were three teenage boys riding in the car. The driver was Matt Duncan, the heavyweight wrestler from Papillion. Duncan was the bigger more experienced wrestler whom Bo had defeated in his last match before his accident. The two others, one who was riding in the front seat and the other in the back, were also on the Papillion High School wrestling team.

After a couple of cars passed through the intersection, a tow truck with a painted side door that read "Bozell Body Shop" and pulling a wrecked car also passed through the intersection. The front seat passenger in the car with Duncan must have thought he saw whom they had come looking for that summer afternoon. Duncan was looking off to his left at the time. The teenage boy next to Matt Duncan pointed at the tow truck as it passed by. "That's him, Matt! Troy said he was working for his old man this summer. I'm sure that was him."

Duncan turned his head around to the front seat passenger. "Did you see anyone with him?"

The other boy shook his head. "No, it looks like he's alone. We're in luck."

As the stoplight changed, Duncan stomped down on the accelerator, his sheepish grin revealing how much he was evidently reveling in the moment. He turned left in hot pursuit of the tow truck. "This looks like it's going to be easier than I thought," he said.

The Ford Galaxy quickly caught up to the truck, and Duncan started honking his horn and flashing its headlights as he was tailgating the car that was being towed. He started waving his arm from outside his open driver's window, signaling for Bo to pull over. The car followed the tow truck for another block and a half before Bo finally signaled a right turn and pulled into an empty church parking lot. He circled around, finally stopping on the far side of the lot farthest from the church just a few feet from a grassy area used for church picnics and youth activities.

Bo slowly climbed out of the truck cab, slamming the door behind him and walking a few steps in the direction of Duncan and the other two boys, who had gotten out of the Ford Galaxy after stopping several feet behind the car in tow. Duncan walked up to Bo as the other two boys stayed a few feet behind him. Big Duncan towered over Bo as the two teenagers came face-to-face. "Hey, Bozell, remember me?"

Bo stood his ground, not flinching or showing any sign of fear. "Of course, 1 remember you, Matt Duncan. I heard you won the heavyweight state championship this year." Bo continued to stare up into the eyes of Duncan.

"Yeah, I did that," Duncan replied.

They continued to stare at each other, almost nose to nose, until Bo finally asked a casual question, trying to break the uncomfortable staredown. "So what brings you and your friends to Plattsmouth?"

Duncan turned away from the stare and spit onto the asphalt before answering, "I decided to come and find you."

Bo gave the appearance of outwardly looking puzzled toward Duncan, but inside his head, he knew instinctively what was going on. "Why would you want to come and see me?"

"Oh, I think you know why, Bozell. You embarrassed me in that match in Papillion earlier this year. I think it was a fluke. I think you just plain got lucky."

Bo stood motionless, not making a move. He knew Duncan could explode at any given moment, but he had a hunch that he wouldn't sucker punch him or anything like that. He had a hunch that Duncan was after greater satisfaction. "I guess you're entitled to your opinion."

Duncan moved even closer and really got into Bo's face. "I knew you were a smart-ass, Bozell! That's why 1 want a rematch! Over there in the grass. Right now, you and me, one-on-one!"

Bo continued to stand his ground, not showing any noticeable emotion. "I'd love to oblige you, but I can't," he calmly replied.

Duncan looked really pissed off now. "What do you mean you can't? Why can't you?" he shouted as he was practically spitting into Bo's face with every word.

"'Cause the doc told me 1 couldn't ever wrestle again."

Duncan appeared like he really wasn't sure how to react to Bo's excuse. He looked dumbfounded for a few seconds. "1 think you're just making excuses, Bozell! 1 demand a rematch! Right now!"

Bo didn't flinch. He looked steely eyed and mysterious like his favorite actor, Gregory Peck. "You know what, Duncan, right now, there's nothing I'd like better than to go over there in that grass and kick your ass. But if I did that, you'd have won, and I would be the loser, maybe for the rest of my life."

Matt Duncan's eyes opened wider, and he suddenly looked cross-eyed. "You're talkin' gibberish now, Bozell. I think you're just plain scared." Then he unexpectedly pushed Bo in the chest, causing Bo to lose his balance and back up a step. Duncan continued with his tirade. "I don't think you've got the guts to take me on. That's what I think."

Bo kept returning Duncan's stare with his own. He hesitated for a few seconds before dropping the bomb on Duncan. "Maybe not, but I do have an ace up my sleeve."

Duncan shook his head as if to shake the cobwebs out. "What the hell are you talkin' about, Bozell? You're wearin' a damn T-shirt!"

Bo had decided it was time for reinforcements. While looking Duncan square in the eyes, he suddenly yelled out, "Ace!"

The big dog, which had been lying low in the truck cab like Bo had instructed, came flying out of the open driver's side window. Ace was barking and snarling all the way, with teeth exposed and eyes blazing like a wild wolf attacking his prey, as he charged toward Matt Duncan. Duncan looked temporarily in a state of shock at this sudden turn of events. He tried to move his legs, but it looked like they were stuck in mud. He was like a dead man walking—or, in this case, standing—like an elk in the crosshairs of a hunter's bow. Before Duncan could probably even think about running for his life, Ace was on him. The dog hit him squarely in his chest with his two front paws, and Duncan fell onto his back like a rag doll.

While all this was happening, his two friends—who were supposed to be providing backup—had beaten feet to the car, quickly jumped inside, and slammed their doors. Ace had big bully Duncan pinned to the ground with his front paws on his chest and his rear paws straddling his legs.

Duncan's face said it all. He looked terrified as Ace barked and snarled, keeping Duncan trapped and helpless. The bullmastiff had the recently crowned state heavyweight wrestling champion pinned to the ground, with his big head inches from the big boy's terrified face.

Bo knew that Ace was waiting for further instructions from his master. What seemed to be a good idea at the time suddenly popped into the master's head. "Ace, 1 think it's time to give Mr. Duncan a bath."

Ace responded to Bo's command by shaking his head back and forth over the boy's face. A flashflood of slobber sprayed and streamed all over Duncan's face and shirt. He was moving his head back and forth, trying to remove some of Ace's drool that was lying on his face like mud puddles in a potholed road. Ace's young master was quite amused that his sudden good idea had worked to perfection, but alas, all good things must come to an end. Besides, he was starting to worry that it could turn out to be the first recorded asphalt drowning in the state of Nebraska. "All right, Ace, let him up."

Ace stepped aside, and Matt Duncan slowly got up from the asphalt surface, pulling up the front bottom of his gray T-shirt to wipe off the dog goobers that remained on his face. As Duncan wheeled around and started to walk to his car, he turned his head in Bo's direction. His eyes looked like they were on fire, just like how they looked in the Papillion gymnasium the night when Matt Duncan lost his only match of the year. He yelled back at Bo, "You haven't heard the last of me, Bozell! You're dead meat now!"

Bo's face broke out into a big shit-eating grin as he answered Duncan, "Oh, you shouldn't have said that, at least not until you're back in your car."

Ace started barking again and chased after Duncan. The boy ran for his car, quickly jumped into the driver's seat, and closed the door. A half second later, Ace rammed into it, causing a noticeable dent in the middle of the door. Matt Duncan fumbled for his car keys in his pocket.

The three Papillion teenagers looked to be in a state of panic at that point. "Come on, Matt! Let's get out of here!" yelled the front seat passenger.

"Ace! That's enough, boy!" Bo yelled.

Ace ignored Bo and went over to the right rear tire and took a chomp out of it with his teeth. The tire quickly lost its air pressure and went flat. Ace was still not done. He trotted around to the other rear tire and lifted his leg on it, the ultimate dog insult.

"Ace! That's enough! They've had enough!" Bo pleaded. He knew that things had quickly gotten out of hand.

The barking, snarling dog then came around to the front of the car and jumped up on the front hood, causing yet another dent in the hood of a car that didn't have as much as a scratch on it minutes before. He moved up until he was right in front of the windshield. The big dog stopped barking and snarling only long enough to grab the driver's side wiper blade in his mouth, ripping it off the car. He then did the same to the passenger's side wiper blade.

The boys in the car were looking very panic stricken at that point. Ace continued to bark, snarl, and throw dog drool all over the front windshield.

Was the monster dog going to start eating the car until he got to them? "Ace! Come here, Ace!"

Ace finally jumped off the front hood of Duncan's car and trotted back over to Bo. This time, Duncan remained silent as he and his two friends probably just wanted the big dog and Bo to go away at that point.

"Come on, Ace, back in the truck." Bo went over to the tow truck and opened the door as the mastiff jumped back into the truck cab. Bo couldn't help himself. He had to get in one last parting shot. "Hey, Duncan! If you don't have a spare tire, I could give you guys a tow to the nearest filling station!" he yelled as he climbed back into the driver's seat before closing the door.

Duncan just glared back at Bo through his mostly closed window without saying a word.

"Sorry! Just thought 1 should offer!" Bo turned the ignition key, and the big engine began to rumble again as he put the truck in gear and drove away.

Inside the tow truck cab, with a scowl on his face, Bo turned to Ace. "I just asked you to scare them, Ace! Did you have to trash their car? 1 didn't say anything about trashing their car! Are you going to pay for the damages?"

"Woof!" the dog answered.

"What with? Dog bones?" Bo looked a little disgusted as he drove back to the shop.

Ace was in agony as he looked at his young master, who was staring straight ahead, giving his full attention to his driving. He wanted to be able to say, *I'm sorry. I know I got a little carried away back there. I just got caught up in the moment. I don't often get the chance to really enjoy being a scary big dog.*

It has its drawbacks though. I've got a splitting headache, and I think I loosened a tooth when I bit into that tire. But it was worth every minute of it. Those boys back there had to be taught a lesson. Besides, it was part of my mission. As for covering the cost of the damages, you're on your own there, kid. There's only so much I can do in my present capacity, like trying to explain my actions with the one-word vocabulary of woof.

Several days later, Bo was picking at his food as he was having supper with Henry and Martha in the Bozell kitchen. He was noticeably upset. Ace was not in the kitchen with them.

"Bo, you've barely touched your food. You need to eat something," said Martha.

Bo continued to stare down at his full plate of food. "I'm just not hungry, Ma."

Henry didn't look like he was having any trouble eating his share of the food. He looked at his son in between bites. "Stop worrying, son. Ace will get to come back home tomorrow."

Bo was thinking the worst, and his father's consoling comments weren't helping. "Not if the judge thinks Ace is a danger to society like the Duncans claim."

"You're worrying over nothing. He didn't hurt anybody." Henry took another mouthful of food before continuing, "You know, if you hadn't picked him up after leaving the shop that day, this never would have happened."

Martha rolled her eyes, surmising that it had apparently become obvious to Henry that nothing he or Martha could say was going to cheer their son up. So in typical Henry fashion, he must have decided that if he couldn't cheer Bo up, he might as well remind him again about what caused the whole mess in the first place. Martha glared at Henry. "Henry, we've already had this conversation. Bo feels bad enough as it is."

Bo had a quick comeback for his father. He didn't need Martha's help. "If I hadn't picked him up on that tow run that day, I might be in the hospital right now. Besides, he was getting awfully lonely stuck in the dog run all the time."

Henry, being the primary source of Bo's comeback abilities, had a pretty good one of his own. "It can't be any worse than being stuck in the dog pound for the past week. But you do make a good point about Ace protecting you against that Neanderthal." Henry really was a good father. Through the years, Martha had always been a witness to the fact that her husband always seemed to try the best he could to balance out his criticism with something positive.

Henry cut, stabbed, and chewed up a couple of more bites of his steak. When he finally broke the silence, he was looking down at his plate, scooping up some com onto his fork. "What are the odds? The only time Ace is with you when you're working, Matt Duncan shows up, causing trouble."

"Yeah, the only time," Bo repeated.

Henry scooped up the last of his corn on his plate with his fork and his left index finger. "You were stoppin' and picking him up every time 1 sent you out in the truck, weren't you, son?" "How did you know?" Bo asked.

Henry continued to chew his final mouthful of corn before answering, "1 didn't, until just now."

"Henry, will you let it go for crying out loud? He's never going to eat his supper if you keep badgering him," Martha implored.

"All right, I'm done. Actually, I'm a little relieved. I was beginning to think that my youngest son was the slowest worker I've ever had. I couldn't figure out why it was taking him so long to pick up the wrecks. Now that I know he was making two extra stops at the house each trip, I feel better." Henry finally smiled, but to Bo, it looked faked. His father slid his chair out from the kitchen table and turned his attention to his wife. "So what time do we have to be at the courthouse tomorrow?"

Martha looked at the clock on the kitchen wall as if she needed help in answering. "The hearing is set for ten o'clock."

It was midmoming in front of the Cass County Courthouse. The Bozells'
attorney, Lloyd Townsend, was running late. Most everyone else was
already inside the courtroom. Leonard Bozell was standing by himself near
the front entrance at the top of the steps. He had gone into the courtroom
with Alice, but he had come back outside when he saw that Townsend
wasn't there yet. He watched Randy Whitfield and Brenda Roberts walk
into view from around the comer and up the steps past him.

Within a couple of minutes, Randy had come back outside to the front
steps as well. He lit up a cigarette as he stood a few feet from Leonard.
It was a beautiful summer morning. The sky was cloudless, and the sun
was shining directly into their faces, causing both men to squint a little
as they seemed to be watching for someone. Randy took a few drags on
his cigarette before glancing at Leonard. "You're Bo's uncle, aren't you?"
Randy asked after exhaling some smoke into the air.

Leonard looked at Randy, trying to remember where he had seen him
before. "Yes, I'm Leonard Bozell," he answered.

Randy stepped over with his hand extended, and Leonard shook
hands with him as Randy introduced himself. "I'm Randy Whitfield. I'm
a neighbor of your brother's family. I've seen you before over at Henry and
Martha's house. I live across the street from them."

Leonard's face produced a smile. "Oh yeah, you're the young fellow
that Sam tried to frame for his pharmacy break-in, aren't you?"

"That would be me," Randy answered as he and Leonard let go of
each other's grip.

"How did you get that black eye?" Leonard asked.

"It's a long story. Let's just say it was a lesson learned," replied Randy. "You should have seen it a week ago. It's starting to look a lot better now."

They both turned their attention away from each other and looked at the comer of the courthouse where it was likely that Lloyd Townsend would appear at any moment. "You just come out for a smoke, or are you waiting for someone?" Leonard asked as he continued to look at the front sidewalk where it emerged from the southeast corner of the building.

"Actually, I was waiting for your brother's attorney," Randy finally answered.

"Oh yeah? So am I," answered Leonard.

Randy, who had still been watching for Townsend, suddenly turned his full attention to Leonard. "If you don't mind me asking, why do you want to talk to their attorney? I assume it has to do with the dog."

"Well, yeah, sort of, I guess," Leonard replied. "Is that what you want to talk to him about?"

Randy didn't answer at first as he looked up at the morning sky to the west before lowering his gaze and staring back at Leonard. "Yeah, 1 just wanted to know if he thought he had a strong defense—you know, if he was completely confident about getting Ace off the hook."

Leonard looked skeptically at Randy. "I know you're their neighbor and all, and I'm sure you're grateful to Martha for what she did for you, but I'm a little surprised that it's that important for you to talk to their attorney before the hearing."

"Well, no disrespect, Mr. Bozell, but I think the same could go for you. Why is it so important to you to stand out here waiting to talk to Lloyd Townsend?"

"Because I don't want to see Ace put to sleep because I think he's a very special dog."

"Are you talking special as in here one second and gone the next?" asked Randy.

Leonard had to digest for a second what Randy had just asked. His face finally lit up as he looked intently into Randy eyes. "You . . . you mean you've seen him do it too?"

"Yeah, I've seen him come and go," Randy said in a surprisingly casual tone.

"And I take it you have as well, Mr. Bozell."

"Call me Leonard."

"Okay, Leonard, why doesn't Ace just simply, you know, disappear to get out of this?"

"I thought of that too. I'm guessing he's not done here yet. If he just suddenly disappeared, he would have a lot of explaining to do once he came back, that is, if he eventually ever did come back. Wait a minute. What am I saying? A dog can't really explain anything. It doesn't matter. I'd like to see him stick around. He was responsible for saving my life. Heck, come to think of it, he also saved Bo's life."

"You can make that three people he's saved. Well, in a way, he saved my life. I know he had a hand in at least prolonging it for me," Randy added.

"Maybe he's supposed to save a few more lives or help more people before he leaves," Leonard hypothesized. "He's certainly done a lot already in the short time he's been here."

They stood in silence for a few seconds before Leonard continued their unusual conversation. "You know, it's too bad we can't be character witnesses for Ace."

Randy chuckled with a smirk on his face. "Oh yeah, I can see the headlines now. 'Two men testify under oath as character witnesses at the hearing for the Bozell dog, claiming that the dog has apparently been sent from God and has the power to teleport himself when he needs to help somebody in trouble.' Yeah, that would make you and me look good and sane, now wouldn't it?"

Leonard contemplated what Randy had just said. He was still worried, but he tried not to show it. "You know what, Randy, we might as well go back inside because there's nothing we can say that would be believed anyway. We're just going to have to hope that old Lloyd Townsend gets Ace off. He's a good lawyer. I'm confident he'll get the job done for us. Hopefully, Judge Murphy won't unknowingly play out the role of Pontius Pilate."

He surely had lost Randy with his last comment as Randy had been missing in action during the years that many young boys and girls, willingly or unwillingly, learned about all the significant biblical characters in Sunday school classes across the country. "Who?" he asked with a perplexed look on his face.

"Never mind. Are you coming back in with me?" Leonard asked.

"Yeah, I'm right behind you. Maybe when this is over, you can tell me more about this Paunchy character. I've been going to church for the past few weeks, and I've learned that Jesus was a carpenter and that some of His followers were fishermen, but I haven't heard about any pirates yet." Leonard just smiled, turned, and headed into the door with Randy close behind him. No sooner had they disappeared through the big double doors than Lloyd Townsend, a heavyset, frumpy-looking older gray-haired man in a wrinkled suit, came walking around the corner, heading toward the steps of the courthouse with his briefcase in tow.

In the courtroom a few minutes later, Henry was sitting at the defendant's table with Lloyd Townsend while Bo and Martha sat right behind them. The Duncans were sitting behind the Cass County district attorney, Martin Brunlow, a sharp-dressed tall man in his late thirties. The judge had not entered the courtroom yet.

There were quite a few people in attendance. Randy Whitfield and Brenda Roberts sat near Bo's uncle Leonard and aunt Alice. Some of Bo's friends, mostly from the wrestling team, were sitting in the gallery that was sectioned off from the front of the courtroom by a three-foot tall railing. Bonnie, Marvin, and Tanya were also there, as well as quite a few curious townspeople who had heard about the hearing. On the other side, sitting next to the Duncans were the two wrestler friends who were with Matt Duncan on the day of the incident. The court reporter was in attendance, and the bailiff was standing in the front corner of the room next to the door where the judge would enter.

The courthouse was old, but it looked well maintained. The courtroom itself had a high ceiling with six big suspended lights, which added to the lighting provided by some large arched windows on the west wall. The entire front wall and judge's bench was finished in light mahogany panels, and the remaining three walls were painted a grayish-white color with some strategically placed paintings of pioneer families and previous Plattsmouth dignitaries.

Henry leaned over to Townsend and whispered in his ear, "1 really thought when 1 offered to fix their car for free, they'd drop their complaint against Ace."

Townsend extended his right hand and patted Henry on his shoulder. "You tried, Henry. Don't worry, we'll save your dog."

Everyone was talking in hushed tones as they awaited the arrival of the judge. Suddenly, a door opened in the front left corner of the courtroom, and a very distinguished-looking older man in a black robe entered and walked to the bench in front. The bailiff talked loudly from the front comer of the courtroom as the judge entered the room. "All rise! The Honorable Joseph P. Murphy presiding." Everyone stood up until Judge Murphy had taken his seat.

The judge was in his early sixties with silver hair, clean shaven, and wearing black-rimmed glasses. He was of medium build and height, but there was an unmistakable aura of authority that emanated from the judge the minute he entered the courtroom. This was his domain. He seemed clearly in charge. Pity any poor fool visiting his courtroom who didn't understand that obvious fact.

Judge Murphy sat down and then addressed the rest of the courtroom. "You may be seated." Everyone sat back down as Judge Murphy shuffled through some papers in front of him.

The bailiff continued with his bailiff stuff—stuff he'd said so many times that he probably could have said the words in reverse just to make it more interesting and less boring for him. "Hear ye, hear ye. Cass County Court is now in session to hear the case of *County of Cass v. Henry R. Bozell.*"

The judge finally began the hearing in the usual manner. "Let the record note that the county of Cass district attorney and the defendant, Henry Bozell, represented by counsel, are all in attendance in the courtroom at this time." Judge Murphy looked at the district attorney. "Okay, Mr. Brunlow, you may proceed."

Brunlow took his cue from the judge and stood up before speaking. "Your Honor, Mr. and Mrs. Daniel Duncan, alleging that Henry Bozell is harboring a dangerous animal, have filed a criminal charge in Cass County." He cleared his throat before continuing, "On the afternoon of June 15, 1969, it is alleged that the dog owned by the Bozells attacked

Matt Duncan, son of Mr. and Mrs. Daniel Duncan of Papillion, Nebraska. The attack occurred in the parking lot of St. Timothy Lutheran Church in Plattsmouth, Nebraska. The Duncans maintain that the Bozell dog is a menace and a danger to the community. Further, because of this dog's size and temperament, he could easily cause serious bodily harm to an innocent person or other animal at any given time in the future. For these reasons, Cass County—on behalf of the Duncans—is seeking the court's ruling that the Bozell dog should be put to sleep."

All the people who were at the hearing in support of the Bozells reacted to Mr. Brunlow's request to the judge that, basically, Ace should be executed. The noise had obviously became too much for Judge Murphy as he grabbed his gavel and pounded it on his bench a few times. "Silence! If we have another outburst like that, I will have this courtroom cleared!"

Brunlow sat back down, showing no expression. The judge continued after the courtroom quieted down, "Mr. Townsend, you may make your opening statements."

Townsend whispered something to Henry and finally stood up and addressed the court. "Your Honor, it is our contention that there were mitigating circumstances surrounding the events that led up to the aggression displayed by the Bozell dog on the afternoon of June 15. The Bozell dog was simply protecting Bo Bozell, son of Henry and Martha Bozell, from the aggressive behavior displayed by Matt Duncan at that time. Unfortunately for my client, the only witnesses at the scene were friends of Mr. Duncan. However, we intend to prove that the Bozell dog acted only when called on by Mr. Bozell and in a manner that posed no direct bodily harm to Mr. Duncan or Mr. Larsen and Mr. Malloy, who accompanied Mr. Duncan on that afternoon." Mr. Townsend sat back down in his chair as there were assorted whispers heard from some in attendance.

Judge Murphy turned his attention to Brunlow once again. "Mr. Brunlow, do you have any witnesses that you'd like to testify before the court at this time?"

Brunlow stood back up and made eye contact with Judge Murphy. "1 do, Your Honor. The county of Cass calls Matt Duncan to the stand." Matt Duncan rose from his chair and walked to the witness stand. The bailiff walked over and placed the Holy Bible he was carrying in front of

Matt Duncan, who then placed his hand on it. "Do you solemnly swear to tell the truth, the whole truth, and nothing but the truth, so help you God?"

"I do."

The bailiff then returned to his previous spot as Mr. Brunlow approached Duncan on the stand. "Mr. Duncan, what were you and your friends doing in Plattsmouth on the afternoon of June 15?"

Duncan looked down at his feet and then returned his gaze to the district attorney before he answered the question. "We drove over to see a friend of ours who used to live in Papillion."

"And how is it that you and your friends came into contact with Bo Bozell?" Brunlow asked.

"We had just gotten into town when we saw Bozell drive by us," Duncan replied, blinking his eyes several times as he answered.

"And how did you end up in the parking lot of St. Timothy Lutheran Church with him?"

Duncan hesitated for a few seconds as though he hadn't heard the question. "I pulled out behind him and started flashing my headlights and honking until he noticed me in his rearview mirror and pulled into the church parking lot," he finally answered.

"Why did you do that?" Brunlow asked.

"We just wanted to catch up on old times with him since we're all wrestlers. I wanted to see if he knew that I won the state heavyweight championship this year. 1 also wanted to see how he was doing since he had given up wrestling."

Brunlow turned away from Duncan on the witness stand and looked at Lloyd Townsend. He brought his arms up and tapped his fingertips together before turning around to face Duncan. He finally continued his questioning. "What happened after everyone exited their vehicles in that parking lot?"

Duncan, who had acted like he was bored with the whole affair, suddenly became more animated with his responses. "Bozell must have felt threatened or something. Before we had a chance to speak, he called his dog, who was hiding in his truck cab, to attack us."

Once again, the Bozell faithful in the courtroom erupted with disapproval over Duncan's remarks. Judge Murphy pounded his gavel.

"Order! Order in the court!" he shouted. The noise subsided from the courtroom gallery as Bo was just shaking his head in disbelief.

"What did the dog do?" Brunlow continued.

"He came flying out of the truck window and attacked us. Brent and Larry ran to the car after Bozell's dog knocked me to the ground. 1 was able to get away and make it into my car just before the dog rammed into my car door. Then he took a bite out of my left rear tire, causing it to go flat. Finally, he jumped up on the hood and ripped off my windshield wipers with his mouth."

Brunlow looked astonished after Duncan finished as though he had just heard it for the first time. This was kind of stupid on his part because there wasn't a jury in this case, and Judge Murphy knew good and well that the district attorney had rehearsed the line of questioning with the "plaintiff" before the hearing. "And then what happened?" Brunlow finally asked.

"Bozell was finally able to get his dog to come back to his truck, and then they left," Duncan concluded.

Brunlow looked at the judge. "No further questions, Your Honor."

"You may step down now, Mr. Duncan," Judge Murphy said as he looked at the big boy.

It was several minutes later when Bo was on the witness stand as the Bozells' attorney, Lloyd Townsend, was questioning him. "Are you in agreement with Matt Duncan about how you managed to come into contact with him and his friends on the afternoon of June 15?"

"Yes, it was like he said. I must have driven by them, towing a wrecked car to our body shop in the company tow truck. I finally noticed the flashing headlights and heard him honking his horn," Bo calmly replied.

"Did you recognize who it was before you pulled into the parking lot of the church?"

Bo didn't hesitate at all before he answered, "Yes. Once I noticed the Sarpy County plates, I knew right away who it was."

Townsend looked at Duncan and then back at Bo. "How could you be so sure?"

Bo also gave a quick glance at Duncan and then looked back into the eyes of Townsend. "Because I was face-to-face with him earlier in the year at a dual meet in Papillion. He and I wrestled each other that night."

"And who won that match?"

Brunlow quickly stood up and looked at the judge. "Objection, Your Honor. That's totally irrelevant to deciding the fate of the Bozell dog at this hearing."

Townsend took his thumb and index finger and rubbed them into his eyes. He then looked at Judge Murphy. "Your Honor, we are trying to prove that there was a reason why this normally docile dog acted aggressively that day, so the question is relevant."

"Overruled, Mr. Brunlow."

"Who won the match, Bo?" Townsend continued.

"1 won," Bo answered.

"And, Bo, you not only won the match but you also won by a pin in the first period, did you not?"

"Yes, I did."

After Bo had answered the question, Townsend again looked at Duncan. He continued with his next question as he had his back to Bo and was looking straight at Duncan, who looked like he had started to get a little fidgety in his chair. "Mr. Duncan has testified that there wasn't any conversation in the parking lot before your dog came charging out of the truck cab. Do you agree with Mr. Duncan's testimony?" "No. We talked," Bo softly replied.

Townsend turned back around and faced Bo. "Can you tell us the nature of that conversation?"

Bo hesitated as he closed his eyes and pinched the bridge of his nose for a few seconds before opening his eyes and finally answering the question. "I can't remember what was said word for word, but basically, Duncan asked me if I remembered him. I said 1 did. Then I told him I'd heard he won the state championship. After that, I asked him why he and his friends were in town."

"And what was Mr. Duncan's response?"

Bo responded immediately this time as he looked intently into the eyes of Townsend. "He said he'd come looking for me, that I'd embarrassed him in the match in Papillion, and he wanted a rematch . . . right then and there. He said my win was a fluke."

"And then what happened?"

Bo glanced at Duncan and then back at Townsend before answering, "I told him that my doctor said I couldn't ever wrestle again. He said I was just making excuses, and he seemed to be getting madder and madder."

"What happened then, Bo?"

Bo glanced at the judge and answered Townsend while still halflooking at Judge Murphy, "He finally pushed me backward. He shoved me in the chest. 1 decided it was time to call reinforcements."

Townsend once again had to coax out of Bo the rest of the story. "Can you be more specific, please?" he asked.

"I called for Ace, my dog."

"What did you expect your dog to do?" Townsend continued.

Brunlow stood up again and addressed the judge. "Objection, Your Honor! How can any human predict what an animal would do in such a situation?"

Townsend calmly looked at Judge Murphy. "Please bear with me, Your Honor. If you will allow the question, you'll soon see that it is indeed a valid question to ask of Mr. Bozell."

Judge Murphy hesitated for several seconds before answering. He touched his left temple with his index finger while seemingly propping up his chin with his left thumb and staring at the back wall of the courtroom. He finally looked at the district attorney. "Overruled, Mr. Brunlow. We're deciding the fate of a family pet here. You may answer the question, Mr. Bozell."

Bo continued as he turned his attention away from the judge and back to Townsend. "Well, to be totally honest, I didn't expect Ace to trash their car. I told him before I got out of the truck that he might have to scare them for me, if I called for him, but I didn't say anything about their car."

"What made you so sure that Ace wouldn't do any more than just scare them?" Townsend asked.

"The same reason Duncan and his friends thought I was alone that day," Bo responded. He then looked at his father before he continued with his explanation. "You see, I wasn't supposed to be taking Ace with me when I was working. So when I'd pick him up after leaving the shop in the tow truck, I made him sit low in the cab when we were in town, in case a friend of my pop's saw us. Ace is a big dog. It wasn't easy for him to stay hidden in that truck cab for so long, especially in the summer heat with no air-conditioning. But he's the smartest dog I've ever known. When I told him just to scare them, I knew that's all he would do. I just wish I'd said something about not trashing their car, or we all probably wouldn't be sitting here today. Ace probably didn't even see Duncan shove me. His head had to be below the level of the windows. Duncan and his friends didn't see him until I called for him. Ace was doing exactly what I told him to do if he heard me call his name."

"How was Mr. Duncan able to get away from your dog after the dog was on top of him?"

"I told Ace to give Duncan a bath, and after that, 1 said he could let him up."

"A bath?"

"Yeah, you know, slobber all over him."

The courtroom erupted in laughter. Daniel Duncan looked at his son with a troubled, disappointed look on his face as Matt Duncan buried his face in his hands. Judge Murphy had to pound his gavel once again. "Order!" The laughter quickly subsided once the judge had admonished those in attendance with his gavel and steely stare.

"No further questions, Your Honor," Townsend said as he looked at the judge. Judge Murphy turned his head toward Bo. "You may step down now, son."

Several minutes later, Lloyd Townsend was cross-examining Brent Larsen, one of the two friends who was with Matt Duncan on the afternoon of June 15. Townsend had already cross-examined Duncan, who had stuck to his story, making the same statements he had previously made to Brunlow. For some reason, Townsend hadn't pressed Duncan on any possible irregularities of his previous testimony. Bo was starting to wonder if his dad had picked the best attorney to represent them. Lloyd Townsend had enabled a lot of crucial and relevant facts to come out during his questioning of Bo, but his cross- examination of Duncan had seemed a bit lame.

"Mr. Larsen, you just told me that you've known Mr. Duncan for six years, is that correct?"

"Yes, that's what I said."

"And what is the name of the person that you all came to visit that day here in Plattsmouth?"

"Troy. Troy Manchester."

"Did Mr. Manchester know that you were all coming to see him?" "Yeah, I called him the day before."

"With your apparent good recollection of time, how long has it been since your friend Troy Manchester moved from Papillion to Plattsmouth?"

"Oh, I'd say it's been about two years probably."

"Is Mr. Manchester in the courtroom today?"

Larsen looked around the courtroom before answering, "No, I don't see him."

Townsend, who had been scanning the other faces in the courtroom along with Larsen, turned back toward him before continuing his crossexamination. "Since you are the one who called him and, I assume, the one who knows him as well or better than Mr. Duncan or Mr. Malloy, can you tell me where Mr. Manchester lives in Plattsmouth?"

Larsen looked at Duncan with a scared and apologetic look, and he still hadn't answered Townsend.

"Mr. Larsen, did you hear the question?" Townsend repeated.

"I'm not sure where he lives."

"You were coming to see him, but none of you knew where he lived?" "We were going to check in the phone book after we got into town."

"Mr. Larsen, if you talked to him on the phone the day before, why didn't you ask him for his address and directions to his house then?"

Larsen mumbled something in response that only Townsend was close enough to hear.

"Mr. Larsen, could you speak up, please? I don't think everyone heard your answer."

"1 didn't think of it," Larsen finally answered with his head down.

"Mr. Larsen, do you have Mr. Manchester's phone number memorized?" Townsend continued.

"No," Larsen quickly responded.

"How did you find the telephone number for Mr. Manchester when you called him the day before you all drove here to Plattsmouth?"

"It was in the phone book."

"Mr. Larsen, aren't the addresses listed in the phone book next to a person or family's phone number?"

Larsen's hands were trembling as he looked away from Townsend and at Duncan again. He finally looked back at Townsend and answered him, "Yes."

"Why didn't you simply note the address of Mr. Manchester in the phone book when you called him that day if you knew you were coming to see him the next day?"

Larsen hesitated and then mumbled his response again.

"Please repeat your response a little louder this time, Mr. Larsen." "I didn't think of it."

Townsend hesitated and looked all around the courtroom before continuing. He finally turned back toward Larsen and leaned on the railing of the witness stand so that his face was very close to Larsen's obviously shaken and worried face. "Mr. Larsen, was there any conversation you heard between Mr. Duncan and Mr. Bozell on the afternoon in question before the Bozell dog appeared from the truck cab?"

Larsen's hands were really trembling now as beads of sweat had formed on his forehead. He sat there, looking like a scared puppy, not answering Townsend's last important question.

"Mr. Larsen, may I remind you that you are under oath?"

Larsen looked down at his feet before he finally answered Townsend, "There might have been some conversation. I was too far away to hear anything."

Townsend stopped leaning on the witness stand railing and walked back toward his seat. He looked pleased. He had whispered to Henry earlier that he didn't really have all the hard facts before the hearing, but he did have a hunch—a very good one as it turned out. "No further questions, Your Honor," he said with his back to the judge so he couldn't see how much he was smiling at the time.

"You may step down now, Mr. Larsen," Judge Murphy sternly said with a cold look on his face. The judge looked at Matt Duncan with the same disapproving look as Larsen stepped down from the witness stand. Brent Larsen had a look of great relief on his face as he walked back to his seat while wiping the sweat from his forehead with his hand. As he walked by Matt Duncan, his friend glared at him.

A few minutes later, Townsend was finishing up with his closing statements. "In conclusion, Your Honor, I think it's clear that we have a difference of opinion about what actually occurred on the afternoon of June 15. Therefore, at this time, I think it is only fair that the object of this hearing be allowed to appear before the court. Any human being that is on trial for his or her life has been allowed to speak before the court to express his or her guilt or innocence before judgment is passed. With that precept, I ask for your indulgence, Your honor, that the Bozell dog be allowed into the courtroom at this time."

Judge Murphy didn't respond to Townsend's request initially. He reached up his right hand and rubbed the back of his neck for a few seconds while looking down at the documents in front of him. He finally looked up at the defense attorney. "Mr. Townsend, this has already been one of the more unusual cases that I have ever presided over. So by all means, bring in the dog." Townsend walked to the back of the courtroom as the people present were speaking to one another in hushed tones. He opened one of the two double doors and motioned to someone outside the door. A sheriffs deputy brought Ace into the courtroom on a leash and walked with him up the aisle and through the gated railing before stopping. Bo got up from his seat and walked over to the deputy, who had the leash in his hand. "Your Honor, will you allow me to take control of my dog at this time?"

"Go ahead, Mr. Bozell. Deputy Salinski, you may temporarily turn over custody of the dog to Mr. Bozell."

The deputy handed the end of the leash to Bo and stepped back to the closed gated railing. Bo unhooked the leash from Ace's collar as he leaned down and got face-to-face with his dog. "Ace, I want you to go up to Judge Murphy's bench and throw yourself on the mercy of the court."

Ace padded slowly up to the front of Judge Murphy's bench with his head down before flopping down on his belly. He stretched his front legs out in front him as far as they would go and rested his chin on the courtroom floor, remaining in that position without moving while rolling his sad-looking big brown eyes up at the judge.

Judge Murphy stood and leaned over his bench, looking down at Ace, who continued to maintain his "please spare me" position with his big droopy eyes, pleading for mercy. "All right, I've heard and seen enough. This case is dismissed," the judge said as he pounded his gavel one last time.

The Bozell faithful erupted in jubilation. Henry gave Townsend a big bear hug while Martha and the rest of the Bozell clan behind were smiling and hugging one another. Finally, things quieted down enough for Judge Murphy to speak again. "Ace, you can go home now."

Ace slowly rose into a sitting position and lifted one paw, waving a thank-you to Judge Murphy, before he looked back at Bo and slowly padded back over to his young master.

Judge Murphy looked at Henry, who was all smiles. "And, Henry, I hope you're not getting any ideas about using your dog to drum up more business for your body shop."

Henry shook his head back and forth. "No, Your Honor, I'd never do that. Besides, he's not my dog. He's Bo's Ace."

While the Bozells and their friends were still celebrating the judge's ruling, Matt Duncan, his parents, and Duncan's friends started to make a quick exit from the courtroom. Their departure was halted when the district attorney motioned for Daniel Duncan to come over to him. They began to have a brief conversation and were quickly joined by Daniel Duncan's wife.

Larry Malloy and Brent Larsen were almost to the door when Matt Duncan caught up to them. "Hold up, you guys," he said in a hushed tone.

Larsen got a scared look on his face before quickly passing through the door, leaving Malloy alone with Duncan. "Brent! Come back!" Duncan called out down the corridor while standing in the open doorway. Larsen quickened his pace down the hallway without looking back.

Matt Duncan took a step back into the courtroom and turned to face Malloy. "That chickenshit. When you get to his car, tell him I'll be calling him later."

"Sure, Matt, whatever you say."

Duncan stepped in closer to Larry Malloy and leaned forward, whispering in his ear, "Son of a bitch, this sure didn't turn out like I thought it would. Now I'm probably in trouble with the old man. But you know what, I don't care anymore. This still isn't over yet. If Cass County won't kill that damn dog, I'll figure out a way to do it myself."

Henry, Martha, and Bo were in the middle of eating supper. Ace was lying in his favorite spot in the corner of the kitchen. The back door was open, with a faint early evening breeze coming in through the outside screen door, and a small fan was sitting on the kitchen counter, blowing air on the highest setting toward the kitchen table. The window above the kitchen sink was wide open as well. Ace was panting more than usual as he lay on the floor. Everybody looked a little sweaty.

Martha, especially, was looking very irritated as she ate her supper. "Honest to Pete, Henry, don't you think it's about time we shut the house up and turned the air-conditioning on?"

Henry swallowed a piece of his ham before answering his wife, "Ah, come on, Mother, it's not that hot out yet. We don't even celebrate the Fourth until tomorrow."

Just then, the sound of firecrackers going off somewhere in the neighborhood interrupted their conversation. When all the loud popping of fireworks finally stopped, Martha glared at her husband. Henry undoubtedly knew the look all too well.

"Since when do we have to wait until a holiday gets here before we can get some relief from this heat? I'm sweating, Henry, and 1 don't like it. I swear, if you looked up the word cheap in the dictionary, it would have a picture of you."

Henry probably already knew that he'd be turning the air-conditioning on at that point. "Very funny, Mother. Did you just make that up?"

Martha was not amused. "I'm serious, Henry! I want the house closed up and the air-conditioning turned on while I'm doing the dishes, and that's final!"

Henry laid his fork down on his plate. "Oh, all right, Martha. Don't get your dander into an uproar. Bo and I will go around and close all the windows when we finish eating."

Ace lifted his chin off the floor enough to let out a weak woof. Henry looked back around at Ace. "Is that how you say 'thank you' in dog talk?"

"Woof!"

Henry turned back around in his chair. "I thought so," he said with a smile.

You wouldn't have that smile on your face if you really knew what I was thinking right now, Ace thought as he stared at the back of Henry's head.

Suddenly, Ace was being admonished but not by anyone in the room he could see. *I'm not apologizing. I know he's Bo's father. Yes, I know why I'm here. No disrespect, but You're not in this skin covered with fur that can't sweat, okay? Oh, You know how that would feel. Of course, You would. Sometimes I forget. Sorry about that.*

Since Martha knew she had won the battle over the hot air, or more appropriately the battle of hot air, she suddenly changed the subject. "Did the Duncans come and pick up their car yet?"

Henry nodded before answering, "Did this afternoon as a matter of fact. Mr. Duncan came and got the car just before we closed today."

Bo looked at his mother and talked while chewing on a mouthful of food. "He apologized to Pop and me. Said he realized now that Matt had lied to him."

Henry chimed back in while Bo was swallowing his food. "Yeah, he also told us even though his son would be on scholarship in the fall, he was making him go find a summer job now." *"Oh really?"* Martha responded.

"Yup. He said he told his son that, apparently, he had too much time on his hands and that he should be working this summer like Bo's doing. He said, for the first time, he didn't think he could always trust his son anymore."

Bo smiled and looked at his father. "Aren't ya glad you don't have to worry about me like that, Pop?"

Henry almost choked on his food before he answered his son, "Uh, Bo, what's the difference between what Matt Duncan did and you sneaking over to the house behind my back to pick up Ace on towing jobs?"

Bo looked downright insulted at what Henry had just said. "There's a big difference, Pop. First, I didn't lie to you. I simply withheld the truth. And second, I wasn't spending my time trying to find somebody so I could beat him up or something. 1 was working."

Henry just shook his head and rolled his eyes. "That kind of logic might work on the high school debating team, but it doesn't fly with me, son."

Bo knew that his father was going light on him, so he didn't push his luck. "1 guess that means you don't want me picking up Ace anymore on company time, huh, Pop?"

Henry didn't even bother to look up from his plate. "1 guess it does," he calmly but sternly replied to Bo.

Ace let out a moan from his corner. Henry looked around at the dog. "Oh, stop it. You're not that deprived. I refuse to let a dog lay a guilt trip on me. You're not riding shotgun in the tow truck anymore." Henry turned back around and looked at Bo. "And, Bo, Marty's going back to driving the tow truck for the next two weeks while you clean the shop from top to bottom."

Bo looked at Ace as he grimaced over what Henry had just told him. "See, Ace? It could have been worse. You only got solitary confinement, while 1 got two weeks of hard labor."

Henry must not have thought that was very funny as he glared at his son. "Should we make it three weeks?"

Bo's smirk turned into a frown. He looked more serious as he lowered his head a little. "No, sir. I'm sorry I deceived you."

Henry looked calm again before having the last word. "Sometimes we just have to learn things the hard way, son."

They all fell silent for a minute while finishing up the last of what was on their plates. Henry finished chewing his last bite of ham and looked at Martha while Bo was loading up his plate again with seconds. His thoughts must have shifted to the funeral they had attended the day before. "I heard it was some of Sam's friends that put up the bail money. It sure would have been embarrassing if he'd been handcuffed at Ida's funeral."

"Handcuffed or not, it was still the strangest funeral I've ever been to," Martha replied. "I couldn't believe the way Ida's father acted. Did you notice how often he gave Sam the evil eye? He seemed more concerned about the humiliation he apparently thinks he's enduring because of his son-in-law's arrest than grieving over the death of his only daughter. Knowing what I know about him, I think it's an ironic twist of fate that he's going through this now. It's like the old saying 'What goes around comes around.'" "Yeah, I noticed that too," said Henry before he took a sip of his iced tea. "He certainly didn't act that way when his wife died a few years back."

Martha nodded in agreement with her husband's observation. "Sam had told me before that Ida had never been very close with her parents, especially her father. She resented the fact that her father had finally told her he was proud of her only after she had married Sam. It was obvious to her that she could never please him on her own accord. It wasn't until she was the wife of one of the most respected businessmen in town that his attitude toward her had changed. He's always been such a phony. I know he never liked Leonard either. I could tell that he wasn't very happy to see Leonard and Alice at the funeral."

"Ah, to hell with him. From what you've told me, Leonard probably had more right to be there than he did," Henry said with a scowl on his face.

Martha normally admonished Henry when he used a curse word at the kitchen table but not this time. She agreed with her husband. "Have you talked to Leonard since we all left the cemetery? I couldn't believe he seemed so calm and controlled through the whole ordeal. I saw tears rolling down his cheeks a couple of times, once at the funeral and once at the cemetery. But overall, he seemed okay. I would have expected him to break down more. I don't understand what happened recently that changed Leonard's emotions so much about Ida."

Henry shook his head. "I don't understand it either, Mother. I pointblank asked him a couple of times, and he just smiled at me and said that he understood now, whatever that means."

"How's he been doing at work the past few days?" Martha asked. Bo started to grin. "Leonard had to fix a job that Pop messed up today. I'd say he's been doing pretty good."

Henry looked a bit disgusted and offended. "Hey, I messed that paint job up on purpose to give your uncle a chance to get his confidence back."

Bo looked at his father and then at Martha with a smirk on his face. "Yeah, you should have seen the acting job Pop put on when he pretended to trip over the hose and sprayed paint all over the place while he pretended to have trouble getting to his feet. I certainly never would have guessed that he did that on purpose."

Bo glanced back at Henry in time to endure the Bozell stare—the steely-eyed stare that Henry must have perfected by watching every John Wayne movie ever made. The best thing to do whenever he was getting the Bozell stare was to either leave the room or change the subject. He changed the subject back to Sam and the pharmacy. "Ma, are you going to stay on at the pharmacy and work for Rick now?"

"Yes, I think so. Rick's a nice young man. Ever since he came to work for Sam, he and I have always had a good working relationship." "What about Terri and Susan?" Henry asked Martha.

"Terri's staying, but Susan gave her two weeks' notice a couple of days ago. I'm glad it was Susan and not Terri who quit. Otherwise, we would have been down to just one pharmacist until Rick could have found a replacement. Good pharmacists are much harder to find than good store clerks. Besides, there was always something about Susan that bothered me. She never seemed quite genuine to me. She was always talking about church functions when Sam was around, but she never said a word about it when he was gone. And she was always badmouthing people, like your father here, who still smoke, even though I could always smell it on her every time she came into work. She never stepped outside for a cigarette while she was on her break, but after she came back from lunch, I could always smell it on her. I guess she never realized, being the closet smoker that she was, that any real nonsmoker could smell it a mile away. She also claimed she didn't drink, but sometimes on Saturday mornings, her eyes were all bloodshot, and she seemed like she was moving in slow motion. Quite honestly, I'm not really going to miss Susan at all."

Henry must have fully digested what Martha had just said about Susan because he looked a little offended. "Martha, you know I quit smoking.

What do mean like your father here?"

"Oh, sorry, dear. I forgot that you still thought I didn't know." "But I really did finally quit, Mother," said Henry.

"Oh really? Don't you have any more side jobs on motorcycle gas tanks lined up that you'll be working on after supper out in the garage?"

"No!"

Martha looked at Bo and smiled. "Gee, maybe he really did quit this time. If your father was listening closely to me earlier, he should know now that he can't make such a claim unless he can back it up."

Henry looked up from his plate and at his wife. "Will you please quit talking about me as if I'm not in the room? I've made it a full forty-eight hours this time."

Martha smiled and looked back down at her plate as she scooped up some com with her fork. "I already knew that, Henry, but thanks for sharing with us just the same."

Henry sighed and shook his head, mumbling something under his breath as he reached over and forked another piece of ham onto his plate. Then he got up and walked over to the kitchen counter, filled up his glass with more ice tea from the pitcher, and walked back over to the table. After sitting down again, he turned his attention to Martha. "Is the sale of the pharmacy completed yet?"

"Not yet," Martha answered. "It won't be official that Sam has lost his pharmacy license until after Judge Murphy sentences him next month."

The front doorbell rang. "Go and see who that is, Bo," Henry said to his son.

Martha moved her napkin from her lap up to the table next to her plate. "Stay put. I'm done eating. I'll go."

Martha got up from her chair and walked out of the kitchen as Henry and Bo continued to finish their supper. When Martha entered the living room, she was quite surprised when she saw who was standing on crutches on the front porch, peering through the front screen door. Her face lit up with a big smile while her eyes welled up with tears of joy. "Ben! You're home! You're home! Why didn't you call us, honey? We could have picked you up at the airport!" Martha tearfully exclaimed as she peered through the screen door at her second son.

"I wanted to surprise you, Mother. Besides, I didn't want any big fuss made."

Martha opened the screen door and wrapped her arms around Ben as his crutches fell to the porch floor. Ben's duffel bag was sitting next to him on the porch, and he was in his summer Marine Corps dress uniform. On his left foot was a white cast that went halfway up his shin, noticeable because of a slit that had been cut in his pant leg, starting from the bottom cuff.

"Oh, son, you just don't know how good it feels to see you and hold you again!" Martha exclaimed as she held on to her son for dear life. If Ben weren't such a strong marine, Martha surely would have cracked a rib or two. "For a while, I thought none of us would ever see you again. We were all so worried about you."

Ben was still wrapped in Martha's bear hug. "I'm sorry I put you all through that," he tearfully replied.

"Oh, my sweet son, it wasn't your fault. You have nothing to apologize for. I'm just so glad that you're finally home. That's all that really matters now."

Ben finally broke free from his mother's embrace. "There's good news and bad news about that, Mother."

Martha looked at her son with a puzzled and worried look. "What do you mean, son?" she nervously asked.

"The good news is I'm home for good. They had to discharge me. The bad news is I'll never be able to walk normally again. I'm just lucky they didn't have to amputate my left foot."

Martha just stood there with her mouth open before she could find the words to answer. "Oh my, let's get you inside so I can holler for Henry and Bo." Martha picked up her son's crutches and handed them to him before grabbing his heavy duffel bag. "How did you get your big bag onto the porch?"

Ben placed the crutches in position under his arms before putting his full weight onto them. "The taxi driver carried it up here for me before he left. He was in 'Nam too. On the ride home from the airport, he and I had a good talk. It helped make up for some long-haired hippie freak calling me a baby killer while I was waiting for my duffel bag at the baggage claim area. I thought about nailing him with one of my crutches while he was walking away, but I decided not to lower myself to his level."

Martha held the screen door open for Ben, pulled the duffel bag through the door, and left it leaning up against the wall next to the front door. "I'm so sorry you were treated so disrespectfully, son. Times have sure changed since your father came home from World War II. If it hadn't been for your grandmother's death at the time, your father would have joined the other returning soldiers, who rode on makeshift floats in a big homecoming parade right down Main Street through the middle of downtown. It was one of Plattsmouth's proudest moments. There might not be any parades anymore, but I'm just as proud and happy as I was the day your father came home. Speaking of your father, Henry! Bo! You need to come into the living room!" she yelled at the top of her lungs.

Ben turned toward Martha as he wiped some sweat from his brow with his arm. "Wow, Mother, it's hotter in this house than the jungles of 'Nam."

Martha frowned and shook her head. "I'm sure you've changed a lot, son, but unfortunately, your father hasn't."

Ben popped himself on his forehead with the palm of his sweaty right hand. "Oh yeah, the old 'waiting till the Fourth of July'—how could I forget that tradition? Believe it or not, I even missed that. I missed everything about this family and this house."

As Ben continued to stand inside the front door, leaning on his crutches, Henry finally entered. Henry's face lit up with excitement and surprise at seeing Ben. He rushed over to him. Ben placed his crutches against the wall, anticipating a hug from his father. He wasn't disappointed. Henry gave his son a big hug, not letting go for a long time. "You son of a gun, why didn't you call us that you were coming home?"

Ben answered his father while they were still locked in the long embrace, "I thought it would be more fun to surprise you."

"Well, it worked. I thought you weren't coming home for at least another week," Henry said as he finally let go of Ben.

Just then, Bo walked into the living room. He reacted in much the same way as Henry. He grabbed hold of Ben and held him tight. "Welcome home, big brother."

Bo's bear hug was tighter than either of his parents was. Ben seemed to struggle to answer. Apparently, his ability to breathe and to speak was temporarily challenged. "Thanks, Bo. It's good to be home again."

Martha looked over admiringly at Ben. "Let's get you into a nice soft chair. I'm sure you're tired from your trip." Martha gave Ben his crutches and helped him over to Henry's favorite chair as Henry and Bo looked on.

Ben hesitated in turning around and plopping down in Henry's recliner. He looked at Martha and then at his father. "Nobody sits in Dad's chair but Dad."

Henry looked proudly back at his second eldest. "It's okay, son. I want you to take my chair. I want you to know how much I love you. I want you to know that, in my entire life, I'll never deserve to sit in that chair any more than you do right now. Sit down, son, and take a load off your feet."

Ben stared at his father with a look that Henry had probably never seen before, and then Ben sat down gently into his father's chair, softly replying, "I love you too, Dad." He eased into the chair.

Everyone else sat down after Ben had gotten comfortable. Sitting on the sofa were Martha and Bo while Henry sat down in the straight chair that Martha normally occupied. Henry finally looked around the living room. "What happened to Ace, Bo? He's usually right on your heels when you change rooms around here."

Bo shrugged at his father. "I don't know. He wanted to go outside when he saw we were leaving the kitchen."

Henry suddenly seemed a little irritated as he looked at Bo. "I thought I told you to keep an eye on him for a while as he's out in the backyard." Bo shrugged off Henry's paranoia. "Don't worry, Pop, he's not going anywhere."

Martha wasn't even paying any attention to what Henry and Bo were talking about. She was anxious to do some face-to-face catching up with her number two son. "Ben, I've got to ask you this, son. Why didn't you tell us more of what happened over there and about what you were going through in rehab since you got back? You only sent us two letters the whole time, and they were short and to the point."

Ben gave his mother an apologetic look. "I'm sorry, Mom, but I just wasn't ready to talk about it. You have no idea what it was like over there." Ben let out a deep sigh before continuing, "I mean, my best friend got blown up right next to me. We were on a night recon mission. Danny and I were just a few feet apart. Then just like that, Danny tripped a land mine, and the force of it blew me out into a ditch where 1 must have hit my head on a rock or something. When I came to, nobody was around. It was dark, but I didn't hear a sound, except for the wind in the trees. I knew that Danny must have been dead at that point."

Ben stared off into space as if he were back across the ocean, reliving the whole experience all over again. He finally looked back at his mother. "I tried to get up, and that's when I realized that my left boot was gone, along with part of my foot. There must have been some shrapnel that hit me farther up the leg and on my left side. I was bleeding badly, but I think it was mostly my foot." He paused a few seconds before continuing his story. "Before it was daylight, I managed to put a tourniquet on my leg, using a twig and some twine I could reach. I tried a few times to start moving, but I just couldn't, so I decided to stay put until the next night. I thought I was well hidden where I was. When daylight came, I realized I was going to have to wait it out even longer. There was Vietcong and North Vietnamese regular army swarming around all over the place, so I decided I better wait until the second night to try to start moving back to base camp. I was in and out of consciousness sometimes. I remember waking up, and it was dark again."

Ben hesitated again before going on with his story. The whole family seemed to be hanging on his every word. But something must have told them to be patient. They probably all sensed how hard it was for Ben to tell this story, so they waited in silence for Ben to continue. "I was so scared, more scared than I've ever been in my whole life. 1 couldn't help thinking that I was going to die there and never see any of you ever again. I felt so alone. I was in the middle of enemy territory with a bum leg. Suddenly, I could feel this big hairy creature almost leaning into me, and then I could hear the panting and feel his hot breath against my skin. And as I focused my eyes more, I could see—thanks to the moonlight—that it was a dog. 1 was too tired and weak to be afraid of him, and the dog let me know right away that he was friendly, and I knew then 1 wasn't alone anymore."

Ace was barking through the open back screen door now. Henry had a hard time looking away from Ben, but he finally turned to Bo. "You better go let him in, son, before the neighbors get upset."

Bo looked back at Henry and then at Ben. "I'll hurry," he said as he scampered out of the room. He looked over his shoulder as he reached the entryway to the hallway. "Ben, don't go on with your story until I get back, okay?"

The back screen door opened and closed as Martha and Henry sat, staring at Ben. Bo hurriedly walked back into the living room, and then

Ace appeared through the doorway. When Ben saw Ace, his jaw almost dropped to the floor. "It's him!"

Ace quickly padded over to Ben and jumped up enough to put his big paws on Ben's lap, and Ace was trying to lick him in the face. "Ace! Get down!" Henry yelled.

"It's okay, Dad, he hasn't seen me for a while," Ben calmly replied.

"I didn't think you had ever met Ace. Did you go visit him behind the hospital when Bo was there?" Henry asked his son.

"Dad, this is the dog that helped me get back to my unit." Ace finally dropped back down off the chair while still sitting close to Ben.

Henry started scratching the side of his head while he continued to look at the dog and his second-bom son. "You must be mistaken, boy. This is Bo's dog, Ace."

Ben became more animated as he continued, "I'm tellin' ya, Dad, this is the dog that helped me survive and guided me back to base camp."

Martha gave a warm and comforting look at Ben. "Now, now, dear, don't get all excited. I'm sure there's a logical explanation here."

Ben was starting to look a bit exasperated at his family. "Mom, he's got the same face, the same markings. It's him, I tell you."

No one seemed to know what to say at that point, especially Bo, who seemed to be preoccupied. Ben finally continued to try to convince his family that he wasn't crazy. "This dog did everything for me. He helped me get water. He found me a walking stick. He dragged me through thick mud. He—"

"Did you just say mud? Lots and lots of mud?" Bo interrupted. Ben had just said something that triggered a response in both Bo and his mother. Bo shot a quick glance at his mom.

Martha started shaking her head. "No, Bo, it couldn't be. You know that. It's physically impossible."

Henry looked back and forth between Martha and Bo with a bewildered look on his face. "Do you two know something I don't? Am 1, once again, the last to know what's going on around here?"

Martha acted like she didn't want to answer Henry. She let out a deep sigh. "Ace was all muddy when he appeared back in Bo's room that morning," she finally said to Henry.

"You mean after he was gone those two days? Wait a minute, what do mean by appeared?" Henry asked in obvious bewilderment.

"He woke me up by licking me in the face, Pop. Ma and I don't know how he got back into my room."

Henry scratched his head and looked at Ben. "No offense, son, but you've been through an awful lot. Now you and I and your mother and your brother Bo all know that the same dog can't have been here and across the ocean in a foreign country at the same time. It didn't happen, and it couldn't happen. And if any of you breathes a word about this to anyone, they'll be takin' us all away to the loony bin."

Meanwhile, Ace was sitting there all frustrated. He was thinking, *Please just let me say three little simple human words—"it was me. " No, never mind. Henry would probably have a heart attack*

Bo apparently wasn't accepting his father's narrow-minded view of the situation as he looked pleadingly at his father. "But he was all muddy that morning, Pop. And there weren't any muddy footprints in the kitchen or down the hallway and up the stairs. You were long gone for work. You didn't let him in. So who did?".

Henry started scratching under his chin as he looked back at Bo. "Ace must have let himself in. You know how smart he is. He must be able to open and close doors."

Martha came to the defense of her son. "How can a dog open a door with his paw, Henry?"

The veins on Henry's neck were starting to pop out as his face turned red. "I don't know. He must use both of his front paws at the same time, or maybe he uses his teeth or something."

Martha fired back at Henry, knowing and sensing that only Henry was unwilling to accept the unexplainable among them. "Okay, but what about what Bo said about no mud anywhere else in the house except on his bedroom floor?"

The adrenaline must have been winding down because Henry seemed to be starting to run out of gas. He sounded calmer this time as he countered his wife's last argument. "Ace must have cleaned it up. 1 don't know, and I don't want to know."

Martha shook her head in disgust as she stared at Henry with a pathetic and disappointed look on her face. "That attitude, Henry, is exactly why you are the last one to know anything around here."

Henry's pulse seemed to quicken again upon being attacked with stinging words of criticism by his wife. He was practically foaming at the mouth at that point. "Give me a break, Mother! How can you expect me to believe something that is as far out as what you are all suggesting?"

Ben looked at his father. "There's more, Dad. Something else happened, something that probably has the doctor who attended to me still scratching his head. You just mentioned about someone who couldn't be halfway around the world but unexplainably was. Well, as it turns out, my unprotected foot was full of thorns and sharp stems when I finally got back to base camp."

At the mention of thorns and stems, Bo and Martha exchanged understanding glances before Bo looked at his father. "Ace had a bunch of thorns and stuff stuck in his paws."

"That doesn't prove anything, son. There's plenty of thorns for a dog to step on around here, right down by the river on the outskirts of town," Henry countered.

Ben ignored Henry's explanation about the likely cause of Ace's thorns. "One of the stems the doctor found stuck in my foot had impaled a leaf from the same plant as the stem deep into the skin. The doctor apparently had done an extensive study on alternative medicines at one time. In particular, he said he had studied healing plants of the world. He identified the leaf and stem as a Hypericum hookerianum. It's a healing plant that's found only in India. He said that the plant probably played a role in saving my foot from amputation. He was at a loss in explaining how that plant could have turned up in 'Nam."

After Ben's revelation about the healing plant, Bo knew he had more information to share with his father to try to convince Henry that there was a connection. "When I pulled the thorns and stuff out of Ace's paws, there was hardly any bleeding. Don't you find that strange, Pop?"

Henry just shook his head with his lips pursed. "Not really. They probably weren't that deep."

Bo looked at Martha for a sign of approval. "Should I tell him about the dried blood and shards of glass?"

Henry's veins in his neck looked like they were about ready to pop. "Dried blood and shards of glass! What in the hell is going on around here?"

Martha glared at her husband for two reasons—his cursing and his narrowmindedness. "For god's sake, Henry, will you get a hold of yourself? You're not saying anything helpful here!"

Henry looked back and forth at Bo and Martha and then at Ben. He once again must have realized that he wasn't, indeed, doing anything helpful to allow Ben to relax and feel safe now that he was finally home. He let out a big deep breath, seemingly letting go of most of his frustration at the same time. "Son, I'm sorry we're carrying on so much after you just got home. You just sit there and get comfortable while I go get you and me a nice cold beer. Your brother here is going to come with me and tell me a little story about blood and glass."

Ace was lost in his own thoughts and questioning his role in Ben's rescue. *I'm so sad about Ben's friend Danny. Why couldn't You have sent me just a little bit sooner? I can't change what is destined? Oh, then does that mean I must be a part of destiny? I'm sorry. Sometimes I have a hard time understanding all this stuff.* Ace's frustration was met with a final reminder of who he was.

Yes, I know. I haven't forgotten that I'm just a big dog.

Ace's telepathic conversation was interrupted by a knock at the front door. Everyone in the living room could see that there was an elderly African American man standing outside the screen door on the front porch. Henry looked at Bo. (Henry never answered the door if there was another able-bodied family member in the house to answer it for him.) "Go see what the old gentlemen wants while I get your brother a beer. You and I can talk later." He headed for the kitchen while Martha continued to talk to Ben.

Bo jumped up and went to the front door. Standing inside the screen door, he addressed the old man. "Can I help you?"

"I come to see my dog."

Bo's jaw dropped, and his face looked like he'd just seen a ghost or something as he stared out at the old man.

Ace had been sitting next to Ben, being petted, until he noticed the old man at the front door. When the big dog saw the old man, he left Ben, padded quickly to the front door, and stopped next to Bo with his tail wagging. He looked out through the screen door at this supposed stranger with an apparent smile on his face. The old man looked down through the screen door and smiled back at Ace. "Hello, Dog. I thought I'd never see you again."

A few minutes later, Bo and the old man were sitting next to each other on the front porch swing. Ace sat so close to the old guy that he was leaning into him on his side of the swing. "I figured Ace had to belong to somebody before he ended up with me," Bo finally said as he looked at his unexpected guest.

The old man looked back at Bo with an inquisitive look. "Ace? Is that what you call him?"

"Yeah. What did you call him?"

"I called him Dog."

Bo wasn't impressed with the old man's apparent lack of creativity, but he tried not to let it show. "Why is that?" he finally asked.

"Because I woke up one mornin', and there he was. I somehow knew right away that God must have sent him to me, so the name came naturally."

Bo was puzzled. "Came naturally? I don't understand."

The old man shook his head and smiled. "Come on, son. Surely you've heard before what God is spelled backward?"

Bo thought about it for a second and then smacked his forehead with the palm of his hand. "Oh, I get it."

The old man and Bo pushed their legs off in unison so the porch swing continued to swing back and forth in the warm summer breeze. Bo finally snapped out of his temporary trance and asked the old man another question. "How long ago was it when Ace showed up with you?"

The old man rubbed his jaw before answering Bo, "I reckon it was about two and a half years ago, about a week after my Annie died. Annie and I had been together for forty-six years. 1 didn't take her passin' too well. All I was thinkin' about was how I wanted to be with her again. I stopped eating. I figured maybe I'd just starve myself to death. Then I woke up one momin', and there he was, siftin' there on the bedroom rug, lookin' right through me. He was. He put me at ease right off the bat. I didn't even think about how he got in until after we got acquainted. He come over to my bed real slow, and then he laid his head on the edge of the bed, lookin' at me like he knew all about me. I started cryin' like a baby as he sat there just lookin' at me, never takin' his eyes off me, not movin' a muscle."

They continued to swing together on the front porch. Bo tried to digest what the old man had just said to him. He really didn't want to take the conversation any further. He hoped at some point that the old man would finally grow tired of the silence and just get up and leave, never to come back again. It finally came to the point where the most patient man would win, and the old man had far more years of being patient than young Bo. "So how did you know how to find him?" Bo finally asked.

The old man kept swinging with Bo and, at first, did not answer. Finally, without looking at the boy about to cry, he answered the question.

"Saw an article in the newspaper the other day." "Oh yeah, the hearing," Bo mumbled.

"Yes, sir. Whoever wrote that article did a fine job. Knew it had to be Dog. Ain't no other dog on God's green earth like this dog." Ace moved forward and placed his head in the old man's lap. Bo looked down at his own feet as the old man continued, "My brother claims he saw Dog one night. Claims Dog saved him and Izzy from a punk tryin' to rob their liquor store. Said he come flyin' through the front window. He did. Bet it happened just like George said."

Bo's eyes got all misty as he continued to look down at the floor. He turned to the old man. "Guess you'll be wantin' to take him home with you then."

The old man didn't even see Bo's tears. He just kept looking forward as the swing kept swinging back and forth. Bo's stomach was knotting up, and he was starting to feel sick, waiting for the old man to answer him. Finally, the old man spoke without looking at Bo. "No, son. He's your dog now. He wouldn't be with you if it weren't where he wanted to be. I just wanted to say goodbye to him good and proper."

Bo breathed a deep sigh of relief. The knots in his stomach were gone, and he didn't feel sick anymore. The old man finally looked at Bo with matching tears in his eyes. "I woke up one mornin' last February, and he was gone. It bothered me somethin' terrible at first, but then I realized it must have been time for him to move on. I finally figured he musta taught me everything I needed to know."

Bo finally found his tongue again after listening to the words of experience and feeling the need to reveal his own recent experience. "You know what, I realize now that I really had a lot of things wrong in my head before Ace came along. I just didn't know it at the time. I always tried to put up a good front, but I had a lot of days where 1 couldn't help feeling sorry for myself. My parents kept driving home the point that I could succeed, no matter what the handicap was that I had to overcome."

Bo briefly paused before continuing, "Ace helped me realize that I shouldn't think about having a handicap at all. I've watched him shake off all my dad's criticism about his size and his drooling all over the place. His unbelievable intelligence seems to always help him usually come out on top. That's no small feat when it comes to my pop. I don't even know why I noticed that, but I did. It got me to thinking. He made me stop and realize that, no matter how many people may think you're big and scary or no matter how many people may think you're a freak because you're wearing hearing aids, you still have your mind to help you overcome it all. I know now that I can overcome my disability. 1 can become anything 1 want to be. I've got two years of high school left, to get my grades up and try to get a scholarship to college. If it weren't for Ace, I wouldn't feel this way now. I'd still be feeling sorry for myself. It was always easy to blame other people for how I felt. I know now that I control my own destiny, only me."

The old man smiled at Bo and then looked back at Ace. "Like I said, boy, ain't no other dog like him."

Bo started to smile as well from ear to ear. "In fact, I think Ace has helped me realize what I want to be someday. I've thought about how he seems to be able to communicate with me, even though he can't talk. That got me to thinking more and more about communication. It's something I really struggled with early in my life. Maybe I can't always hear everything, but that doesn't mean I can't express myself, especially when I write my thoughts down on paper. I've decided I want to major in English in college. My teacher gave me an A+ on my last assignment for sophomore English class before the semester was over this year. She too encouraged me to pursue English as my major," Bo said as he smiled at Lester.

He continued his conversation with the old man on the front porch. "The last assignment was to write a poem about someone we knew, someone that has had a positive influence in our lives. I wrote a poem about my pop. In fact, I've got it in my pocket here. I've been carrying it around ever since school let out, trying to decide when I should let Pop read it. Even though I got an A, I'm worried that he might not like it. You want to read it?" "Sure, boy.

Let's see what you got."

Bo reached back, fished the folded sheet of paper out of the back right pocket of his faded blue jeans, unfolded it, and handed it to the old man. Lester pulled an old pair of reading glasses out of his front pocket and slid them onto his nose. He read Bo's poem very slowly.

The Old Man

My old man's a tough old bird carved from toil and sweat. In fact, he is the toughest man that I have ever met. His daddy died before his time, which made Pop grow up fast. He had to learn that life was hard and good times didn't last.

I can't imagine how he felt to lose his dad so soon. There must have been emptiness in each an' every room. This early dose of death could have taken the old man down. Instead, I'm told he made himself the toughest man in town.

Getting older helped me realize what my pop has done for me. Even though I'm just sixteen, it's become quite plain to see. He's always there for me and gives all that he can give. In many ways, he shows the world how every dad should live.

Now I'm not saying my old man is perfect in every way. He's short tempered, impatient, and has far too much to say. But the soul of the man is sound, and his love is always free. And I hope I've somehow told him just how much he means to me.

The other old man sitting next to Bo on the porch swing smiled big as he handed the poem back to him and slipped his glasses back into his front shirt pocket. "I think your teacher's right, boy. You do write well. When ya gonna show that to your papa?"

Bo shrugged. "I don't know. I guess when I think the time is right."

"Well, don't wait too long, boy. You never know what tomorrow brings." The wise old man slowly rose out of the porch swing and leaned down, giving Ace a hug as the mastiff licked his face for the last time. "You cherish this dog, son. You don't hafta take care of him. He'll always take care of you." He looked down at Ace before leaving. "And thank you, Dog. Thank you for everything. I can see now you had a higher callin'."

The old man left the porch and walked to his old pickup truck. Ace followed him off the porch but stopped halfway to the old man's truck, standing in the yard as the old man got closer to the curb. Bo got up and walked to the edge of the porch by the front steps. He yelled out to the old man as he was getting into his truck. "I hope you're not all alone!"

"Nope! Got another dog now! 'Course he ain't like him, but he'll do! He'll do just fine! In fact, he's so smart he was the ring bearer for my niece's wedding a couple of weeks ago!" He climbed into the driver's seat and closed the door. The pickup truck's engine revved up, and he drove away as Ace finally turned around and trotted back to Bo. The relieved teenager petted Ace on the head and opened the front door for him as they both went back into the house.

Henry, Martha, and Ben were all still sitting in the living room. Henry turned his head from Ben and looked at Bo as he sat down in the living room with Ace at his side. He must have failed to notice Bo's red eyes and tearstained cheeks. "What did that old man want, Bo?"

Bo couldn't answer Henry at first. He was lost in thought, digesting what he and the old man had just shared together.

"What did he want, son?"

Bo finally quit staring into space and looked back at his father as Ace decided to return to Ben and lie down by his feet. "He just wanted to say goodbye."

"What?"

"Never mind. I'll tell you later when we're talking about blood and glass."

It was a bright, sunny Saturday afternoon in late July. There was a usual gathering of mostly Plattsmouth residents at a small sandpit lake near the Missouri River. The sandy beaches around the lake allowed for an assortment of summer activity, making it one of the most popular swimming and recreational sites close to Plattsmouth. It was only a tenminute drive by car from town. Even boys and girls on bicycles, still stuck in those awkward early teen years (too old to be seen in public with a parent and too young to drive), could make the trip with minimal effort in about thirty minutes.

If you didn't want to put up with the town's only swimming pool with the whistle-happy teenage lifeguards and too much chlorine in the water that burned your eyes, this was the place to be on a hot summer afternoon. There was only one lifeguard on duty at a time at this county-run lake site, and he or she was always an older college student in his or her twenties, someone who understood how annoying a shrill whistle would be in such serene surroundings. The other advantage it had over the swimming pool was for the benefit of families who had four-legged furry friends that didn't like being left out of a family outing. Pets were allowed around the lake and within the grounds of the park.

There were children swimming as their mothers or elder siblings were sunbathing on big beach towels or in lawn chairs in the sand. The small concession stand housed in between the men's and women's restrooms and showers was busy selling snow cones, popcorn, hot dogs, and pop. There was a group of teenagers playing sand volleyball over in the northwest corner of the beach near the front entrance from the highway. The girls were in mostly two- piece swimsuits, and most of the boys were shirtless and wearing blue jean cutoffs. They had asked Bo and Bonnie to play, but Bo had respectfully declined primarily because they had excluded Marvin and Tanya. Bo had simply said no to the invitation while not elaborating on why. He wasn't in the mood that day to strike a chord for social injustice. This was a day to just relax and soak up some summer sun.

Five miles away, on the same winding highway that passed by the sandpit lake, a dark blue Ford Galaxy was traveling at a high rate of speed. It had just passed a slow-moving pickup truck, starting the maneuver at the beginning of a curve in a no-passing zone. The driver in an oncoming white Chevy Camaro convertible had to tap his brakes a couple of times to allow the Ford to safely get back into its lane. The bald middle-aged man driving the white Camaro laid on his horn as he passed by the Ford Galaxy moving in the opposite direction.

"Don't you think you better slow it down a little bit, Matt?" said the nervous front seat passenger in the Ford.

"Lighten up, Larry. I've got everything under control," the cocky young driver calmly replied as he gave a quick glance at his front seat passenger before returning his eyes to the road.

"Grrrrr! Woof!" said the agitated dog from the back seat.

"Come on, Matt. Take it easy, would ya? You're makin' Caesar all nervous back here," the third teenage boy in the back seat said excitedly to the driver.

Matt Duncan looked in his inside rearview mirror with a smirk on his face at his whiny friend in the back seat before he tromped on the accelerator even more, sending the car fishtailing around a curve. "Perfect, Brent! I want your dog to be madder than a hornet by the time we get there!" he shouted over the roar of the engine.

"I still can't believe Manchester actually called you after seeing Bozell and his deaf-mute friends driving in as he and his buddy were leaving. I'd think it would be the last thing he'd want to do after we got him involved in the hearing over the Bozell's dog," Brent Larsen said from the back seat.

"Woof! Grrrrr!"

"Caesar! Shut up!" Larsen yelled at his dog while the dog strained to stick its head out of the partially open rear window.

Duncan smiled into the inside rearview mirror, probably knowing that Larsen could see his face from the back seat. "Oh, I guess I forgot to tell you two. About a week after the hearing, I took a little drive by myself to Plattsmouth. I found Troy's house. His parents and his elder sister were all working, so good ol' Troy was home alone. He and I had a nice little talk on his front porch that afternoon. I guess I have a way of being convincing when I need to. He he. He promised me he'd give me a call if he ever spotted Bozell and his dog around town."

"Grrrrr! Woof! Woof! Woof!"

"Shut up, Caesar! You're driving me crazy!" Larsen scowled at his dog as he held him close on a short leash.

"Let him bark, Brent! Get 'em, Caesar! Get 'em!" Duncan yelled as he watched the salivating, snarling dog in his rearview mirror.

There were some young children throwing a beach ball back and forth in shallow water near the beach on the northwest shore. Some other gradeschool-age children from Iowa School for the Deaf and a mother of one of the children were playing Frisbee with Bo and Bonnie. They were just a few feet southeast of the lifeguard tower. Marvin and Tanya were lying on beach towels and catching some rays near the concession stand. Ace and Lucy were romping around together along the beach, and then they ran into an area of cottonwood trees and disappeared.

The trees were in abundance along the other side of the narrow gravel road that led to the restrooms and concession stand in the wooden shack near the lake. The gravel road was in a horseshoe shape as it surrounded the lake. There were a west entrance from the highway and a south entrance from a gravel road. The south entrance was handy for the older kids on bicycles who had made the thirty-minute ride from town while avoiding the fast-moving highway traffic.

Cotton balls were blowing off the tree limbs and drifting gently down to the ground from a soft summer breeze. Some had made it to the edge of the lake, where they were bobbing gently on the water, looking like snowflakes that wouldn't melt. There were a few smaller family dogs running around, happily playing with little children. One little terrier was fetching a ball thrown by the mother of some children who were swimming.

A long rope with plastic bobbers attached every few feet cordoned off the shallower swimming area. It stretched the length of the lake from one shore to the other. In the middle of the swimming area was a fifteen-footsquare wooden platform that swimmers could dive from or use as a rest stop from the fatigue of swimming.

Bo and Bonnie finally quit playing Frisbee and sat down on beach towels. Bonnie reached over and took a couple of cans of cold pop out of a Styrofoam cooler near the towels and handed one to Bo. "Thanks, and thanks for coming over today," said Bo as he wiped some sweat from his brow.

Bonnie replied to Bo using sign language.

"Yeah, I guess it has been since the hearing. This is my first Saturday off in three weeks," Bo answered.

Bonnie once again asked Bo another question using sign language.

Bo responded by speaking out loud, face-to-face with her. "1 finally finished up my two weeks of extra duty at the shop last weekend. I don't think Pop and the guys give cleaning a very high priority during the year. It was so disgusting our shop cat, Murphy, kept coming up and thanking me." Bonnie laughed a silent giggle at Bo's last remark.

He continued, "I thought I was going to get a chance to do more than grunt work at the shop when my two weeks of scraping and scrubbing was over. My uncle Leonard had volunteered to go with my brother Ben up to Chicago this week, so I thought we'd be shorthanded for the next few days, but yesterday, Ben ended up flying up there by himself. He told us he was still staying for a whole week, with or without Leonard going along." Bonnie signed a long question to Bo.

"My brother's marine buddy from 'Nam lived in South Chicago. My brother was standing right next to him when he was killed over there. I guess they had talked about visiting each other's mother after they got back. Since this guy never made it back, my brother is fulfilling his promise to visit his mom.

"Ben said he needed to stay for maybe a week so he'd have time to find and hire a good lawyer for his friend's brother. I guess the guy in 'Nam convinced Ben that his brother had been convicted of a crime that he didn't commit. Finding the lawyer wasn't part of the promise, but Ben's gonna do it just the same," Bo explained.

Bonnie signed to Bo, curious about why his uncle was going to go along and then didn't go at the last minute.

"Well, the reason Leonard was going in the first place was to appease my ma, who was worried about Ben going into South Chicago by himself. Ma thought it could be too dangerous for him," answered Bo. "But apparently, Leonard and Ben had a little talk a couple of days ago, and then they went and convinced Ma that Ben would be just fine by himself."

Bonnie looked very confused at that point, expressing her confusion with rapid-fire hand signals.

"I'm not really sure, but 1 think they somehow convinced Ma that if Ben did run into trouble, he'd be protected. Besides, my uncle finally admitted that he was afraid to fly."

Bonnie had a suspicious look on her face as she signed once more to Bo.

"What do mean you think I know more than I'm letting on?" he asked, trying to look surprised and slightly offended. She kept staring at him. "I swear, I really don't know for sure."

They sat on their beach towels in silence for a couple of minutes before Bonnie began signing again to Bo.

"You're uncle Charlie is living with you now?" Bonnie nodded yes to his question.

"So what happened?"

Bonnie signed a response to Bo.

"You finally told your dad, and he asked you to take him to his brother, huh. Wasn't your uncle mad when he realized you had told your dad?" Bonnie signed her short reply to Bo.

"Wow, so Milt had left town by then, leaving him alone down by the river. Your uncle started to cry when he saw the two of you? And your dad and your uncle just stood there hugging each other for several minutes without talking. Must have been an emotional experience. I'm glad you don't have to worry so much about your uncle anymore." Bonnie wiped away some tears and signed to Bo.

"Yeah, family is important. I hope your uncle can hold down the job your dad found for him."

Bonnie answered Bo with rapid-fire signing as a smile reemerged on her face.

"No. Even if he doesn't keep the job, it really doesn't matter anymore, does it?"

Ace and Lucy came running by, having returned from the trees near the river. One of the deaf children threw the Frisbee off course, and it flew out into the water, bobbing up and down from the waves created by the swimmers. Ace charged into the water after it. When he finally reached it, he scooped it up into his mouth and headed back to shore, giving it back to the little boy who last threw it.

The mother who was playing with them went and sat down near Bo and Bonnie. The children started throwing the Frisbee so that Ace and Lucy could take turns trying to catch it in their mouths. Lucy finally tired of the game, came over to Bonnie, and lay down, panting. Bonnie apparently had finally given up on trying to make sense of what Bo had told her about Ben's Chicago trip, and the two of them were now lying flat on their beach towels, sunbathing.

As Ace continued to play with the children, the dark blue Ford Galaxy pulled up. It parked in the middle of a line of cars that were all parked diagonally along a stretch of gravel that was sectioned off from the lake by buried wooden posts with a metal cable running through them. The posts were evenly spaced apart in a curved line behind the concession stand and restrooms.

The driver of the Ford Galaxy was Matt Duncan, with Larry Malloy riding shotgun and Brent Larsen in the back seat. The fourth passenger in the back seat of the car was a very vicious-looking rottweiler, and it obviously didn't have a very gentle disposition, especially after Duncan's attempts to rile up the big dog on the trip from Papillion. The dog was already growling after getting a glimpse of some of the other dogs that were there, and he hadn't even been let out of the back seat of the car yet.

Brent Larsen was holding his snarling dog on a short leash. He had mentioned his concern to Larry before Duncan had picked them up about the possibility of Caesar scratching the back of Duncan's front seat. He apparently knew that if the dog caused any noticeable damage, there would be hell to pay, even though it was Duncan's idea to bring the dog along in the first place.

Larry Malloy didn't look like he was too comfortable with the situation as he sat in the front passenger seat next to Duncan. Brent Larsen also had a very worried, nervous look on his face. Duncan could see Larsen in his inside rearview mirror. "Matt, I don't think this is a good idea. There's too many people here."

Duncan's face suddenly changed from sullen to animated. His cheeks started to turn red, and his nostrils flared, much like the nostrils of the rottweiler riding in the back seat of his car. "I don't care! When else are we going to find Bozell and his dog out in the open, away from his house?

Don't chicken out on me now, Brent. Besides, you owe me with the way you *wimped out* on me at the hearing."

Larsen had often admitted to Malloy that he had always been afraid of Duncan. From Larsen's point of view, their shallow friendship had been based on fear as much as it had been mutuality of interests. Brent Larsen seemed a little defensive but appeared to be treading lightly when answering his bully brother-in-arms. "Bozell's lawyer was asking about stuff that we didn't think of ahead of time. I didn't have a choice, Matt. He boxed me into a corner."

Larry Malloy was almost as big as Duncan but had always shared the same sentiment with Larsen when they had previously discussed in private how to deal with their big bully of a friend. He turned to Duncan in the front seat after surveying the situation for himself. "Brent's right, there are too many people here. Why can't you just let it go, Matt?"

Duncan slammed the top of his steering wheel with the palms of his hands so hard that the plastic wheel quivered back and forth like a tuning fork from the impact as he glared back at Malloy. "Twice now, Bozell has made a fool out of me! It's finally payback time! Then I'll let it go!"

He took a deep breath and turned his head around toward the back seat, showing Brent Larson the fire in his eyes before continuing with his instructions. "Now get Caesar out of the car, but keep him over on the passenger side out of sight, until I tell you to unleash him."

Larsen and Malloy both shrugged and obeyed, much like they had so many times before that day. They, with the rottweiler, slowly got out on the passenger side of the car while Duncan slid out of the driver's seat, slamming his door and hurrying around to join them on the other side. Caesar had leaped out of the open car window, not wasting any time before starting to lunge forward on his leash, all the while barking and snarling while Larsen tried to keep him under control as they crouched down behind the passenger side of the car.

"How do you know Caesar will go after Bozell's dog?" Duncan asked. Larsen looked back at Duncan with a reassuring look on his face. "He always goes after the biggest dog. He's a rottweiler."

Duncan didn't seem totally convinced, but it was apparently the only plan they had, so it was time to proceed. "Yeah, well, whatever. Go ahead and do your thing."

Larsen, crouching down low, brought his dog up to the right front fender of the car. He peeked around the corner of the car and brought Caesar around so the dog could see the beach area. Duncan and Malloy stood up straight and looked over the top of the Galaxy in the direction of where Ace was playing with the children.

Larsen started talking to his dog and getting him fired up while he pointed at Ace. "There he is. He's the one you want. Now go get him, boy! Get him, Caesar!" Larsen unhooked the leash and slapped Caesar on the buttocks as the frenzied, foaming-at-the-mouth dog bolted away in the direction of Ace.

Bo and Bonnie were still lying down, sunbathing, oblivious to the danger that was at hand. As the rottweiler charged toward Ace, the children who were playing Frisbee with the gentle mastiff all got scared and started running away. Other frightened children, obviously not knowing for sure who the rottweiler was after, started screaming and crying, running in all different directions.

The commotion finally came to Bo's attention, and he and Bonnie rose to their feet. Ace stood frozen in place, not moving a muscle, as the rottweiler got closer and closer. The rottweiler's jowls were flapping around as he galloped forward with clenched teeth and wild eyes. The short hairs along his back all the way to his tail were standing straight up. He wasn't barking, but he was growling, snarling, and throwing spit in all directions as he got ever closer to Ace.

Bo didn't know what to do. He was temporarily in shock as he just stood there with his mouth hanging open. Finally, Bo yelled to his dog, "Protect yourself, Ace! Ace!" For a fleeting second, Bo had a terrible feeling that this was how it had to end for his beloved dog. The bullmastiff remained motionless as the rottweiler closed in on him.

Just as the rottweiler leaped into the air, ready to tear into Ace, the mastiff quickly moved a little to his right, avoiding the frontal assault from the lunging dog. As witnesses would reluctantly attest to later, it seemed like Ace moved out of the way a bit quicker than the eye could follow. As the rottweiler came flying by just to the left of Ace, unable to change the direction of his leap in midair, the big dog lunged at him, clamping down on the attacking dog's neck. The two dogs tumbled to the ground.

The bullmastiff was on top of the rottweiler, continuing to hold him by the throat in his big jaws. Ace had enough weight to be able to keep the other dog pinned to the ground on its backside. He kept enough pressure on Caesar's throat to let him know it was over. The rottweiler probably knew instinctively that it was time to submit.

Bo, Bonnie, and several other grown-ups and teenagers hurried over to the two dogs. Brent Larsen was on a dead run, maybe thinking that Ace was going to kill his dog. Duncan and Malloy were behind Larsen but not moving quite as fast. Ace continued to hold Caesar by the throat, making sure the rottweiler had given up before letting go of him.

Finally, Ace let go, and Caesar rolled back up onto his feet, running and whimpering to his master. The crowd of people started cheering and clapping when they saw that it was over and that Ace had prevailed. Larsen put the leash back on Caesar. He then checked the dog over, noticing a little bit of blood around his throat. Other than that, the shaken and defeated canine seemed okay. Maybe he wouldn't be so eager to attack another dog for a long time to come. Duncan and Malloy finally joined Larsen next to Caesar.

Bo looked at Duncan with a scowl on his face. "I might have known you were behind this, Duncan. Don't you ever give up?"

Duncan shook his head a little and had a look of surprise after Bo's accusation. "1 don't know what you're talking about, Bozell. It was an accident. The dog got away from Brent. He couldn't stop him."

Bo wasn't buying Duncan's excuses. "Yeah, right, it was an *accident.*" Bo turned his head and looked at Larsen. "Ace could have killed your dog just now. You know that, don't you? Was Duncan's revenge really worth the chances of losing your best friend?"

Larsen didn't seem to understand. "What do you mean?"

With Bo realizing that Larsen didn't get it, he got even angrier. *"Your dog,* dummy! Don't you care enough about your *dog?"*

Larsen remained silent, looking back down at Caesar.

"Apparently not," Bo concluded, shaking his head in disgust.

Duncan must have finally decided that he'd been once again humiliated enough for one day. "Come on, you guys. Let's go."

Duncan, Malloy, and Larsen, with his dog tight on his leash, walked to Duncan's car. Malloy got back into the front passenger seat, and Larsen opened the back door for his dog to get inside. As Duncan opened his car door and was about ready to slide in, Bo yelled over to him, "Hey, Duncan!"

"Shut up, Bozell!"

"All 1 was going to say was good luck at college this year!"

Duncan shook his head, obviously not understanding why Bo would be wishing him good luck at that point. He closed his car door, started the engine, and backed up a little, and the blue Ford Galaxy pulled away down the narrow gravel lane, heading for the highway exit.

Bonnie used sign language to ask Bo a question.

"Because he's clueless," he answered. "He just doesn't get it. 1 wished him luck because he's going to need it. Hate brings nothing but trouble."

Bonnie smiled at Bo while placing her open right hand on his left cheek. Ace and Lucy were rubbing noses. Lucy then circled around Ace, rubbing up against him. Bo picked up the Frisbee as the two dogs now stood several feet away. Lucy then moved farther away from Ace, wagging her little bobtail like she was ready to play again. Bo yelled to the two dogs, "Who's gonna catch the Frisbee?" He threw the Frisbee so that it was sailing high right in between the two of them.

Ace and Lucy both leaped high into the air. Their mouths touched the opposite sides of the Frisbee at the exact same time as they were suspended off the ground, frozen in time—simple love personified. As the two dogs landed again in the sand on all fours, Ace—being the gentleman that he was—let go of his side of the Frisbee so his girlfriend dog could take full possession of the prize. She dropped the Frisbee into the sand as he rubbed the top of his head against her neck. He couldn't help asking, *Can't I stay here a little longer this time? Lucy's hot.*

A couple of minutes later, without any apparent reason, Ace took off on a dead run for the trees near the river. Lucy followed in hot pursuit. After several minutes, Lucy reappeared from the trees by herself. She ran back to Bonnie whimpering. Bo and Bonnie had lain back down on their beach towels with their eyes closed. Several minutes passed with Lucy sitting near her master, still whimpering and whining.

The dog finally nudged her master's arm. Bonnie leaned up on one elbow and stroked Lucy's back with her free hand, trying to calm her while looking down at Bo, who was still lying on his back with his eyes closed. She finally stopped petting Lucy and rousted Bo back up into a sitting position. With a concerned look on her face, she made it clear to him that his dog hadn't come back, asking him in sign language if he was going to go looking for Ace.

Bo, at first, looked surprised to hear the news of his dog's most recent disappearance. He thought about her question for a few seconds. Even though he initially looked a little worried, having surmised the probable reason for Ace's sudden disappearance, he calmly answered, "Nah, he'll be back, just like I know that Ben will be back in a week."